ALWAYS ON MY MIND

ALWAYS ON MY MIND

CARYS GREEN

Harvill
Secker

1 3 5 7 9 10 8 6 4 2

Harvill Secker, an imprint of Vintage, is part of the Penguin Random House group of companies

Vintage, Penguin Random House UK, One Embassy Gardens,
8 Viaduct Gardens, London SW11 7BW

penguin.co.uk/vintage
global.penguinrandomhouse.com

First published by Harvill Secker in 2025

Copyright © Carys Green 2025

Carys Green has asserted her right to be identified as the author of this Work in accordance with the Copyright, Designs and Patents Act 1988

Penguin Random House values and supports copyright. Copyright fuels creativity, encourages diverse voices, promotes freedom of expression and supports a vibrant culture. Thank you for purchasing an authorised edition of this book and for respecting intellectual property laws by not reproducing, scanning or distributing any part of it by any means without permission. You are supporting authors and enabling Penguin Random House to continue to publish books for everyone. No part of this book may be used or reproduced in any manner for the purpose of training artificial intelligence technologies or systems. In accordance with Article 4(3) of the DSM Directive 2019/790, Penguin Random House expressly reserves this work from the text and data mining exception.

Typeset in 13.5/16 pt Garamond by Jouve (UK), Milton Keynes
Printed and bound in Great Britain by Clays Ltd, Elcograf S.p.A.

The authorised representative in the EEA is Penguin Random House Ireland, Morrison Chambers, 32 Nassau Street, Dublin D02 YH68

A CIP catalogue record for this book is available from the British Library

HB ISBN 9781787304574
TPB ISBN 9781787304581

Penguin Random House is committed to a sustainable future for our business, our readers and our planet. This book is made from Forest Stewardship Council® certified paper.

For R. G. Always.

Happiness is not a possession to be prized, it is a quality of thought, a state of mind.

Daphne du Maurier

Unity Quick Start Guide

The chip is only activated when both parties are conscious.

The flow of thoughts can be controlled and managed by the main user.

The host's thoughts will always take precedence within the host's mind.

The aim of Unity is to enhance the thought process via revolutionary cerebral-sharing technology.

If there is an issue with your chip, please contact your implantation centre at your earliest convenience.

Both participants must be over 18 years of age.

A Unity chip can only operate on a dual wavelength, so only between two consenting individuals.

Everyone's internal thought process is unique to them. At Unity we embrace this.

Please refer to the terms and conditions for further details and a comprehensive list of potential side effects.

Prologue

She needed to stop thinking.

Her mind. It had to be empty. Still.

Silent.

It was dark within the walk-in wardrobe. The only movement the gentle rocking as Anna shifted back and forth, knees bunched up tight to her chest.

Don't think.

She wanted to listen out for a creak. The thud of a footstep. Anything. But each time she stilled her breath enough to focus, her thoughts began to betray her.

Jack and Jill.

Anna felt the heat of a tear streak down her cheek, tasted its salty death on her lips.

Went up the hill.

She just needed to wait. Wait and not think. She could do that, couldn't she? Her thoughts were hers alone to control. Only—

To fetch a pail of water.

There was movement just beyond the wardrobe. Was someone in the bedroom?

Jack fell down.

She rocked back and forth. Back and forth.

Rain whispered against the windows but Anna couldn't

hear it, barely any sounds reached her within the wardrobe, her chosen prison. Pressed suits and elegant tea dresses hung just inches above her. Carrying the scent of him. Of her.

And broke his crown.

Perhaps it wasn't perfect, but she had to hide somewhere. Hide and gather her thoughts. Smother them.

Another noise. This one closer. Anna clenched the breath within her chest, refused to release it, ceased rocking.

And Jill came tumbling after.

1

TWO MONTHS EARLIER

Anna was late. As usual. She was rushing through the city as twilight crept in, leather satchel smacking against her hip. She shouldn't have stayed so long in the little art shop off Dormer Street. She'd intended to spend only ten minutes there, maybe twenty. But a whole hour had passed before she had returned to the whispered hum of electric engines and stepped over puddles again. It was too easy to chat with Marcus, the owner, who had endless stories about his life in Italy before he came to London. It was too easy to get lost among the shelves of oil paints. Horsehair brushes. Anna loved the waxy smell, the way the world seemed to still when she was in there. But all too quickly, as the bell above the door jingled behind her, the spell was broken. The sounds of the city came screaming back to her. Like a serpent at the door, always waiting. The hustle. The grind. Anna feared there was no way to truly escape it.

Elijah will be pissed.

She pictured him at home, tracking her progress on his

phone, annoyance levels rising. She wondered if he was cracking his knuckles as minutes slipped by, listening to the pop, jaw clenching.

He hates it when I'm late.

As she hurried for her train, she considered tucking into a shop and firing off a quick text to her husband. A chance to explain herself. Elijah was as precise as he was handsome. Punctual, reliable, envied by others, it was like being married to a Rolex watch.

There's no time.

Better she catches the earlier maglev train than sacrifice a few moments to send a message that would only serve to cement her tardiness. She knew Elijah was finishing early that afternoon, that he was probably already in their kitchen, chopping tomatoes as he leaned against the polished marble surfaces, some pasta boiling on the hob. Elijah's attention to detail made him a good cook. 'I'm more of a "shove it all together and hope for the best" kind of girl,' she'd told him when they first started dating back in the Student Union of the University of Manchester. Anna winced at how that felt like a lifetime ago.

Was his phone on the countertop, alerting him to her progress? Was he asking the AI within their home to confirm his wife's location? She knew signal could be sketchy in the depths of the city as she flitted between hotspots. Elijah was always telling her to keep her data on, all the time. But Anna refused.

'It drains the battery.'

'That's not the point. I like to know where you are.'

A double-decker bus sped past her, buffeting her away from the kerb. An advert for a new film was playing on its side, a woman twisting through a meadow, smiling beneath a golden sun. Anna kept walking, clutching her bag more tightly to her side. She tried to calm the hem of her skirt which had flown up, ran her fingers through her dark fringe, hoping to tame it. Already she could feel the throng of people around her, all heading for the same destination.

Why did I stay in the city so long?

She knew why. As soon as Marcus asked how her latest piece was going, her inner timekeeper switched off. Anna no longer cared. There were some things where her passion was so great, it could swallow everything else whole. Her art was one such thing.

'Going well.' She smiled kindly to the ageing man behind the till point as she picked up a palate of watercolours, cheeks aching from the effort of lying.

'From Spain,' came Marcus's silky voice, 'best there is. Would be perfect for you.'

'Mmm.' Anna turned them over to assess the digital price tag, which winked red at her. Fifty pounds. Ouch. More than she should be spending on supplies, especially considering she hadn't sold a single piece in three months. At first, she'd had a steady assortment of customers for her work, but it had dwindled. Not that she wanted to admit as much to Marcus. Besides, Elijah wouldn't mind the splurge; it was their anniversary, after all.

'When can I see the new piece?' Marcus asked as he rang up her order. 'I keep waiting for you to have a proper exhibition. I would be first in line.'

'Thank you.' Anna gave a courteous smile, hoping the despair she felt at the word 'exhibition' didn't show in her eyes. How she'd love one. A chance to feel admired, validated. But as Elijah had told her so frequently, 'Lofty ambitions rarely come true, only sometimes.'

They did come true. *Sometimes.* That's what Anna clung to.

She remembered the first time she'd shown her work to

Helen. Back before all the kindness between them had eroded away.

'Your work reminds me of a painting I saw in Venice,' Marcus began wistfully. 'Though that had a bear in, I think. Or perhaps a lion. Still, it was quirky. Fun.' In the store it had begun, Marcus's reliable trip down memory lane. Anna was more than willing to go with him if it meant forgetting about her lack of sales, or showcases. For a moment she got to join him in the sun and it was glorious. But it couldn't last.

Body coiled tight within itself Anna stood on the tube, one hand clinging to a nearby rail. People jostled around her with the motion of the train. The interior lights flickered a hazy blue, supposedly to reflect the sky outside so that they didn't feel like rats in a tunnel. It was busy, though a few seats were vacant. Not that Anna would ever consider sitting on one.

'How many asses do you think land on those *a day*?' Mandie had declared on their first tube ride together six years ago. Just like that, Anna's days of sitting down on the underground were over. Even though on bitingly cold days she did glance longingly at their plump cushioning, missing their heated infrared touch.

She was thinking of the sun. Of warmth. Things she greatly missed as London failed to embrace spring as quickly as she would like. It was almost mid-March and still the wind had teeth, still the rain felt like ice when it fell. What she wouldn't give to be somewhere hot.

Leaning back, Anna let her eyes close for a blissful moment and remembered where she was ten years ago. Sand between her toes. White lace against her legs. The tube juddered to a halt and her eyes snapped open, thoughts of her wedding day instantly gone. A hologram on the inside of the train caught her attention: a couple hand in hand in a field of flowers, gazing at one another. She realised it was the same image she'd seen earlier on the bus. Only it wasn't a trailer, it was an advert. One she now recognised. The couple vanished, replaced by text across a perfect blue sky.

Unity. Where true love becomes real.

She turned her back to the advert, not that it did much good. The signs for Unity seemed to be everywhere. She must have walked past twenty holograms on her short trip to the tube station and at least half were for Unity. Some of them spoke, trying to draw in passers-by.

'Never again wonder where he is.'

'Never again wonder how she feels.'

'True connection is Unity.'

The doors to the tube hissed open and several people got off. Anna inhaled the dry air of the station, needing to think again of sunnier days. Elijah had told her he had a surprise for their ten-year anniversary.

Please be a holiday.

Anna had done her best to leave not-so-subtle hints around their three-storey townhouse. A laptop open on a hotel website here. A bikini on the bed there. Even bringing her suitcase out from the wardrobe and stacking it by the bedroom door. Her husband was an astute man; she knew he'd get the message.

She tingled at the thought of it. The excitement of champagne on the plane, cocktails by the pool. It would be bliss. And an added bonus: time with Elijah. Just the two of them, without life intruding at every given opportunity. Someone was always buzzing or pinging him, demanding his attention; his job forever blurring the boundaries between work and life.

'Never again argue over what to have for dinner. Unity. For true closeness.'

The advert was talking again.

Anna wished she'd remembered her earbuds so that she could drown it out, but of course she'd forgotten them. In reality, they remained in the gift box Elijah had presented her with two Christmases ago.

'I don't get it,' he'd comment whenever he caught his wife using a CD or writing a note in her diary. 'There's a whole wealth of technology around to make your life easier, Anna. Why not embrace it?'

'Because I'm old-fashioned,' she'd remind him, smiling cutely, 'and you love that about me, remember? Besides, you churn through tech like it's going out of fashion.'

'That's called progress, Anna. A new model comes in, an old one becomes obsolete.'

'We have a cupboard full of all your obsolete models,' Anna told him. 'Is that where I'll end up one day?' she mocked.

'Never.' Elijah kissed her temple. 'You'd be impossible to upgrade.'

Within her satchel, Anna's phone buzzed. That was one piece of technology she'd had to get acquainted with. She felt like she wasted a wealth of time uploading pictures of her art to social media, but it did occasionally result in a sale. Though not nearly as many as she'd like.

Babe, where are you? x

Shit.

Clearly the tracker on her phone wasn't being as reliable as Elijah would like.

Anna hated to think of him at home, dinner prepared,

crestfallen that the guest of honour still hadn't arrived. She began hurriedly typing out her reply.

> I'm so sorry, I'm nearly home, it is just insanely busy in the city.
> A few tube lines are shut. Be back soon xxx

A little white lie to smooth over his feelings. Best he didn't know her lateness was due to lingering within Marcus's shop for too long. And if the tracker kept dipping out, there was no harm in it anyway.

> You're late x

No shit. Sometimes Anna wished her husband could unwind, just a bit. Everything didn't have to be on such a tight schedule. The holiday he'd surely planned for her, they both needed it. A chance to reconnect. Relax. Celebrate ten years of married life. Anna was smiling as she stepped off the tube at her station. Even when she reached the street and cold rain pelted her, her good mood held. She just needed to practise her surprised face for when her husband revealed they'd soon be jetting off to paradise.

2

Anna was on her street, walking the stone pavement that was lined with luxury cars, some omitting a gentle glowing pulse as they began to charge overnight. The wrought-iron railing that snaked up her steps towards her navy front door was in sight. A pulse against her side. Within her bag. Anna paused, folded the flap and fumbled for her phone.

'Hey,' she answered breathily.

'Why are you answering your phone?' Mandie's voice was sharp in her ear.

'Sorry?'

'I was all ready to deliver a beautiful, loving message to your answerphone. So either you've skipped it or you're late for your anniversary meal.'

'I'm late.' Anna kept walking. 'So why not deliver the loving message directly to me?'

'You know how it goes: happy anniversary, babes; so happy for you, blah blah blah,' Mandie said in an overtly sweet voice. Anna imagined her friend sprawled out on the double bed in her studio flat, probably with a glass of champagne in hand. Mandie always liked to boast how she was living 'a champagne lifestyle on a lemonade budget'. She felt that life was for celebrating. Even if she was struggling to pay her rent, she'd still crack open a bottle of something bubbly every evening. Her vibrant attitude was one of the things Anna loved most about her.

'So anyway,' Mandie continued, 'what do you think the big anniversary gift will be?'

'I'm hoping a holiday, somewhere warm.' Anna slowed as she reached her house, peering up at the roof and the pewter sky above.

'No,' Mandie said with confidence, 'I'm guessing diamonds.'

'Ooh.'

'Or a threesome.'

'Wow.' Anna looked down to her rain-splashed ankle boots. 'Thanks, Mand.' Her friend's bluntness was something she loved a little less than her vibrancy. 'I really can't see that being Elijah's style.'

'I'm just saying,' Mandie yawned languidly on the other end of the line, 'men in their mid-thirties, they get restless. Start to wonder about all the sexual horizons they've yet to explore.'

'I don't—'

'And a threesome really isn't so bad. Trust me. Just make sure you vet the person first.'

'I think Elijah would have an aneurysm if we invited someone else into our bedroom.'

'He might surprise you,' Mandie declared suggestively, and Anna just knew her friend was raising her pristine eyebrows as she spoke. 'No matter how much we think we know someone, we never truly do.'

'I'm pretty sure Elijah would most definitely not want a threesome.'

'I guess if he did, he'd ideally look at getting you cloned. Two Annas at once.'

'That's . . . troubling.'

'He's completely infatuated with you.'

'I still think one of me is more than enough for anyone,' Anna joked. 'Besides, cloning is, like, ten years off.'

'I don't know,' Mandie sounded thoughtful, 'I've heard that tech is closer than you think. More like five years, max. You could pretend to have a twin. Or a doppelgänger. Would you be the good one or the evil one?'

'On that uplifting note, I'm here; I've got to go.'

'Okay, well keep me posted.' Mandie made a kissing sound and then hung up. Anna returned her phone to her satchel and looked at her front door, its polished silver knocker which gleamed even in the gloom. The camera embedded above the doorbell to the right of the door, waiting to scan her face. Ever watching.

A threesome.

She chewed her lip. Was that really something Elijah would want? It would be completely incongruent with who he was. Her husband was shy, private. It was typical Mandie, thrusting a firework into an empty room, waiting to watch everything explode. She never understood the quietness of Anna's life, her marriage. And Anna *knew* Elijah. Didn't she? The camera beside the doorbell shone green, the door opened and her husband peered down the steps towards her.

'Hey, you okay?' he asked tersely. 'What are you standing around outside for?'

'Sorry.' Anna brushed away the conversation with Mandie and climbed the steps, the rain now turned to mist. As she removed her boots and coat she felt her husband watching her. 'I know I'm late.'

'It's fine.' Elijah moved close, folding his arms around her, but there was a stiffness to his touch.

He's mad at me.

'Please, Elijah. I've said I'm sorry.'

Her husband stared at her but she failed to read his guarded expression.

'You know I came home as soon I could, that I've been excited for tonight.' She added a gentle lilt to her voice, reached up to place her hands upon Elijah's shoulders. She pouted slightly, noticed his mouth lift at the corners.

Elijah smelt of coffee and cologne. 'I'm just glad you're back so that we can celebrate.' His lips pressed against her cheek. Soft. Just like his hands.

'Well, I'm starving.' Anna peered round him towards the door to the kitchen.

'Good.' He took her hand in his and guided her towards the dinner he had prepared. Anna followed, dwarfed by his six-foot-two frame. Elijah was lean. When she'd met him, he was like a streak of lightning. All bones. But he'd filled out over the years, taken on a more manly shape. His russet-brown hair was neatly cut, face freshly shaven. He turned to smile at her, chestnut eyes crinkling with excitement.

Anna felt butterflies in her stomach. Mandie didn't know what she was talking about. This was her husband, her Eli. She'd known him for almost twenty years. They'd been inseparable since that first awkward kiss at the Student Union. She had been his first. His only.

'Oh, Eli,' Anna gushed as she saw the dining table: two settings; wine poured; candlelight flickering, the wick already half burned down. 'You didn't have to go to all this trouble.'

She leaned up and kissed him.

'And wine too; I didn't think you'd be drinking.'

'Well, it's a big occasion.' His hands were on her shoulders, warm. 'This is our ten years; it's special.'

'Can you believe that a decade ago we were in Santorini?' Anna smiled wistfully as she sat down.

Elijah took the chair opposite, twisting his wrist to check

the time on his Tag Heuer watch. 'I think ten years ago, around now, Gavin had started vomiting in the pool.'

'Oh, God, yeah.' Anna laughed at the memory – the best man doubled over by the edge of the pool; Helen hysterical at his side, telling him not to get any sick on his suit. Instead, it all landed in the aquamarine water, curdling and spoiling it.

Helen.

Once she had been Anna's closest friend, back at university where their lives tangled together. They'd take shots together all night, spend days curled up in their pyjamas on Anna's single bed bingeing countless TV shows. Anna felt an ache in her chest. How she missed that connection. That feeling.

'He was really on one that day,' Elijah recalled, drawing her back into the moment. 'I mean, he always drinks a lot, but I think he outdid himself in Santorini.'

'He did.' Anna speared a piece of pasta with her fork. As she placed it in her mouth, she could tell it was freshly made, not store-bought and from a bag like the pasta she served. It tasted divine. 'You made this?' she asked between mouthfuls. 'Like, rolled out the pasta and everything?'

'No.' Elijah gave a soft shake of his head, still smart in his shirt and trousers from work, though his jacket and tie were gone. 'I can't take all the credit. Celine went out and grabbed most of it for me while I was in meetings.'

'Ah,' Anna felt her body tighten, 'how nice of her.'

Celine. Her husband's new assistant. Twenty something. French. With legs for days and hair so dark and glossy it surely couldn't be natural.

'Oh fuck,' Mandie had exclaimed when Anna showed her a social media picture during one of their lunches out, 'she looks like a bloody model. Watch that.'

What Anna had needed to hear was, *Yes she's gorgeous but your husband adores you; you have nothing to worry about.* Mandie and her honesty. Dammit. Now Anna flinched whenever she heard the woman's name.

Thanks, Mand.

'She really goes above and beyond as an assistant,' Anna remarked icily. Elijah grinned, oblivious to her tone.

'Yeah, she's great.'

Of course she's fucking great. She can probably speak five languages, listens to classical music and if she made art, you could bet it would sell.

Anna swallowed, the pasta thick in her throat.

'Gavin is forever hovering round her,' Elijah added, expression darkening.

'Mmm,' Anna noted, dismissive.

'I guess Helen is just used to his antics,' Elijah remarked as he raised his glass and sipped on red wine. Anna watched the muscles in his neck working as he drank, wondered how many glasses he was planning on having.

'She's always been a pushover with him,' Anna rolled her eyes, 'ever since uni.'

Uni.

The ache she felt in her chest over her friend felt stronger. Sharper.

'Happier to turn a blind eye than rock the boat.'

'Can we talk about something else?' Anna speared another piece of pasta. 'About *us*.'

It is our anniversary, after all.

Elijah thoughtfully chewed his pasta before he responded. 'Hmm? Sure. So where were you again? In the city? I don't like it when the tracker drops out.'

'Getting art supplies,' Anna explained with a sigh.

Though sometimes I wonder why I bother.

'Why did you need art supplies?' Elijah asked as they

continued eating. 'Last time I checked the studio was pretty well stocked.'

'I was really just looking, seeing what's new. I didn't know you checked my supplies.'

Elijah raised his eyebrows but said nothing else.

Of course he checks the studio. He checks everything.

'And then the trains were playing up and—'

'It's important you make sure you have data on, with your phone,' Elijah interrupted, looking at her, tone stern. 'I need to know where you are, Anna. It's a big city.'

'I know but . . .' She exhaled, keen to not tumble into an argument. 'It's not like I track your phone.'

'You could if you wanted.' As if to prove a point, he pulled his phone from his pocket and placed it face up on the table. 'You just need to get the app. I showed you what to do.'

'Yeah . . .' Anna shrugged half-heartedly. Why did everything have to be a pulse on a screen? Every step accounted for? 'Anyway,' she smoothly changed the subject, 'the piece I'm working on, it feels a bit different from everything else. I think if I can nail it, then, you know, it might be the start of something for me.'

'As long as you're happy.'

Happy.

He knew she hadn't been happy with her art for years. How could she be? But in his eyes it was just a hobby. Not her career. Not her life. She wasn't serious about her future. Not like Celine.

Fucking Celine with her catlike grace. Her kindness. Her enthusiasm.

Her career.

Anna sank low in her chair.

'Hey, come on, smile. This is our big night.'

'Sure.'

Elijah raised his glass to his wife. 'Thank you for ten wonderful years.'

'Thank you.' Anna managed to smile as their glasses clinked together.

'So, do you want your gift?' Elijah asked playfully, knowing she did. Anna loved gifts. Every Christmas and birthday she'd preen and coo over turquoise boxes containing silver, gasp when she opened designer handbags. She loved to be adored and Elijah loved to adore her. It was a formula which had served them well throughout their relationship. Still, she always did the dance when talk turned to gifts.

'You didn't have to get me anything.'

'Don't be ridiculous.' Elijah's gaze was warm as he watched her. 'This is a big occasion, and a big occasion calls for something extra special.'

Anna's stomach turned over nervously. She thought of her original gift for her husband – a portrait she'd spent a month painting out in her shed at the back of the garden. Only two days ago, after a night on the prosecco with Mandie, she decided the gift was too paltry. Too pathetic. She went out to the edge of their little garden, grabbed it from its easel and burned it while her husband slept in the house behind her. Anna stood and shivered as she watched flames consume his brown eyes, his thick hair, his boyish grin. She waited until it was ash and then she joined him in their marital bed, hating the fact that the thing he truly wanted, the thing he yearned for, she could never give him.

'I keep thinking about how close we are.' Elijah's fingers drummed rhythmically atop the beech-wood surface of the table.

'Okay . . .' A bubble of nervous laughter erupted from Anna. Stupid Mandie, getting in her head.

Please, not the threesome. I love my husband, I do, but—

'I want us to get closer.' Suddenly a large white box was on the table, adorned with a scarlet velvet bow. Elijah slid it across to his surprised wife. 'Happy anniversary, darling.'

Anna grabbed the box, eager. Hands atop it, she felt the coolness of its surface, levelled her gaze to stare at her husband.

'I know how you keep beating yourself up about stuff that is beyond your control,' he said gently, 'how you keep worrying about things.'

Anna blushed. Had he known about the fire? Had he peered out and seen her studying the flames like some demented person? But then why hadn't he spoken up? Carefully, Anna began to untie the bow; it felt soft against her fingers, like the fur of a puppy.

'I'm hoping this will make things better for us,' Elijah continued as Anna gently raised the lid from the box. 'I feel like with this, we will be perfect.'

3

The lid came off easily. Within the box there was a cushion, the same colour as the bow. Merlot red and soft to the touch. Atop the cushion a single piece of gold card, embossed with words. Anna delicately picked it up, candlelight winking against its shiny surface.

'What is . . . ?' As she brought it closer, she noticed the shape of a logo. A heart within a heart. Hers almost stopped. Anna didn't move. Didn't speak. She just stared at the golden card within her grasp. Across the table, Elijah awkwardly cleared his throat.

'Well, what do you think?'

What do you think?

Anna blinked, feeling unsteady. The card and its neatly embossed text blurred in and out of focus.

'Sweetheart?'

She drew in a long breath, anchoring herself. Then she silently read the card.

Executive Package
Elijah and Anna Weston
24th March
True connection is Unity

'It's . . .' The date was just under a week away. Anna read it again. And again. Then peered up at her husband, half of his face in shadow, the rest bathed in the fluttering golden glow of the candles.

'I know it's a lot.' He gave her a shy, lopsided smile. It made him look so much like the fidgety boy in the Ramones T-shirt she'd met all those years ago. It was rare to see him like that these days: unguarded. Vulnerable. Anna coughed, trying to find her voice.

'U-unity?'

He reached for one of her hands, knocking over the box. The velvet cushion slid free, as dark as a beating heart. 'It will be good for us. Great, even.'

'You really . . .' Anna looked to her other hand, which still gripped the golden card. The shock was easing. As it abated, she gained clarity. Elijah had always been drawn to technology, fascinated and entranced by it. Every new product, he simply had to have. Their home was a shrine to every technological advancement over the last decade. The doors, the windows, the toilet, even the heated sheets on the bed, everything was controlled by an app on their phones. Everything opened or closed at the touch of a button. They could be on a beach in the Bahamas and still able to turn on a tap in the kitchen. To Elijah, Unity was surely just the next logical step. A piece of tech they could be a part of.

'Everyone at work talks about it.' Elijah spoke quickly. 'Wishing they could get one. It's extremely exclusive. Appointments are insanely hard to come by. And the reviews are just ridiculous; people say it completely changed their marriage. Their life.'

Anna grimaced. 'I wasn't aware that our lives needed changing.'

'No, no, I'm not saying that.' His fingers dug into her hand as his hold on her tightened.

'Hmm.' Anna kept looking at the golden invitation.

'And we have the Executive Package,' her husband enthused, 'which means the procedure is minimally invasive, just a single incision behind the left ear.'

Anna's fingers strayed to the point he spoke of, tracing the curve of her skull.

'It comes with a ten-year guarantee.'

'Right.' Anna turned the card over, the heart logo large upon the back.

'We go in, have our own treatment room, all completely luxurious.'

'Sounds like a spa day,' Anna replied flatly.

'It will be like that,' Elijah's eyes were wide, imploring, 'just like that. Relaxed. Informal. Just you and me.'

'But then . . . then you get to hear my every thought?'

'And you get to hear mine,' Elijah countered. 'Think how much better that will be for us. How you can stop being suspicious of Celine.'

'I'm not—'

'Anna, I know you. You worry, you fixate. You dwell on things.' He sucked in a breath, looked pained.

Anna hung her head. 'Maybe I don't want to know what you truly think of me.'

'But you should,' Elijah reached again for her hand, 'because I love you. Anna, I love you more than anything. When we are apart, I miss you. Even when I'm just at the office. This way, we will always be connected, always a part of one another's day. Promise me you'll think about it?'

'I mean, does it, you know, turn off?'

Elijah shifted awkwardly.

'It switches *off* when we sleep,' he told her, savouring the chance to be knowledgeable. 'We both have to be conscious to hear one another's thoughts.'

'Right.' With a slow exhale Anna placed the card on the table. Now flat, it no longer sparkled in the candlelight.

'And you can tune in and out of one another's thoughts. It is all very intuitive, apparently.'

'It's just . . .' Anna stared at the card. 'Hearing each other's thoughts, all the time. Don't you think it's a bit much?'

He wants to be in my head.
He wants to hear everything.
I can't let him do that.
Fuck.
This is too much.
I can't let him know about—

'No, I don't think it's too much.'

'I mean . . . *all* our thoughts, Eli?'

'Sweetheart, it's not as daunting as it sounds.'

'Because it sounds pretty daunting.'

Anna continued to stare at the card.

He'd hear everything.

'There is nothing to worry about,' Elijah continued.

All my thoughts.
All my worries.

'Eli . . .'

Everything.

'I really think we should do this, Anna.' Elijah's gaze grew glassy. 'I think this will make us as close as we can possibly be. I'd always know where you are, if you're okay, if you're safe. Don't you want that? Don't you want us to be even closer?'

I don't want you in my head.

'Aren't we close enough?' Anna looked up at him, pulse thick in her ear. He moved to raise the bottle of wine, a glugging sound filling the space between them as he refilled her glass.

Why does he want this?

'Eli, I . . . I have an app on my phone so you can track me, we have cameras all over the house that you watch when you're at work. We have—'

'I want to be as close to you as I possibly can be,' Elijah told her earnestly, placing the bottle down. 'I put all those things in place to protect you, Anna. To keep you safe. And I bought the Executive Package because you deserve the best. I work so very hard to give you everything. To give you all of me.'

'I know.' Anna's voice was small. She was thinking of her studio, her paintings, the bills she failed to pay anything towards.

I work so very hard to give you everything.

Elijah had built an entire world for her; all he was asking was for her to share it with him. To let him in.

My every thought.

My every worry.

My every reaction.

My every regret.

Anna's pulse began to quicken. 'I need some fresh air.' As she stood, her hand knocked her glass. It tipped to one side, wine flowing out like blood across the table. It spread over the golden card, drowning it. 'Shit, sorry, I'm—'

'I've got it, go.' Elijah dismissed her with a wave of his hand. 'It's fine.'

Within the garden Anna paced, an e-cigarette between her fingers, its tip glowing neon blue in the gloom of the night. She shivered in her dress, wishing she'd grabbed a coat before heading out, but she'd been moving quickly, without thought.

Now, phone in one hand, e-cigarette in the other, she paced back and forth. There was no moonlight, just the glow from the nearby patio doors. The rain had moved on and now the city sounded close. The hum of car engines and horns piercing the night. The rattle of an outdoor bin chirping as it closed, digital lock in place. The rasp of a dog barking. Anna kept smoking as she scrolled down the screen of her phone. She had intended to look up Unity. Do some actual research. She'd seen the adverts, the holograms, everyone had. But she never gave them more than a passing glance, sensing that all it sold was an unachievable dream. A reality that could never exist. But when her husband saw those adverts, he saw something else. In the sickening couples gazing adoringly at one another, he saw *them*. Or at least, what he hoped they might become.

Are we not already perfect?

Anna's chest ached. She knew they weren't.

Is he restless? Bored? Tired of it being just the two of us?

One hand pressed to the flatness of her stomach.

A surname. A mortgage. A home. A life. Already they shared so much.

Her gaze flitted to her studio.

'It's a shed,' Mandie had remarked the first time she came round.

'No, it's my studio,' Anna had corrected her.

'Shove fairy lights, easels and an electric heater in there, but it's still a shed, sweetie.'

Did Elijah take her work seriously? Or did he also see just a shed?

I'll find out soon enough.

Could she handle that? What if her husband was actually just humouring her?

Shit.

She couldn't do it. How could she? It was too much. Allowing someone into your mind?

Not someone. Eli. Your husband.

Anna blinked back tears, head throbbing. Turning towards the house she saw his silhouette in the bedroom window. He was there for a second before withdrawing from the glass. Already she denied him so much. The empty spare room was a painful reminder of her failures. Her shortcomings. Anna took a long drag on her e-cigarette.

Every conscious thought. Would that be so bad? Anna groaned, knowing it would be. But he loved her. Through it all, all the heartache and pain, he continued to love her. Elijah. Her Elijah.

You know him. Better than you know yourself.

And he loves you, despite all that has happened.

Within her hand, her phone trembled. A message from Mandie.

> So, how was it? Need me to suggest some decent escort websites? x

Anna's laugh was brittle against the cool night air. She suddenly wished Elijah had suggested a threesome. It would have been much simpler. Quickly she wrote a reply and hit send.

> We need to talk xx

And say what?

Wearily, Anna closed her eyes and tipped her head skyward. More than ever, she needed her friend's pragmatism. Needed to be told if her husband had just suggested the most ludicrous thing ever for their anniversary.

Everyone at work talks about it.

How Elijah loved to gloat to his colleagues. Always

needing to be the best. First with golf, then poker, then all the VR games and headsets. Whatever the hobby *du jour* was, Elijah had to master it, and fast. With Gavin hot on his heels, their university rivalry having graduated into the workplace. But this was all too far, surely? Anna slowly twisted her head to look back up at the white walls of her home, at the distant green blinking of watching cameras, her husband now nowhere in sight. If she could read his mind in that very moment, would it reassure her? Anna's phone illuminated with Mandie's reply.

That bad? Xxx

It wasn't, was it? Anna blew bubblegum-scented smoke into the air, watched it drift away.

She tapped out her reply.

More like complicated xx

Mandie's reply was swift.

Nothing a good lubricant couldn't sort xx

Anna laughed. It was a rough bark of a laugh, from her belly. And it felt good. Cigarette finished, she went back inside the house, back to her husband.

4

Anna loved the stillness that settled within her house at night. Even with all the gadgets and apps Elijah insisted on cramming into every available space, the floorboards on the stairs still creaked, the wind still gently brushed the curtains when a window was left open. The house had always felt classic, inviting. And at night, with the lights dimmed, it was at its best. Beautiful and welcoming. Like something from a television show, an image of what a happy marital home should be.

But Anna felt uneasy as she padded up the stairs to bed, one hand following the curve of the banister. The bare wood of the steps hard beneath her feet. If only he'd let her carpet them, soften them.

'But that wouldn't be in keeping with the classic style of the house,' Elijah told her. Anna pointed out that all his technical additions were hardly in keeping with the house either.

'That's different,' was his curt reply. And she knew not to press it. The staircase would remain wooden and bare. Hard.

The third step released a creak as she stepped upon it.
My thoughts.
She reached the landing.

My head.

He wants to be in my head.

Her temple throbbed with the weight of it all. Sliding into bed, Anna chanced a furtive look at her husband where he sat beside her, soft pillows propped at his back, a tablet glowing in his hands.

'I'm just really not sure about it,' she admitted, watching Elijah's expression harden. 'I think hearing each other's thoughts is . . . it's *intrusive*, Eli. It's too much.'

'Anna.' He sighed as he said her name. 'This is . . . this will be good for us. This level of connection, we need it.'

'Do we?'

'Yes,' he told her with urgency. 'I want to be in there.' He reached out and tapped her forehead. 'I want a level of intimacy neither of us has experienced before.'

'Sure, but—'

'Just think how intuitive it would be in the bedroom.' His eyes burned with excitement.

Anna drew her mouth into a hard line. 'I'm perfectly happy in the bedroom.'

'But if I could know in the moment exactly what you wanted, imagine how amazing that would be.' He reached for her, slowly grazed his fingers against her cheek.

'Elijah—'

'I wouldn't even suggest this if I didn't think it would work.'

'I'm just saying,' Anna inhaled slowly, deliberately, 'I think this is too far. I mean, don't you, really? Our *thoughts*, Eli? Aren't you happy as we are? The two of us? This life we have built?'

'It's just the two of us, and I'm fine with that, but why not add this other dimension? Be even closer than we are?'

Just the two of us.

'I love this life I've built for us.' Elijah offered her a smile.

I've built.

'There's nothing wrong with pushing for the next step. We have been through so, so much. Much more than a couple should ever have to endure.'

'Eli—' She felt guilt gripping her chest, strangling her.

'Anna, I love you.' He reached across the bed, grabbed her hand tightly, squeezed it. 'I've loved you since the moment I met you.'

Anna felt tears in her eyes that weren't yet ready to fall.

'I love you too.'

That moment, their meeting, she didn't want to go back there.

I can't let him know.

'I'm asking you to do this for me, Anna.' Elijah studied her as he spoke, hand still gripping hers. 'After everything, don't we deserve this?'

She couldn't find her voice, could only nod.

He means after everything I've put him through.

She tried to imagine it, Elijah in her mind.

'Please, Anna.'

Anna recalled all the times he was at her bedside within yet another hospital, clutching her hand as he was now, promising he wouldn't let go.

'You struggled so much when . . . when we lost them.'

A gasp of a startled breath. Anna looked into her husband's eyes, fearing he was already there, in her thoughts.

'Eli—'

'Do you have any idea how much that all scared me? Seeing how hurt you were? How much you went into yourself?'

'Elijah, I was . . . I was grieving.' She heard her voice crack.

How can you grieve for something you never had?

And yet you could. With a pain so raw, so isolating, that some days it had the power to take your breath away.

'I was there, Anna, even when you were at your lowest. I wanted to be closer but you pushed me away. Now . . . now that would never happen again.'

'Eli—'

'Let me be there, Anna, protecting you as much as I possibly can. Let me in. I can't . . . It kills me worrying you might slip away again. It's exhausting.'

Anna clenched her teeth together, wondering if it was as exhausting as losing a baby, over and over?

'We need to do this.' Elijah raised a hand to stroke the curve of her jaw, lowering it to the sweep of her neck. 'Can you do this for me? After everything I've done for you?'

How can I say no?

He's right . . . That time . . . it was so dark. And I felt so alone. Maybe . . . maybe this would help.

Anna shifted her body, crossing the expanse of the bed so that she was directly beside her husband, able to kiss his soft lips. 'I'll do it,' she declared gently, 'for you, I'll get the chip.' As Elijah wrapped her in his arms, drew her closer, the house groaned and creaked as it did every night, releasing the tensions of the day.

5

'You can't be serious!' Mandie shrieked, loud enough to turn a few heads within the bar they were in. She peered at Anna over the vast glass of lime-coloured cocktail she clenched between both hands, the colour clashing hideously with her neon-pink jumpsuit. Anna's expression didn't shift. 'Oh my God, you're serious.'

'He's booked us in for next week.' Anna attempted to be bold but feared her words were coming out with the timidity she felt.

'For Unity? The OneMind shit?' Mandie stared at her friend, eyes wide, before drinking deeply from her glass. 'Honestly, Anna, you can't be serious.'

'I am . . . He is. We are.'

'You're going to give him access to your every thought?' Mandie lowered her glass, ice cubes clinking loudly as the green ocean settled. 'Your *every thought*?' She pinched the tips of her fingers together, long purple nails meeting one another.

'Not exactly *every* thought,' Anna corrected her feebly. 'You can sort of tune in and out from one another. And it doesn't even connect when one person is asleep.'

'Right, so just *some* thoughts, then.' Mandie theatrically threw her hands up in the air and leaned back in her chair. 'Well then, that's all right.'

'Please don't be like that,' Anna mumbled, tugging on the edge of her fringe and looking at the table.

'Like what? Reasonable? Honest?'

'I just . . .' When Anna glanced over at her friend her eyes smarted with the desire to cry. 'I love Eli. I know him. I know him better than I know myself. I know every mole on his face, the way he takes his tea, the fact he can't put on socks unless they've been warmed in the microwave.'

'*What?*' Mandie grimaced. Then she shook herself and resumed her line of thought. 'Your husband's strange quirks aside, how can you possibly think that having access to everything he thinks is a *good thing*?'

'Because . . .' Anna wedged her thumbnail between her teeth and began to gently chew it.

'Just because he gives you so much flex with your art, that he pays for your shed, your supplies, makes it so you don't have to work . . . Him doing all that doesn't mean you owe him anything.'

'Studio,' Anna mumbled.

'Hon, it's a shed. Not that it fucking matters, your art is the shit. You know I love it. Like I love you.'

'I know.'

'I just don't want you doing something that is going to be an epic mistake.'

'The reviews for the chip are amazing. So many couples rave about it,' Anna offered, reaching for her own drink and swallowing a few sips of the sour-tasting cocktail.

Mandie rolled her eyes. 'Uh-huh. You know any of them?'

'No, but they say it gave them this new . . . new closeness. That it's amazing.' Anna's voice was strained. Desperate.

'Who are you trying to convince? Me or you?' Mandie gave her a level look.

Why does she always have to be so right about everything?

'Anna, you're better than this. Unity is bullshit. Our mind . . . in this crazy fucked-up world, is the only place that is truly *ours*. Don't give yours away so easily.'

'I'm not.' Anna released her thumb and wiped at her cheeks, searching for tears she feared had fallen. 'Do you not think I've thought all this? As soon as he gave me the card, I panicked.'

'I bet,' Mandie remarked sagely, gaze darkening. 'If you let him into your mind there will be nowhere to hide.'

That's what I'm afraid of.

'I know.'

Because if he finds out about—

'Nobody completely knows anyone.' Mandie gazed into Anna's eyes, searching them. 'Remember that.'

'I *know*.' Anna looked down at her hands, clenched together atop the table.

'Bet you're wishing he'd asked for a threesome now,' Mandie added wryly, sensing the need to lighten the mood.

'You know what Elijah is like.' Anna reached for her glass and drank, liking how it brought some clarity to her thoughts, stilled her manic heartbeat. 'He's obsessed with any kind of new tech. Lives for it.'

'Your house is next-level ridiculous.' Mandie drained her glass and then raised her hand towards a young waiter to order a fresh round. 'Two.' She smiled sweetly, gesturing across to Anna even though her glass remained half full. 'Remember that time I got trapped in your downstairs loo?'

Anna spluttered her drink. She did. In the moment it hadn't felt quite so funny, when she was frantically trying to understand the various settings in their control app housed within the tablet mounted on the wall in the hall. Lights were turning on and off all over the place, the robot hoover fired up, all while Mandie banged the door and complained she was in the dark and the toilet kept squirting water at her. It was only once her friend was finally free that they both doubled over laughing. Anna had vowed to get to grips with the house app. Though like so many things, it slid to the bottom of her to-do list, forever replaced by something more pressing. Something that held more interest to her.

'Look.' Mandie's tone grew serious as their fresh drinks arrived. 'Do you want this? The Unity thing? Never mind what Elijah thinks.'

Anna considered the question. It was one that had been running over and over in her head for the past twenty-four hours. She loved her husband. Truly. Completely. She loved that he supported her art, that he gave her the space to chase her dream. She loved how he made her breakfast every morning, even though he was the one heading out to work. Elijah was kind. Loving. And every day she feared he was going to be snatched away from her because of the child she couldn't give him. How long until she hit forty and he decided he didn't actually want it to be just the two of them? How easily he could replace her with a younger, fertile model.

Someone like Celine.

But if Anna knew what he was thinking, she'd know when she risked being pushed out. Would know when to fight. When to worry. When to cut and run. She'd know it all.

'Don't let it be the baby thing,' Mandie suddenly blurted.

Anna baulked, cheeks red.

'I don't need some piece-of-shit microchip to know what you're thinking,' Mandie continued with a delicate smile. 'We're best friends. It comes with the territory that I know what's going on in that head of yours.'

'It's a factor, yes,' Anna admitted quietly. Then she drank. A long, draining drink from her cocktail, knocking it back until her teeth hit the cool glass and all she could taste was blueberry and gin.

'You know that it shouldn't be.'

Anna said nothing. She finished her first drink and reached for her second.

'Because what happened wasn't your fault,' Mandie pressed on, brow furrowed. 'You can't keep beating yourself up about it.'

'I'm not, but ...' Anna cradled her head in her hands, drawing in a long breath. 'Eli and I ... we share a life. A history.'

'And soon a mind,' Mandie added grimly.

'Besides, it won't last. It's just a fad. He wants to try it out, test the technology. That's all. Have bragging rights. I guarantee that in a month we will be having our chips removed.'

Mandie winced.

'You know how he is; when something is all shiny and new he has to have it. Then a new thing comes along and he upgrades, moves on.'

'Is he trying to upgrade *you*?'

'It's a simple procedure,' Anna explained, ignoring the comment. 'They make a cut here,' she turned her head and held her hair back, 'and then insert the microchip. All you feel is a tiny scratch. Then it's synced with the partner device.' She hated how much she sounded like the adverts she tried to avoid through the city. 'Fuck,' she blew out a tight breath, 'I sound like such a dick.'

'Yes,' Mandie agreed. 'You do. As long as you only *sound* like a dick and don't get in the habit of thinking about other dicks.'

Anna blushed.

'Hadn't thought about that, had you?' Mandie pointed a long finger at her. 'Because if you have this, you'll need to watch it. Me, I could never...' She gave a rueful shake of her head. 'While we've been sitting here I've scouted four guys I'd consider taking home. One girl.'

'That's because you're an animal,' Anna teased, grateful to turn the subject away from Unity.

'It's because I'm alive and making the most of it,' Mandie countered. 'Monogamy isn't for everyone.'

'I know.'

'And he'll doubtless have thoughts about other women; he's a man with a beating heart, after all. Are you prepared for that?'

No.

'Yes.' Anna drank again.

'Bullshit.' Mandie lifted an eyebrow at her.

'It'll... it'll be fine.'

Elijah wouldn't risk this if he thought about other women.

'And how often do you think about other men?'

'I don't,' Anna replied sharply, quickly.

'I call bullshit again.'

Fuck.

Mandie sighed as she watched her friend. 'I'm just saying, we are all human. We think things. That's how it goes. You sure Eli is the kind of guy who could deal with an errant thought?'

No.

'He wouldn't suggest it if he wasn't,' Anna replied unconvincingly.

'I just fail to see what good can come from any of this,' Mandie continued.

'It's about connection,' Anna offered, beginning to feel woozy, the kick of the cocktail hitting her system. 'Like... the ultimate connection.'

'And you want that?'

'Yes.' Music from the bar was pulsing in Anna's ears. She felt restless. 'I want that.'

I owe him that.

'You might think now that you can control your thoughts all the time, but hon, you can't. No one can. Our thoughts betray us.'

'Like I said, it's not *all* the time. You tune in, tune out.'

'What if you hear something you don't like?' Mandie was having to raise her voice over the building pulse of the music. She looked into Anna's eyes. 'What if he hears something *he* doesn't like?'

'Come on,' Anna swallowed, stood up, legs wobbly, and reached for her friend's hand, 'I need to dance.'

'I still think it's a bad idea,' Mandie called as she followed her towards the dance floor. Anna ignored the comment and threw her hands up, swaying in time to the music. It was an old song. One that came out when she was a student. When she first felt the sting of true love.

'I love him,' Anna declared as she twirled around.

'I know.' Mandie ceased gyrating to the music and embraced her friend. She kissed Anna's cheek, leaving a crimson print. 'I'm just worried about you.'

'Don't be,' Anna assured her brightly, drunk. 'It will be fine.' She tried to focus on how happy all the couples in the adverts look.

All fake. All staged.

But there hadn't been anything negative in the news about Unity. Had there? Perhaps everyone who went there was truly happy.

My thoughts, I can control them. Can't I?

She trusted Elijah, his instincts. He'd bought the house

they lived in, the car outside their home. The clothes on her back. Why would he push her to do something that risked burning everything down?

No errant thoughts.

He won't even hear everything. He will tune out.

Beside her friend Anna kept dancing to the song, remembering a different time, the flash of disco lights in the SU. A face in the crowd, staring. Burning her with their gaze. Anna slapped the heel of her hand against her temple.

Stop it. Stop thinking. Stop it.

'Babe?' Mandie threw her a concerned look.

'Headache,' Anna shouted over the bass. Her thoughts, she was going to have to get a lot better at controlling them. And fast.

For me, Unity was about safety. I work as a paramedic, which involves late-night shift work, prolonged times when I'm away from my partner. Now we can interact simply and instantly. It is more than reassuring. It feels like having him there with me. Now my shifts fly by. As a medical professional, I can't recommend Unity enough. I rave about it to everyone I meet. It is so, so very simple to have the chip implanted and the benefits are truly extraordinary.

The trust that comes from knowing someone completely is so rare, so special, and Unity captures that. Knowing, first hand from him his thoughts, how much my husband cares for me, makes me feel valued, secure and loved. In a job that involves many high-pressure moments, this sense of security has really changed things for me. I don't need to wait until I'm home for a reassuring kind word. It is already there. He is my life partner, my guide. Our love has only been strengthened by Unity.

Karen Roberts, Unity User

6

THEN

The bass thumped through the walls. Anna lingered shyly in the corridor, assessing the darkened room before her, the strobe of neon lights.

'Come on.' Helen held her hand, alabaster skin cold. 'It's going to be fun.'

Anna wasn't so sure. The minidress she'd put on hitched too far up her thighs, making her self-conscious. And already her feet ached within the strappy sandals she'd worn.

'It's Freshers' Week,' Helen was tugging her towards the darkness, 'we are meant to be having fun.'

It was only Tuesday, though to Anna it felt like a month had passed since her dad had waved goodbye from the car park outside her halls of residence. The little room that was to be her home for the next several months felt bleak and impersonal. More a cell than a bedroom. Walls of bare plaster, a single sink that carried the scent of mould. A wardrobe that whined every time it opened and a bed that was stiff and wedged beneath a single, smeared window. It was far from the ideal Anna'd had in her mind, fed to her through television shows over the years.

'It will be the time of your life,' her dad had said as he leaned in to kiss her cheek. 'I met your mother in my first year.' He'd eased back from her, taking his air of sadness with him.

'You just need some fairy lights, posters . . .' Anna turned to see a willowy redhead behind her, leaning into the doorframe to assess the bedroom. 'I'm Helen.' She extended a long-fingered hand and smiled.

'Anna.'

'Anna, hey, what are you studying?'

'Media studies.'

'Ooh, fun.'

'You?'

'Maths.'

'Intense.'

'I hope so.' Helen had blue eyes that held a coolness which unnerved Anna. 'I've got some fairy lights that my cousin gave me; they're not really my thing but you can have them.' She gestured across the hallway, to her own room. 'No posters, though. But it's a start.'

Almost everyone in their corridor wanted to go to the Student Union. But the first night Anna stayed in her room and Helen hung back with her. They talked. For hours they talked about who they were, where they were from. What they wanted for their futures. As their housemates rumbled back in around two in the morning Anna felt warmed by the developing fire of friendship. She was going to try hard at university. She'd promised her father as much. No more going off the rails. Rebelling. Drinking until she blacked out.

'People tolerate it right now because of losing your mum,' a college tutor had sternly warned her, 'but that goodwill is going to run out. Remember that.'

Anna vowed to be a new version of herself at university. A better one.

'I love this song,' Helen declared loudly over the music as she led them towards the bar. Anna wore her keys on a lanyard around her neck which rattled when she walked, her money for the night stuffed into her push-up bra. The music drilled through Anna as Helen ordered double vodka and lemonades. 'Here.' She pushed a plastic tumbler into Anna's hands. No ice. No frills. Just the drink as it came. 'To university.' Helen knocked her cup into Anna's.

'To university,' Anna echoed, bringing the cup to her lips and drinking down the sweet, slightly warm contents.

The alcohol helped. It shut down the voices in her head which continually fretted. Anna joined Helen and some of their housemates on the dance floor. Arms up. Head thrown back. She didn't even know the song that was playing but in the moment she felt alive. Free. And it felt good. As she danced and turned, the lights flashed in her eyes. She caught glimpses of figures gathered around the dance floor, shadowy and distant. And then she locked eyes with someone in that crowd. Only slightly taller than her, with dusty blond hair that messily tumbled over his forehead. He wore jeans, a T-shirt and faded Converse. In his hand he held a bottle of beer. When he caught her eye the faint crinkle of a smile pulled on his lips. Anna turned her back to him, laughing. Blushing. She wondered if any of the make-up she'd carefully applied in front of her little mirror back in her room had smudged. Not that she really cared. The vodka in her system was boosting her up so high that nothing could bring her down.

'Hey.' Breath on her cheek, warm and laced with hops. She turned as a fresh song started up. The blond guy was beside her on the dance floor, comically twisting his hips.

'Hey.' Anna stifled a giggle. 'Nice moves.'

He ceased moving, extended his hand to her in an oddly formal gesture. 'I'm Gavin.'

She slid her delicate hand into his and he made a show of shaking it theatrically. 'I'm Anna.'

'Anna.' He placed her name in his mouth like he was trying it on. Checking it fit.

'And I'm Helen,' another voice piped up, eager and bright.

'Helen, hi.' Gavin gave her a courteous nod. 'That's our crazy mate, Oscar.' He glanced in the direction of a short redhead who was dancing manically, seemingly alone beneath the flashing lights. 'And this is Elijah.' He drew forward a figure who lingered reluctantly behind him. Tall and slim, brown-eyed and nervous. He clutched his bottle of beer to his chest like a shield.

'Hey.' He directed his greeting at no one in particular.

'He's not much of a dancer,' Gavin said apologetically with a roll of his pale grey eyes, 'and apparently also not much of a talker.' He leaned towards his friend, whispered something to him and then nudged him in the ribs.

'Well, we love to dance,' Helen declared with confidence. Anna nodded, having to admit that it was better than being back in her room, back with her thoughts. 'I love this song.' Helen grinned, reaching for Gavin's hand and drawing him to her. 'It's so good!' Anna watched how naturally they slotted together. Helen's long arms around his neck, his hands on her hips, swaying and moving in time to the beat. Anna glanced back at Elijah, who had drifted away from the dance floor, back to the shadows, to a barstool beside an empty table. She looked to catch Helen's eye but her friend was entranced by Gavin.

'Not having a good time?' Anna lifted herself up on to the stool beside Elijah. It was slightly quieter away from the dance floor but she still had to raise her voice to be heard.

'No, I am . . .' He twisted the bottle of beer in his hands, head bowed. 'This is just . . .' He shrugged self-consciously. 'It's not really my scene.'

Anna cast her gaze back at the dance floor, at the rhythmic movement of all the bodies beneath the lights. That had been her scene. The dancing. The drinking. The creeping home at dawn and pretending her mother wasn't dying. Because if she drank enough it stopped being true. Anna disappeared into darkness and it was blissful.

But that was the old Anna. The one who had danced with dozens of boys like Gavin. Let them kiss her neck. Place their hands between her legs. Even dated a few. She knew guys like him. Dizzying. Intoxicating. She didn't know guys like Elijah.

'What are you studying?' she asked him. He ceased turning his empty bottle and looked up at her, dark eyes wary.

'Maths.'

'So, you're an egghead like my friend,' Anna teased. Elijah just looked wounded by her words. 'I mean, you're smart. Doing a serious course.'

'And you?' He didn't look at her when he spoke to her. 'What are you studying?'

'Media studies,' Anna explained. The vodka had made her confident. Open. Bold. 'I'm a bit of a dreamer,' she went on. 'I want to be a painter one day. Just like my mum was.'

'Huh.' Elijah rewarded her with a half-smile. 'That sounds . . . different.'

'Yeah.' Anna laughed nervously. Saying it out loud – her dreams, her aspirations – it made them feel more real, less like a castle in the sky. The previous night she'd confessed to Helen what she wanted and had been met with warmth. Kindness. Now Elijah wasn't dismissing her dreams either. It was as though here, at university, they were more than valid. They were accepted. Gone was the scorn of her college tutors lamenting that she needed to be realistic in her choices. Gone was the worry of her father, who feared she was clinging to someone else's dream as a coping mechanism.

'I hate this song,' Elijah admitted stiffly, shoulders hunched.

'It's not so bad.' Anna tilted her head, studying him. 'You regretting coming out tonight?'

Elijah suddenly looked up, staring right into her eyes. 'No. Not at all.'

As they talked Anna failed to feel the heat of Gavin's gaze each time he twisted on the dance floor and found her within his eyeline. Which was often. She was wrapped up in Elijah. In the differentness of him. The night slipped away in what felt like minutes and Anna knew she needed to see Elijah again. Her world suddenly seemed supernova bright with the prospect of all that might come to pass. It was a welcome change to all the darkness she had known.

When I first came to Unity, I'll admit I was scared. I had no idea what to expect. Would it be strange hearing my wife's thoughts? What if we ended up hating one another? What if she thought things I didn't want to know about? But I needn't have worried.

I used to always worry about my wife. She's blonde, petite, a target for anyone with a pulse, really. If she didn't text back quick enough, or got held up in traffic on the way back home, I would be beside myself. The issues we have faced in the past – her straying, and my parents' dislike of her – I wanted to put it all behind us. I saw Unity as a fresh start. A start we so sorely needed.

But that day of our procedure, I nearly backed out of it. I kept wondering if she'd see me differently, knowing what goes on in my head 24/7. Would she stop loving me? She didn't. Of course she didn't. I should have known this would only make us stronger. We've been inseparable since we met. And now I know everything that is going on as it happens. I no longer need to be consumed by my phone, by my worry. It has been beyond liberating. My wife and I are happier, and stronger, than ever. And we are even due to welcome our first son next month. No arguing over names since we both know what we think straight away. Unity has made me a happier, more relaxed man. A better, less stressed husband. I owe Unity everything.

Max Peters, Unity User

7
NOW

The sun was pale overhead, having not yet fully broken through the morning cloud cover. Elijah was clutching Anna's hand as they pulled up outside Unity. Leaning towards the window, she peered up at the vast building. It stretched up and out of view, singular and sleek.

'Thanks, mate.' Elijah nodded to the driver and then opened the door. It was cold out. Cold enough for Anna to wish she'd brought a coat with her. As she'd deliberated in their hallway, touching first her jumper, then the coat on the rack, then asking Alexa what the weather was, Elijah came up behind her and laughed. 'I'd ask what you've decided on the coat front, but this time tomorrow I won't need to.'

'Yeah.' She'd quickly abandoned all thoughts of the coat.

'You ready?' Elijah squeezed her shoulder as they lingered at the entrance to Unity. Gilded revolving doors, a single plaque beside them indicating where they led.

'Ready as I'll ever be.'

Hand in hand, they walked in. Within the lobby of the building the air smelt different, sweet. The floor was walnut and in the centre of the room was a marble desk, behind which there was a marble façade on which 'Unity' was mounted in large gold letters. Vast bouquets of red roses were placed at either end of the desk in golden vases.

'Good morning.' The slim woman behind the desk quickly locked eyes with Elijah. She had a slight accent, high cheekbones and white-blonde hair. 'Do you have an appointment?'

'Yes.' His grip on Anna's hand briefly tightened. 'Mr and Mrs Weston.'

'Perfect, come with me.'

The woman's black stilettos tapped sharply against the floor as she led Anna and Elijah towards the brushed-steel doors of a lift. 'I'm Sylvia,' she told them, always looking first to Elijah. 'Just go to the eighteenth floor and everything will be taken care of. Enjoy.'

Enjoy.

As though they were embarking on a luxury holiday. Anna joined Elijah in the lift, which was just as sumptuous as the lobby. Gold rails. Marble floor. A mirror above them and the soft plucking of a harp being piped in.

'This all seems really nice,' Elijah commented as he glanced around, stealing a moment to check his reflection and readjust the collar of his jumper.

'Very fancy,' Anna muttered, stomach flipping as the lift rose. It moved quickly, efficiently, not stopping on any other floors. They arrived at eighteen and as the doors parted silently Anna noticed the subdued light, the rise in temperature. Here, the floor and walls were all wood. And a corridor snaked away from them that they instinctively followed. Anna smelt vanilla. And cocoa butter. It made her think of being on a beach.

'Ah, Mr and Mrs Weston.' They rounded a corner and a tall man with curly hair and an Australian accent was there to greet them. He wore a pale grey suit and held a digital monitor that he briefly glanced at prior to addressing them. 'So good to have you both at Unity. Welcome. Welcome.' He gestured for them to follow him to a waiting area where the floor opened up. Numerous sofas, all unoccupied, were scattered around a room which had floor-to-ceiling windows looking out over the city. There were more roses, a buffet station along the far wall; Anna clocked a coffee machine and a basket of pastries. Not that she was in the slightest bit hungry.

'I'm Murray; I'll be your liaison for today.' Their guide touched a tanned hand to his chest, nails immaculate. 'First, take a moment to relax and unwind in our waiting room. Then, when it is time, we will call you through for your appointment.'

'Great.' Elijah was already moving towards the coffee machine. Murray grinned and seamlessly checked his monitor again.

'And you're having the Executive Package. Wonderful. I'll just need you both to sign some waivers.' His fingers began to patter across the screen of his monitor.

'Waivers?' Anna shot her husband a worried glance.

'All standard stuff,' Murray said with confidence as Elijah made himself an espresso, the machine hissing.

'I just . . .' The monitor was suddenly in her possession, a screen glowing with a box that required her thumbprint. She looked at Murray, whose smile never fell. 'Can I read the waiver?'

'There's a video that will commence shortly prior to your appointment which will answer all your questions.' He smoothly gestured to a blank wall opposite the buffet station.

'Okay, but—'

'It's a lot,' his warm hand was suddenly on her wrist, 'I know it's a lot. My husband and I had it done eighteen months ago and let me tell you, I was a nervous wreck,' Murray laughed at his past self, 'but it was the best thing we've ever done. Truly. It's brought us a closeness I didn't even know existed. And I was so blown away by it all I simply had to come and work here.'

'So you can hear him right now?' Anna looked into Murray's eyes, wondering what was going on behind them.

'He's bored and in a meeting at work, so yes,' Murray's face crinkled, smile still in place, 'but I get to instantly reassure him. Experience it with him. Normally we'd wait until the end of the day to talk, to connect. Now we don't have to.'

'It's not . . . distracting?' Anna enquired carefully.

'Not at all.' Murray beamed at her, effusive. 'Think of it like having a radio playing in the background all day. If you tune in, focus on what's happening, you get to listen to something interesting. And if my husband wants me, he can direct thoughts to me; it's all extremely intuitive. Our thoughts, we control them. And here at Unity, we get to share them with the people we love.'

Elijah strolled back over, small mug in hand, a Danish in the other. 'Honestly, sweetheart, I've read up on everything. We're good.'

Anna thought of Mandie, how adamant she was that she should not go through with it. But then Mandie wasn't married; she didn't understand how complicated long-term relationships could be. She hadn't had to look at Elijah's face, wounded, each time Anna pissed on a stick and it gave the wrong result.

'The doctor said it could happen, though . . . right?' her husband would ask, voice brittle with hope.

'Yeah.' Anna would force a smile when all she wanted to do was weep. What the doctor had actually said was that after all her miscarriages it was *unlikely* she would get pregnant again. Then they said something about build-up of scarring, of damage. But Anna was barely listening, watching Elijah, holding her breath.

'Unity is all about connection,' Murray's enthusiasm was almost contagious.

'And it's all your . . . *conscious* thoughts, right?' Anna heard the anxious inflexion on the end of her question.

Murray nodded emphatically. 'Yes, that's right. Only *conscious* thoughts. All the things running through your mind day to day. Nothing subconscious, the chip enters stasis mode when you sleep.'

'But you can, like, tune in and out?' Anna pressed.

'Exactly.'

'What if there was . . . ?' She wrung her hands together. *Something I didn't want him to hear.*

'As I said, it's all extremely intuitive.' Murray's smile never faltered.

'Right.' Anna bit her lip, nervous.

'It's going to be fine.' Elijah met her gaze, his expression warm, open. 'Trust me, sweetheart, I've read up on it all. You know me, when it comes to tech I do my research.'

'I know.'

'You are both going to *love* it,' Murray enthused. 'Trust me.'

'Right, great. Sure.' Anna pressed her thumb to the monitor, felt the brief heat of a sensor and then an upbeat chime. It was done. Signed. Elijah repeated the action for himself without hesitation.

'It will all be over soon.' Murray gave her elbow a gentle squeeze. 'They sedate you, so you won't even feel the chip going in.'

The lights in the room dimmed and the blank wall came to life, clearly housing the kind of concealed television that Elijah had been so keen to install in their front room.

'Welcome to Unity,' a serene voice began as the video

showed couples walking hand in hand, laughing freely, 'where OneMind brings true happiness.'

As the video played Anna perched stiffly on the edge of the sofa, while Elijah leaned back, arms spread wide.

'First there will be a minor procedure under mild sedation. The Unity data chip, less than half a centimetre in length and paper thin, will be inserted behind your left ear. Afterwards you may feel foggy. Some people report a slight headache, but it's nothing regular pain relief won't alleviate.'

Anna's heart rate began to climb.

'Once the chips are successfully implanted and synced, you will gain access to your partner's conscious thoughts. Think of it as a secondary conversation to your regular day. An enhancement to your inner monologue.'

Anna stole a glance at Elijah, noticing the strength of his jawline in profile.

'The host user can tune in and out of their partner chip's channel. This will come surprisingly easily. Within hours it will feel like a completely organic process. The scientists here at Unity worked tirelessly to ensure a completely seamless experience. In short, if you think about it, you will summon it. Their thoughts, your mind. And while you sleep the chip enters a stasis mode and ceases transmission.'

Elijah reached for Anna's hand, entwined his fingers through hers.

Am I really going to do this?

'More than anything, Unity is about togetherness. One-Mind. We so readily share our lives, our hearts. The next step was naturally our thoughts. We hope you have a wonderful connection.'

The video ended and for a moment they were plunged into darkness. And then their names were called. Anna looked to her husband as the lights began to come up.

Tell me you've changed your mind. Tell me we can go home. Don't let me disappoint you again.

When Elijah turned to face her he was smiling, excited.

He truly wants this.

Anna returned his grin, steeling herself for what was to come.

They were taken to a private room. Anna lay on a bed covered in pure white linen. Elijah was a few feet away from her, on a different bed. The lighting in the small room was low, the walls showing footage of the rainforest, the gentle hiss of rain all around.

'Now,' a woman in pale blue scrubs was at Anna's side, raising her right hand, 'there will be a slight pinch as I apply the sedative.'

Anna looked to the ceiling, tried to listen only to the rain and the rustle of leaves. But her mind was pulling her back to a different moment, a bleaker moment. She was on a hospital gurney, needle thrust into the back of her hand, someone parting her legs, worried whispers floating up to her.

'It's such a lot of blood.'

'Something's wrong.'

'Have you had cramps?'

So many appointments. So many strangers staring up into her core. Finding only darkness there. And always delivering the same, finite answer.

'Are you ready for Unity?' the doctor asked quietly as something cold rushed up Anna's arm. A metallic taste at the back of her throat. Then she began to feel heavy, sleepy.

'I love you,' she heard Elijah call to her.

Or had she dreamed that?

It was impossible to tell.

One of the biggest problems I faced when I came on board at Unity was taking a complex data chip and making it not only small enough to seamlessly fit into a regular person, but also strong enough to handle the endless flow of thought data which would stream through it.

Early models were a lot larger than the final Unity chip. It took years of painstaking research and a team of the finest minds I've ever worked with to produce the data chip we know and use today. Built with carbon fibres, it will not erode or warp during a person's lifetime. The silver coating ensures it is antibacterial while the interior capabilities are housed in a durable shell with zero omissions. It is a one-of-a-kind piece of technology never seen before on the mass market.

When a chip is implanted, it is placed against the dominant hemisphere, the left side of the brain. As this is where speech and language are controlled, making it the easiest, most accessible path to thought patterns. The chip contains bio-nodes which pulse out from the main chip and attach to nerves on the outer hemisphere. It is important to always keep this attachment at surface level. Too deep and you begin to mine excessive mental data function. And at Unity, the focus is on thoughts. Only present. Thoughts cannot be recorded or contained within the chip, only read in the moment by the user.

> Once a chip is embedded, it is synced to a secondary, partner chip. A chip can only transfer data between two units. To add additional recipients would greatly enlarge the size of the chip, which would be counter-productive to its service requirement.
>
> Isaac Rogers, Chief Science Operator, Unity

8

THEN

Anna smoothed her hands down the soft silk of her dress, loving how it fanned out into exquisite lace. It felt so delicate to the touch, clung to her body like a second skin.

'You look stunning,' Helen commented from where she stood a few inches away, throwing the bride an admiring glance.

'Thank you.' Anna checked her reflection in the vanity mirror, twisted the white lily tucked into the bun at the nape of her neck. Her wedding dress was elegant, simple. Timeless. Helen wore a floor-length lavender gown, along with the three other bridesmaids. Helen's red hair snaked down her shoulder in a plait laced with flowers. Anna's fingers found the pearl necklace at the base of her throat. It had once been her mother's. She swallowed, throat dry.

Something old.

Did it also count as something borrowed when it couldn't be returned?

'I still can't believe how beautiful this place is.' Helen padded across the hotel room to the window which peered out onto the azure sea, sunlight catching like diamonds on its surface.

'It's so lovely,' Anna agreed, releasing the necklace to sip her champagne. It was barely noon and she was already on her third glass. But then it was her wedding day; she was entitled to some indulgence.

'Did you pick the island?' Helen asked, still looking out. Anna locked eyes with her reflection, frowned. Helen knew full well that Elijah had chosen the location. His parents owned a villa on the island, which was where the groom and his groomsmen were currently holed up. Anna idly applied more mascara to frame her honey-brown eyes. In less than an hour she would be Mrs Weston. Her hand trembled.

'We came here that summer after graduation, me and Eli, so it felt perfect to come back here to get married.'

Anna didn't mention how stifled that summer had felt, so full of sadness over Oscar. It reminded her of losing her mother, that wicked poison of grief seeping into her blood anew. Anna had felt herself sinking all over again, so she'd clung tightly to Elijah. Held on to him with all that she had.

'Sure, it's a beautiful place.' Helen moved to stand beside her. So tall and statuesque she could almost be made of marble like the Greek gods carved in stone. Anna envied that ethereal air her friend had. Head and shoulders above everyone else, always looking at others with something between scorn and disinterest. When people looked at Anna they didn't see a goddess. They just saw someone delicate, small. Someone who could be ignored.

'It still feels strange when we all get together, and it's just, you know, the four of us, even after all this time. No Oscar causing chaos in the background,' Anna admitted softly.

'I feel like Gavin has picked up that mantle with relish,' Helen remarked drily.

'He's not that bad.'

Helen's hands were on her shoulders, fingers hard and cold. 'You and Eli are so perfect for each other.'

'Thank you.' Anna peered at her friend in the mirror and smiled. 'Just like you and Gavin.'

'Hmm.' Helen dropped her hands, went to the small table on the other side of the room and picked a half-empty bottle of champagne out of the ice bucket, beads of water sweating on its side as she refilled her glass. 'We are rather sickeningly sweet, all of us meeting at university, being friends, still being together despite going through so much.'

'True.' Anna again fiddled with the lily in her bun, wondering if she should keep it in. As Helen sipped her champagne her expression turned mournful, mouth dipping at the sides. 'It'll be you next,' Anna gushed, keen to make her friend smile.

'I've no doubt,' Helen replied, blue eyes fixed in an icy stare towards the window facing the ocean.

'Ooh, has Gavin said something?' Anna asked brightly. She imagined a proposal from him would be most elaborate, probably involving a flash mob. He didn't do anything by halves. And he'd also be trying to outdo Elijah's modest proposal over a candlelit midnight picnic in the back garden. Anna had loved it – it felt romantic, intimate. When she thought of Gavin trying to upstage them, the champagne in her mouth soured. She swallowed it with a grimace, unsure when their friendship group had switched from companionable to competitive. It wasn't a change she welcomed.

But it wasn't always like this.

Once they had all laughed together until their faces ached, until they couldn't see for tears. Once their lives had been full of joy. Of dreams. Of potential. And when Anna looked to her friend she still felt it: the tug of those strings that tied them together. The shared history.

'No, he's not said anything.' Helen kept looking to the window, detached. 'But now you're married, I'm sure he'll ask me.'

Back on their sticky kitchen floor at university Anna had lay drunkenly beside Helen and together they had described their dream weddings, vowing to of course have one another as bridesmaids. And Anna was honouring that promise, even if Helen seemed withdrawn. The magic, their youth, Anna feared she'd waste a lifetime trying to recapture it.

She opened her mouth to speak but was interrupted by a knock at the hotel-room door. Her cousin, Caroline, poked her head around the door, face flushed. 'Almost time,' she declared excitedly.

'Quick.' Helen marched back to the ice bucket, hastily pouring a fresh glass of champagne, not caring as some spilt over her fingers and on to the floor. 'Get another one of these down you. Enjoy your final moments of freedom.'

They said 'I do' on a small beach, watched by forty guests. Just like the engagement, it was small, intimate. Elijah's mother wept audibly from the front row. Anna and Elijah stood beneath a canopy of flowers, hands clasped, the sun on their backs. Her bridesmaids beamed with pride, holding their bouquets of lilies. It was only Gavin who smeared the serenity of the scene. Anna knew the second she appeared at the end of the short aisle, her father holding her arm, that something was wrong. His tie was loose, hair falling into his eyes. And while the other groomsmen were still, hands clasped before them, he swayed gently to and fro. As Anna walked up to meet her groom, she noticed how Gavin didn't raise his head to look at her, not even once. He was drunk.

Of course he was. Looking to ruin everything, to upstage Elijah with his antics.

To punish me.

And if anyone questioned him on it he'd surely blame Oscar, as if that wasn't a burden they all carried. Anna knew Gavin didn't even feel that raw over it all, not any more, it was just an excuse. Pushing down her fury she locked eyes with Elijah and tried not to cry. In his gaze she saw true happiness. True adoration. It was the fairy tale she'd been told to chase since she was a little girl.

After the speeches they all settled down to enjoy dinner on the beach, candles now burning as dusk began to spread along the horizon, the sky pink and glowing. To her surprise, Gavin managed his speech perfectly, cracking some jokes which went down well. Always the people pleaser. Helen's face was sour throughout the dinner; Anna assumed she too was angry about the state her boyfriend was in.

'You're perfect,' Elijah kept telling her over dinner, grinning madly. 'This is all just perfect. You're my wife.'

'I know.'

'My wife,' he kept repeating. It seemed that drunkenness was catching. With Elijah it happened quickly, his usual aversion to alcohol abandoned for the night. Since uni, he always tried to drink a little less. But not on their wedding night. And Anna had to admit that she herself was more than a little tipsy. The champagne just kept flowing. Beneath the sun it was too easy to keep drinking. 'I can't wait for everyone to fucking leave, though,' Elijah declared before dessert arrived.

Anna smiled at him. There was her antisocial husband that she loved. Forever keen to be in their bubble of contentment, loath to share it with anyone else. 'Then it can be just us.' Under the table he reached for her leg, began to move his fingers beneath the soft silk, towards the top of her thigh.

'Eli.' Anna playfully swatted him away. 'Behave. My dad is just over there.' And he was: a small, diminished man with the same eyes as Anna. He'd pulled away from her when her mother died, let her time at university forge a canyon between them. And while she'd thought he too was struggling with seemingly bottomless sorrow he was actually courting someone new. A nurse he'd met on the cancer ward. The betrayal of it all felt so bitter. So sordid.

'I can never replace your mother,' he'd insisted when he told Anna about Elaine.

'And yet you have,' she told him sadly.

Elijah's gaze was bright, joyful. 'You're mine now. My wife. Mine for ever.' Then he was on his feet, demanding a fresh toast for his new wife. 'Look how beautiful she is,' he called to his guests, posture swaying, as everyone made all the suitable sounds of admiration and affection. As Elijah slumped back down in his chair Anna glanced past him and noticed Gavin was gone. But Helen remained, picking at her piece of wedding cake with a look of disdain, pretty nose crinkled.

'Everything all right with them?' Anna nodded in the direction of her bridesmaid, causing Elijah to turn.

'Who the fuck knows?' Her husband leaned close to her, nuzzling her neck. 'I don't want their drama today. Or any bloody day.'

'They're our friends; we should care if they're all right.'

'They're fine.' Elijah's tone became icy. 'I'd rather, on our wedding day, all your attention was on me. Your husband.' He said his new label with pride, chest swelling. Anna couldn't help but adore him for it.

'You're right.' She kissed his lips, tasting of champagne. 'I promise that tonight, when all the guests are gone, you'll get my complete, undivided attention.' He kissed her hard, savouring the promise of what was to come.

When the stars came out, the reception moved from the beach to the hotel. Everyone gathered around the pool, drinking champagne and cocktails, giddy from a day celebrating. Anna kept sipping champagne to push through her mounting fatigue. What she wouldn't give to go back to her honeymoon suite, collapse into the mountainous king-sized bed and fall asleep listening to the sounds of the waves lapping back and forth outside.

'So how does it feel, Mrs Weston?'

Anna had been peering down at her reflection in the pool. She turned with a start to find Gavin at her side, tie now completely removed, eyes bloodshot.

'You're drunk,' she told him curtly.

'So what?' he sneered, raising a beer bottle to his lips. 'It's a wedding, you're meant to get drunk.'

'Helen's going to be pissed.'

'Let her be.'

'Eli, too.'

'And you?' He fixed her with a watery stare. 'Am I also falling short of your expectations?'

'Gavin—'

Someone jumped in close by, splashing Anna's silk as they landed in the water with peals of laughter.

'Fancy a swim?' he smirked.

'No, I—'

Then he doubled forward, hands on his knees, beer bottle falling to the tiled floor, and threw up straight into the pool. A murky cloud of vomit spreading out into the pristine water. People screamed and began rushing to get out. Others laughed.

'Jesus Christ, Gav.' Helen was suddenly there, forcing him to stand straight, berating him shrilly. 'Why are you in such a fucking state? Why do you have to ruin everything?'

'I didn't ruin anything,' he noted darkly, peering at her from behind sweaty strands of hair.

'You're such a bloody mess.'

'Does she know what she's getting into?' He swerved around Helen to stare at Anna, eyes wide. 'Do you know?'

'Enough,' Helen warned through gritted teeth.

'He should be here, you know. Oscar.'

They all went silent at the sound of his name. For a moment there was only the whisper of the wind lifting in off the sea.

Then Gavin snorted. 'Why am I even wasting my time?' He attempted to shuffle closer to the pool.

'We need to get you to bed.'

'I'm King of the World!' Gavin drunkenly exclaimed, thrusting his arms wide. Helen gripped him beneath his shoulders, steadying him, glancing back at Anna and mouthing the word *sorry*. Anna watched them stumble away.

Mrs Weston.

She rolled her new name around her mind.

It was going to take some getting used to.

9
NOW

Slowly Anna's eyes fluttered open. She felt like she was rousing from a deep sleep. As everything slid into focus, she noticed the rustling leaves of the digital rainforest around her. Then she heard the rush of rain. A hand, gentle against her shoulder.

'There we are, Mrs Weston. It's all done. How are you feeling?'

'I'm . . .' Her voice when she used it felt raw. As though she'd not spoken in days. 'I'm okay.'

I guess.

She blinked lethargically and reached her hands to the side of the bed in an attempt to sit. The hand on her shoulder suddenly pressed down hard.

'Just take a few minutes to rest, to let yourself acclimatise to this change.'

The rain hissed around her. Anna wished they'd just switch the damn projection off. It wasn't relaxing her. It was making her feel anxious, trapped. And the rain. Why was it so loud? She groaned, temple throbbing.

'You may experience some slight discomfort at first but it will soon wear off.'

Anna grimaced. Slight discomfort. Now that the fog of sleep was thinning away, she felt pain. Raw and real. Like waking with the mother of all hangovers.

'It will pass, just draw in some deep breaths and—'

'Eli?' Anna rasped, twisting her head and seeing her husband's slumbering form on the other side of the treatment room. Did he feel like someone was using a jackhammer on his skull like she did?

Anna?

She gasped. His voice. In her head. As surely and easily as she heard her own.

Ohmyfuckinggod.

Sweetheart, are you all right?

OhmyFUCKINGgod.

Am I saying this or thinking this? Shit, I can't tell. Stupid sedatives.

I'm going to be sick.

Anna?

'I'm going to be sick.' Anna pushed herself up suddenly, leaned to the side of the bed and dry heaved.

Fuck.

Are you all right?

'I really need to be sick.' She looked at the doctor beside her, who nodded with understanding.

'Okay, let's get you to the bathroom. Come with me.'

Anna twisted and lowered her legs from the bed, stance uneven.

Anna?

Without looking back, she followed the doctor out of the treatment room, back into the waiting area.

'Anna!' Elijah called after her hoarsely.

I need to be sick.

Now the smell of coffee and pastries was nauseating. Anna

clasped a hand to her mouth as she hurried towards the panelled door being held open for her, soft light pooling on to the walnut floor. Anna was on her knees, gripping the cold porcelain of the toilet and expelling everything she'd eaten that morning.

Are you all right?

Anna, is everything okay? Where did you go?

Fuck.

Fuck.

FUCK.

She bowed her head and heaved again, throat burning.

Sweetheart, where—

I'm being sick. Leave me alone. I need a minute.

Okay. Sorry, I . . . Shit. Is she all right? Should I go? Do I need to go? Where has that doctor gone? I need to ask her and—

Eli, clear your sodding mind for one minute. Please. I need to . . . tune you out.

Closing her eyes, she found the quiet that she sought.

Shuddering against the toilet, Anna managed to straighten, reach for toilet paper and wipe her mouth.

'Christ,' she panted as a gentle knock came at the door. 'Come in.'

It creaked open and the doctor appeared in the gap, thin face pinched with worry. 'I'm afraid sickness is a rare side effect from the treatment. We have some anti-nausea medication you can take.' The door opened wider and she proffered two crisp white tablets and a tall glass of water.

'Thank you.' Anna hastily accepted, swallowing the tablets down, head still pounding. 'Could I . . . ?' she gasped, feeling wretched. 'Some pain relief too, please?'

'Of course.' The doctor disappeared and the door closed.

For a moment she remained on the cool floor, listening only to her shallow breathing.

Anna?

Eli's voice in her head. So clear. So close. Her vision swirled, disorientated by his presence.

Sweetheart, are you feeling okay?

No.

I'm just leaving the treatment room. I'm heading to the bathroom. Okay?

Anna curled her knees towards her chest. How many times had she been alone and unwell in a bathroom? Usually peering down at the bloodied mess which had left her. Usually weeping at what it meant. Always alone. Wiping the tears off her face and forcing herself to stand, to carry on.

I'm outside the door. Baby, I'm here.

Now she wasn't alone. Not truly. Elijah was with her.

I'm scared.

Don't be.

My head feels fucking awful.

It will pass.

When the door to the bathroom opened again the doctor was joined by the welcome sight of her husband, who smiled through his worry when he saw her.

'Here.' The doctor handed Anna more tablets. 'These will help with the pain. If you feel up to it, come and sit in the waiting area. The effects will be wearing off very soon.'

Anna made it to the sofa, allowing Elijah to fuss over her and bring her a hot tea, which she gently sipped.

'You look pale.' He cautiously stroked her head.

'I feel like shit.'

His fingers lifted her hair beside her ear. 'Is it really bad?' Anna wondered, frowning.

'No.' She felt the warmth of his touch around an area that was numb. 'It's covered in a small dressing so I can't see the actual incision, but it doesn't seem too big. Check mine.'

He turned and Anna leaned close and drew his left ear forwards. Sure enough, there was a white plaster neatly applied behind it, hiding away any cuts. 'It does seem small.'

Is she all right? Is it normal to be sick like that?

'Thanks.'

'Fuck.' Eli pressed the heel of his hand to his temple. 'Sorry, honey. I just . . . I'm worried. It's very rare to be sick.'

'Yet here we are!'

'Just try and be calm.'

Try and be fucking calm. Nice. When I'm the one hauling my guts up.

'Anna,' Elijah's tone was stern, 'I'm just trying to help. This is going to be good for us.' He rested a hand on her knee.

'Is it, though?' she quickly countered, finally coming to the surface of her discomfort and tasting fresh, clean air. The drugs they'd given her worked quickly. 'Already we are arguing with each other. And now there's no filter, no way to get away from it.'

'When I woke up and you weren't in the room I was scared, but I could contact you right away, no phone. No shouting out. No searching.'

Because we are connected.

'I know but—'

'Anna, we've done the right thing. Now you'll never be alone again.'

Anna's expression soured. *Why are you bringing that up?*

I'm not meaning that specifically, but—

Please don't bring that up.

The first miscarriage. When Elijah was in New York with work. Anna had felt so adrift, so afraid. She'd called him and kept going straight to voicemail. She'd wept as she cleaned herself up and curled up on the sofa, pressing a hot-water bottle to her abdomen, hating how empty she felt. How alone. When Elijah finally called her back that was what she told him through her tears: 'I just felt so alone. So utterly and awfully alone.'

I just never want you to feel that way again.

Elijah stroked her cheek tenderly. Anna had to admit that between the pills and the sweet tea, she was beginning to feel like herself again.

I love you.

A kiss upon her cheek.

I love you too.

They left Unity as they'd arrived, hand in hand. Murray was in the lobby to wave them off, smile wide.

'This is what we like to see,' he waggled his finger at them, 'happiness, the pair of you are radiating it. I just love it!'

'Thank you.' Elijah nodded politely at him. 'It was a bit rocky for a moment.'

You can say that again.

'My wife was quite sick when she woke up.'

Murray's face was solemn. 'It happens, it happens. As with any medical procedure, it's a lot for the body to get used to. But I promise, it passes quickly. The worst is over and look at you now, beaming and bright.'

'Thank you,' Elijah repeated, their taxi drawing up to the kerb outside.

'You know, I'm honestly jealous of you both.' Murray smiled warmly as he tapped a hand to his chest. 'You're about to enter the most exciting, most illuminous phase of your marriage. I hope you're ready.'

How much do you think they pay him to be this fucking upbeat all the time?

I reckon they slip something to him each morning.

Or pipe it into the building, through the air conditioning . . .

That's what actually made you sick. You're allergic to such high levels of enthusiasm.

Hilarious.

Anna gave her husband a subtle pinch as they waved to Murray and stepped outside.

'See, this is going to be good.' Elijah kissed her before Anna slipped into the back of the waiting taxi.

'Sure.' She sucked in a lungful of city air; it wasn't fresh but it was good. The car pulled away and the sleek building of Unity slipped into the rear-view mirror. Elijah reached his hand across and held hers.

What do you think happens when one of us dies?

Christ, aren't you a ray of sunshine this morning? Her husband laughed drily as the car moved through the busy city streets.

I'm just asking.

Wonderful, I now get a front-row seat to all your strange, morbid thoughts.

Buckle up.

'Thank you for doing this.' His eyes glistened with sincerity as he looked at her.

Like I had much choice.

A furrow appeared in his brow, Elijah's mouth dipping.

Got you. Anna forced a bright smile, heart racing. *Try not to be so easy next time else this new dimension for us won't be any fun at all.*

I'll try. He clasped her hand tightly as the car bounced over a speedbump, causing fresh pain to spread from behind Anna's ear, from where the dressing had been so carefully applied.

10

Anna, are you all right?
Elijah's voice pressed into her thoughts. Kneading her temple, Anna swallowed against the wave of nausea rising within her, momentarily disorientated.

Just give me a . . . a minute.

Somehow she felt both jet-lagged and hungover. It made for an unpleasant sensation.

Anna's mouth hung open wide as she yawned, a hot stream of urine sliding down the inside of the toilet. She winced as she formed her thoughts back to her husband, still adjusting to the feeling.

Yes, I'm all right. Just about.

Okay. Good.

Standing, she flushed, washed her hands and stared at her reflection. Eyes almost black against the pale pallor of her skin. She had not slept well. All night she'd felt a pounding in her skull that refused to ease even as she wandered into the kitchen and popped several painkillers.

My headache wouldn't go.

You take something for it?

Is it normal for it to last this long? Should I call Unity?

'Stop worrying. It's been less than twenty-four hours since you had it put in.'

Her husband's actual voice from the bedroom behind her was suddenly jarring.

Fuck.

What?

'You scared me.' Anna padded into the bedroom on bare feet, folded back the duvet and rejoined Elijah in bed.

'How?'

'I feel like I'm not sure how I'm going to hear you, like is it in here,' she tapped a finger to her temple, 'or, you know, more normal.'

'Okay.'

Anna moved to press her cold feet against Elijah's back, needing his warmth.

'Hey,' he complained playfully. 'Enough of that!'

Anna's laughter fell away as she rolled on to her side. 'I just think, maybe, we need, like, a system.'

'A system?'

'For our thoughts.' Rolling again, on to her back, she looked up at the ceiling, at the woven lampshade they'd brought back from Morocco. She always loved how it twisted the light at night, casting strange and wondrous shapes upon the dove-grey walls.

We don't need a system.

'That's what I mean.' Striking out, Anna jabbed her husband square in the ribs. 'I don't like it when you . . . switch.'

'Yes,' Elijah rolled on to his side to look at her, studying her in profile, 'but the more we use our . . . internal voice, the more comfortable you'll be with it.'

'Hmm.'

You need to give it a chance. Remember what the guy at Unity said, it's basically a radio station playing.

'How about, if we're in the same room, we talk. Like, properly.'

'And when we're not?'

'Then be in my mind.'

'That's the system you want?'

'That's the system I want.'

Elijah leaned over and kissed her lips softly, cementing their agreement. Then he stretched and left the bed. Anna heard his movements drift through the house, listened to the slap of cupboards opening in the kitchen beneath her.

I fancy eggs for breakfast.

Oh, okay, so now we like speaking this way. Now we can give orders.

Poached. Two pieces of toast.

Yes, your majesty.

And juice.

Got it.

Tea too.

Not so bad, is it? Lying there in bed reeling off your demands.

I'll admit I could get used to this.

As penance you have to entertain my very dirty thoughts about you.

Okay.

Especially given how good your arse looked this morning when you got up.

Feel free to get filthy.

Oh, I will.

By lunchtime Anna was in her studio, the small heater in the corner humming loudly while she stood before a blank canvas.

'Come on.' She chewed the end of the paintbrush she had clenched between her teeth, fingers pinched around its head.

She wanted to do something brilliant. Original. Striking. A piece that demanded to be seen, that was impossible to ignore.

Not fucking cats.

Think . . . think more like Randall. His style. What he would do.

For so many years she had painted cats. Initially careful portraits of them, usually the tabby who would strut along their back fence each morning. Then Anna began putting the confident tom in surreal situations: driving a car, on a sun-lounger. She was told her paintings were quirky, fun. She never heard the words she was striving for.

Stunning. Exceptional. Epic.

She originally considered that painting quirky cats could be her brand. Her thing.

'Oh, Anna Weston, yes she does those adorable cat portraits.' She would daydream about an advertising deal with someone like Cadbury, where she would paint different cats eating different brands of chocolate bar in various locations. Anna imagined the pictures everywhere, on the back of magazines, billboards, the sides of buses.

Randall?

The thought pierced through Anna's pondering and she straightened. Blinked. Canvas still frustratingly empty.

Christ, Eli. You scared me.

Why are you thinking about that Randall guy?

I . . .

Anna was shaking her head, caught off guard, the stitches against her chip beginning to burn.

I was thinking about his style. How he—

Were you thinking about how he likes to paint topless? Ridiculous gimmick. He's a poser. Nothing else.

How do you even—

You mentioned him back at uni, cited him as your favourite painter. I figured he still was.

I did? I mean . . . he is.

I remember everything, Anna.

I like his style and—
Clearly, you still enjoy thinking about him.
About his art, Elijah. There's no need to be so jealous.
Should I start thinking about topless women?
Eli—
I like the cats. Keep them.
No, I need something new. Something special.
What's wrong with the cats?
I need to be noticed.
You are noticed.
Anna breathed out loudly through her nose.
No, I'm not fucking noticed, Elijah. Not by people who matter.
With a grunt she pulled the paintbrush from her teeth, angrily struck her canvas with its soft end.
And now we're having a goddamn argument without you even being in here. Fuck.
Anna turned and kicked at the heater.
You wanted to be inside my head, Eli. Well, I'm pissed. I'm fed up. Fed up of being so fucking . . . mediocre.
Don't cry.
Dammit.
The heater kept humming, caring not for her kicks.
Dammit. Dammit. Dammit.
The door to the studio creaked open. Elijah cautiously walked in, eyed his wife tenderly.
'Sweetheart, I know you're frustrated.'
'You've no idea.' Anna clasped the sides of her head with her hands and paced back and forth within the tight dimensions of her studio. 'I don't tell you the half of it because . . .' She paused to look at Elijah.
I'm a failure.
I'm a failure and now I can't hide that from you.
I failed at this and I failed at—

His warm arms were around her, head bowed as he peppered her in kisses.

Stop, sweetheart, stop. You're not a failure.

'I am,' Anna objected, voice muffled.

You're a beautiful, talented painter.

'Eli—'

'And one day the rest of the world will see that.' He eased back and cupped her chin in his hand. 'One day your cats will be appreciated in all their glory. I just know it.'

'I don't.'

'Well, I do,' he said firmly. 'Besides, it's not like you *need* any of your art to sell. You already have everything you could ever want.'

'Mmm,' Anna replied weakly.

Lucky me.

You're welcome. Elijah pressed a kiss upon her lips, like someone slapping a seal on an envelope. Claiming her.

As the sun dipped low in the sky Anna had managed to paint the start of a background. A beach. No cat yet, but it was a start. She looked to the small window that was angled over the garden, towards the house, and saw the lights coming on. A dozen golden rectangles pushing back the strength of the night. And within one window she saw Elijah pacing back and forth. She knew he was on a work call thanks to snippets he'd been thinking:

Fucking prick.

I don't think so.

Twat.

While she worked she tried to tune in and out from his thoughts, like twisting the dials on a radio, chewing on the end of a paintbrush as she focused her mind.

Anna rolled her eyes when things became negative, zoning

Elijah out. She liked caring only about the stroke of her brush against the canvas. It felt so Zen. Helped her own thoughts carry away, let her be calm.

Bad call, I take it.

I'm losing my mind.

I can tell.

There was silence within her head. All Anna could hear was the hum of the heater, the caress of paint upon canvas. For twenty minutes she was absorbed in her work. She didn't notice the day slip over into night, a cold creep in that even the little heater couldn't stave off.

Bitch.

Sorry?

Anna jolted, brush dropping suddenly, striking a red smear across her picture.

'Fuck.'

This, this is why I didn't want to hire her.

Eli?

I should have known she'd do this.

Everything okay?

Says she didn't expect it to happen so soon. Bullshit.

Eli, just take a breath and—

I told Gav it would be like this. He knew. And now here she is announcing her pregnancy like she's having the Messiah and we all have to pretend we give a shit. My whole team is fucked now. Fucked. While she swans off for nine sodding months to stay at home.

Look, Eli, I don't think—

We never should have hired her. I can't even ask if she's coming back. Oh no. HR made that very clear. Telling me to just keep being positive. While she screws us all over.

ELIJAH.

I told Gav never again. No more hires of women under thirty. It's just a shit show. And I know why he did it, why he likes her. Because she—

Elijah!

Fuck.

Babe.

Shit.

Eli . . . you need to calm down.

Just a bad call at work.

Real fucking bad.

Are you seriously that pissed off about someone being pregnant? Do you know how unreasonable that is?

I didn't mean, I don't—

You made me mess up my painting.

Shit. Shit, I'm sorry.

Take a moment. Realise you're being a dick.

You don't understand, it's really going to mess things up at work and—

People are allowed to have babies.

I know.

And you're allowed to feel . . . I don't know.

Anna placed the tip of her paintbrush between her teeth. Began to chew.

Jealous. You can feel jealous. Angry. Annoyed. That's okay. But don't be . . . don't be cruel.

It's not that, Anna.

Are you sure?

A snap. A stab of something sharp within her mouth. The coppery taste of blood.

'Ah.' Anna withdrew the paintbrush, looking down at its splintered tip now glistening red.

Anna, I'm sure. It's more . . . Look, I don't expect

you to get it. It's a corporate thing. Honestly, don't stress. Just a bad day. That's all.

Okay then. Love you.

Love you.

Anna tossed the broken paintbrush into the small bin by the door and moved to prepare some fresh paint on her palette, keen to fix her mistake before she called it a day, tongue throbbing painfully within her mouth.

Dammit.

Just breathe.

I'm angry.

I can tell.

So angry.

Eli . . . just . . . just don't think about it. I know it's hard not to feel . . . emotional over it all.

It just really messes up the dynamics of a workplace.

It will be all right.

Gav agrees.

Of course he does. Will blue or green work?

Anna swirled her paintbrush against the palette and carefully raised it towards her canvas.

Not like he will be having a baby anytime soon.

Sorry? Anna froze, brush in hand.

He says they stopped having sex.

Since when? She needled the fresh wound upon her tongue.

Don't know.

Shit. Helen hasn't said anything.

With a tilt of her head Anna studied her work in progress and asked aloud, 'Why would she?' She felt the drip of blood out of the corner of her mouth.

Helen and I barely talk any more. Not like we used to.

The truth of it stung.

I'm worried he's going to fuck someone at work and get fired because of all the MeToo bullshit.

Bullshit?

Anna, I'm not in the mood to debate popular soapbox causes.

He's not dumb enough to have sex with someone who doesn't want it.

All women want him. That's the problem.

Anna dropped her brush. 'Fuck,' she whispered as she bent down to fumble for it, a smear of paint staining the floor, crimson like the crust forming beside her mouth.

Women can't help themselves around him.

That's not true.

It is. I think he's seeing someone.

Oh?

I think maybe he is. Yeah.

That would surely be enough for Helen, though, right? Like you can only turn a blind eye so many times. And if he plays around as much as you say he does—

He does.

Then why would Helen tolerate something serious? She just wouldn't. Even she has her limits.

Maybe you don't know her as well as you think you do.

I used to know her better than I knew you.

Things change.

Anna inhaled slowly, contemplating her painting. It was passable. For now. Mistake still clear just beneath the surface.

Do you ever wonder what Oscar would have been like? If he'd have got married, settled down?

No.

Really?

What do you want for dinner? I can't be arsed to cook.

Me neither. Indian?

Chinese.

Okay, but you order it in.

You need to get used to the hologram waiter app.

I'm still adjusting to the latest piece of tech you wanted us to get.

Fine. You want the usual?

You know it.

Anna moved to switch off the heater, the studio instantly feeling cold and damp without it.

See how good this is? Usually you'd have had to stop working and trek all the way back into the house to have this conversation?

And as a bonus I get to enjoy all your work-related meltdowns.

She is a bitch.

For being pregnant?

No. She was a bitch before.

I see.

Prawn crackers?

Is the Pope Catholic?

You all done out there?

Anna wiped at her mouth, taking away the blood that had crept towards her chin.

Just about. Want me to come inside and take your mind off work while we wait for dinner?

Yes. Very much so.

Good.

You were talking about fucking, right?

Right.

Well then, hurry up and get your arse in here.

Giggling, Anna turned off the lights in her studio and closed the door. The garden was thick with shadows as she hurried inside.

11

THEN

Anna felt light-headed as Oscar handed her a small shot glass filled with what looked like water from a swimming pool.

'You're a bad influence, you know?' she shouted over the thump of the bass as she knocked the blue liquid back in a single swallow, its sweetness tacky against the back of her throat.

'Bad influence or just fun?' Oscar grinned, cheeks as red as his hair, which was plastered to his temple.

'Do you ever just . . . stop?' Anna wondered as they lingered by the bar, a rare moment of just the two of them. Usually Oscar was with Elijah and Gavin, ordering in drinks until Elijah began throwing up and Gavin laughed and bowed out. Constantly pushing them.

Oscar arched an eyebrow at her. 'Where's the fun in that?'

All he seemed to do was dance. Drink. Fuck. His bedroom door slapping open in the middle of the night as yet another conquest was ushered out into the cold to conduct the walk of shame back to their own halls. 'We're at university.' Oscar draped an arm around Anna's shoulders, smelling of sweat and cheap beer. He wore a green T-shirt and dark jeans, coupled with flip-flops. 'We are meant to be having the time of our lives,' he told her, breath warm on her cheek.

'I know.' She gestured to her now empty shot glass, which rested on the sticky surface of the bar. 'But you, you know. You try so hard.' Anna looked into his eyes.

'I'm just trying to enjoy myself,' Oscar protested.

'Enjoy yourself or forget yourself?' She held him in a steady gaze. 'I know the signs; I went through it myself before coming here and—'

'This isn't a therapy session this is a drinking session,' he cut her off.

'Sure,' Anna said with a light roll of her eyes.

'We're not meant to be, you know, getting serious.' He shot a sideways glance towards the table where Gavin and Elijah were laughing together. 'We're not meant to be falling in love. They're both fools.'

'Gavin doesn't love Helen.' The words tumbled out of her, fast and urgent. How much had she drunk? Fuck. She was clearly wasted. Cringing, she tried to turn away from Oscar but he followed her body language, leaned in towards her shoulder.

'I wasn't talking about Helen,' he informed her coolly. 'Both those guys,' he prodded a stout finger towards his friends, 'need to stop being so pussy whipped and just let loose.'

'Like you do?' Anna eased away from him, lifting her gaze to defiantly meet his. His eyes were bloodshot, as usual. Anna had long speculated that he did more than just drink on nights out, that he was snorting something far stronger in the privacy of his own room. Oscar, who seemed not just drawn to the edge but desperate to vault it. He moved like his past was snapping at his heels and he poured every ounce of his energy into trying to outrun it. In his rare sober moments Anna saw an aching pain behind his eyes, almost understood the urgency to self-medicate. The hole left behind from her mother, she knew it would never be filled. Loss. Oscar was as familiar with it as she was. Only his pain seemed to torture and twist him, while Anna's so often left her hollow.

'I'm having fun,' Oscar declared, gesturing to the pretty blonde behind the bar for another drink, cementing his order with an overt wink. 'There is nothing wrong with that. And I'm going to teach those two to start having some more.'

'Well, good luck with Elijah,' Anna remarked, scanning the dance floor for the shape of Helen, keen to move away from their friend. It had become a running joke between them that Oscar was like a gremlin: if he were fed and watered after midnight he became a monster. And the clock had not long slipped past one, so Anna wanted to make the most of her last few hours dancing with her friend, before she had to help her boyfriend stagger back to halls.

'He's got such a serious rod stuck up his arse I'm surprised you can't see it when he opens his mouth to go down on you.' Oscar snorted at his own comment and then eyed Anna wryly. 'No offence.'

'Mmm.' She gave him a tight smile.

'When we go to Kavos this summer, we will finally get to have some fun.' Oscar was looking once more to his friends.

'Because me and Helen won't be there?'

'Exactly,' he replied quickly. Then, swivelling to face her, his mouth creased into an apologetic smile. 'I know I'm sounding like a twat. But I had this . . . you know, this vision of uni. Of being with the lads and going wild and it all being so . . .'

'Fun?' Anna offered drily.

Oscar spluttered into his fresh bottle of beer. 'Yeah, fun. And this . . . this coupling up. It's not . . . it's not what I envisioned. I didn't want to be,' he looked down at his drink, 'alone in this.'

'I get it.'

'My brother . . . he was too serious. Too uptight. Couldn't have a laugh. And look where that got him.'

'Look, Oscar—'

'I just want them to be my boys, my wingmen. To be enjoying themselves for once. To get out of their own heads. To live in the moment with me.'

'Is that why you're forever pushing Elijah's buttons?'

'No,' Oscar said, a touch defensively. 'I'm just . . . I test boundaries. That's all. Would I rather they were footloose and fancy free like me? Yes. I'm not about to stand here and lie to you, Anna. You're nice.'

'Gee, thanks.'

'They'll just never get this back. This time. Life is so fucking, brutally short. Before they know it they'll have ties around their necks like nooses: mortgages, kids. It all falls apart after uni.'

'That's your idea of things falling apart? Adulthood?'

'It's a prison.' Oscar winced, leaned against the bar. 'Before I get locked up, I want to have all the fun I can.'

'I feel like you're having plenty of fun.' Anna nodded towards the blonde behind the bar who kept smiling in Oscar's direction.

'Which is how it should be.' He span back to the bar and slapped the dark, stained surface with enthusiasm. 'I just wish those two weren't in such a hurry to pin it all on one girl.'

'Maybe the girl is worth it,' Anna retorted cockily.

'Trust me,' Oscar finished his beer and then smoothly ordered another, 'no one is worth it.' And for the briefest moment she saw it: a flash of pain behind his eyes that he normally concealed so well with his wildness, his zealousness. A sip of his new drink and it was gone. Anna blinked, wondering if she'd even seen it at all. 'Kavos.' He smiled at her, though his body was now facing the blonde. 'That's where it will all go down. That's where hearts will be broken.'

'As long as it's not Elijah's,' Anna said sweetly, turning away to notice Helen upon the dance floor, swaying back and forth beneath a strobe light.

'Well, that's on you,' Oscar remarked before leaning towards the next potential notch on his bedpost. He was about to flash her a smile when a hand clapped him on the back.

'All right, mate?' Gavin leaned in close to him, voice loud. 'Are you getting this round?'

'Sure.' Oscar gave a drunken nod. 'What about smiler back there? What's his poison?' He shrugged in the direction where Elijah lingered behind them, hugging the edge of the dance floor, expression stony. 'Real ray of sunshine your fella.' He poked Anna sharply in the ribs, causing her to twist back round to him.

'He's just shy.'

'Mmm.' Oscar made an elaborate show of waving at Elijah, merely getting a shrug in response. 'He doesn't like me much.'

'Because you're a loudmouth,' Gavin teased as he accepted two fresh bottles of beer from the blonde behind the bar.

'Maybe,' Oscar agreed lightly, then, looking only at Anna as Gavin and Elijah shuffled back towards the darker depths of the club, new drinks in hand, 'or maybe because I see things. And he doesn't like that, does he? Doesn't like to share his toys.'

'You're wasted.'

Oscar gave a loud bark of laughter. 'True.' He drank deeply from his own beer and swiped a hand across his mouth. 'You should go dance with Helen. She looks lonely.'

'Yeah,' Anna agreed absently, looking to where Gavin and Elijah had disappeared to, the music pounding in her head, the floor shifting beneath her feet. All of them had drunk far too much.

Since having our Unity chips, my wife and I love to recite poetry to one another throughout the day. A sort of unravelling love letter. We try to outdo each other, finding the most beautiful sonnets we can. It has definitely encouraged me to be more creative in my marriage. And more appreciative of every kind word, kind thought. When I'm in a stressful meeting, I can't tell you how elevating it is to have her soft voice enter my thoughts and recite Shakespeare. It is truly a heavenly experience. One I simply wouldn't be without. Unity has improved the quality of my day-to-day life. I used to be so stressed with work, so anxious. My worst self, really. Unity changed that. Now if I'm having a bad day I can instantly speak with my wife, hear her calming voice. Know that I'm not alone. The world is this vast, scary place. Having a partner, truly knowing a partner, changes all that. I've learned so much about my wife since we joined Unity, including how she knows all the words to every *Carry On* movie. Together we laugh. Together we learn. Together we love. I am eternally grateful to Unity for giving us this ongoing gift of romance.

Tom Myers, Unity User

12
NOW

When Anna awoke the room was dark, the only light a band of gold beneath the bathroom door. She curled on to her side, realising it was still early. She closed her eyes, with every intention of drifting off to sleep.

But Elijah's voice filled her mind.

Singing.

He was working through the opening lines of 'Always 'On My Mind'. In his mind. In Anna's mind. She smiled to herself, peered over at the closed door, considering how she might surprise him beneath the flow of hot water, even if his choice of song was a little maudlin.

Do good today.

The singing had stopped.

Just focus. Don't let him get in your head. You deserve this. All of this. You're hot shit, got that?

Anna pressed a hand to her mouth, suppressing a burst of laughter that almost escaped.

You are the man. The fucking man. She loves you, she's happy. Stop worrying.

Squeezing her eyes shut, Anna willed herself not to think,

not to engage. She felt like she had intruded upon some private moment, some thoughts that were never meant for her to hear. Was it something her husband did every morning? These little pep talks?

Dammit, sorry, Anna.

Oh, Eli. She winced within the bed. Caught out.

Baby, sorry if I woke you. Sometimes I think . . . I think weird shit before work. Ignore it. Please.

No, no you're fine.

I thought you were asleep.

I was.

Then just, yeah, forget it. Please. Go back to sleep.

Okay. But only because you're hot shit.

Anna!

This time she let her laughter leave her loud and clear, echoing off the walls, reaching all the way to the bathroom. She was laughing so hard her chest hurt. All prospects of sleep suddenly gone, she decided to join Elijah in the shower after all. Besides, there wasn't that long until she'd need to get up and get ready for her lunch date with Mandie.

Anna pushed the rice around her plate with a fork, free hand occasionally lifting to touch the space behind her ear where there was now a slim ridge. It continued to feel tender and at night it throbbed in time with her pulse.

'Is he talking to you right now?' Across from her, Mandie ceased eating her noodles. 'What's he saying? Is it weird?'

Anna frowned, focusing, tuning in to the internal thoughts within her mind.

I've told her twice that the numbers are off and yet here we are. Again. Another mess for me to clean up.

'No, it's not anything weird.' Anna's hand drifted back

towards the table and her uneaten meal. 'He's not really thinking much right now. Work stuff, I guess.'

Toilet break. Again. The man must have a bladder the size of a bloody peanut. We need to just get this done. I can't believe he wore that shirt. It's more pink than a dog's arse.

I need a sandwich.

Anna withdrew from his thoughts, letting Elijah quieten within her mind so she could focus on her lunch.

'I still can't believe you had it done,' Mandie exclaimed, pinching thin, greasy noodles between her wooden chopsticks. 'How does it feel?'

'Strange,' Anna instantly blurted.

Mandie leaned back, bemused. 'That was quick.'

'I kind of have to answer quickly.' Anna made a tower of rice and then swiftly chopped it down. 'If I, you know, deliberate then I . . .'

'Think?' Mandie concluded for her, voice rising with concern. 'So what, you say everything you're thinking instead of . . . thinking it?'

'Sort of.' Anna felt herself growing hot. She wished she'd worn something lighter than a cable-knit sweater dress and calf-length boots; she was sweltering within her clothes, arms and chest itchy.

This bloody dress. I'm never comfortable in it. Dammit. This is what I get for trying to compete with Mandie's level of style. I'm a twat. Now an itchy twat.

Anna abandoned her dinner to scratch at her lower arms. 'If I say something I'm not thinking it. And as Elijah can hear *all* my thoughts, like when he wants to, when he's tuning in, I'm just . . . trying to not send out a tsunami of them.'

'Well, that doesn't sound healthy,' Mandie said between mouthfuls of noodles.

'It isn't,' Anna admitted with a downwards glance. 'But it... I guess it works. I don't want to bore Elijah with every thought I have.'

'Mmm.' Mandie pushed her empty bowl away and cradled her chin in her hands, staring at her friend. 'Is it that you don't want to bore him with every thought, or that you don't want him to know every thought?'

Why does she have to be so good at this?

'The latter,' Anna admitted quietly. Shamefully.

'Babe, I love you, but this whole Unity thing is madness.'

Who is good at what?

Nothing. Shit. Sorry.

You okay?

You surprised me.

Are you out?

Yes. With Mandie. My data is on, I'm sure you've checked my location.

I'm at work. In meetings. I'm busy. How's Mandie?

Fine. She's fine. You get your sandwich?

Bacon. Yes. Having it now.

Any good?

Mandie clocked Anna's distracted expression. 'Oh my God, he's legit talking to you right now, isn't he?'

'He is, yeah.'

'Wow.' Mandie released a dry laugh, sitting up and spreading her hands wide, like fireworks. 'It all blows my mind. Like, truly.'

'It's definitely strange.'

Yeah, it's good. What's Mandie said?

Eli, hang on. Let me focus.

'I'm struggling a bit.'

'How long has it been?' Mandie reached for her glass of water and sipped at its straw.

'Three days.'

'Okay, well, three days isn't anything. I thought Unity was, like, permanent though.'

Anna's hand lifted to stroke the fresh wound behind her ear. 'Like I said, I can see Eli getting pissed off with it within a month and us getting it removed. We have a graveyard of abandoned tech back home, laptops, tablets, VR sets. So much stuff he swears becomes obsolete within a year.'

'Uh-huh.' Mandie nodded as she continued to sip her drink. 'And how's he finding it?'

'Same. I think. Although . . .'

'Although what?'

'It's meant to be like a radio playing, right? His thoughts just always in the background, a strange soundtrack in my head I can dip in and out of. It's just . . . taking some getting used to, I guess. Sometimes there's a lot of back and forth; other times it's more quiet.'

'Maybe he's just not got much going on up there,' Mandie teased, tapping her forehead.

'Please.' Anna laughed, then, stomach clenching. 'He's, like, the most thoughtful person I know.'

'If I were you I'd appreciate the quiet moments.'

'I do.'

'And it'll take a while to get used to it all. To figure out all the kinks.'

'I guess.'

'There has to be an upside to it all, though, right?' Mandie pursed her lips, glossy and cherry red.

'You don't need to do that.'

'Do what?' Mandie queried sweetly.

'Try to put a positive spin on it all. You always do that.'

'I'm just trying to help you feel better. Anna, it's three days in. It's a huge change. Maybe you just need more time.'

'I mean . . .' Anna sighed, nudging her plate away from her. 'It is nice to know what he's thinking. There's a . . . security to that.'

Mandie clicked her fingers. 'There you go, that's a positive. Why bother putting a ring on it and sharing a mortgage when all you need is to sync consciousness?'

'Don't put it like that.'

'I'm teasing.' Mandie tapped the table to activate the dessert menu.

'Nothing for me.'

'You've barely touched your dinner. At least share some cheesecake with me.'

'I've felt sick all week,' Anna moaned, stomach churning as if on cue.

These bloody headaches.

Are you still bad? Shall I call the doctor?

What? No. No, it's fine. Eli, I'm with Mandie. I need some space.

But if you're feeling bad.

Drop it.

I'm trying to help. Don't snap at me.

Anna winced, cradling her head in her hands.

'You all right, hon?' Mandie peered up from the illuminated table. 'You said in your message that you threw up after having it done. Maybe it's still messing with your system.'

'Maybe.'

'If it goes on for more than a week you should really go back.'

'I will.' Anna nodded weakly, the ridge throbbing beneath her fingertips.

'And stop playing with it.' Mandie arched an eyebrow in warning. 'The last thing you want is it getting infected.'

'Although they would then be forced to take it out,' Anna noted.

'True.'

The restaurant was lively around them, people in suits scattered among tourists. Anna liked the place. Its low lighting and leather booths gave it an old-worldy atmosphere. And they served the best ramen in the city. Which accounted for how busy it always was, never a table spare. The clutter of cutlery, the pinch of chopsticks, the murmur of voices, it felt so loud to Anna. She winced, hand to her forehead.

I feel sick.

'You okay? Hon, you look kind of pale.'

Anna. Anna, are you all right?

Eli, just—

'Do you need to go the bathroom or something?' Mandie was staring at her, concerned.

No.

Then, remembering herself, 'No.' She released a heavy sigh. 'I feel like I'm more sensitive to sound.' Anna squinted against the glare of the table.

I need to lie down somewhere quiet. Somewhere still.

'Is that a side effect?'

'I guess so.'

Has it always been so fucking loud in here?

'Well, fingers crossed you just need to last a few more weeks and it will all be over. Elijah will have got his need to know everything you think out of his system.'

'Hopefully.'

Are you all right?

Fine. I'm fine.

But you just—

I'm tired, that's all.

'In the meantime, have you thought about what you're going to do?'

'What do you mean?' For a moment Anna's vision blurred, like she was on the cusp of a migraine.

'I'll have the white chocolate raspberry cheesecake.' Mandie was glancing up to the server at her side. 'As will she.'

'Mand, I'm really not in the mood for something sweet.'

'No problem, if you don't want yours I'll doggy bag it and enjoy it later.'

'I keep worrying I'm allergic to the sodding thing.' Anna pressed the heels of her hands into her eyes, not caring if she smeared her mascara.

'It's just a lot. A lot going on in one person's head.' Mandie swiped her hand across the table and it grew dark, menu disappearing. 'How's it been with Elijah? Learned anything?'

'Not much. He mainly just thinks about work.'

'I always figured he was the "still waters run deep" kind. Like, he's all quiet and shy on the surface. But underneath—'

'He does get angry about work, though. A lot.'

'Ooh, okay.'

'But I already knew that.'

'I mean, I guess if nothing scandalous crops up in his thoughts, that's reassuring, right? And what you were after from all of this?'

'Yeah . . .' Anna sighed, lowered her hands. 'Yeah.'

'And what about you?' Mandie eyed her friend shrewdly.

'Me?'

'You feeling so shit because you're struggling to manage your every thought now you have an audience?'

Anna cringed.

Am I really that transparent?

'I just . . . I never know when he's there. When he's tuned in. And sometimes . . .' Anna raised her thumb to her mouth, began to chew upon the ridge of her nail.

'Sometimes . . . ?' Mandie prompted, leaning forward, expectant.

'Sometimes he hears stuff he doesn't like. Minor stuff,

you know? Like, I'm just thinking about some guy, some artist.'

And he's angry.

Anna bit down harder on her nail, making her eyes smart.

What if he hears something worse than that? What will happen then?

'I figured.' Mandie gave a rueful nod. 'Sounds like we just need a plan, a way to help you manage what's going on in that pretty little of head of yours.'

A plate was placed in front of Anna. A generous slice of cheesecake atop it, velvety smooth and drizzled with coulis as dark as blood. Bile crept up the back of her throat. 'I'm really not hungry.'

'More for me, then.' Mandie slid the plate over to her side of the table and picked up a fork. 'What about songs?'

'Songs?'

'Yeah, like when you're stressed or thinking too much, run songs over in your mind.'

'Mmm.'

'No, something simpler. Something that requires no energy.'

'Like what?'

Mandie thoughtfully chewed on a forkful of dessert. 'Ooh.' She suddenly angled the stainless-steel piece of cutlery at her friend. 'What about nursery rhymes?'

'Nursery rhymes?'

'They're, like, deeply ingrained in our psyche. So it will take next to no effort to remember them.'

'I don't know . . .'

'I used to do it when I was sick,' Mandie stated quickly, digging into her cheesecake with more fervour.

'Oh?'

Anna felt tentative. Mandie rarely spoke about being unwell. It had happened before they'd known each other, when she was a teen. When she explained to Anna about having Crohn's disease, and an ileostomy, she was always so factual. Emotion never crept in.

'I got sick at twelve, had like over twenty major surgeries, really fucked up my guts, and ended up with a stoma for my troubles. So no kiddos for me. Like, ever. But I get to eat as much as I want. And trust me, when your body denied you food for being sick for so long, you learn to *love* it.'

Anna tried to glean more information as the years went on but Mandie kept her past locked away tight.

'Don't look so scared.' Mandie smirked at Anna's wide stare. 'I'm offering good advice here. I used to get these, like, intense stomach cramps. It'd feel like being gutted from the inside out. I'd sit on the toilet for, like, *hours*, while my insides poured out of me. And to keep myself from freaking out and losing my mind, I'd sing nursery rhymes to myself. Over and over.'

'That all sounds so awful.'

'No,' Mandie clicked her fingers, frowned, 'this isn't an invitation to launch a pity party. This is me helping you. Got it?'

'Got it.'

'Anyway, the rhymes were good because they were simple, easy and, you know, weirdly comforting. I think because they transported me to better times, when I was a kid and I still had all my organs.'

'Mandie—'

'I'm saying try it. When you feel like your sanity might snap with the effort of trying *not* to think. Or when you want to make sure Elijah can't get in your head, nursery rhyme.'

'Like "Baa Baa Black Sheep"?'

'"Three Blind Mice" was a favourite of mine.'

'It's kind of dark,' Anna recalled.

Mandie shrugged. 'Yeah, they lose their tails, but maybe they shouldn't have been scampering around the farmer's wife's kitchen, you know? I feel like all nursery rhymes are dark as they hide some message for kids.'

'I guess.'

'What about when you sleep?'

'When I sleep?'

'Yeah, can you still hear him then?'

'No.' Anna shook her head. 'If either of us are sleeping the chip stops transmitting.'

'Ooh, okay. Well, worst case, dose yourself with NyQuil and just be comatose the next few weeks.'

'That's definitely last-resort territory.'

Mandie smirked. 'Sure.'

Why does Gavin have to be such a piece of shit? Why is he circling the Roberts deal like that?

Anna bowed her head and dragged her fingers through her hair.

'Hon?'

'I'm fine, it's just . . . it's weird. We are having a conversation and now Eli is moaning about work. About Gavin.'

'Ooh, okay. How is Gavin?'

Anna flinched before slapping her palm against the table. 'I'm going to give the nursery rhyme thing a go.' She nodded decisively, voice bright and keen.

'I mean, it's worth a shot.' Mandie finished her cheesecake and then gently pushed Anna's plate back towards her. 'Maybe if you stop feeling so stressed, the other side effects might ease.'

'Maybe.'

'Take a bite, trust me. It tastes divine.'

He thinks he can have anything he wants. He's never respected boundaries. Now I have to sort his fucking mess.

Anna placed a forkful of cheesecake in her mouth, stomach still turning over. She swallowed, the base catching in her throat. Then came the taste. The sweetness. The vanilla-laced richness of it all. She nodded as she went for a second bite. 'Okay, I'll give you that. It's delicious.'

'See,' Mandie beamed, 'I know what I'm talking about. Stick with me, kid.' She winked jokingly.

'What would I do without you?' Anna smiled.

'You'd quite literally go mad.'

'True.'

On the train ride home, as the carriage hovered along the electric tracks, Anna leaned her head against the window and tried Mandie's advice. She didn't want to think, didn't want her thoughts to stray too far, too wide.

I'm on the way back.

Okay, sweetheart. See you soon. I missed you.

Missed you too. How's work?

Lame as always.

Why are you so angry with Gavin?

You know how he is, always stirring stuff up.

I don't want to think about him.

Me neither.

Three blind mice. Three blind mice.

You okay?

See how they run. See how they run.

Anna?

I'm just trying to keep myself awake.

Okay.

They all ran after the farmer's wife.

She cut off their tails with a carving knife.

You know that's originally about Protestant loyalists who were accused of plotting against Mary the first. They were all burned at the stake.

Did you ever see such a sight in all your life as three blind mice?

Unity

Where true love comes together

At Unity we promise complete togetherness with our innovative OneMind technology. Never again wonder where your partner is. What they are doing. What they want for dinner.

All of your relationship questions will be answered with our simple microchip. From as little as £40,000, true, transparent happiness can be yours.

Why not visit Unity today and see why so many couples are opting for OneMind, One Choice. One Happily Ever After. Start your forever together, today.

13

Elijah had gone into the city. Anna was still in bed when she heard the front door close behind him.

Shit. Sorry, overslept. Have a good day.

Didn't want to wake you when you seemed so peaceful. I'll be back by six.

It didn't surprise Anna that she had slept through the alarm. All night she had tossed and turned, twisting beneath the duvet. It felt as though, once Elijah drifted off to sleep and his thoughts silenced, her own became infused with a manic energy.

What the fuck am I doing?
I can't go on like this.
How can four days feel like four months?
Why won't the damn chip stop throbbing?
Is that normal?
Am I okay?
Mandie was right. This is madness. All of it.

Eyes wide, she stared into the darkness with only her thoughts for company. There was something blissful about the one-sided nature of her inner monologue, even if she was spiralling.

He's going to tire of this, as he tires of all new pieces of tech. Everything ends up being old. Useless.
I hate this.

You know Eli. He's a good man. He's done this because he loves you.

Anna thought of Murray at Unity. Of his wide, insincere smile. Did his husband's thoughts really penetrate his own throughout the day? If so, how was he not slowly going insane? Anna feared for her own sanity thinning to the point where it risked shredding altogether. Already it took so much effort to control her thoughts, to not let them run away from her.

So much fucking effort.

In Eli's absence the house was still. Anna sat up in bed, hugging the duvet to her chest. She heard the ticking of the clock on the wall. The distant hum of the rush-hour traffic. The gurgle of the infrared heater kicking in.

Everything is going to be fine.

You okay, babe?

Anna's hands made fists against her bedding. She pictured her husband on the tube, one hand holding the rail, head bowed, smart in his navy suit, leather satchel at his side.

Is Gavin there too?

Gavin? Why are you asking about Gavin?

I'm just . . . picturing you going to work. You alone?

He gets on at the next stop.

Yes, of course.

With Helen. I just know she'll have a face like a smacked arse as usual.

Ha, yes. Helen.

'Helen.' Anna said her friend's name aloud as she moved from the bed to the bathroom, satin pyjamas whispering with each step. 'Why haven't I told Helen about all this shit?' She paused at the sink and spoke directly to her reflection. 'Because she'll tell me what Mandie did, that this is all bullshit. Even though I know full well that if Gavin asked her to do it she'd be at Unity in a sodding heartbeat. When he says jump, she leaps. It's been like that since that first night at uni.'

That first night.

Fuck.

Anna's shoulders sagged and her gaze dropped to stare at the plughole, hands cold against the sides of the sink.

'I'm talking to myself,' she declared breathily. 'Rather than having any actual thoughts, I'm saying everything aloud like a . . . like a crazy person.'

What the hell is he wearing?

Do you still think he's seeing someone?

Why would you ask that?

Just being nosy. Aren't you interested?

Is he really smiling? Who smiles this bloody early? And that God-awful green—

Eli, I've woken up with a headache again, I need some quiet.

Anna's temple throbbed. She tried to focus, slowed her breathing in an effort to tune her husband out. But his thoughts were so loud, so persistent, determined to get through.

Who wears a green suit? Honestly. He looks like the fucking Joker. No one is going to take him seriously today.

Eli—

Not that they ever do. He's always so . . . so brash. An anecdote for every moment—

Elijah.

Anna raised her head slowly to look at herself, hair shiny in the glow of the spotlights that covered her bathroom ceiling. Her pink pyjamas hung delicately against her slender frame. A Valentine's gift that she knew cost over a hundred pounds. The bathroom, fitted with marble tiles, a waterfall shower, an electric toilet that washed you after you went and even played a soothing melody. Her entire world glittered. Dripped expense.

'You're lucky, you know that?' She held her own face in a steady stare. 'Remember that.'

Splashing cold water onto her cheeks she rose, expression steely, determined to face the day.

I just need to keep busy.

If your headache is bad, try and rest.

No, no. I need to keep busy to take my mind off it.

So Anna kept busy.

She hoovered the entire house, all three floors, even though they had a cleaner, Jayne, who came once a week on Wednesday mornings. Then Anna polished. Every surface; duster in hand she spritzed and she scrubbed. When the house smelt of lemons and everywhere was smear free, she baked.

Anna made a lemon cake, making the kitchen hot and balmy, the aroma intoxicating. Panting, she closed the oven, silenced the electric timer, and realised it was just past two in the afternoon.

There was nothing left to do but go to her studio and paint. Tying her hair into a ponytail, Anna ate a sandwich and then stalked across the garden, grass damp from earlier rainfall. She faced her half-finished canvas.

It's shit.

'Stop thinking,' she scolded herself. 'I don't need Eli's pity over this.' She recalled the last time she'd felt low over her art and he anonymously ordered four cat prints from her website. Originally she'd been so elated by the order.

'Oh my God,' she'd gushed over dinner, phone in hand. 'They've ordered four pieces, can you believe it?'

Eli had nodded as he chewed his plant steak. 'I can believe it, babe. Your pictures, they're so good. I told you to have faith.'

It was months later that Anna uncovered the truth, when she'd been in the cellar searching for a screwdriver and happened upon a piece of tarp right at the back. Pulling it down she'd gasped to be faced with the tabby doing the can-can she thought she'd sent away to her enthusiastic buyer. It turned out they'd been delivered to a friend of Eli's and then returned to him. Left in the back of their cellar to rot. Anna could barely see through the tears which burned as she fled from the canvases.

'You're mocking me,' she'd screamed at Elijah when he returned home from work. Pale and crestfallen he'd shaken his head.

'No, sweetheart, no. I was just trying to help, to make you feel better.'

'I don't need your pity. Your charity.' In a frenzy, Anna had run back to the cellar, to her paintings, carried them up and out into the garden, pushing aside the table and chairs on the patio.

'Don't do this,' Elijah had called as he ran after her.

'They're worthless,' Anna had howled, snot blending with her tears. 'Totally worthless. No one wants my work. I'm a failure.' She'd wanted to see them burn, see the cats get ripped apart by flame and then carried away as ash on the breeze. But her husband had grabbed her from behind, so strong, held her as she squealed and cried until the anger drained out of her. Once she went limp he'd released her and then silently carried the canvases back to the cellar, back to their purgatory beneath the tarp.

I should have burned those pictures.

Even in the pale light of day, Anna thought of the canvases. How she loathed what they represented.

Anna?
Sorry, bad day in the studio.
It'll be okay, sweetheart.
Not studio, shed. I'm in a sodding shed and I need to admit that. Stop calling it a fucking studio.
Anna—

She tilted her head back, hands on the base of her spine. The skin around her chip pinched, burned. And she felt the promise of a headache in her temple, dull and stinging.

Breathe.

'Stop thinking,' she shouted aloud. She wore her paint-splattered dungarees and Crocs, the fleece-lined kind. Anna was at her most casual, most relaxed. At least outwardly. Inside she felt a war waging.

It's raining, it's pouring.

She stomped towards her latest piece of art, brush in hand.

I'm about to go into a meeting, is everything all right?

The old man is snoring.

The cat in the centre of the canvas had been cavorting in a field. Anna dipped her brush in some brown paint from her palette, made a large sweep across the base of the picture.

Now the cat would be digging his own grave.

He went to bed.

Banged his head.

Remember I'll be home soon, at six.

And never got up in the morning.

At four o clock her headache felt like someone with a pneumatic drill was trying to break into her skull, so Anna took a NyQuil and chased it down with a shot of vodka. Collapsing on to the bed upstairs she stared at the ceiling, listening to the clock, waiting for the inevitable.

'Anna?'

She awoke with a jolt. Pressure at her side. 'What the . . . ?'

It took a moment for the thickness of sleep to ease away. Blinking, she winced against the brightness of the central light that had been turned on, at the looming figure of her husband staring down at her, tie tight against his neck. 'What the hell, Anna! I've been phoning for the last half-hour!'

'You have? Oh.' Woozy, she tried to sit up, the room beginning to tilt. 'Sorry, I just came for a lie-down and . . .' She noticed that Elijah was staring at her bedside table, face thunderous, at the packet of medication and glass tumbler. He reached for it, drew it close to his nose. 'Hey, don't—'

Anna reached to stop him but wasn't quick enough, reflexes sluggish thanks to her sleep-addled brain.

'Vodka, really?' Elijah sneered, putting the glass back down. 'What is going on with you? Is this,' he gestured between them, 'is this new thing with us really so hard?'

Because I like it.

Headaches, Eli. I keep getting them.

Anna looked down at her lap, wishing she didn't feel so sick.

They'll pass.

You don't know that.

You're just adjusting to the chip, that's all.

There was an old woman who lived in a shoe.

'No.' Elijah clicked his fingers in front her face, shocking her. 'No more stupid fucking rhymes. Anna, what's wrong?'

'It's just a lot.' Anna fell back against her pillows dramatically. 'Letting you in like this, it's hard. And my head keeps . . .' She cradled her head in her hands, almost dizzy.

Elijah exhaled loudly, hands on hips.

'The things I think, they're not always pretty and trying to . . . to control things is . . .'

'I didn't expect your thoughts to be pretty.' He loosened his tie and then climbed on the bed beside his wife. 'But, Anna, this will only work for us if we allow it to. The headaches will ease in time. Forcing yourself to sleep so that you can avoid me being in your thoughts, that's not healthy.'

None of this is healthy.

You're being too negative. You're not giving it a chance.

Slowly, Anna turned on to her side to look into Elijah's eyes.

'Hey,' he greeted her softly.

'I don't want to disappoint you,' she admitted in a whisper. 'I feel like I'm forever disappointing you.'

'I am in no way, nor have I ever been, disappointed in you.' Raising a hand, he touched her cheek, taking away a tear. 'Anna, I love you.'

And hearing my thoughts should prove that to you.

'You get pretty pissed at work.'

'You get pretty pissed over your art,' Elijah smoothly countered with a half-smile.

'True.'

'While you napped, I was doing some planning.'

'Oh?'

'I think we both could use a break. OneMind is an adjustment, it takes time. So I thought we could go over to that cabin we like, up in Sherwood Forest.'

'I do love it there,' Anna admitted.

I love listening to the rustle of the wind in the trees.

'I thought you'd like it.'

And that private patio, where we toasted marshmallows and had a barbecue every night.

'We can do all that this weekend.' Elijah drew her close and gently kissed her mouth.

And when you fucked me in the Jacuzzi.

That, we can most definitely do this weekend.

Anna reached for the back of Elijah's head, pulled him to her. Kissed him hard. She didn't need to say anything, think anything. He knew her body, what she liked. Together they fell into an easy, pleasurable rhythm.

That night, Anna fell asleep thinking of the little log cabin in the woods. One of her favourite places in the world. The serenity. The stillness. For the first time since her visit to Unity, the pain behind her ear faded away.

14
THEN

The light beyond the kitchen window wasn't yet golden, the darkness of night still holding on. Anna was at the table, stiff in a plastic seat, cradling her head in her hands, shivering within the toga she still wore. Already the revelry of the night was fading away, diminishing to a dull ache behind her temples.

So much drinking.

Dancing.

Chanting.

Helen had swirled her beneath the lights, laughing loudly in her ear as they tumbled together like atoms destined to combust. And all the while Elijah lingered on the edge of the dance floor. Watching. And drinking.

The door to the kitchen slapped open and Oscar sauntered in, wearing only an oversized pair of black boxer shorts, openly scratching at his crotch. 'Hey,' he greeted Anna, voice hoarse.

'Hey.'

He went to the fridge, stooped down and pulled out a bottle of beer. There was a soft hiss as he twisted off the cap.

'Penny for your thoughts?' he asked, dropping into the seat opposite her, eyes bloodshot, pupils large.

'I just . . . can't sleep.' She thought of Elijah sprawled across her single bed, snoring louder than a thunderstorm, body slick with sweat as all the alcohol of the night began to leak from his pores.

'Can you hear Gav too?' Oscar laughed drily. 'I swear he has more stamina than me. Fucking beast.'

Anna's face briefly fell.

'Ah, well, he'll wear himself out soon.' Oscar sipped from his beer. 'What you need is a drink.' He clicked his fingers at her and moved to stand back up.

'No, no.' Anna stretched out a hand, motioning for him to stop. Her tongue felt so thick within her mouth, like a vast dry sponge. 'I've had enough to drink tonight. We all have.'

'If you say so.' Oscar rolled his eyes and downed more of his beer.

'That's the problem,' Anna muttered bitterly. She was so tired, lingering in the awkward space between being drunk and hungover, head already pounding with the threat of what was to come. How many shots had she even done with Helen? Four? Five? She was lucky she hadn't just passed out. Like Elijah.

'Hmm?' Oscar looked at her, lowered a hand beneath the table to scratch again at his balls.

'Does it . . . ?' Anna blew out an awkward breath. 'You know . . .' She pointed to the beer, then demurely lowered her gaze.

'Huh?'

'You drink as much as Elijah. More. Same as Gavin.' Her gaze tilted towards the door, the corridor, his bedroom beyond.

'I like a drink, yes,' Oscar agreed slowly.

'But does it, you know, impede things?'

Oscar studied her, lifted his eyebrows in realisation. 'Ah. Okay. For me, no. Gav, no. I'm guessing it's an issue for Elijah.'

Anna clasped her hands together, twisting them, fearing she'd said too much. 'Really, it's just, no, nothing, I'm only—'

'It would explain a lot,' Oscar interrupted her, musing to himself. 'I find you in here most nights, waiting on the dawn. And I catch you looking at him a lot.'

'Elijah?' Anna hugged her arms tight to her chest, a shield.

Oscar raised his eyebrows again, sipped his beer.

'I've asked Gavin, but could you try and get Elijah to drink less. Please?' Anna asked.

'I'm not his mother.'

She shook her head, smarted, realising her mistake. Oscar wasn't like Gavin; he was harder, less concerned over her feelings. Over anyone's feelings.

'Forget I said anything,' she muttered tersely, getting up.

'Wait,' Oscar called after her, turning in his seat to look up at her as she stood by the door. 'I'll try. I promise. But guys like Elijah, they exist in their own head too much. Always trying to keep up with the guys, keep up with his girl. My mum used to say still waters run deep. Be wary. He's so much like my brother was.'

'You don't talk about him much.'

'Why would I?' Oscar turned away from her, massaging the back of his neck.

'Oh, look, I'm sorry, I know what it's like—'

'No,' when he turned sharply back towards her his eyes were ablaze, 'you don't know, Anna. No one does. That's the fucking point. You all think I'm just this clown out for a good time; I'm just trying to survive.'

'I get it,' Anna assured him strongly.

'Elijah keeps too much up here.' Oscar pounded his thumb to his temple. 'It's not good. It's unhealthy. People should live in the moment more.'

'He's just thoughtful,' Anna said defensively.

'Yes, but too thoughtful. He's always got something on his mind, that one, something that is driving him crazy. I know how that goes.'

'Better than being an empty fucking shell like you,' Anna snapped, and then regretted it. Fatigue was lighting her fuse much faster than she'd have liked. 'Sorry.' She looked into Oscar's eyes, blushing.

'Don't be.' He held her in a pitying gaze. 'If I wasn't getting any I'd be a total bastard too. There has to be something to brighten the darkness, right?'

'I'm not—'

Oscar raised his hands, still clutching his bottle, in a sign of submission. 'We never had this little chat. Okay? And I'll tell Elijah to go easier on it when we're out.'

'Thank you.'

'But there's a bigger issue here.'

'Goodnight, Oscar.' Anna turned away, entered the corridor, too tired for any mind games.

'I think you'll find it's morning,' he called after her, his voice bouncing off the blank walls of the shared kitchen. 'Sweet dreams, Anna.'

She paused outside Helen's door, stilling her breath to listen. There was no sound within, no smack of a headboard against a wall. Her shoulders loosened and she breathed a soft sigh of contentment? Relief? Anna wasn't sure. With the onset of a savage headache she kept walking to her own room, entered the heavy darkness in which Elijah lay, lost to sleep, unaware that she'd ever even left his side.

15
NOW

The cabin was as Anna remembered it, nestled within tall oaks like something from a fairy tale. She climbed out of the car, savouring the freshness of the air, the gentle trill of birdsong.

'I love it here.'

'Me too.' Elijah hauled a suitcase from the boot.

'We were lucky to get it.'

'Term time.' Elijah grunted as he pulled the suitcase down the short path to the front door. 'Means it's cheaper too.'

'Sure.'

Anna followed him to the door, waited as he tapped the wristband they'd each been given on their drive in against the lock, causing it to illuminate green. The door clicked open. Anna's boots echoed against the wooden floor in the hallway. Already she felt better, looser. Freer.

'Is this the one we had last time?' She glanced about at the polished kitchen to her right, then strode towards the living area, noting the corner sofa across from a wall that held a concealed television. And opposite the sofa a large dining table of solid oak. The walls were either covered in a wallpaper design of twisted tree limbs or boasted a digital skin of woodlands where the leaves flickered and birds darted between branches.

'No.' Elijah propped the suitcase at the foot of the stairs which led up to the bathroom and two bedrooms. 'But close enough. Same style.'

Anna had reached the French doors and was already hastily twisting their locks, throwing them open and looking out into the dense woods just a few feet away. Redwoods and oaks stretched up to a pale blue sky. Anna stepped on to the patio, went over to check the Jacuzzi, cover still atop it.

'Want me to set that up already?' Elijah asked from inside.

Keen. I like it.

'It's just my favourite part.' Anna moved from the Jacuzzi to open the door to the outside sauna, letting a memory of heat escape past her.

'Mine too.' He was behind her now, hand squeezing her shoulder.

'Do you think we could do it in the sauna?' Anna peered in, studied the slatted benches, wooden walls.

'I mean,' Elijah nuzzled her neck, 'probably. But we risk overheating.'

'True. Jacuzzi it is.'

She rarely saw her husband move with such speed as when there was the prospect of sex. He was removing the cover for the Jacuzzi, checking the water, turning it on, listening for the gurgling of fresh bubbles. All while Anna drifted back inside, content in the tranquillity of it all. The woods. They soothed her. Nourished her.

Tea?

She went to the kitchen and flicked on the kettle.

After.

Anna laughed. One thing she could always count on with Elijah is that he made her feel desired.

'So the sex is still good even after all these years?' Mandie had asked over cocktails the previous month.

'Yeah, the sex is still good,' Anna confirmed. 'I mean, we have to mix things up sometimes, to keep it exciting.'

'I hear that.' Mandie smirked and clinked her glass against Anna's.

'I mean, it's never *great*,' Anna admitted quietly.

'Great sex is like lightning in a bottle,' Mandie affirmed. 'It comes along every now and then and is fucking wonderful, but you can't build a life on great sex.'

'True.'

'You and Eli had great sex back when, though, right? When you were two horny students who couldn't get enough of each other?'

'Of course,' Anna gushed, drinking deeply from her glass, unsure why she'd lied. 'I did have great sex at uni,' she added, wishing they hadn't started down this road.

'Well, I had great sex last week,' Mandie declared brightly, 'which I think deserves a fresh round.'

By their second cocktail, talk had shifted to which cast member in *White Lotus* they were most likely to sleep with, Anna always favouring more retro television programmes. And from there, holiday destinations that were on their bucket list. But Anna couldn't stop thinking about Elijah, about sex, about how it was perpetually good but never great. Was Mandie right? Was it impossible to have long-term great sex? Was that the white whale that all single people wasted time chasing? Anna felt like her body still remembered the great times, taunted her in quiet moments, skin prickling, stomach dipping in that delicious way. Betraying her.

*

Anna was staring out of the kitchen window at the embankment which led up to the trail that snaked through the woodlands and connected all the cabins. With a start she realised that her mind had drifted back to that conversation with Mandie.

Fuck.

Jacuzzi all set up.

Okay. Great. Anna abandoned the tea she was about to make and began shedding clothes as she walked back towards the patio. If she'd given anything away in her thoughts, Elijah seemed undeterred. She joined him in the warm, bubbling water, birds flitting among the nearby trees. The woodlands were thick with shadow, even beneath a bright sky.

Anna was reading her book on the patio, savouring the quiet. Elijah had gone upstairs. 'I'll be back in a minute.' She assumed he was getting his boots. Grabbing a coat. She turned a page when his thoughts interrupted her, loud and sudden.

Urgh, just get out.

She folded down the page she was reading, closed her book.

What did I eat? Fuck.

A tremor of laughter moved through her as Anna pressed her hand to her mouth.

It must have been that burger. Dammit. Christ. Need to crack a bloody window. Or light a match.

Outside, Anna snorted.

Argh, there it goes. That's better.

Umm, honey?

Shit. Sorry, baby. Sorry. I'll be right down.

No, no you're fine. Take your time.

By now she was laughing so hard her eyes had misted.

Really, Anna, I didn't mean to be so gross.

Be gross. This is what we signed up for, right? Complete closeness. Total unity. Wonder why they don't mention listening to your partner shit on the adverts?

I'm glad you're amused.

Make sure you crack that window on your way out, babe.

You're hilarious.

The day moved quickly and easily. They hiked a trail. Ate lunch at an Italian restaurant. Hired a pedal boat and spent a blissful hour on the lake, talking about nothing and everything.

'I like being here like this, with you,' Anna admitted as she looked across the grey water, watching a pair of ducks paddling side by side.

'I told you it'd do us good.' Elijah smiled at her.

And help you get more at ease with things.

I'm getting there.

And I really needed the break from work. From the city.

'Everything all right with work?'

'Yeah.'

No. It's Gavin. It's always fucking Gavin. We've got this mega important client coming in next week and he's not prepared a deck, doesn't seem to give a shit. And the CEO insists on Gav presenting as he's so fucking personable.

'Everyone likes him,' Elijah concluded sharply.

'Including you,' Anna pointed out. 'He is your best friend, after all.'

'Yeah, but,' Elijah kept pedalling morosely, 'he's like family now. I'm stuck with him. Whatever shit goes down between us, we always smooth it out eventually. We're like brothers.'

'You're definitely love–hate like brothers.'

'Sometimes I worry it's more hate than love,' Elijah admitted with a lofty sigh. 'But then, I guess, there was love there once. We will get back to it, eventually.'

'Do you think?'

I fear I'll never get things back with Helen. Not like how it was.

'But you and Helen are not like sisters.' Elijah rolled his eyes.

'We were once,' Anna stated, dejected. Back in those heady first days of university, Helen was her closest, dearest friend. She told her everything. They spent nights getting drunk at the SU, days struggling with hangovers, dragging themselves to lectures and eating junk food while watching *Sex and the City* and *Gossip Girl*. It happened slowly, their drifting apart. Now Anna only saw Helen when they all went out as a group.

'You have Mandie.' Elijah kept pedalling, moving the boat around to the far end of the lake. 'I like her, she's fun.'

'She's mega fun,' Anna agreed.

'She makes you happy, I like that about her.'

'You don't think Helen makes me happy?' Anna turned to look at her husband, who shook his head.

'No, not at all. You're always your worst self after seeing her.'

'Huh.' Anna dwelled on the comment as she kept pedalling.

I suppose I always feel like I have to live up to her.

You know that's crazy, though, right?

Helen has her shit together, her high-end job. She wears suits to work. Designer dresses. I wear fucking dungarees. Like a toddler.

I like your dungarees.

For a few minutes they just pedalled, the water sloshing against the base of the boat.

Do you think they'll have children? Anna stared straight ahead as she thought the question.

They'd need to start having sex again first.

It's a serious question.

Then no.

They started to pedal back to the dock, their hour slot almost up.

But if we'd had kids, then yes, I think they would have.

Why does he have to turn everything into a competition? Even his life?

Because he's like a brother.

I find it exhausting.

Me too. I feel like . . .

Like what?

Like I need a drink.

You barely drink these days.

I know. Can still feel like I need one, though.

I didn't think you missed it.

Well, now you know.

The boat butted against the dock.

When night fell it was thick and velvety. The stars shone brighter than they did in the city, not having to fight with all the streetlights for dominance. Anna and Elijah sipped wine in their Jacuzzi as the air chilled around them. Then they went in the sauna, then up to bed, skin pink and tingling. Anna was exhausted. The good kind.

Sometimes I think with Gavin . . .

Hmm?

Anna was sitting on the edge of the bed, body heavy with the blissful anticipation of sleep. She turned to her husband, who was already lying down, eyes closed.

We're so close because of Oscar. It'd have been his birthday this week.

'Oscar?' Anna breathed the name into the room. It felt like calling to a ghost. Elijah had never been the same since the incident back at university. The holiday Oscar never returned from. 'What do you mean?'

Elijah's breathing slowed.

What do you mean, because of Oscar? Like it bonded you or something? Elijah?

There was nothing, he was gone. Slipped away into his dreams. When Anna's head hit the pillow she was too tired to wrestle with her thoughts, or worry about the pain behind her ear. She just slid into darkness, let it carry her away.

'What are you fucking doing?' The air was hot, sticky. There was music playing somewhere, loud and thumping like an erratic heart.

'I said we need to get out of here.'

Anna looked down the length of the beach, where drunken figures tottered along the raised shoreline, waves bubbling up to meet distant rocks. A girl doubled over to throw up, someone rubbing her back as she retched into the ocean. Another couple were entwined around one another on a white plastic lounger, the girl's skirt tucked high around her waist, bikini top on the floor, breasts wobbling with abandon as she bounced atop her partner. The wind that rattled them all was sharp and purposeful, lifting in off the water.

'Hey.' A hand on her chest and Anna was staring into Gavin's eyes. In the moonlight they were the softest pale grey, sandy hair blowing in the wind. His breath smelt of tequila. 'Stop dicking about, we need to go.'

Anna looked down and noticed that the hand against her chest was shaking.

'He's dead.' Gavin drew closer, hand now on her shoulder, pinning her in place, his eyes awash with tears. 'Are you listening to me? He's dead. He fell into the fucking water. We seriously can't be here right now. We have to get out of here.'

Now there were shouts along the beach. Wild and panicked. Anna felt her pulse begin to rise. Turning she ran, Gavin at her heels, footsteps awkward and disjointed. But she knew she had to move. She hurried towards the lights beyond the cliffside, the throb of the town. People were spilling out of nightclubs, hanging off picnic benches. She smelt the grease of a takeaway and tried to fight the urge to vomit. Standing beneath a lamppost she bowed her head, let her sick splash on to the ground, her feet, swaying unsteadily. It looked almost neon green.

'We shouldn't have done those fucking shots.' Gavin was at her side, casting nervous glances back towards the beach. 'I kept telling him over and over to chill out. Fuck! We need to get back to the hotel.'

Anna woke in the stillness of the cabin, breath fast and sharp. She shifted beneath the white sheets, disorientated. As her eyes settled to the dimness, she saw the shape of Elijah beside her, lost to sleep, his chest steadily rising and falling. Quietly, she climbed out of bed and made for the bathroom. She could still taste the cocktail-laced sick. Could still smell the salt of the ocean and the grease of the kebabs being hastily bought along the shorefront.

A dream?

She splashed cold water against her face. It had felt so real. And Gavin, he'd been there.

Anna looked at herself, stomach twisting.

Could it have been more than a dream?

She recalled the holiday to Kavos that Gavin and Elijah

had gone on during the summer after first year at uni. With Oscar. How excited they had all been, and then on their return so closed off. Because only Gavin and Elijah came home. At first, they refused to speak about what happened, but snippets seeped out to their friends. Oscar had drowned. Drank too much and fallen from a cliff after a particularly wild night out. He became a cautionary tale of not living to too much excess. The university held a memorial. Then life moved on in the callous way that it has of refusing to stop even for the gravest of tragedies. It was almost November when Elijah finally opened up to her, drunk in her little single bed in the house she now shared with Helen and a few others.

'We should have helped him,' he had told her, eyes wide and slick with unshed tears. 'You know how he is, drinking so fucking much. Then we argued and he just slunk off to the beach and we never saw him again. He was just . . . he was gone.'

'Oh my God.' Anna had drawn him to her, wanting to take away the pain. 'That sounds awful. What did you argue about?'

'Nothing,' Elijah had twisted away from her, 'just, you know, bullshit. It didn't even matter, and he fucking drowned out there alone because we let him walk off. Because we didn't look out for him like friends should.'

No wonder they'd been so quiet on their return, Anna thought. Elijah had seemed so troubled when he spoke of it, clearly disturbed. Filled with guilt. Regret. How many times he must have run that night over in his mind, wishing it had gone down differently, if only he'd called Oscar back, begged him to stay at the bar. Anna stroked his hair while he fell asleep, loving how sensitive he was. How he had opened up to her. It felt like one of the many turning points in their relationship.

But this was no dream. Anna looked away from the bathroom mirror, towards the bed where Elijah lay sleeping. She felt suddenly cold, a shiver racing up the length of her body. No, what she'd experienced lying beside her husband was not a dream.

It had to be a memory.

And in it her husband wasn't confused in some bar, or waking up in a hotel room wondering where his friend was. He was on a beach. And he was running away.

This time when Anna closed her eyes her mind took her to a dream that was most definitely her own. She was back in the kitchen of her old university halls, the strip light that speared the ceiling garishly bright against the backdrop of black through the curtainless window which overlooked a busy street. Anna's breath was shallow, fast. Lips against her neck, hands firmly gripping her thighs. This was a dream she had lost herself in many times before.

With a jolt she was back in the bed, in the cabin, beside Elijah. Heart racing, a pleasant warmth lingering between her legs.

Shit.

She turned to look at Elijah. His back was to her, his breathing level and deep. Her husband remained within the fog of sleep. Anna reached out a hand to stroke his thick hair.

Her dreams.

His.

Were they so intermingled?

What can you see?

Her body became cold with dread.

Where I see a beach, do you see our old kitchen?

Of course, Elijah couldn't hear her, his chip in stasis mode while he slept. Anna remained wide-eyed, knowing she would not rest until the dawn. She wasn't willing to close her eyes for fear of which part of the past she might fall into next.

16

'So, how was the weekend away?'

It was warm in Mandie's flat, the radiator on the far wall humming, rain peppering the window which looked on to a bustling street. Anna was on the peach-coloured sofa, mug of tea between her palms, as her friend spread herself across an armchair, legs hanging over the armrest, a fluffy purple throw cast over her lap.

'It was . . .'

Strange. Just say it was strange.

'Fuck.'

'What?' Mandie swung herself to sit with her back against the cushions.

'Sorry, I need to talk quickly so I don't, you know, overthink things.' Anna tapped her temple and gave an apologetic shrug.

'Okay, so, *quickly*, how was the weekend away?'

'Strange.'

Mandie's eyebrows both lifted, interest piqued. 'Strange how? Like good strange or bad strange?'

'I don't know.' Anna looked down at her tea, knowing there wasn't time for deliberation, for her thoughts to get away from her. 'I had this dream.'

'Here we go.' Mandie's eyes shone with excitement, she drew her legs up beneath her, leaned forward.

Anna? You all right?

Yep. Just at Mandie's.

What was strange?

The tea she gave me. She used almond milk and I just wasn't feeling it.

She on another health kick?

Something like that.

'Hello?' Mandie clicked her fingers.

'Shit, sorry. So yeah, I had this dream and it was, like, so real, you know?'

'Uh-huh.'

'I'm on this beach and Gavin is there.'

'Gavin?' Mandie asked, pensive.

'He's on the beach, talking to me, telling me to leave. There are people shouting, some people having sex on a lounger.'

'Oooh.'

'He tells me someone has died and we need to leave. And I can . . .' Anna extended a hand forward, trying to recapture the feeling. 'I can smell everything. Taste everything. It's like I was really there, on that beach.'

'Okay.'

'And I think it's because I *was* there.'

'Come again?' Mandie furrowed her brow.

'Not me, *Eli*.' Anna groaned, hating how she sounded. 'It sounds ridiculous. I know it does. But, like, I swear, it was a memory. One of *his* memories.'

'How is that even possible?'

'It's not.' Anna shook her head, frustrated. 'I spent all day yesterday poring over the terms and conditions from Unity. They mention headaches, hallucinations, phantom voices, but nothing about access to the other person's memories.'

'I mean, are you sure that's what happened?' Mandie rested her slender elbows on her knees, frowning. 'Maybe you guys talked about a beach, or Gavin, before you went to bed, and it was just on your mind.'

'I guess . . . maybe.'

'Well then, there you go.'

'But it . . . this felt different. It felt . . . *real*. Eli, he told me years ago about how our friend Oscar died on a beach when they went for a lads' holiday to Kavos.'

'And you think this dream is connected to that?'

'Only . . .' She picked at the ends of her nails. 'Elijah was never there when our friend died. They had an argument and Oscar left the bar, walked along the cliffside and fell because he was so wasted.'

'So it was just a dream?' Mandie was still frowning, trying to piece everything together.

'It felt real.' Anna gave her friend an imploring look. 'I know it makes no sense. Elijah said he was never there when it happened and yet . . .'

'You think it's a memory?' Mandie asked quietly.

'Yeah.' Anna's voice became shaky. 'I just . . . I didn't think we could do that. You know, have access to memories like that?'

'Maybe it was just a blip,' Mandie suggested. 'You said yours had been aching right? Your chip?'

'Yeah.'

'And you threw up right after, right?'

'Right.'

'So maybe yours is, like, a little faulty.'

'Maybe.' Anna chewed her lip as her tea grew cold. 'I struggle to . . . tune out. His thoughts seem to find me even when I'm focusing on something else.'

'Is that meant to happen?'

'I think strong thoughts always break through to the other person. As it's kind of like . . . internal shouting.'

Mandie's voice lifted with concern. 'Is Elijah shouting a lot?'

Anna quickly shook her head, causing the skin beside her chip to throb. 'N-no.'

'Has Eli mentioned having strange dreams?'

'No.'

'Well, there you go.'

'You think he'd tell me if he did, right?'

'Well, you'd know,' Mandie countered, tilting her head. 'Because,' she tapped her fingers upon her forehead, bracelets sliding down her arm, 'you can't hide anything from each other.'

'Mmm.'

'Only you've not told him about the dream,' Mandie deduced.

'I just don't know what it is yet and I don't want to worry him.'

'You think he'd be worried?'

'I don't know.' Anna stood, lowered her tea to the small side table shaped like a pineapple and paced over to the window. 'I didn't sign up for potentially accessing each other's memories.'

'I bet.'

'I didn't . . . I wouldn't . . .' Anna felt her heart rate climbing as panic knotted between each breath.

He can't know. If he'd seen me and—

Anna discreetly fisted her hands into a ball, her nails leaving tiny half-moons within her skin.

Humpty Dumpty sat on a wall.

'Is there something you're trying to hide from him?' Mandie gave her a concerned look.

Humpty Dumpy had a great fall.

'Because you know you can tell me, right? You can tell me anything.'

All the king's horses and all the king's men.

Anna was shaking her head again. 'Really, it's . . .'

Couldn't put Humpty together again.

'You can't keep this up for ever, hon,' her friend said softly. 'I'm worried about you. Talk to Eli, just tell him your chip is playing up, say whatever it takes to get the damn thing taken out.'

Everything okay?

Fine. I'm fine.

You don't sound fine.

Eli, I'm—

She shook her head, tried to banish him.

I didn't know you were . . . there. Tuned in. I'm with Mandie.

Okay, as long as you're all right. I worry about you.

I know.

I like to know what you're doing.

I know.

Anna watched the rain hit the glass and tremble down, the people below blurred and obscured as they hustled beneath umbrellas and hoods. 'Thing is, he really likes it. Having the chip. I worry he'd not believe me about the dream; he'd think I was just looking for an excuse to end the whole Unity stuff.'

'Isn't it a legit reason to take the chip out, though?'

'I'm so certain it was a memory, not a dream.' Anna sighed, chin dipping to her chest.

'Maybe you should just ask him about it.'

'You're right.' Anna withdrew from the window, returned to the comfort of the sofa. 'He's working late again, putting in a day at the Manchester office. I'll ask him tomorrow, when he's home and rested.'

'Or just ask him now,' Mandie suggested with a waggle of her eyebrows. 'After all, you are connected, *true unity*.'

'Better we talk in person.'

'Why didn't you just ask him when you were at the cabin?' Mandie rearranged the throw across her lap, picking at some loose threads.

Anna considered this.

Ladybird, ladybird, fly away home.

'Because you could have just had it out with him then,' Mandie continued.

Your house is on fire and your children are gone.

'I could have talked to him about it then,' Anna admitted. 'At the cabin.'

All except one.

And her name is Ann.

'But Mandie, there was something about the dream.'

And she hid under the baking pan.

'Something that scared me.'

Mandie dropped the throw into her lap. 'Like what?'

'Just the . . . the tone of it. I *felt* Eli's fear in it. Back when he told me about what happened, back at uni, he was so torn up about it. He's a sensitive guy and . . .'

'You're worried it'll be difficult for him to talk about?'

'Yeah.'

No.

'You might be right. But hon, you won't know until you ask. And don't look so worried; it's not like he can hear us talking right now.'

'I know.' Anna sniffed, chewing on a thumbnail.

'It's only your mind that has been hacked.'

Anna's shoulders sank low.

'Oh, I didn't mean to—'

Anna extended a hand towards Mandie, cutting her off.

'No, don't worry. I appreciate your honesty. Love you for it. But with Eli, I keep thinking . . . what if he's reliving it night after night because it traumatised him so much? What if there's a reason he lied about being on the beach that night?'

'Sweetie, I don't know what to say. This really feels like a conversation you should have with Elijah. If he does have unprocessed trauma, he can get help for that.'

'Urgh.' Anna leaned her head back against the sofa, looked up the emerald lampshade in the centre of the ceiling. 'I just wish it hadn't happened.'

'Another worm to crawl out of the Unity can,' Mandie said with an eye roll. 'I mean, you're getting to know your husband better, for sure. But is it maybe *too* well? Or,' she pointed at Anna and nodded thoughtfully, 'maybe it is a good thing. Like, now you know he's dealing with this . . . this memory, you can help him through it.'

'You're right.' Anna looked to the window, to the worsening rain. 'I really need to head back.'

Mandie followed her gaze. 'Or you could stay here tonight, like old times? I've still got that spare duvet in the cupboard.'

'The *Moomin* one?'

'The one and only.'

Anna smiled. 'Thanks, but I need to get some painting done this afternoon. Besides, don't you have a gig later?'

'Gig schmig,' Mandie scoffed as she walked her to the pink front door. 'They want me to open for that comedy club on Clapton but that basically means entertaining drunk people while they wait for everyone to arrive.'

'But does it pay?'

'Poorly.'

'You going to do it?'

'Maybe.' Mandie fluttered her long eyelashes in frustration. 'Sometimes I wish the bohemian life hadn't chosen me. She's a cruel mistress.'

'Mand, you're a fantastic singer and one day someone is going to see that and give you the record deal you deserve.'

'Hmm, I've been waiting for that train to roll into the station for ten years now. I'm tired.'

'I hear that.'

They hugged in the stairwell, Mandie holding her tight. 'You know I'm always here if you want to talk, right?'

'Right.' Anna kissed her friend's cheek. 'I'd be lost without you.'

'Ain't that the truth?'

Anna stepped out into the rain, raising her umbrella.

'And try not to worry about the dream, okay?'

'Okay.' Anna waved before starting to power along the street, towards the tube station. She didn't want to admit to Mandie that what she truly feared wasn't the dream on the beach, it was what her husband might be dreaming about beside her. What she might be subconsciously sharing.

On the train there was too much time. Too much space for her thoughts to fill.

How's Manchester?

They rattled past a station.

Eli? You in a meeting now?

Rain speckled the glass; a few seats behind her, a baby began to cry. The sound brittle, jarring, like breaking glass. Anna kneaded her temple, closed her eyes, tried to find some calm.

Elijah? Are you there?

Anna focused on her thoughts, her connection. Tried to find her husband. He had just been there, back at Mandie's, worrying over her. Forever caring. Forever there.

Elijah?

Eli?

Are you all right?

Now she just had her own thoughts for company. So she chanted a short rhyme over and over until the train pulled into her station and behind her the baby continued to cry.

Ladybird, ladybird fly away home,

Your house is on fire and your children are gone,

All except one,

And her name is Ann,

And she hid under the baking pan.

You love your rhymes about Catholics being burned at the stake.

Eli! There you are!

Can you not think of happier things?

Welcome to my head, it's a hot mess in here. You busy? You went quiet for a bit.

Yes. Very. I miss you.

I miss you too.

Funny that Ann is almost Anna.

Yeah, very funny.

17

THEN

It was cold in the waiting room. Anna pulled down the sleeves of her lilac hoodie to cover her hands, trying not to catch the eye of any of the other women sitting on plastic chairs around her, their stomachs swollen and ripe.

Elijah was next to her, laptop open, tapping away. 'Did you have to bring that?' she asked hotly. Each tap of a key was like a bullet through the stillness of the waiting room.

'Yes,' Elijah responded through gritted teeth. 'You know how busy things are at work; I couldn't afford to take an entire afternoon off.'

'We won't be here an entire afternoon,' Anna retorted.

'It's already been forty minutes.' As they talked, her husband's gaze never left his screen, his fingers never ceased tapping.

Tap.

Tap.

Tap.

Ping. A new email.

Anna turned her body away from him, trying to study the room as discreetly as she could. She couldn't handle another knowing smile from an expectant mother. How their gaze would get misty when they looked at her, one hand rubbing the orb that gathered at their core. She knew what they were thinking: that she was at the start of her journey. Wasn't it all just wondrous? Weren't they so very lucky? How fucking wrong they were. Anna wanted to scream at each smile; instead, she would stiffly return it, hating herself.

There were almost a dozen other women waiting on appointments. Some alone. Some with partners. One woman had brought along a snot-ridden toddler who she kept plying with crisps that left his hands and face covered in orange dust. One woman was so engorged she could barely stand. Each time she went to the use the toilet – which was often – she huffed and panted like she was breaching the summit of Everest. Face red, ankles like trees, she'd shuffle past Anna.

'She must be about to drop,' she heard someone mutter in the woman's wake.

'At the end, you just want them out, that's all that matters.'

A middle-aged doctor with small eyes and a patchy beard appeared at the mouth of the corridor that led away from the waiting area. He tapped the tablet he was holding. 'Anna Weston.'

'Hi.' Anna meekly raised a hand, then elbowed Elijah. 'It's us, come on.' Together they followed the doctor into a windowless room with a single desk, two chairs on the far side for them, a filing cabinet wedged near the door and a gurney opposite it, plastic hidden beneath a fresh sheet of blue paper towel.

'Sorry to keep you waiting,' the doctor grumbled as a formality, certainly not sounding like he meant it. Head tipped towards the tablet now on his desk, he scrolled through numerous pages while Anna and Elijah nervously sat across from him. Laptop finally in its bag, her husband reached for her hand and squeezed it. When she caught his eye he smiled and mouthed, *It'll be fine.*

'So, Mrs Weston, we've gone over the results of your tests.'

'Okay, great.' Anna smiled tightly. The tests. The endless instruments that got shoved into her while she was told to just 'relax'. How were you supposed to relax when it felt like you might get torn in two? Her hips would buck, sweat slick on her forehead. All while a probe examined her from the inside out. Looked for mistakes. Flaws. Between the scans and the blood tests, Anna felt as though she had no secrets left, no part of herself that had gone unexplored.

'We wanted to get to the bottom of all the miscarriages,' the doctor went on.

'Yes,' Anna agreed, voice high, strained. How drained she felt after three years of trying and failing. Never even making it to the twelve-week scan. The elation she'd feel when she saw the lines on the pregnancy test, the digital baby dancing in the window, how soon it all curdled to fear. She never had to wait long for the bubble to burst.

'This time will be different,' Elijah kept saying, forever hopeful.

But after the third miscarriage, Anna knew. Something within her was broken. 'We need to get help,' she told her husband as she mopped up the blood of the child that might have been.

'How have you been feeling?' the doctor asked, suddenly raising his head to look straight at Anna, eyes like raisins. Shrivelled and dark. 'Have the iron infusions helped?'

'Yes, a bit.'

'She's still quite tired, though,' Elijah added, concerned.

'It's to be expected.' The doctor was again looking to his tablet. 'Most women go through bouts of depression when they have multiple miscarriages.' His tone was cold, clinical. Anna clenched her free hand into a fist. 'It's the hormones.'

Elijah quickly spoke up before Anna could say anything, sensing his wife's growing despair. 'Well, what did the scans show? Do we need to go down the IVF route? We are more than happy to do so.' He gave her hand another squeeze.

A sigh from the doctor. 'You could, but I'm afraid that isn't a particularly viable option.' He raised his tablet and turned it around to face his patient. Anna was looking at something dark and alien. Shadows. Curves. Was this what she looked like from the inside? 'If you see here,' the doctor traced a finger along the edge of the image, 'this is the lining of the uterus. It should be smooth. What we are looking at is intensive scarring.'

'Intensive scarring?' Elijah asked while Anna stared at the image, transfixed.

The doctor lowered the tablet and cleared his throat. He was now staring solely at Anna. 'You mentioned a traumatic termination in your late teens?'

'Umm.' She blinked herself back into the moment. 'Yes, when I was at university, I was . . . yes, nineteen.'

Elijah's hand was still atop hers.

'Having accessed the files from that procedure, it would seem you had a reaction to the medication, shedding more than the required amount of the lining and suffering internal burns. As a result, your uterus is now lined with scar tissue, thus rendering it inhospitable for a foetus.'

For a moment Anna couldn't breathe. She was back in that awful moment, in the top bedroom of the house she shared with Helen and several other girls, watching as the floor beneath her turned black. Helen bursting in, screaming, then shouting for someone to call an ambulance.

'What are you saying?' Elijah snapped, turning hostile.

'I'm saying that due to the damage, your wife won't ever be able to carry a baby to term.'

'So we can't get pregnant?' Elijah's hand was too tight against hers now, causing her fingers to grow numb.

'You can get pregnant,' the doctor countered calmly, 'you just can't stay pregnant. And each failed pregnancy makes it even harder for a future one to catch.'

'Can't you do anything?' Elijah demanded. 'Remove the scar tissue?'

'Really, she'd need to have a transplant of a new uterus and that's not something we do. You'd be wiser to consider surrogacy, or adoption.'

'So that's it, you can't help us?'

'I've helped all I can.'

Anna stood, needing to leave. The air in the room was too stale, choking her. In the back of her throat she could smell the coppery tang of her own blood, even after all these years. She said nothing, for fear that if she did nothing coherent would come out. Instead, she marched back to the waiting area, not even pausing to see if Elijah was behind her. She strode through the winding corridors of the hospital, making it to the car park, the day dull and grey. Hands to her knees she leaned forward, drawing in long breaths.

'Sweetheart.' Elijah was there, hand on her back. Then he was pulling her to stand, wrapping her in his arms. 'Oh, baby, I'm sorry, I'm so sorry.' He kissed her forehead and clutched her against him. 'That guy, he was such an insensitive prick and—'

'I'm sorry.' Anna pressed her face into the softness of his oatmeal sweater. 'It's my fault; it's all my fault.'

'No. No.' Elijah's voice was stern as she leaned back. He clasped her face within his hands, honey stare warm and glowing as he studied her. 'This is not your fault, baby. Not one bit. We both made that decision. Together. We both said we didn't want a baby then.'

Hot tears sliced down her cheeks. 'But you're not the one broken, Eli. I am.'

'No, we both are.' He kissed her lips, tasting her tears. 'You and me, Anna. Always you and me. We made that decision together; we'll handle the consequences together. You're not alone in this, baby. We're in this together. I love you.'

He hugged her again. Held her as a heavily pregnant woman waddled past them. 'There are other options,' he said quietly, stroking his wife's hair. 'We could still look into IVF, get a second opinion.'

'Can we just go home?' Anna pleaded. All she wanted was to lie down in bed, close her eyes and sleep away the rest of the day.

'Of course.'

Hand in hand, they walked back to the car. Elijah drove through the city while Anna studied the buildings blurring by outside, stomach churning.

'Don't be sad,' Elijah pleaded as he drove. 'Let's just try to make the best of it all, okay? How about we have a takeaway tonight? I'll even watch *Moulin Rouge* if you want.'

'Sure.' Anna's eyelids felt heavy. Knowing the truth was exhausting. Back when it happened, she felt a fire burning within her, but no one would listen. Pinched-faced nurses scowled in judgement as she howled in a hospital bed. Eventually her blood levels were deemed too low and Anna was given an infusion. No one cared about her insides, what damage might have been wrought upon them. They seemed to care only about what she'd given up.

'Be more careful next time, yeah?' a stony-faced doctor told her when she was discharged a day later. 'There's a whole world of birth control out there. I suggest you get acquainted with at least one of them.'

Anna hung her head, eyes puffy, and said she would. She hadn't been expecting any of what had happened. The pregnancy, it had crept up on her. Through the haze of nights out and countless shots and bottles of bright blue drinks, Anna had lost track of time. Of dates. She missed her period once, twice, before the realisation set in.

'Weren't you guys being careful?' Helen had asked in a tight whisper when Anna told her what was happening.

'I guess not careful enough.'

Anna took the second pill alone in her uni room, listening to Adele, assuming everything would be fine. Assuming she was doing the right thing. She didn't expect her decision to echo through her life. To change everything. But it did.

Over the last six months Unity has seen a market share growth in excess of 80 per cent. Which is unprecedented. Quite frankly, we can't keep up with demand. Since we launched, we have been booked solid at our flagship London site. With plans to open Unity in Paris, New York and Sydney over the next year.

Month on month there is a significant rise in our share prices as the market reacts to our developing popularity. Our estimation is that by 2045, 30 per cent of 18–45s will be Unity users. We have seen the highest level of engagement within this age bracket. Young newlyweds, in particular. So many people seek the reassurance which only Unity can bring. All of our data chips are patented and we are confident that rival companies are still three years out from being able to safely launch their products to market. Unity was always ahead of its time and is now riding this wave.

When it comes to Unity, the results speak for themselves.

Howard Benson, COO, Unity

18
NOW

Anna held an onion in one hand, the long handle of a knife in the other. With a fluid motion, she chopped it in half. She was in the kitchen, the sky a sickly yellow across the garden as the sun failed to penetrate the sullen cloud cover. Her morning had been spent painting. Or rather, spent in her studio. Shed. She had stared at her canvas, her half-completed cat, willing herself to do something. Anything. But after an hour she gave up and withdrew to the house, choosing to focus on making dinner instead.

I'm making lasagne.

Nice. I'll be back by eight.

As she chopped, she listened to the smack of the knife hitting the wooden board beneath it, the wet whisper of the onion as it was shredded. Again and again she sliced. Diced. Eyes smarting. On the far wall, an oversized clock with roman numerals ticked by each passing second.

'We don't need a clock,' Elijah had objected when she spotted it in a garden centre. 'We have our phones, the smart monitor. No one has a clock any more.'

'Well, I like it.' Anna admired its copper tones. 'It's timeless. Pun very much intended.'

'Sometimes I think you're stuck in the past.' Her husband had shaken his head at her as he carried the large clock up to the till point, tapping his smart watch against a monitor to pay.

'I'm just classic.' She'd smiled sweetly at him. 'Not everything has to be digital, controlled by technology.'

'It's the way the world is going.' Elijah had hefted the clock out through the glass doors towards their car. 'If you don't keep up you're just going to be left behind.'

Something chirped and then the house was eerily silent. Then a scream of bells from outside. The alarm.

Anna brought down the knife and gasped. 'Shit.'

Fuck.

She looked down and saw a droplet of crimson blooming from the tip of her finger. She placed the finger in her mouth, sucking hard.

Goddammit.

Anna? What's wrong?

Cut my bloody finger chopping an onion. And it looks like the power is out and the sodding alarm is on.

Chopping? With what? Why not just use the dicer?

Can you not!

It's efficient.

Urgh, this shitting alarm.

I don't even know why we keep those chef's knives. We barely use them.

I literally just used them.

And now you're bleeding. They should go.

Eli—

Sucking on her finger, Anna moved to the digital display in

the hallway that managed the alarm system for the whole house. Upon the wall it glowed red in warning. Beyond the front door she could hear the howl of the shrieking alarm bells.

I'm about to go into a meeting. It's a big one. Do you need me?

The alarm, Eli! We've had a power cut! The alarm is going ape shit.

Like I said, I'm going into a meeting and—

I just need the passcode. It's asking for a passcode.

'Fucking thing,' Anna seethed at the digital display, asking her to use the touch screen to punch in six digits. Six numbers she didn't know. Elijah had set up the security system; as with anything in their home, it was synced with his phone.

Jesus, Elijah, help me.

Anna continued to suck her finger. Tasting iron.

Elijah.

Elijah, where the hell do you keep going? I'm meant to be able to hear you all the time? All the fucking time, and I keep getting silence! Nothing! Where do you go?

I'm always here, Anna.

The passcode, Eli. Please. It's going nuts here. Help me.

She could feel the alarm pounding through the house, surely squealing down the street, attracting anxious stares.

It's your date of birth.

Anna punched in the relevant digits, the sirens instantly ceasing. Exhaling, she released a shuddery breath. A chirp from the kitchen. The power was back on.

Well, that was a fucking stress.

Anna wondered back into the kitchen, harassed. She looked down at the diced onion now splattered with her blood. Unusable. After carefully twisting a pale plaster around her finger, she shoved the onion pieces into the bin.

'I just can't get anything right today.'

Slamming down the lid of the bin, sound rattling through the kitchen, Anna peered again through the window, towards the far end of the garden.

Did anyone else lose power?

She knew there was a way to check, online.

I'll check later.

I could go and paint.

Make myself useful.

It was what she was supposed to be doing, painting. Creating. While Eli spent his days in the office, in the city, she spent her days in her studio. That was the deal.

Some good it's done me.

Stop it.

Anna felt her shoulders droop.

Eli, don't.

I'd say everything has worked out pretty well for you.

She looked around at the smooth surfaces of her large kitchen, jaw clenching.

'Easy for you to say,' Anna muttered through clenched teeth. She glanced at the clock face on the oven, flashing the time from ten minutes ago, begging to be reset. That would have to wait for Elijah.

At least the sodding alarm stopped.

She willed the rain from the previous day to come again, to give her ample excuse to stay inside, to ignore her work. But the sky remained sickly, the ground dry. Anna made a cup of tea, abandoned her lasagne, and headed for the front room. On the sofa, tucked beneath a blanket, she watched several of her favourite shows back to back, finger throbbing, letting herself become absorbed in their stories. When her eyelids grew heavy she didn't fight the feeling, allowing herself to drift into a shallow sleep.

*

I'm going to kill her.

Anna's eyes flew open, heart instantly pounding.

I'm going to fucking kill Julia.

She glanced around, disorientated.

How dare she embarrass me like that? Who the hell does she think she is?

Startled, Anna gathered herself into a ball, noticing how the light of the day had slipped away while she slept. Now it was almost dusk, the room gloomy around her.

And then she had the nerve to look at me and smile. Like she hadn't done anything wrong. Smug. So smug. Bloody bottle blonde who always looks strung out.

Eli?

Always batting her lashes at the CEO like it'd do any good. She's only even in that room because she's a woman.

Elijah?

It's all gone too fucking far. Now we're letting in incompetent people like her and ruining everything. I keep saying over and over, it should be a meritocracy not a chance to tick boxes and fucking virtue-signal.

Elijah!

If she ever does that to me again, I'll have her neck in a noose and I'll enjoy listening for the snap.

Eli!

Anna had her hands in her hair, eyes closed in frustration. Sweat beaded on her forehead as she tried and failed to tune out the heated thoughts which kept coming at her like tiny daggers.

Just . . . stop!

Shit. Sorry, babe. Very bad day at work.

Jesus, Eli.

Like I said, I'm sorry.

You . . . you . . . that woman. How can you think like that, Eli?
I can only say sorry so many times.
You thought about . . . about . . .
Her breath caught in her throat, causing her to stoop forwards, struggling.
Killing her.
Hands shaking, Anna drew the blanket protectively around herself, staring ahead, pulse racing.
That . . . it's not—
It's a fucking bad thought, Anna. We all have them.
Not like that.
Can we not? I'm stressed enough as it is.
Anna's eyes were wide. Fearful.
Things got heated, yes. Don't you ever do things you don't mean?
Sorry?
Don't you ever think things you don't mean?
Anna held her head in her hands, forehead throbbing with the threat of a migraine. Her fingers moved to stroke her microchip, the skin around it hot.

'Does he know?' she whispered to the empty room around her, voice brittle. 'Does he imagine my neck in a noose?'

I'm just heading for the train.
You seem really angry.
I am.
You've scared me, Eli.
Eli?
That wasn't my intention.
What did Julia even do to make you so mad?
Nothing. No. I don't want to talk about it, okay? Gav is here now. I could actually use his take on Julia. He does a brilliant impression of her from the last office party.

She pictured the two of them laughing together on the train.

Anna blinked at the space around her. The living room so still, so calm, compared to the tempest that had just been raging in her mind.

'He gets so angry,' she told the stillness. 'I didn't know he got so angry.' Needing to occupy herself, she went back to the kitchen, to her abandoned dinner, and began throwing mince into a frying pan.

London Bridge is falling down.

The meat sizzled.

Falling down, falling down.

The smell sickened her to her stomach but she kept cooking, afraid to have her husband come home to an empty table.

Afraid of him coming home.

London Bridge is falling down.

She was dicing a carrot when she glanced up and noticed the digital clock on the oven. How it had changed.

My fair lady.

It was blinking at her furiously, stuck on a single moment, a moment that wasn't the time that the power went out. Anna felt herself frowning, recognising the alignment of the digits, failing to understand why they were there.

08:12.

Her birthday.

'Smells good,' Elijah declared when he came through the door and removed his long black coat.

'It's almost ready.' Anna stepped out of the kitchen to join him in the hall, wiping her hands on a tea towel, taking a moment to tuck a strand of hair behind her ear, grazing her chip, plastering on a tight smile.

'Don't you look the image of domesticity?' he teased, coming to kiss her cheek. 'Usually when I get in, you're covered in paint and telling me to order a takeaway.'

'Well, I wanted to keep busy.'

'So I see.'

'You're not the only one who can cook, you know.'

'Did you use the smart oven?' Elijah paced into the kitchen, glancing around at the dirty sideboards, the onion peel by the sink. 'It will just finish when everything is cooked.'

'I just set a timer.'

'Okay, but like I said when we got it installed, it removes the possibility of human error and—'

'Can you just go and sit down and wait for the meal I've slaved over for you?'

'Slaved over?' he repeated in jest.

'Go.' Anna nudged him away from the kitchen. 'I'm glad you've come home in a decent mood.'

You were so angry earlier. Gav manage to cheer you up?

It's his single most endearing skill and why I keep him around.

So why does he keep you around?

Because I have something he wants.

'Sorry?' The word left Anna in a squeak as she stood, a mouse before a lion.

'My title.' Elijah gave her a cold smile. 'He's been after my role from day one.'

'R-right.'

'Is there at least wine?'

She pointed to a bottle of Merlot with a single glass near the kettle. 'There is wine.'

But I figured you'd not be drinking.

I'm drinking.

Eli, are you sure—

'After my day I need it,' he snapped at her, nostrils wide. Anna was silent, taking him in. 'Besides, I won't have *too* many, if that's what you're worrying about.'

I'm not worrying about that.

You sure? You seem to enjoy keeping tabs on my drinking.

That's not true.

And back then it was anxiety, Anna. You know that. Not the drink.

I didn't say anything.

I'll take a glass, just the one. I promise.

'You sounded pretty pissed at that woman. Janine.' Anna folded her arms as she looked at her husband, her body growing cold as she recalled the violent image he'd placed in her mind.

'You mean Julia,' he corrected her with a grunt. 'And yes, I was. Still am.'

'You seem to get angry at work a lot, Eli.' Anna continued to stare at him, fighting against the fear that was building within her. She looked at the ring she had placed upon his finger.

Her husband gave a nonchalant shrug. 'Doesn't everyone?'

'Not like that.' Her words were barely a whisper.

You get very, very angry.

'Sweetheart,' his hands rested gently on her shoulders as he leaned down to kiss her cheek, 'everyone thinks bad things. Awful things. It's human nature. I might think bad things, but I never actually do them. There's a difference. A huge fucking difference.'

'Yeah, sure.'

'Look, I'm sorry you had to hear that. I didn't expect to get so riled up. Maybe when I'm in a big meeting you can, you know, make sure you tune out. Just for a bit.'

'I tried but . . . but heated thoughts, emotional ones, they always come through.'

'Well, I can't help feeling emotional.'

'I just . . . You wanted to *kill* her, Eli.'

'An errant thought.' Eli was pouring himself a large glass of wine. 'Nothing more. We all have those, right?' He regarded her coolly, and beneath his gaze Anna grew hot, uncomfortable.

'Perhaps we can . . .' Anna paused to clear her throat. 'Perhaps we can try and not, you know, imagine truly awful things—'

'Anna, don't make this into a thing.' Elijah sighed. He looked at her, extending the freshly poured glass of wine. An olive branch. 'Yes, what I said was ugly, I know that. But it's me. Unfiltered me. I want you to have access to that, Anna. I do. The good and the bad. I want us to completely know one another.'

'I don't know.' She accepted the wine, fingertips laced with sweat.

'Urgent thoughts push through, Anna. You'd know that if you read the damn manual.'

'I've read the manual,' she muttered, knowing that she hadn't, not really. Not thoroughly. Not like Elijah, who would have inhaled every single page.

'The chip is about connecting us through the good and the bad. Remember how dark things got after that third miscarriage?'

Don't. Anna felt tears gather behind her eyes.

Elijah calmly poured himself a glass of wine as he spoke.

'You couldn't get out of bed for days. You were in such a bad place. I was terrified what you might do.'

We don't talk about that.

'But we should, Anna,' Elijah sipped his wine, stepped

closer to her, hand on her waist. 'I want to be able to understand you. Protect you. Even from yourself.'

'From myself?' Anna rasped.

'Back then, there was no telling what you might have done.'

She imagined herself hanging from the miniature chandelier in their hallway, neck snapped at an unnatural angle, eyes glassy and unseeing.

'I'm sorry if I shocked you,' he came close to kiss her temple, 'but know that you shock me too sometimes.'

She glanced at his wine glass, almost full to the brim.

Anna, don't. I've had a day.

I know but—

'Let's just enjoy our dinner.' He gave her a tired smile. 'This is the best part of my day, you know. Coming home to you.'

Anna squirmed beneath the intensity of his stare. 'Yes, yes I know.'

Mine too.

Turning from him she locked eyes with the oven and its digital clock, reading the correct time, and felt her stomach dip.

Anna was in her pyjamas, at the sink, teeth freshly brushed. Her fingers were pressed against her microchip, the skin sore to her touch.

In the bedroom Elijah was sitting up in bed, reading an article on his tablet, the screen casting a blue glow upon his face.

Anna was pressing hard, feeling the ridge of the chip.

She drew in a long breath. Looked at her reflection. Sighed and dropped her hand. Then she padded back to the bed, climbed in beside her husband and reached for her book from the bedside table.

'Is there any way to control more ... heated thoughts coming through?'

'I'm reading up on it now,' Elijah explained, showing her the tablet's glowing screen. 'Apparently we might need to get them reconfigured.'

Or you could calm down at work.

Elijah ignored her and carried on reading. 'It says urgent thoughts will always push through,' he stated, 'and they list side effects here.' He read from the tablet. 'Nausea, hallucinations, feelings of being disorientated.'

She traced the line of the chip with the tip of her finger.

'Is the skin around it still hot?'

She pushed down harder. Nodded, eyes smarting.

'So maybe it's infected or something. We should really have them take a look at it. Have you had any other strange side effects?' Elijah asked, peering at her.

'No.' The lie came so easily she didn't fight it. The sand on her feet, the salt in the air, Gavin's fearful face. It had all felt so real. Could it have just been a hallucination?

'Can you call Unity tomorrow?'

Yes. Sure. We'll get it sorted.

Elijah leaned over to kiss her. 'Until then, I'll try and be less angry at work, okay?'

'Okay.'

Anna attempted to read her book but the words kept blurring on the page, her mind too distracted. Finally, she clicked off her lamp and stared into the darkness. With Elijah already asleep she was finally alone with her thoughts. She was thinking of the pink peonies Helen had sent her after that third miscarriage. The one where Anna fell into a pit she feared she'd never climb out of. How the flowers had filled the lounge with their sickly sweetness.

The pinkness. The plumpness of the petals. They looked

like the kind of flowers you sent someone who'd just had a bouncing baby girl. Not someone who'd lost one.

Helen hates me.

But the thought sank beneath the tidal wave of sadness that soon claimed her. When her whole world went dark.

'She's just being kind,' she remembered Elijah saying, admiring the blooms. 'She's just being there for you.'

But Anna knew better. She remembered the Helen of old, the one who did truly care, who would eat ice cream from the tub with her cross-legged on the cold student kitchen floor as the sky turned golden outside. The Helen who never judged, who always held out her arms for Anna to collapse into when things went wrong. That Helen was gone.

'You're going mad,' Elijah kept telling her with certainty. 'Helen loves you.'

Was that the case? Was Anna losing her grip on reality? Locked in a dangerous cycle of trying to dig up the bones of the past?

In the end Anna had thrown the flowers in the recycling bin, comforted by the thought that they would soon be reduced to pulp.

19
THEN

Her hangover was wicked. Anna could taste Taboo in the back of her throat, making her want to vomit again. She was crouched over the toilet, strings of greasy hair falling into her eyes. Carefully, she tried to angle her stream of piss on to the plastic stick she was holding. She kept telling herself that it couldn't be real, any of it. That she'd merely messed up her days. People missed periods all the time, right?

That night, in the union, as The Killers blasted in her ears, she slipped over from fun drunk to messy drunk. Helen found her weeping in a corner, empty plastic shot glasses littering the table in front of her.

'What's wrong?' Helen, so slender in her monochrome bodycon dress. She sat beside Anna, reached for her hand. 'Is it Eli?'

'I'm late.' Anna blurted the thing that had been festering for weeks. Now months. The worry she kept suppressing with every sweet-flavoured alcohol-laced drink she could get her hands on. And now she was too intoxicated to lie, to pretend everything was all right.

'How late?' Helen asked, expression calm.

'I've missed one,' Anna hiccuped over a sob, 'maybe two.'
'Christ.'
'I know.'
'Have you taken a test?'
'No.'
'Anna!'
'I know.' Anna's face crumpled like stale pastry, more tears falling freely.
'It's okay, breathe. We'll get you a test and go from there, okay?'
'Okay.'
'Eli,' Helen scanned the bodies dancing a few feet away from them, 'does he know?'
'No.'
'Okay.'

Helen was good to her word. On the way back to their house they staggered into Asda, managed to find the pharmacy and grab a test. Helen paid for it with her chin held high, matching the assistant's judgemental stare. Anna leaned into her, needing her friend's strength, her certainty. Helen was always a lighthouse in a storm, guiding others. Anna knew that without her she'd have crashed upon the rocks long ago.

'Try not to worry.' She shoved the test into Anna's clutch bag. 'We don't know anything yet.'

It was easy to hide the purpose of their supermarket trip from the guys. Elijah and Gavin were completely pissed, laughing outrageously, faces flushed, slumping to the side when they walked. It felt like their world had become a cycle where they were either completely drunk or too hungover to function.

Back in her bedroom Anna hid her bag beneath the bed while Elijah drunkenly undressed. Naked, he pinned her to the bed, breath heavy with beer. 'I love you,' he panted, leaning down to leave sloppy kisses upon her neck. 'I love you so much.' He pushed up her skirt, pressed his body against hers. She felt the flaccid shape of him against her thigh.

'Fuck,' Elijah grunted in dismay, rolling off her.

'You need to stop drinking so much,' Anna said, turning on her side to conceal her relief.

'It just keeps fucking happening.'

'Try not to stress about it.'

Moments later, his breathing thickened and he was asleep. Anna was frozen, not daring to move until she was quite certain he was completely gone. But somewhere between waiting for her to chance to leave the bed and listening to Eli, sleep came for her too. When she next opened her eyes golden sunlight was threaded across the textbooks and clothes strewn across her bedroom floor. Quietly, she lifted from the bed and made for the bathroom.

Anna's hand trembled as she held the pregnancy test, studying it, waiting for something to happen. She could hear movement downstairs, the padding of footsteps, the slam of a cupboard. It wouldn't be long before someone was knocking on the bathroom door, needing to be let in.

'Fuck. Come on.'

Were two minutes supposed to feel this long? She bounced from foot to foot, dressed only in one of Elijah's Tottenham T-shirts.

Then the test changed. First one line. Then a second.

A positive test.

Anna let out a low howl.

'Fuck. Fuck, fuck fuck.'

It was one of those things that, growing up, Anna had harboured a fantasy of: how it would be when she first got pregnant. She'd be married, living in a big house, with a dog, and a long garden that slopped down towards a river. For as long as she could remember, this was the dream she'd held in her mind. She would run a successful art studio, drive a big black car. And her husband would wear suits to work and adore her. Because that was how things were supposed to go. Supposed to work out.

She wasn't supposed to be starting the second year of university, sitting in a room that had mould bleeding out from the far corner of the ceiling, in a shitty part of town, without even having a driving licence. Or a job. This was not the plan. The bleakness of it all seeped into her as she returned to her bedroom and watched Elijah sleeping. The air in the room was stale. Anna had vomited twice since seeing the test and now her throat felt sore, as though she'd spent the night drinking sand not shots and alcopops.

'Hey.' Elijah stirred, rubbed his eyes. 'Is everything okay?'

'No.' Anna didn't want to hold it in any longer, didn't want to continue suppressing her fears, especially now she knew they were real. She sensed a huge clock above her ticking down to doomsday. She had to act. 'Elijah, I'm pregnant.'

His eyes flew open. 'Woah. Shit.'

'Mmm.'

He scrambled to sit up, to face her on the same level. She could see the desperate processing going on behind his eyes. 'W-what ... what do we do?' he asked, looking between Anna's pained expression and her stomach. 'Fuck, Anna, what do we do?'

She liked that it was we. Straight away, Elijah never made her feel alone in it all, not for a second. He was even there with her, two weeks later, at her first doctor's appointment, holding her hand.

'It's the right thing to do,' he kept saying on the walk over. 'We're not ready to be parents. Not yet.'

'I know.'

'We'll get our chance again. I know we will.' He paused to stoop down and kiss her lips. 'This will just be something we look back on, part of our story.'

He said all the right things. That he loved her. That this was all fine. Though he never once suggested keeping the baby. That first morning, as soon as he knew, he began googling abortion procedures. And Anna understood. It was inconceivable for them to keep the baby. How would they cope? Where would they even live? She kept imagining her father's disappointed face when she came home for Christmas, belly beginning to swell.

No one knew she was pregnant other than Helen and Elijah. And Anna wanted to keep it that way.

As Anna waited for her appointment, she glanced around at the other people gathered in the waiting area of the GP surgery. Some she vaguely recognised from uni. Other people were older, their expressions guarded.

Elijah's knee kept bobbing up and down. 'I suppose we need to start being more careful.'

'Yep.'

'I need to stop getting so drunk.'

'Yep.'

'Most mornings, I don't even remember doing it,' his knee jerked faster, 'no offence.'

'None taken.'

'But I'll do better.' He tightened his grip on her hand. 'I'll stop getting so fucked up with Gavin.'

'Look, it's okay—'

'This is on both of us.' Eli's voice was low and serious as he leaned close to her. 'I should have been being more responsible. And moving forward, you should think about the pill. Because I'm serious about this, about us. This is just a blip in the road, okay?'

'Okay.'

'One day, years from now, when we're ready, we'll start a family. We'll paint the nursery and build the cot. I always thought my kid would have a wall painted like a blue sky, like in *Toy Story*.'

'That sounds nice.'

'And when they're born I'll take leave from work and we'll go for long walks in the woods together. And they'll have your eyes . . .' He gazed at Anna, smiling.

'And your brains.'

'They'll be unstoppable.'

Elijah kissed her and for a blissful moment Anna was swept away by the promise of it all. Of what would come. They wouldn't always be students. Weeknights wouldn't always be spent sweating beneath strobe lights, drinking cheap shots. As much as Anna loved the hedonism, it comforted her to see an end of it. To see an eventual world of stability. And Eli could give her that. Would give her that. Even with all the drinking, he was on track to get a first in maths. He was going to go places. Lead a decent life.

A nurse came out and called her name. Anna stood, expecting Elijah to stay in his seat and meet her afterwards. But he too got to his feet, kept holding her hand. He wasn't about to let her go alone and she fell a little bit more in love with him there and then.

20

NOW

Going to the game.

Anna was on her doorstep, clad in leggings and a T-shirt, hair drawn back in a ponytail, prepared to leave.

His little lad's first game, can you believe it? Six. Christ. That's when Dad took me. We had those hot dogs that burned my tongue and I shouted so hard I lost my voice. The programme, he kept it. In that desk drawer. It's special. That first game.

Anna could picture it: little Elijah, with a crop of dark hair, beaming up at his father as they both roared down to the players on the pitch. Savouring the energy, the moment. Their time together. It was both fleeting and timeless.

I'm sorry.

The thought fluttered like paper in her mind, brittle and light. A hot tear upon her cheek, she forced herself to jog down the remaining steps, head low, back to the camera that watched her as she moved away.

Oh, Anna—

Elijah, I'm sorry.

John at work was just talking about how he's taking his lad to the game tonight and—

And you don't get to do that. Ever. Because of me.

Anna—

Tune out. Or something. Please. There's only so many times I can apologise, Eli. Only so many times I can flagellate myself before there's nothing left to even punish.

Remember I'm going through all this too. It affects us both.

Stop talking to me.

A minute passed. Anna felt bold enough to pick up her pace, face damp with tears.

Anna was running through the park. Arms pumping at her sides. Sweat beaded across her forehead. She swerved around a plump woman with a shrieking Pomeranian; she powered along the river, breathing hard. She was almost at the next turn when a clammy hand clasped her shoulder, forcing her to stop.

'Oh . . . my God.' Mandie was doubled over, gasping for breath, cheeks ruddy. 'You said to meet you in the park for a . . . *jog* . . . remember? Not a fucking,' she sucked in air and slowly rose to stand, 'sprint. Sweet Jesus. I've been chasing you down . . . for . . . five . . . minutes.'

She reached for the water bottle from her backpack and drank deeply.

'Sorry.' Hands on hips, Anna took long, steady breaths. 'I guess I just got distracted.'

'I'll . . . say.' Mandie wiped her mouth and returned her bottle to her backpack. 'I've not run that fast since I ticket-dodged on the tube.'

Anna looked across at a nearby pair of people with pushchairs, laughing as they walked and pushed, chubby little babies happily kicking their legs as they bounced along the path.

'What's up with you?' Composure regained, Mandie gave her friend a serious look. 'You seem kind of off today.'

A hand instinctively flew to her left ear, the chip behind it. 'My Unity chip,' Anna explained with a sigh. 'I think it's definitely faulty. The skin around it . . .' She trailed off, shaking her head.

Mandie made an 'O' shape with her mouth.

'And I keep getting headaches.'

'Well, that's not good.'

'And then there's the . . .' She sucked in a breath, curved her spine as she leaned back, eyes to the sky.

'Dreams?' Mandie concluded for her.

'Yeah.' With a sigh, Anna straightened.

They walked side by side, following the path that led through the park. Daffodils were pushing their way through patches of soil, trees stretching green leaves towards the sky.

'I just want it gone.' Anna was glad she was facing ahead so she didn't have to see the judgemental expression she was certain Mandie would now be wearing, one eyebrow haughtily lifted.

'I bet.'

They walked in silence for a few paces.

'Have you considered muting it?' Mandie ventured, slowing.

'I'm sorry . . . what?' Anna stopped walking completely, turned to face her friend.

'Muting it,' Mandie repeated simply. 'Strangely, I was chatting to a guy last night at a gig who has one and he mutes it all the time. Did you know you could do that?'

Anna paled.

'Oh.' Mandie's eyes grew wide. 'Shit, hon, sorry, I—'

'I thought we could only tune in and out of our thoughts. I didn't know you could . . . *mute* it?' She gave Mandie a questioning look. 'Are you sure the guy wasn't just talking about tuning out?'

'Definitely not. He said to mute his wife he holds down on the chip for ten seconds and then, boom, twenty minutes of silence.'

'Twenty minutes?' Anna felt dizzy. She leaned forward, hands on her knees, taking deep breaths.

'Maybe, maybe I'm wrong,' Mandie said hurriedly, rubbing Anna's back and leaning down beside her. 'Perhaps I got confused by what he was telling me. Is there anything about being able to mute it in the guidelines?'

The fucking guidelines.

Anna had spent so long fumbling through the side effects she hadn't even looked over the actual guidelines in their entirety.

Fuck.

'I've not . . .' She was struggling to find her breath, to admit her fault. Her failure.

Always failing.

Why am I always failing?

Anna? Are you painting? I thought you were out for a run.

NOT NOW.

'He . . . he should have told me,' Anna rasped, realisation coming up to greet her like a tsunami of ice, chilling her to the core.

Where are you?

'Or maybe, hon, you should have read up on all this a bit more.'

Anna felt the comment land like a gut punch. Mandie was right.

It's raining.

'Do you think, maybe, you didn't read up on it all, because, you know, if you didn't you could kind of pretend it's not happening?'

It's pouring.

'Yes.' Anna's voice was as small as she felt.

'I get wanting to be in denial. I do. But this is happening. To you. Right now. You can't just keep burying your head in the sand.'

The old man is snoring.

'I know.'

'You always do this, let Elijah get swept up in some shiny new gadget and then doubt that you'll be able to understand it too. Like the time I—'

He went to bed and he bumped his head.

'Don't say got locked in the bathroom.'

'Okay, I won't. But you get what I'm saying.'

'I do.' Anna paused, leaned back and looked at the sky, at the feathery wisps of cloud that streaked across the blue. 'I think I'm mad at myself as much as him.'

'Okay.'

The lady with the Pomeranian passed them, this time with the dog less agitated and trotting purposefully at her side.

And couldn't get up in the morning.

'So . . . why not try it? The mute thing?' Mandie asked as they slowly resumed walking.

'Okay . . .' Anna blew out hot air, the hand that lifted to her chip was trembling.

'You hold it down for ten seconds,' Mandie explained as she read from her phone.

What you having for lunch?

'One . . . two . . . three . . .' They counted together, walking side by side.

Anything nice?

Sandwich. Probably. What's with the rhyme?

'Nine . . . ten.'

Nothing. What sandwich?

No idea. You're making me hungry.

Anna shook her head in annoyance and gave Mandie a fraught look.

'No dice?'

'No. Like I said, I'm pretty sure mine is faulty.'

'What about Elijah's? Can he mute his?'

'Nope.' Anna blew out a tense breath, wishing she was still running. It was a lot harder to talk while running. 'I mean . . .'

Can he? All this time has he been doing it?

'Well, that's shit if he can't either.'

Who's doing what?

'Isn't it?'

Just some guy Mandie was seeing.

A group of men ran past them, all muscles in their vest tops. Mandie followed them with her eyes, momentarily distracted.

She sure knows how to pick them.

'I called Unity about my concerns,' Anna explained. 'With the chip still hurting and the bloody headaches. They told me to come in next week.'

'Oh, good. So they'll sort it?'

'Hopefully. I can't . . .' Anna gave a sad shake of her head. 'There's something wrong with it. I just know it.'

They reached a green bench and sat down. Mandie withdrew her water bottle and drank the rest of it down.

'You're sure the guy was muting his chip?'

Mandie reached for her phone, highlighted to the article explaining the mute function within Unity chips, silently passed it over to Anna.

'Fuck.'

'Indeed.' Mandie nodded solemnly.

'Why wouldn't he just tell me about it?'

'I'm guessing, because he didn't want you to know.' Mandie pursed her lips in annoyance. 'Or at the very least, didn't want you using it. Which, it seems, you can't anyway.'

'Do you think he can?' Anna felt worry curdle in her gut, raw and nauseating.

'Sweetie, I'm not in your head. What do you think? How often do you hear him?'

'He . . . he comes and goes.'

Mandie sighed, put her empty bottle away. 'But you're probably just tuning him in and out, right? Like he's actually, always there.'

Always there.

That's my fear.

'I'm worried that it might, you know, malfunction,' Anna admitted, tapping the place behind her ear that still burned.

'I bet. This isn't some lock on a toilet door that's playing up. This is, like, your mind.'

'I know.'

'Have you heard about anyone else having issues with the chip?'

Anna groaned. 'Not really, no. It's all still so new, there's not much information out there about it. I've been looking.' As they spoke she discreetly held down her chip for a further ten seconds.

'Have you, though?'

Anna felt seen by her friend's dubious response. Beside Mandie she always felt so transparent.

'Clearly I've been a fucking twat and not read up on anything about it enough.' Her voice caught and Anna buried her head in her hands.

What's your fear?

'Don't be so hard on yourself.' Mandie shuffled closer to her, wrapping her arm around Anna's slim shoulders. 'It's all . . . a lot. The chip. Tuning people out. Muting. Whatever. Maybe the guy I met had a different package. A different type of chip. In fact, I'm sure he said he did.'

'Liar,' Anna sniffed, voice muffled.

'We don't *know* anything for certain,' Mandie offered kindly. 'Let's gather up the facts first, yeah?'

'I'm going to ask them about the dream, too. Unity. When I go.'

'Has it happened again?'

Again, the guy Mandie is seeing.

'No.' Anna looked down at her knees. 'But it . . . it worried me.'

'Maybe it was just a hallucination or something,' Mandie offered.

'It felt too real for that.'

Oh, right. Sounds like a keeper.

'Okay, well, once the chip is fixed, or replaced, it should stop, right?'

'Right.'

I hope so.

You do?

Crap, not. I hope not.

'I'm worried you kind of rushed into this,' Mandie admitted quietly, dark hair tangling in the breeze.

'Same.'

'You know, you can't go on feeling guilty for ever about that spare bedroom still being empty.'

'I know.'

'Why don't you guys consider adoption?'

'We will.' Anna clasped her hands together, skin dry.

'Anna, it's not your fault you can't have kids – you get that, right?' Mandie's hand was on her back, voice soft.

'Then why does it feel that way?' She couldn't raise her head, couldn't turn to look at her friend.

'Well, it's not. Trust me. People have abortions every day. For a number of reasons. You made the right decision for you back then. You can't keep beating yourself up over it. You can't keep feeling like you owe Eli anything. You don't owe him your sanity.'

'But he's always been so good about it, so supportive.'

'Because it was his choice too,' Mandie lamented. 'It takes two to tango. He did the dance, he decided with you not to keep the baby, right?'

'Right.'

'Then you've nothing to feel guilty about. So stop letting him infect you with his bizarre addiction to tech. I'm worried you'll be bionic before you're forty.'

'In a weird way it has been good for us,' Anna said, peering at Mandie tentatively.

'You can't kid a kidder, babes.'

Anna nodded slowly in sad acknowledgement.

'Get it looked at,' Mandie urged. 'Better yet, get it taken out.'

Anna sniffed. 'I just . . . the mute thing. Throwing up after it was fitted. The headaches. It still hurting. I feel like mine needs to go.'

'I'm sure they'll just take it out.'

'And the dream.' Anna chewed her lip. 'Do you think it happened because mine is faulty.'

'I mean, I guess so, yeah.'

'I keep wondering if it happened to Elijah.'

'Have you asked him?'

Anna shook her head.

'Can I trust him?' she rasped. 'If he knew he could mute it, why didn't he . . . ?' She felt engulfed by sorrow anew, thrusting her fingers against her scalp, digging against her hair. 'I mean, is he seeing things too? I just . . .'

'Sweetie, *is* there something you don't want him to know?'

Anna scrunched her eyes closed, angry.

Stop. Don't think. Don't do it.

'I . . . I agreed to let him into my thoughts. But my past . . . That's different.'

'I get that.' Mandie leaned into her, sighed. 'Your thoughts, you can kind of control those. But your past, your history, that's beyond private. That's, like . . . sacred. And what's done is done.'

'I don't want my past appearing in his dreams,' Anna admitted tightly.

'Well, if his chip isn't faulty they shouldn't do. See what they say at Unity. And confront him about the mute thing.'

'Yeah.'

'Although it could just be me, hon. Getting things wrong, wires crossed. You know how I can be.'

They smiled awkwardly at each other, aware of the truth.

'I'm glad I have you.'

'Ditto.' Mandie grinned without missing a beat.

They got to their feet, approached the pathway that curved away from them, wrapping around the bend of the river upon which several swans glided serenely.

'How bad is it?' Mandie asked as they started to jog. 'The thing you don't want Eli to know about?'

Anna threw her a warning glance.

'Okay, okay. Try not to get too knotted up about it. He adores you. I'm sure there's a perfectly good explanation about the mute thing. And I'm sure he'd love you no matter how many skeletons you've stashed in your closet.'

'No,' Anna began running faster, 'he wouldn't.'

When she got to her front door she was breathing hard. Anna had run all the way back from the park, legs pumping high and fast. Like she was being chased. On the top step she wilted before the camera, glanced up so that it could sweep her, recognise her face, and unlock the door. Yet another gadget Elijah had been adamant they get. Instead of the usual bright chirp that foretold a green light, the camera grunted at her. Flashed red.

'What the . . . the . . . hell?' Anna struggled for breath, straightened, squared her shoulders and stared into the camera face-on. A pause. A grunt. A red light. 'Dammit.' She slapped the front door with the palm of her hand. She'd come out with no key. No phone. Just the shoes on her feet, the clothes on her back. She knew Elijah would hate it, but she needed the space. The lightness. The liberation.

The fucking door is broken.

Anna stood firm again, chin raised, waited for the camera to sweep her.

A flash of red.

Elijah, the stupid camera isn't recognising me. Can't you just override it or something?

The camera continued to grunt angrily at her.

Seriously, help. I'm a sweaty mess, I need a piss. Let me in.

A flash of red. Another digital grunt of disapproval.

ARE YOU MUTING ME?

STOP FUCKING MUTING ME.

I told you to always take your phone with you when you go out.

There you are! What the hell! What is this? Fix the damn door!

Why didn't you take your phone?

Are you doing this? Are you messing with the door?

Anna's hands formed fists as she breathed hotly through her nostrils.

Let me in, Eli.

This isn't me, it's just playing up.

It's never done that before.

I guess there's a first time for everything.

Can you help? I need to get inside.

Elijah?

A chirp. The camera suddenly glowing green. Anna burst through the front door as though the step were ablaze beneath her. Doubling over, hands on knees, she drew in long, stabilising breaths.

Next time take your phone.

Did you fuck with the door?

Of course not. I need quiet now; I'm going into a meeting.

Fucking mute me then.

Anna, I don't know what you're raging about. Just tune me out, please. No hysterical thoughts.

Mandie said we can mute our fucking chips! How could you not tell me!

Of course she said that. Thanks, Mandie. Bloody typical. Anna, our chips don't have the mute function.

She exhaled through her nose, air hot.

Why not?

Because what would be the point? We wanted closeness with our chips. Togetherness. I don't want to be muting you. Tuning out is different.

So we just . . . can't mute our chips?

Right.

But other people can?

Right.

All we can do is tune one another out?

I wish you'd stop taking what Mandie says as gospel. I'm going into a meeting. Calm yourself down. You look a mess.

With a start Anna looked back towards the closed front door.

Savage, thanks.

Eli?

Anna gulped down a strained breath.

Love you.

Elijah? Love you!

Love you too.

Anna closed her eyes, the start of a headache building like a storm.

21

She stepped out of the shower, steam rising around her. Anna reached for a towel, pressed it against her salmon-pink skin. She'd always liked her showers hot.

'You're poaching yourself,' Elijah would tease. But it felt good, that scalding sensation, the tingling. The way her body would hold the warmth even once she stepped out of the cubicle.

Anna dragged a comb through her hair, hoped the painkillers she'd swallowed earlier would start to take effect, pulled on some joggers and a soft jumper. Her legs were beginning to ache from her run that morning. She'd pushed herself further than she'd intended to. Locking eyes with her reflection in the mirror above the sink, Anna used her fingertips to make circles on her cheeks, dragging and stretching her skin. There was an ache behind her ear, beside her chip, an ache that seemed to reach all the way to her temple, like a fire moving through her entire brain.

I miss my wall of clouds.

She froze, hands still against her cheeks.

Eli?

Eli, are you home?

He wasn't meant to be. Was he?

You said you'd be in the office all day.

When did you get back?

It had to have been while she was in the shower.

She hurried from the bathroom, across the landing to the spare bedroom that housed a small sofa, a tall fern and a standing desk Elijah occasionally used if he was working from home. He turned when she walked in, face burning.

'Sweetheart, fuck, I'm sorry.'

Anna's vision blurred as she started to cry. She span, gesturing to the wall the sofa faced, decorated with a single print of a tree on a hillside. She'd always found something haunting about the image, it made her think of Cathy lost on the misty moors forever seeking Heathcliff.

It was one of the few pieces of art within their home which Elijah had approved of, had consented to buy her.

'Elijah.' She said his name with a mixture of disdain and despair. 'What the hell?'

'Oh, baby, I'm sorry. I'm so sorry. I came back and I was just in here working and my thoughts . . .' He bowed his head and gestured to the wall, to the picture of the lone tree.

'And you thought about the blue sky and clouds that should be there.' Anna sniffed, dragged the back of her hand across the base of her nose. 'Thought about the baby that *should be there.*'

'Please, don't get hysterical. It was just a passing thought.'

'You come home, don't even check in on me after the thing with the damn door, come straight up here and what, brood? Sulk?'

'Look, sweetheart—'

'Is this what you wanted?' Anna was shouting now. 'Is this what Unity is for you? A chance to punish me? Make me feel bad? Let me know how you truly feel about me? About us?'

Don't do this.

Fuck you.

You forget that I lost something too that day.

Don't.

'It was a fleeting thought, Anna. Don't over-dramatise this.'

'Like the one earlier? About the game? How many *fleeting thoughts* am I going to have to endure?' She blinked back fresh tears. 'And the mute button. Why didn't you tell me that was an option?'

'Do we seriously need to go over this again?'

'You never told me about it; don't bullshit me about connection.'

'Anna, it's not bullshit.' Now Elijah's voice was rising too. 'I do believe it's important we have connection. That we didn't have the mute function enabled. Yes, sometimes I have regrets about us not having a baby. So fucking sue me. It's a burden we both carry, but it's a burden all the same.'

You hate me.

'I love you. I think I've made that completely apparent.' He gestured to his ear, his own microchip. 'I want you in my head, Anna.' Slowly he approached her, placed his hands on her slim shoulders, looked down at her. 'You already own my heart.'

'Do you have any idea how insanely cheesy that sounds?'

'Yes,' he said with a half-smile. 'But it also happens to be true. I'm sorry you heard some random thought about a life that might have been. A life that is gone. Yes, I mourn it sometimes. As do you. But the life we have now is pretty bloody great.'

'Did you not want me to mute the chip? Is that why you never told me about it?' Anna pressed.

'Yes.' Elijah dipped his head, sighed. 'Because I know you. If you knew you could do it, you'd do it all the time. You'd keep hiding from me.'

'You don't know that.'

'I do.'

He lifted a hand and grazed her cheek with his thumb. 'I want to see you, Anna. All of you.'

'What if you can't handle the bad stuff?'

'I can.'

Anna swallowed. 'And what if I can't handle your bad stuff?'

'I'm such a dick, shit.' He enveloped her in an embrace. 'Baby, I'm sorry. I'm sorry.' He kissed the top of her head.

'I didn't even know you were coming home early,' Anna muttered, frowning. 'Why didn't you tell me?'

'I thought I did.'

'Did you . . . ? Are you sure you can't mute your chip?'

'Anna,' he released her and moved to close his laptop where it stood open on the pine standing desk, 'neither of us has the ability to mute our chips. We both have the same model.'

'Right.'

'And we will figure out why you keep having headaches.'

'Yeah.' Anna hugged her arms to her chest. 'Unity can fit me in next week.'

'Great.'

'They asked if there had been other issues.' She studied Elijah's face carefully.

'Other issues?'

'Yes, like . . .' She paused, choosing her words carefully. 'Hallucinations. Strange dreams.'

He pursed his lips. 'Not for me. Why, have you been having other problems? Are you seeing things?'

He stepped closer and Anna saw her pale face reflected in his chestnut eyes. How small she looked. How fragile.

'No, nothing. But I thought I'd mention it, since they asked.'

'Sure.'

Elijah was withdrawing from her now, tucking his laptop under his arm and making for the doorway.

'It's all covered with the Executive Package,' he explained, 'any, you know, alterations or anything.'

But not the mute function.

That's an optional extra.

'Need me to come with you?' Elijah lingered on the landing, looking back at her.

Anna gave a swift shake of her head. 'No, no it's fine. They said they only need to see me.'

'Well, you know,' Elijah smiled and pressed a finger to his temple, 'I'm here if you need me.'

Anna stood and listened to her husband's footsteps move deeper into the house as he went downstairs. For a moment she just stared at the image of the tree, listening to the throb of her own pulse as it drummed in her ears. Then she moved to turn off the light. She really didn't need to use the switch, it was a force of habit. All she actually needed to do was clap her hands. Almost everything in the house could be controlled via the app on their phone or some gimmick. Well, on Elijah's phone, since Anna still needed to install it. He could turn lights on and off, activate locks. Even the windows held the turquoise glow of being linked. With the press of a button anything could be activated. Anna both marvelled at and feared it.

'What if there's a fire?' she'd asked when Elijah had the digital locks placed on the windows.

'There's a failsafe,' he'd smoothly assured her.

'But if there's a fire, and a power cut,' Anna had pressed, 'how do we open the windows?'

'In a power cut everything opens.'

'So if there's a power cut, we are vulnerable to being bloody burgled?'

'I can set everything to remain locked if there's loss of power,' Elijah had offered, tapping on his phone. 'Or just some windows to open?' Anna had waved him away with a dismissive hand, too weary to think about the logistics.

Hand on the light switch she plunged the room into darkness, looking again at the lone tree on the canvas, now swallowed by shadows and barely visible.

Rock a bye baby.

She pictured instead a wall of clouds, a room filled with light.

On the tree top.

With laughter.

When the wind blows.

She knew Mandie was right, that she had no need to feel so guilty.

The cradle will rock.

But that didn't stop the feeling writhing within her, choking her.

When the bough breaks.

And now she'd heard how Elijah truly felt.

The cradle will fall.

'I've ruined everything,' she whispered into the dark, afraid to think the thought but needing to release it.

And down will come baby.

'It's all my fault.'

Cradle and all.

22
THEN

'I always feel kind of ... awkward.' Oscar was sprawled across a sofa tucked away in the back of the chain pub they were all sitting in when he made his admission.

Anna chewed thoughtfully on a chip as Gavin barked, 'Bullshit.'

'Seriously,' Oscar raked a hand through his russet hair, 'you guys see me drunk off my tits most of the time.'

'Pretty much all the time,' Elijah remarked drily.

'But it's because, you know . . .' He let his hand fall to his side, a slight blush upon his cheeks.

'I'm just surprised you were dressed before noon and up to eating lunch with us,' Helen noted from where she was sitting beside Gavin, legs gracefully crossed over his lap, their bodies so close, almost knotted together.

'I'm not a total vampire,' Oscar told her. 'But like I said, without a drink in my hand I feel . . .' He gave a light shrug. 'Yeah, awkward.'

'Exposed?' Anna offered, looking at him. Seeing him.

He shot her a look of annoyance. 'I just don't ever want to be a downer. And you guys are always . . .' He gestured to the two couples flanking him. Helen, catlike across Gavin; Anna and Elijah side by side on the other sofa, sharing a plate of chips. 'I want to live my life in colour,' he told them grandly. 'I want to see everything, do everything.'

'I hear that,' Gavin mumbled.

'You're well on the way to doing everything,' Elijah said with a slight roll of his eyes.

'Don't hate,' Oscar chided with a slight smirk.

'No, I don't. I . . .' Elijah doubled back. Anna felt him stiffening at her side. 'You want this full life, I get it. But you need to think beyond today. Beyond now.'

'All right, Dad,' Oscar said drolly.

'I'm serious. How many lectures have you missed this semester?'

Oscar gave a languid shrug.

'That's my point. All the carpe diem shit only goes so far. What about after uni? After graduation? What then?'

'We don't all have this grand plan.' Oscar locked eyes with Anna for a moment. 'And tomorrow isn't promised so I don't act like it is.'

'Yes, but you still need to be responsible for—'

'What Elijah is inelegantly saying,' Gavin eased into the conversation, gently nudging Helen off his lap so he could lean forward and look directly at his friends, 'is that yes, have fun while you're here. It's good to let loose a bit. God knows, I do it enough. But what he fails to understand is that some of us want more than a mortgage and a decent car.'

'A stable future is important,' Elijah chided him, 'a stable *career* is important. Dreams can only take you so far.'

'It's not about taking me somewhere.' Oscar crinkled his nose in distaste. 'It's about feeling. About leaving a mark on the world. Caring about something more than the mighty dollar. You get it, right?' He looked again at Anna.

'I—'

'Anna's decision to be an artist isn't on trial here,' Elijah interjected.

'But mine is?'

'No, he's right.' Anna spoke up, strident. 'We both want to be artists down the line. And that's different to chasing a corporate dream.'

'Good luck paying the bills.' Elijah raised an eyebrow at her. 'My goal is to have a job that pays, and that pays well. Because that's how the world works.'

'Like you need to worry about money,' Gavin muttered into his drink.

'You don't want more than that?' Oscar countered. 'You don't want to do something that means something?'

Pain flickered across Gavin's face as he glanced at Anna.

'Just because it's art doesn't mean it means something.' Helen was drawing her long hair back into a ponytail, a flash of her perfect cheekbones.

'Maybe it says something.' Oscar stole a chip from Anna and Elijah's plate. 'Maybe that's what it's about. Saying something. Making sense of the world.'

'It's about understanding things.' Anna sneaked a smile at Oscar, who gave her a soft nod of acknowledgement.

'Well, you two can understand your way through as many splattered canvases as you like,' Gavin was rising to his feet, pulling his wallet from his back pocket, 'but I'm thirsty. What we drinking?'

'I shouldn't.' Oscar turned up the collar of his polo shirt, sunk into it.

'Aww, man, come on; we rely on you to get the party started.'

'I've got a lecture at three.'

'Studying some dead artist won't make you a better one,' Gavin said before sauntering over to the bar.

Oscar watched him go, face pinched with indecision.

'We could just go back to halls,' Anna offered, leaning close to Elijah. 'Have a quiet afternoon.'

'Doesn't the SU open at two?' Helen wondered.

Oscar was again tugging his fingers through his hair. 'You know what, fuck it.' He sprang to his feet and chased after Gavin. Anna heard him add a round of shots to their order.

'Can't resist a fucking drink,' Elijah whispered to her, judgement high in his voice.

'It's not like that,' Anna replied sadly. 'He doesn't like being in his own head too much. It scares him.'

'I bet.' Elijah drained the last of his glass of Coke and kissed Anna's temple. 'I imagine it's a mad house in there. Not like in your mind.' He moved to kiss her lips. 'I'd spend all day in your head if I could.'

'Weirdo.' Anna smiled before kissing him back.

'Get a room,' Gavin scolded playfully as he walked back with a tray of drinks, Oscar close behind, watching them all, taking it in.

23
NOW

Anna shivered within her studio. Rain tapped against the roof, the heater in the corner humming loudly. All morning she had stooped over her canvas, stared at the colours until her vision blurred.

'Just paint something,' she told herself through gritted teeth. But how could she when she felt so tired, so drained?

There were only two days until her appointment at Unity. The thought of being able to understand all the functions more clearly filled her with relief. She was becoming increasingly convinced that her chip was faulty. First the memory, then Elijah's erratic presence in her mind. And the headaches, how she seemed to chain them. 'Just keep going,' she commanded both herself and the brush she was holding, sweeping it in a gentle arc across her canvas, intending to leave a smear of sky blue. But instead she kept it millimetres from connecting, letting the soft bristles catch only air. 'Come on. *Paint.*'

Do you intend to stay out there all day?

Anna's jaw clenched. She didn't move but she imagined Elijah at the window, looking out at her.

Please, come inside. I know you're mad at me. I've said I'm sorry a thousand times.

I'm working.

She scowled at her canvas, at her lack of progress. Angrily, she swept her brush across it. Once. Twice. Changed out the colour on the palette, kept painting. The previous blue she'd applied now turning moody and dark.

Anna, please. You must be freezing out there. Just come in.

I'm working.

And finally she was. Fast and furious, as though in a trance. The paintbrush caressing the canvas on each inhale. It had been *years* since she'd found that kind of flow.

Just come inside.

I'm fine.

She wasn't. Her hand shuddered from the cold, which had set deep in her bones. Too long she had petulantly placed herself within the shed. But now she was actually painting, creating something. Panting, she let her hand fall to her side and looked at the canvas. As she gazed upon it, the cold from outside truly settled in her veins.

She was looking at a beach.

I've made you a hot chocolate.

A beach with a high cliff, beneath a dark sky. A beach she recognised.

'Shit.' The word quietly left her in an icy cloud.

Anna bit on the end of her paintbrush, panicked. If Elijah saw it, would he recognise it? Would he know?

I've added marshmallows. And whipped cream.

She threw her paintbrush to the ground, then turned her easel to the wall, removing the beach from view. Just looking at it made her heart race. She needed to get out of there.

I'm coming in because it's cold. That's it.

The door to the shed smacked shut and she strode the length of the garden towards the warmth of the house, breath harried. She entered the utility room, kicked off her boots and pushed her feet into plush ankle-boot slippers, savouring the delicious sensation that then tingled at her toes. Opening the door to the kitchen, she could smell the hot chocolate. The toasted cocoa made her salivate. She was about to glance around for her drink when she noticed the red roses. Four bunches of a dozen roses, all displayed in clear glass vases along the length of the marble island that stood centrally in their long kitchen. Anna inhaled a sharp breath of surprise.

'I know I fucked up,' Elijah peered at her from where he stood by the hot drinks machine that hissed and growled whenever they pressed a button to create a café-quality cappuccino or espresso. 'And you've been mad at me for days. Rightly so. But baby, please. I'm sorry. I'm so, so sorry.'

'That's a lot of flowers,' Anna commented as she walked along the island, one hand stroking the cool surface of the marble. She had to admit how beautiful the roses were, the rich, deep red of their velvety petals.

'I had a lot of apologising to do.'

Elijah had always bought her flowers. And never just a single one, always by the dozen. The first Valentine's Day they'd spent as a couple he'd barely been able to get through the door to their uni halls due to the pink blooms he carried.

'You're trying too hard,' Gavin had sneered from along the corridor, not having even bought Helen a card that year.

'Maybe you're just not trying hard enough,' Elijah had countered.

'They're beautiful,' Anna rounded the end of the island.

'You think I'm trying too hard,' her husband said quietly,

defeated. She stared at him, confused. He gave her a sad smile. 'I don't always need to hear your thoughts to know what you're thinking.'

I like the flowers.

But . . .

'But I don't like knowing that you wish we had a child.'

'Anna.' He came over, held her against her. He smelt of coffee and mint. 'Sweetheart, it was a stupid thought. Nothing else.'

'Yes, but,' her shoulders dropped, 'it's a decision you don't have to make. Whereas for me, decision made.'

'We're in this together,' he told her firmly. 'Always have been.'

'Eli—'

'I'm sorry you heard it. I am. But even hearing it doesn't change anything. Anna, I'm happy. You make me so, so happy.'

Anna looked beyond him, to the row of roses. 'I just fear I won't always be enough.'

'You will be.' He purred the words into her ear as he held her to his chest. 'You are more than enough.'

'Maybe we should start talking more about adoption,' she suggested cautiously.

'Maybe.'

But I don't know if it's for me.

He released her, moved back. 'Do you want your hot chocolate?'

'What do you mean?'

'Baby, not now, okay? We can always discuss it later.'

No, now.

'Adoption just isn't for me, all right? I'd rather carry on just you and me than raise someone else's child.'

Anna froze, absorbing his words.

'I'm happy now,' Elijah insisted. 'If we had our *own* baby, great. Part you, part me. That'd be perfect. But taking on a child we don't know, have no idea about their genealogical past, that doesn't interest me.'

'We could do a DNA test, we could—'

'Do you want that? Really?'

'I want a family,' Anna said simply, 'however that looks.'

'Look, well fine.' Elijah motioned to the side where a mug overflowing with whipped cream and pink marshmallows was waiting. 'Hope that warms you up a bit.'

'You always said you'd consider it.' Anna didn't move towards her mug; she stayed in place, staring at her husband.

'I did and I have.'

'I don't think we should just be closing the door on it so quickly.'

'What would you rather I do, Anna? If I want my own child, it's the wrong thing; if I say I'm not keen on adoption, that's wrong too.'

'This doesn't need to be about you.' Anna felt her face getting hot even though her bones still carried the cold from the studio. 'It needs to be about both of us.'

I need to get back to work.

Elijah began stalking towards the kitchen door.

If you wanted that blue sky wall so badly you wouldn't shut this down.

Fine. We can talk about it. Later. Right now I'm just pissed with work.

What's new?

Don't be like that. It's tough at the moment, with the merger.

Every week it's something.

Anna, please, I'm just stressed. I don't need additional aggravation at home.

Seriously? I'm stressing you out! How do you think I feel when you're in my head? All. The. Time. Always on my mind, constantly.

Please, Anna. I know you're worried about the chip but calm down.

It's fucking faulty, Eli.

'Just like me.'

Upstairs a door slammed. Alone, Anna breathed in the heady perfume of her flowers, felt it catch in the back of her throat. They bloomed seductively against the navy cupboards and marble surfaces. Placing her elbows atop the island, Anna cradled her head in her hands. She pictured another life, one where she'd kept her baby. Had another. The fridge door covered in pictures lovingly created out of crayon. The hallway cluttered with small wellies and child-sized scooters. The concealed television in the lounge would glow all day long, playing cartoons about canine families and girls who played with ducks. That one choice had sent her entire life in a certain direction.

How different might things have been?

She reached for the rose closest to her, plucked one of its petals free, rubbed it between her fingers. What if she'd made other choices, at different points in her life? What if she'd—

Anna, please don't be morose. I told you, I'm stressed. I've apologised. I've bought flowers. Please, let's move on from this. I love you.

I'm not being morose.

Things can't be different. They are as they are. That is the way of life. We made a choice, we live with the consequences.

Not everyone can be as pragmatic as you can.

More's the pity for them.

Why do you always buy me roses?

Because they're classic, like you. You're a typical English rose. Dark eyes, pale cheeks, pink lips. If you were a flower, that's what you'd be.

Even with the thorns?

Most definitely with the thorns.

Anna kept looking at the flowers, trying to shift her focus as it kept wandering back to the canvas in her studio, the first time she'd not painted a cat. Now there was a beach upon it. She felt her cheeks beginning to burn, needing a distraction.

Perhaps I could somehow render this down for a colour? She reached for a long, green stem.

They're your flowers, sweetheart. Do with them what you want.

Anna held the long rose, lifted it higher into the light cast by the window behind her.

Oh, before I forget, we're having dinner tonight with Gavin and Helen.

Shit.

She caught a thorn against the inside of her finger. Dropping the rose to the ground she looked and saw a dark bead of blood expanding between her thumb and forefinger.

It won't be so bad.

No, not that. I just caught a thorn.

Be careful.

Anna sucked on the blood, wondering if she'd need a plaster.

I'm so fucking accident prone lately.

You need to be more careful.

Stooping to pick up the rose from the floor, she carefully returned it to its vase.

Do we really have to see Gavin and Helen?

We've already put them off twice, so yes.

I'm just not in the mood to hear how busy she is at work and have you and him in a night-long pissing contest about who had the best figures last month.

Her fingers tentatively traced the space around her chip, behind her ear, the skin still so hot. So sore.

We won't be like that.

You're always like that. And I always have to get drunk to cope with the pair of you.

It'll be fine. I'll drive, that way you can drink as much as you want.

I'm pretty sure Helen hates me.

Of course she doesn't hate you. You just run in different circles now.

She never messages me any more.

Do you message her?

Anna laughed drily, the sound bouncing back to her.

Fair point.

Tonight will be nice. I've booked a table at Nicco's.

Do they know about the chip?

A creak on the floorboard overhead.

Eli?

They know.

And?

It's Gavin.

What does that mean?

It means, unless he had it first, he's against it.

I really don't want to go.

Baby, I've promised. It'll be awkward if we bail again.

At least consider adoption.

For you?

For me.

For you I'd consider anything.

It's why I keep you around.

Anna was smiling as she pulled open a drawer and picked up some scissors. She approached the roses, holding the stem more carefully as she removed the tallest bloom from the vase. With a swift snip, the head fell away from the thorn-ridden stalk.

When I give the signal, we leave.

Do we need a signal?

Anna laughed again.

I guess not. I'll just tell you when I'm done.

Fine.

She snipped more and more roses, the island becoming cluttered with their detached flower heads.

I've found a use for the roses.

They were pretty useful looking beautiful on the island.

Do you want me to accept your apology or not?

Okay, what's the use for them?

Pot-pourri.

Anna's lips lifted into a smile. She'd put a pot in each room downstairs; fill the house with the soft, elegant fragrance.

So, am I forgiven?

Am I?

Anna—

Even if the family we end up with isn't the one we originally pictured, that's not so bad, is it?

I suppose perhaps not.

I mean, is this the life you always pictured having?

Always.

Anna stiffened, scissors in hand.

Seriously?

From the moment I saw you, dancing in the SU, I knew I wanted to build my life with you.

Really?

Really. Did you not feel that way when you first saw me?

Anna thought of that moment, music pounding, back sticky with sweat, the taste of cheap vodka on her tongue.

Oscar dancing manically near the bar, Gavin on the dance floor.

You had to grow on me.

Cheers.

There was a face in her mind's eye. Anna blinked, trying to banish it away. Then she furiously cut the last of the roses, detaching them from each stem, determined to keep herself busy. As she cut, she replayed a nursery rhyme in her head.

Row, row, row your boat.

Snip.

Gently down the stream.

Snip.

Merrily, merrily, merrily, merrily.

All the roses had been beheaded.

Life is but a dream.

24

They had their usual table at Nicco's: a booth at the far end of the restaurant, where the lights were dim and the air thick with garlic. Red leather upholstery against bare brick walls. Anna had always liked it there. But tonight her calamari starter curdled in her stomach, the Merlot in her glass stung her tongue, tasting like vinegar.

I don't feel great.
You'll be fine.
They'll think we're crazy.
Let them think it.

The judgement from across the table, she'd been braced for it. It arrived just after the plates for the main course were taken away, Anna barely able to touch her risotto.

'Seriously?' Gavin's mouth widened into a laugh, one hand casually cradling his glass of wine, elbow resting on the table. 'You guys *seriously* got it done?'

'Yes,' Elijah confirmed sharply.

'And you have it, like, *right now*.' Gavin wasn't even trying to conceal his amusement, the wine he'd already drunk making him loud, verging on aggressive.

I knew he'd be like this.
Typical Gavin.

'We really like it,' Elijah insisted. 'It's given us,' he reached for Anna's hand, squeezed it, 'a real sense of intimacy.'

'Don't bullshit me.' Gavin's gaze flitted between them, settling on Anna. 'You can't seriously tell me you like this?'

'She wouldn't have got it if she wasn't serious,' Helen intercepted smoothly, face held in a sombre stare as though she were cast from marble. 'She gave her heart to Elijah, why not her mind, too?'

'Because it's ridiculous,' Gavin lamented loudly, 'absolutely bloody ridiculous. You shouldn't give anyone any part of yourself. You belong to you.'

'Not everyone has a marriage like ours.' Helen threw Gavin a look, arm shifting above the table as though they were now holding hands beneath it. Anna felt the acidic burn of wine in the back of her throat.

'Eli, mate, I'm worried you're losing your damn mind.'

'The technology behind it is fascinating.' Elijah grew more animated as he spoke, releasing Anna's hand. 'What I'm drawn to is the cerebral interception they've managed to lock onto. The ability to track and control conscious human thought.'

You and your tech.

As he spoke Helen caught Anna's eye and gave her a sympathetic smile. 'He does love his tech,' she noted.

She thinks I'm just your dumb little guinea pig.

'Oh yeah.' Anna laughed tightly as she finished the dregs in her glass of wine. As the alcohol began to hit her stomach she wished she'd eaten more. 'He's obsessed with it.'

'It's almost his biggest obsession,' Helen agreed, eyes gleaming.

'So, learned anything interesting?' Gavin leaned back against the booth, his arms straddling the back of it. Anna threw him an icy stare. When he'd walked in he'd looked impeccable: sleek in a navy suit, dirty blond hair smoothed back. Now strands fell into his eyes, his shirt jacket discarded, his tie loose over his half-unbuttoned shirt. He was more like the Gavin Anna had first met at university: chaotic, brimming with a frenzied, uncontainable energy. The Gavin who—

She pinched her leg to stem her thoughts and met Gavin's stare. 'Nothing we didn't already know.'

'You're not really selling this whole Unity thing to me.' Gavin gestured between Elijah and Anna. 'I'm still not getting it.'

'What's to get?' Elijah straightened, his tie still pinned tight to his throat. 'It's about complete transparency. Not to mention the safety aspects.'

'See,' Gavin gritted his teeth, 'none of that appeals to me. And it's hardly conducive to a decent marriage.'

'How so?' Elijah's knee jiggled furiously beneath the table. *Keep still.*

'Relationships thrive on secrets.' Gavin smirked and drained the last of his wine before reaching for the bottle in the centre of the table. 'What fun is it if you know everything?'

Anna reached a hand beneath the table, clasped Elijah's knee and stilled it.

Elijah opened his mouth to respond to Gavin just as their desserts arrived. Anna took one look at the moist curves of her tiramisu and knew she couldn't face it. Excusing herself, she went outside to the patio at the back of the restaurant. She inhaled deeply on the e-cigarette she'd brought in her handbag.

Don't be smoking.

I came tonight to keep you happy, permit me this.

She exhaled a long plume up towards the distant night sky.
I worry about the long-term implications.
I worry about my short-term mental health. I'll be back in five.
Heads-up, Gavin is on his way.
Figures.

Anna kept her back to the door which led back into the restaurant, not turning as it creaked open and the sounds from inside briefly flooded the small patio.

'Hey.' She could smell the smoke curling from Gavin's e-cigarette. It smelt of coffee and chocolate.

'Hey,' Anna replied, still not turning around. They were alone in the small courtyard, surrounded by four walls of neighbouring buildings. The picnic benches scattered about were empty, no one else wanting to brave the chill of the night air. Anna lingered close to an outdoor heater, savouring its warmth.

'So, is he in there right now?' Gavin came to stand beside her, so close their elbows were almost touching.

'Not right now, no,' Anna told him icily. She hugged her arms tight to her chest. 'I knew you and Helen would,' her voice became small, 'judge me on this.'

'I really can't imagine it.' Gavin inhaled on a long drag, laughed as he blew it away, smoke shooting from his nose. 'If Helen was in my head all the time it would drive me fucking mad. I know she'd be firing chores at me non-stop.'

'It's not,' Anna was looking down at her feet, 'like, *all* the time. You can tune in and out from one another.'

Unless he's angry.

'I still don't get it. It doesn't seem like something *you* would do.' She could feel him staring at her but didn't look up.

'Eli – he thought it'd be important for us, *good* for us, to have more connection.'

Anna kept her head down, refusing to look at Gavin. But

he moved to stand before her. 'So you just went along with it and now you're listening to radio Elijah all day?'

Slowly she lifted her head and gave him a level stare but said nothing. Gavin inhaled, laughed, crease lines deep around his mouth. 'I swear, you two are losing the plot.'

'Maybe we just wanted complete closeness. No games. No secrets.'

'No secrets?' Gavin raised his eyebrows at her. 'Everyone has their secrets.'

Anna looked away, face flushing crimson, blowing smoke towards a nearby picnic table.

'Are things so bad between you two that you had to resort to this to spice things up?'

Anna scowled at him. 'No. Of course not. We don't need *spicing* up.'

'Sure,' Gavin scoffed.

'Since we're discussing bedroom antics, how are things with Helen?' Her face was burning.

'Fine,' Gavin instantly replied. 'Why?'

'It's just . . .' She studied his face, the way his hair fell into his eyes making him appear younger than he was. 'Nothing. I'm glad you two are fine.'

'Yeah, we're fine. Happy. Are you?'

'Of course,' Anna snapped.

'Yeah, you just radiate happiness these days.' Gavin gave her a wry look.

'Maybe you and Helen should give Unity a try,' Anna suggested haughtily.

'Oh, yeah, great idea,' Gavin laughed. 'That'd go down like a lead balloon. She and I . . . It works. She wants me for me, I respect that. Marriage is an agreement to share a life not a bloody brain. Besides,' he blew smoke directly into Anna's face, 'my mind is my own. No one else gets to access it.'

Anna's eyes smarted as she languidly waved a hand before her face, remaining composed. 'What about your heart? Being married, you already share that.'

'A heart is merely an organ that pumps blood.'

'Wow, ever the romantic.'

Gavin laughed then looked her in the eye. 'You heard his temper with that thing?'

A flash of worry streaked across Anna's face.

'Thought so.' Gavin eased back from her, thrust his free hand into his trouser pocket. 'He can get so worked up sometimes. And it's weird, because he'll go from zero to, like, fucking losing his mind. Ten minutes later, zero again. Been that way since . . .' His voice trailed off. He bowed his head, suddenly seeming distant.

'I've heard him getting wound up at work sometimes,' Anna admitted, 'but then, we all get pissed off at work.'

'True,' Gavin dragged out the word, nodding, 'but he's like a nuclear power station, everything is great until two bad things collide. And then,' he dropped his voice to a whisper, 'boom.'

'You're one to talk,' Anna countered tersely. 'You forever act with anything other than your head.' She didn't mean to glance down but her eyes betrayed her.

'Is that what he tells you?' Gavin twisted away from her, a slight blush on his face as he frowned. 'Fucking typical.' He released a deep sigh. 'So what little secrets has Eli learned since fitting you with a chip?'

'None.'

Gavin arched an eyebrow at her.

'We already knew everything about each other.'

He looked at her, drew his e-cigarette to his lips. 'Bullshit.'

'Elijah and I have no secrets.'

'We both know that isn't true.' He lazily blew out his heavily scented smoke. 'You know, I thought better of you. This . . . this whole Unity crap, it's beneath you.'

'It's about being a decent wife, having a . . . a strong marriage.'

Everything okay?

'It's about you being his little doll.' Gavin scowled. 'A toy that he likes to preen over and play with.'

You've been out there a while.

'Fuck off.' Anna was shoving her e-cigarette back into her bag.

'You don't need some sodding chip to be a decent wife. He doesn't see you, Anna. Sure, he can hear you now, but that's not the same.'

'Oh my God, Gavin,' her voice became shrill, 'as if I'm going to stand out here and listen to you tear apart my marriage.'

'I'm not tearing it apart.' Gavin reached for her wrist, clenched it within his hand. 'But I'm worried about you. I know what happiness looks like, Anna.'

'One thought . . .' She glared at him, pulse racing as she felt the heat from his fingertips against her skin. 'One thought and Elijah would be out here.'

Anna?

I'm fine.

'And what then? He tells me every day what he thinks of me, how I'm just some charismatic screw-up who continually gets lucky riding on his coat-tails. Which isn't true. I don't need a chip to hear that from him.'

'Let's just go back inside.' Anna raised her chin, Gavin's hand still holding on to her.

'Did you have any say in it?' His voice grew softer. 'The chip?'

Anna tried to shake him lose but he wouldn't let go.

'Just because he built you a gilded cage doesn't mean you have to stay in it.' He looked at her, pupils large.

Anna shrugged him off, snatched her hand away from him. 'You're drunk, Gavin.'

'Quelle surprise.'

'Just because Oscar loved to play the drunk doesn't mean you have to fill his role.'

'Is that all you thought he was? Some drunk?' Gavin looked at her, crestfallen.

'Of course not.'

'I still miss him, you know.'

'Yeah, me too.'

'Does he . . . ?' He nodded back towards the door which led inside. 'Does he think about him much?'

Anna clenched her jaw.

The dream.

She ground her teeth together, needing the conversation to end before her thoughts started to run away from her.

'Thought not,' Gavin deduced drily.

'Why don't you stay out here and cool off?' Anna said tersely, striding away from him.

'I hope you're keeping them in check,' Gavin called after her as Anna opened the door to Nicco's. She didn't turn back as he added, 'Your thoughts.'

Anna was silent on the car ride home, forehead pressed to the cool glass of her window, watching the lights of the city morph and blur.

'You all right?' Elijah drove with his shoulders squared, jaw clenched.

Anna, are you all right?

I just feel sick, that's all. I drank too much.

Did he say anything when you were outside?
The usual.
Helen seems so exhausted by him.
I'm not surprised, he's getting worse.
I don't get it.
Elijah stopped abruptly at some red lights.
Sorry.
It's okay.
His whole lovable drunk act was okay at uni, endearing even.
Like Oscar's was.
But not now. Every time we go out it's like he's trying to drink himself into oblivion.
Do you miss him?
Like tonight – I'm sure he had two bottles of Merlot to himself.
Elijah?
Anna's stomach lurched, her own consumed wine sloshing side to side.
Yeah. Sure. Of course.
We never really talk about him.
There's nothing to talk about.
We can talk about missing him and—
Did Gavin say something?
No.
We're lucky, Anna. We're happy, always have been.
Sure.
I think that's a big part of his problem.
Gavin's?
He's jealous of us. He can't stand how happy we are, when he isn't happy. He's always been the same.
He and Helen looked pretty happy at dinner tonight. Holding hands under the table. Sharing smiles.

You don't hear what he tells me at work.
Like about how he's seeing someone?
Why are you bringing that up?
I'm just saying, you always paint this picture of him being a total dick to her but when they're together, I don't see it. They actually seem . . . happy.
It's all a fucking act, Anna.
How can it be? They've been together as long as we have and—
Can we drop this please?

Anna felt the wine beginning to shift within her stomach, beginning to climb.

Stop the car.
Anna, I'm just by a crossing, can—
Stop the fucking car.

The hum of the electric stopped suddenly as Elijah veered up on a kerb, slamming on the brakes. Anna cracked her door, the night fresh against her. Leaning out, she bowed her head and vomited, painting the pavement a milky shade of red.

Jesus Christ, Anna.
Sorry. I'm sorry.

She retched again.

'Here, let me help.' Elijah was unbuckling his seatbelt, moving across to draw her hair back as she continued to throw up.

I drank too much. I'm so fucking sorry. I should have eaten more.
It's okay.
Are you mad at me?
You always get like this.
What?

'No, I'm not mad at you,' Elijah loudly confirmed. 'I just worry about you. You need to start drinking less and eating more when we go out. Okay?'

Okay.

Anna's throat burned. At the back of it she tasted coffee and chocolate.

Fucking hell. Do you think Gavin's being sick?

'I seriously hope so,' Elijah remarked as he continued to hold her hair.

But you know he won't be. He'll wake up tomorrow fresher than us.

You think he's really lucky.

He is.

Do you think he feels that way?

Probably not.

Anna vomited again, this time spitting out only bile.

That's the thing, we never see ourselves as we actually are. Are you done?

For a moment she shuddered, rasped into the night.

Yes, I'm done.

Unity

Executive Package

£60,000

With our luxurious Executive Package, you and your partner can enjoy all that Unity has to offer while discovering true togetherness with OneMind.

Unwind in our guest lounge prior to your appointment, taking in beautiful vistas of the city and enjoying complimentary refreshments from our award-winning pastry chefs.

Become OneMind, true Unity, in our bespoke treatment rooms. Select an immersive experience with our wraparound technology, ranging from the depths of the rainforests to the peaks of Everest. Wherever you want to be, we can place you there.

The Executive Package has unlimited aftercare for you and your Unity partner. A lifetime of happiness starts today. Click here to discover more. Book now for a 10 per cent discount.

25

Sleep took her like an ocean in a storm, roiling her as she tossed beneath the duvet. She didn't hear Elijah fretting over her as he carried her up the stairs, as he carefully removed her clothes. The drunkenness had claimed her.

It was past three a.m. when Anna surfaced from the depths of sleep, fragments of a dream still lingering: her old kitchen at uni, a face just inches from hers.

Dammit, stop, she ordered herself, throat raw, eyes burning.

'Fuck.' Grumbling, she rolled on to her side, heard the gentle rumble of Elijah's breathing beside her.

Why did I drink so fucking much?

Awkwardly, she stumbled out of bed, shoved her feet into the plush softness of her slippers and staggered downstairs to the kitchen, desperate for a glass of water. As she slumped over the sink she noticed she wore her silk pyjamas but had no recollection of putting them on.

I should have eaten more. Goddammit.

Is Eli pissed at me?

She tipped her gaze towards the ceiling, instantly feeling dizzy.

'Urgh.' Anna massaged her temple, drank deeply from her glass, the water unpleasantly cold against her teeth, tasting of metal. She didn't care. She just drank until her throat no longer felt like brittle parchment.

At least I went to the sodding meal. Put up with Gav and his judgement. Thinking he's so above it all.

She could still smell the smoke he'd billowed in her face.

He's just jealous because he'd never do it.

Anna poured herself another glass of water. She remembered being in the courtyard, the stars watching overhead. Gavin mocking her, goading her. But then it all started to blur and slip away, the wine owning the rest of the night. From the burn in her throat she sensed she had been sick.

Eli is going to laud that over me.

She hoped her husband had been understanding. After all, it was at his insistence that they were even there. She would have happily stayed home, avoiding the double date.

I miss the old Helen.

Glass in hand, Anna left the kitchen, flicking off the lights and padding back up the stairs.

Helen used to like me.

The house was so still around her, as if frozen until awakened by a new day.

And I used to like Helen.

Why did I have to fuck it all up?

I miss more than Helen.

It was harder now, to be close. Helen, whose aloofness had once seemed endearing, intriguing, now felt cold, distant. She worked long hours, wore tailored suits and drank chai lattes every morning. She never said it, but Anna sensed the contempt she had for her lifestyle, her art. The way her stony face would crinkle, just a little, whenever she saw Anna in joggers or dungarees, blue eyes cold.

'Some of us need real jobs,' she'd once declared after one

too many glasses of Chardonnay. Later, she'd insisted the comment wasn't directed at Anna.

'Sweetie, of course not, I wasn't talking about you; I was referring to, you know, influencers, all that bollocks. Some of us need to have real jobs to pay our mortgages.'

Money.

It was always the silent companion at any of their outings. Less so in recent years now that Gavin and Helen both had successful careers. And Gavin surely earned close to what Elijah brought home.

But Elijah was from money. The rest of them weren't. Anna wasn't blind to the advantages that gave them: help with buying their home, paying for the wedding. Even the flexibility for her to work from home as she did, focusing on her art – she knew a small part of that was attributed to the help that came from his parents.

'At least you'll always be comfortable,' Gavin had drunkenly remarked at Anna and Elijah's engagement party. Anna had seethed at the comment.

'Marriage is about love, not comfort,' she'd told him self-righteously.

'You sure about that?'

Fucking Gavin.

Pressure behind her eyes; pain pulsing, growing. A migraine was coming. Sometimes Anna lay awake and imagined poison seeping out from her Unity chip, soiling her brain, blanketing every soft expanse of tissue, every neuron.

She rounded the top of the stairs and entered the bedroom. She hated how Gavin could always get under her skin, knew what to say to wind her up.

How Helen puts up with him I don't know.
He's such a know-it-all.
So arrogant.

So bloody cocky.
And yet—
Stop.

She squeezed her eyes closed in frustration. *Just stop fucking thinking.*

The air in the bedroom was thick. Elijah was tucked on his side beneath the white duvet, chest rising and falling. Anna tiptoed around the end of the bed, passing by her mirrored vanity, the doors that led to the en suite and the walk-in wardrobe. She noted the shadowy shapes of all her bottles of perfume, some make-up scattered about.

'Try and be a bit tidier,' Elijah was always imploring her.

'You like that I'm messy,' Anna would playfully remind him.

His bedroom at university had always felt so formal to her. Bed made, only ever navy bedding. Books lined on a bookshelf, a guitar in the far corner. No posters. No knick-knacks. All clothes neatly folded away in the wardrobe.

By contrast, Anna's room looked as though either someone had broken in or a homeless person had taken up residence there. Her bedding was often bundled up in a ball on the floor, clothes strewn across the bare mattress. Books everywhere. Posters were tacked to every piece of wall she could reach. James Dean. *Breakfast at Tiffany's*. Marilyn Monroe. *Lord of the Rings*. Her choices were chaotic, unorganised. Eclectic. A true reflection of who she was. There were even some cat posters dotted around; she'd been drawn to them even then. Make-up covered what should have been her desk. Along with hairspray, perfume, tubs of lip gloss with missing lids and finger indentations. Fairy lights were strung around the headboard.

'I find your room intense,' Eli once complained.

'Well, I like it,' Anna countered. 'Being in here comforts me.'

Helen's room was simpler, cleaner. No posters, no debris.

She placed potted plants on her desk and window sill that she remembered to water. Anna knew that if they were in her room they'd be dead within a month. Helen's room was like her: cool, austere. Anna's was pure madness. Unorganised, cluttered, yet strangely welcoming. At least, that was how it felt to her.

Climbing into bed, Anna curled against Elijah's back, feeling cold. The wine which had worked so well at making her pass out was now firing up her synapses, making her stare wide-eyed into the darkness. She listened to Elijah's breathing, low and level, checking she had not woken him.

He hates it when I wake him up.

Anna tried to absorb her husband's warmth.

Just go to sodding sleep.

She remembered the nights in her single bed at university, Elijah pressed up against her back, an arm around her waist, both of them slipping over into sleep when he'd whisper in her ear, breath hot, 'If you ever leave me I couldn't bear it. You're mine, Anna. Mine.' His grip so tight around her and then his head heavy on the pillow as he slipped away but never let go.

I need to sleep.

The next day would be a busy one; she needed to journey into the city, to Unity. Elijah had offered to drive but Anna felt the need to be alone, to ride the tube. Possibly even find time to visit her favourite art shop on Dormer Street. Not that she was short on supplies, she just enjoyed the ambiance in there. The cluttered shelves, the smell of oil. It almost felt like stepping inside a painting.

Somewhere around four in the morning, Anna again slipped over into sleep.

There was sand beneath her feet. The sea was close, roaring as dark waves lapped at the shore.

'We need to get out of here.' Gavin, young and afraid, at her side. 'Seriously, stop dicking about.'

Anna looked about and recognised the beach. The couple fornicating on the plastic lounger. The smell of spiced kebabs carrying over from the lights near by. The distant hiss of waves hitting rocks. Her stomach churned.

'He's dead, he's fucking dead.' Gavin grabbed her shoulders, gave her a slight shake. She must be drunk as the world seemed to tip back and forth on its axis. Her throat held the burn that only vodka shots could give. 'He fell and . . . Shit. Shit! Let's fucking go.'

Gavin smacked her shoulder and her legs began to move, to run. The sand made it hard going, pulling her down with each step. Up the beach she heard shouting. Saw the shadows of people moving. They made it up the stone steps, on to the street. It was so bright, so loud. Anna winced. A motorbike sped by, cutting so close to the kerb it almost took her with it. There were revellers mingling about, girls in skirts so short you could see their arse cheeks, tottering in plastic heels. Guys followed them like salivating dogs, usually in polo shirts with the collars tucked up high, too much gel in their hair.

And above all of it, above the murmur of chat, the rumble of engines, the giggle of drunk girls, came the wail of a siren. It screamed mournfully, demanding to be heard.

'Shit.' Gavin was tugging on her elbow. 'I think the hotel is this way, come on.' Head down, she followed her friend, bile rising in her throat. A neon-yellow van flew past, lights blaring. 'Ambulance.' Gavin tossed the word over his shoulder as they ducked into a side street. Cafés had bistro chairs spread along the cobbled street, most of them occupied by people still drinking, smoking, savouring the last of the night. Gavin weaved between them, throwing anxious glances back in Anna's direction. 'It's just up ahead.' Anna stumbled after him, legs weakening. She felt the strange stirrings of pain in her joints, though she was still too drunk to fully feel them. 'We just need to go up here.' Gavin pointed to some steps which led up to a white building. Anna looked up at it and felt a flicker of recognition.

Their hotel.

'I just need you to keep it together, okay?' Gavin was right in front of her now, hands on her shoulders, looking into her eyes. 'Can you do that?'

Anna felt herself nod.

'I'm serious, Elijah. Keep it together. Things are bad enough as it is. We can't be found out here, do you understand?'

Anna blinked and heard a voice which wasn't her own say, 'Just get me to the hotel. Get me to the hotel and everything will be all right. I promise.'

Anna woke up cold, skin clammy. Anaemic light gathered behind the curtains. It was the morning of her appointment at Unity. Beside her, Elijah still slept. Breathing in long, nervous breaths, Anna tried to anchor herself in the moment. She felt like she could still hear the sirens moving along the beachfront, feel the heat of the motorbike that had swept up so close to her.

Another dream?

She leaned up on one elbow to look down at her husband. Then she flicked her gaze to the headboard, the glowing circle within it which was now yellow. She knew that meant that the alarm would be going off imminently. Once it turned green the curtains would automatically part as birdsong played from speakers built into their divan. She looked at Elijah, wondering if he was still there, at the bottom of those steps, heading to his hotel. Because that had to be what was happening, didn't it? Were they sharing dreams? Or was she accessing her husband's memories? Both possibilities left her nauseous. The events of the previous night came back to taunt her, wine curdling in her gut. Anna hurried from the bed, made it to the bathroom and curled over the toilet. She retched but nothing came out, she had nothing left to give. Exhausted, she slumped against the tiled floor, head pounding.

These fucking dreams.

For a moment, she closed her eyes, saw Gavin's face again, pinched and afraid. How bad had it been, what they'd seen on the beach that night? Why had they been there? Did she dare ask Gavin about it? And he was so young in the memory, face open and full of possibilities. Was that the summer they went with Oscar? Were they talking *about* Oscar? But they both always maintained that he just went missing. Disappeared after a particularly heavy night out, washed up broken on a beach three days later. It was tragic. It was awful.

Were they lying to her?

Anna grimaced as fresh bile tried to burn its way up her throat.

No.

She coughed awkwardly in an attempt to dislodge it.

Elijah would have told me. Wouldn't he?

Anna massaged her temple, trying to latch on to more details from the dream . . . the memory. Could she pinpoint the country? The date?

Fuck.

She needed to understand what had happened, but Eli had always seemed so crippled by it all that Anna had never dared question him about that night, never dared mention it and risk further fracturing her husband. Which left Gavin. She needed to speak with him. But given his mood at dinner the night before, she doubted he'd want to help her. He'd surely just find it hilarious that she was facing yet another malfunction from her Unity chip.

'I told you it was a ridiculous thing to do . . .' She could already hear him saying it.

But Gavin was in the dream. Memory. Whatever the hell it was. And he'd been there in Kavos. Where Oscar disappeared. Which meant he should know what the hell was going on with it all. Did Anna want answers? What if Elijah was seeing scraps of her past and trying to piece them together each morning?

Her stomach cramped and Anna again tipped her head over the bowl of the toilet, coughing and spluttering, spit dripping from her mouth, a sour taste lining her throat.

She needed Unity. Her chip fixed. And answers. She needed answers.

26

'We are, of course, so sorry to hear you've not been having the ultimate experience with your Unity chip,' Murray said, smiling tightly as he led Anna to the waiting room. She settled on the same sofa she had before her initial appointment, a cup of tea in her hands. But she had no desire to drink it. The blinds were up on the floor-to-ceiling window, revealing the sprawling city below. The sky was clear and blue, making everything feel luminous. Anna had wanted to soak up the sunlight as she was rocked by the tube on her journey in, but between her hangover and the lingering feelings from her dream, a cloud settled over her that even the brightest sky couldn't clear.

'I'll just go and gather your files.' Murray beamed at her before striding away, leaving her alone.

Anna stirred a teaspoon in her tea, letting it knock against the china edges of her cup.

Will they change my chip here and now?

Shit, what if I'm sick again?

She blew out a long breath, hating how wretched she felt. Everything was sore. Her brain, her back. Even her eyes ached from the effort of being held open. Anna remembered when she was young and felt almost made of rubber, able to bounce back from the heaviest of nights without a second thought. She'd sit up downing shots until dawn, blearily watch the sky begin to burn on the horizon from the kitchen window of her student digs. All she'd need to wake herself up for lectures was an ice-cold shower and a pint of orange juice. Now her body reeled for days whenever she committed the slightest act of hedonism.

'It's called getting older,' Mandie had stated sourly one morning when she couldn't get out of bed and insisted on wearing sunglasses even though the curtains were drawn, 'and it fucking sucks.'

I'm in the office. If you need me just shout. Okay?
Okay.
I should be there with you.
Really, it's fine.
There's a big meeting at eleven but if you need me, I'll skip it.
Is Gavin in?
Not yet. Sure he'll drag himself in with five minutes to spare, looking wretched, and still everyone will eat up whatever he says in the demo.
Just try to relax. It'll all be fine.
Same. But if you're sick, if you even feel a bit queasy, just let me know.
I will.

'So . . .' Tablet in hand, Murray came to sit beside her on the sofa. He smelt of chamomile tea. 'When you called you mentioned an issue with the site around your chip?'

'Yes.' Anna lowered her tea to a nearby side table, nodding. 'It doesn't seem to be healing as quickly as it should. It still . . . stings. And I've been having headaches.'

'And is your partner having similar issues?'

'No.'

'How is the transmission site? You mentioned soreness. Does the skin feel hot?'

'Sometimes.'

'May I?' He gestured to her left ear.

'Sure.' Anna turned, drawing her hair back. She felt Murray's tentative touch around the site of her chip.

'Well, you're right; it doesn't appear to be healing as quickly as we'd like.' He dropped his hand and lifted a small black device that was beside him on the sofa. Sleek in design, almost like a mobile phone. He held it close to her ear, pressed a button and Anna felt slight heat against her chip. Then the device beeped loudly three times.

'Ah, okay.' Murray withdrew the device and tapped its front, which now glowed with information. 'So it does seem that there is a slight fault within this chip, which I imagine has been causing the soreness and headaches. At first glance it appears to have been embedded too deeply. I am so, so very sorry, Mrs Weston.' He looked at her as though he were about to burst into tears. Anna stiffened awkwardly at the sudden display of emotion.

'Oh, well, you know. I just want it sorted, really.'

'Of course, of course. We can replace that chip for you at no extra expense.' Now he was back on the tablet, scrolling furiously. 'We want every couple to have the optimum experience here at Unity.'

'What about the mute function?' Anna asked, her hangover making her bold, her tolerance levels dangerously low.

'Sorry?' He ceased scrolling to throw her a puzzled look.

'The mute function,' Anna repeated, her smile failing to meet her eyes. 'I was wondering if it would be possible to have that fitted into my new chip. I didn't realise before that it was an option.'

'Of course,' Murray replied smoothly with sincerity. 'The mute function is described within all the literature you'd have been sent prior to your appointment. We don't tend to overtly talk about it once you're here because, well, we want to encourage couples to have complete togetherness.' He beamed at her.

'Sure.'

'But now you've realised you'd like that added to your package, that's no problem at all, we can get that activated for you.'

'Do you use yours?' Anna stared at him, her veneer of politeness completely crumbling away.

'My?'

'Mute function. Do you use it?'

Murray tilted his head, gave her a diplomatic smile. 'Sometimes, yes. Generally, no. I'm sure you and your husband have found, as I did, that there is something so reassuring about having instant, unimpeded access to your significant other.'

'I guess.' Anna's response was flat.

Murray went back to scrolling on the tablet. He suddenly tapped it, grinning. 'So, we have a slot here when we can do a standard reissue of your chip and also add the mute capability.'

'Okay, great, when is that?'

'The second of August at ...' Murray squinted at the tablet. 'Three p.m.'

'Sorry,' Anna felt heat rise up her neck, 'August? That's ... that's three months away.'

'We are experiencing very high levels of demand at the moment.'

'My chip is *broken*,' Anna told him sharply, teetering on the brink of tears. 'I ... I can't stop these headaches. It's simply ...'

Fucking hangover.
Keep it together.

'It's not good enough,' she concluded. Murray pursed his lips, looking aggrieved.

'Mrs Weston, I am so, so sorry you're in distress. Here at Unity, that is the last thing we want. I appreciate it must be unsettling to know your chip is *slightly* faulty. But, as we have laid out in our terms and conditions, it can and does happen. That does not mean that there isn't a simple fix. Which there is.'

Anna? You okay?
Yes. All good.

'I'm . . . Three months.' Anna bowed her head. She needed to keep calm. 'It's just . . .' She shifted to peer up at Murray, whose face was open as he patiently watched her. 'In the terms and conditions,' clearing her throat she straightened, clasped her hands together, 'it mentions hallucinations.'

'Have you been hallucinating?' Murray asked slowly, his accent thickening.

'No.' Anna chewed her lip and then corrected herself. 'Well, yes. Sort of.'

'Can I ask if you're taking any medication at present?'

Anna gave a brisk shake of her head. 'No.'

'Okay, well—'

'The chip,' she interrupted, nodding at the black device now placed between them on the leather sofa. 'Mine is most definitely faulty, we know that.'

'Ah, but as I've said—'

'The terms and conditions mention hallucinations. Tell me, can someone ever access more than conscious thoughts? Possibly subconscious ones, like dreams?'

For a moment Murray turned grey. His mouth opened and closed several times before he righted himself, dragging one hand through his thick hair. 'Sometimes, though *extremely* rarely, an individual's chip might be embedded slightly too deep into the frontal lobe, which can result in an extended connection.'

'By extended, you mean linking dreams?' Anna's chin began to tremble.

'When we say dreams, we mean more like—'

'Linking memories?' she asked in a whisper.

'Please, Mrs Weston, do not despair. I'm sure you just have an issue with the transmission site, nothing more. Try not to—'

'Tell me,' she insisted uneasily, swiping a hand across her cheeks to knock away tears that had begun to fall, 'if a chip was embedded *too deep*, like mine is, what physical reaction would you expect from someone?'

Murray was silent.

'Vomiting perhaps?' Anna enquired quietly.

'Perhaps.' He gave her a pitying look. Anna tilted her head to the ceiling, blinked rapidly, trying to calm herself. 'I'll see if we can maybe find you a cancellation at an earlier date.' Murray started scrolling anew on his tablet. 'I'd hate to think of you suffering additional distress.'

'If I can see his memories,' Anna almost didn't dare ask it, but she had to know for sure, 'can he see mine?'

Murray looked pained. 'I wouldn't like to speculate when—'

'He can, can't he?' Anna read the older man's expression and ground her teeth together. 'Shit. Shit!'

'Please, Mrs Weston—'

'I didn't sign up for him being able to see my bloody *memories*.' Fat tears rolled down her cheeks. 'Thoughts . . . fine. Thoughts I can control. But . . .' Her hand fluttered upwards, to her mind.

'Mrs Weston, I understand.' Murray spoke loudly, calmly. 'There is a cancellation a month from now. A late appointment, I'm afraid: ten p.m. But does that work for you?'

'A month.' Anna sank into the sofa, deflated.

'You're doing just fine,' Murray consoled her. 'Just because you're having... hallucinations, does not mean that your husband is too. Let's not jump to conclusions. He's more than welcome to come in to ensure his chip isn't also defective.'

'A month,' Anna said again, reaching for her tea with a shaking hand.

'Four weeks, no time at all,' Murray said with forced brightness.

'But what if he can see my memories?'

'Has he said he can?'

'No.'

'Well, then let's operate on the assumption that he can't. And in one month we'll remove your current chip and even fit you with an upgraded model that comes with a lifetime guarantee,' he quickly lowered his gaze to assess the information on the tablet, 'as currently you only have the ten-year guarantee.'

Anna didn't reply. She downed her cold tea, almost baulking as it slid down her throat, slimy. But she needed the sugar hit. The caffeine.

'I understand you are worried,' Murray suddenly held her in a level stare, voice grave, 'but please, Mrs Weston, whatever you do, don't try to remove the chip yourself.'

Anna looked at him, wary.

'If you attempt removal yourself, you risk permanent cerebral damage. Do you understand?'

'Has that happened before?'

'Please, Mrs Weston, allow us to do our job. Do not put yourself in harm's way.'

'How many chips malfunction?'

'Hardly any.' He gave her his salesman smile, but he faltered when he saw the raw pain in her eyes. 'It's a new technology, barely in the public domain; we've not reached a year in circulation yet. There are going to be speed bumps, but I can assure you that everything here is done to the highest standards, with your safety in mind.'

'Did the waiver cover speed bumps?' Anna asked tightly.

'It did.'

She closed her eyes, exhausted.

'And are you feeling closer, since coming to Unity?'

'Yes.' There was no denying that having Elijah's voice in her head made her feel closer to him. But the jury was still out over whether that was a good thing. 'If I get my chip fixed, the dreams, will they stop?'

'It will be fitted at a more temperate level for you.' Murray smiled.

'Would you let your husband see your memories?' Anna asked.

Murray's smile fell. 'Tell him they're hallucinations,' he told her.

'I can't.' Anna looked down at her hands, noticing how worn low her nails were. She must have been biting them more than usual. Her fingers flexed, wishing she could smoke her e-cigarette in there. 'He'll know they're not hallucinations.'

'Look, Mrs Weston, I can—'

'Does he have it?' Anna tightened as she asked the question. 'Does my husband have the mute function?'

I need to know.

The flicker of movement. Clenching in the jawline. But other than that, Murray's expression remained smooth, calm. 'Mrs Weston, we—'

'I just feel that perhaps, if our chips aren't *completely* aligned, that might be part of the issue.'

'I'm afraid I can't disclose information about your husband's chip,' Murray's voice was suddenly firm, eyes kind, 'company policy.'

'I see.'

Does he have it? Has he had it all this time?

'One month.' Murray clasped a hand to her shoulder. 'One month and you'll be back here again brightening up my day.'

'I'm pretty sure I've done the opposite this morning,' Anna told him with an apologetic smile.

'You most certainly have not.'

She admired how he remained so affable even when faced with a possible calamity. Calm and confident, Murray walked her back to the lift. In the lobby she was given a gold-embossed card with the date of her next appointment etched into it. Anna thanked the blonde woman behind the desk, walked outside where the sun burned bright against the pavement, doubled over and threw up the tea she had drunk, not caring about the scornful looks she attracted.

27

It was warm on the tube. Anna held her bag on her lap, leaned into it, as the carriage rocked her back and forth. Sitting down – something she loathed doing, but she was too exhausted to stand.

How did it go? Where are you now?

On the train.

Across from her a group of young women were laughing raucously, nudging one another, peering down at a phone. So much about them sparkled, from their large earrings to the flash of their nails. Anna envied them.

What did they say at Unity?

My chip is broken.

Oh shit. How? Is it linked to your headaches?

Yeah. And it's . . .

Anna squeezed her bag tighter, studied the people in the carriage around her, wondering if any of them were currently having internal conversations.

My chip is just fucking broken. Embedded too deeply.

Above the jubilant women, Anna spotted the glimmer of turquoise water. Then, striding into it hand in hand towards a golden sunset, a man and women. They turned to one another, laughing as the image changed to reveal the Unity logo.

Unity.
Where happiness is togetherness

Anna wanted to scream.
I've got to wait a whole fucking month until they can sort my chip. A month.
Okay, well that's not too bad.
It's all a lie. What they promise. He said lots of chips malfunctioned.
Who said?
Murray. At Unity. He also said . . .
Anna scraped the back of her hand across her eyes, needing to hold it together, at least until her stop. Her throat was raw, legs tired.
He said to expect hallucinations. At least until it's fixed.
Oh, fuck. Sweetheart. Are you all right? Have you been seeing things?
I just want it fixed.
And they can't do any earlier than a month?
No, that was the soonest they could fit me in.
I can call them. After this meeting, I can call them and—
I just want to go home and rest.
They reached her stop and Anna climbed the stone steps, up into the sunlight of mid-morning, which seared against her eyes.
'Fuck.' She shielded her gaze, feeling the pulse of a potential migraine in the back of her head.
I just need to get home.
As she walked she drew out her phone and opened up the Unity terms and conditions, poring over them. The terminology was so vague, so evasive.

You may encounter discomfort
You might experience discharge at the access site

What sort of discomfort?

What kind of discharge?

Anna, I'm worried about you.

I'm fine, really.

Why are you going over the terms and conditions again?

I'm just worried about mine being defective.

Do you want to just take it out?

Yes.

I'll call them right now, say we're not happy and need to book a removal.

Is that . . . is that okay?

Sweetheart, if it's stressing you so much, and we know yours is broken, let's just get them out.

Okay, great. Thank you.

Relief swelled within her.

I just want it gone, Eli.

I understand. I'll call them now.

She walked faster, harder, heading home. But at the end of the street where she normally turned right, she took a hard left, feet guiding her down a slope, across a set of traffic lights and into a darkened pub set amid a row of terraced houses. Anna quietly approached the bar and ordered a vodka tonic. It was empty inside, the pub having only just opened for the day.

'Hair of the dog, is it?' the portly bartender asked her. He had a dimple on his chin and dark, greasy hair that was poorly combed over an obvious bald patch.

'Something like that,' Anna muttered as she carried her drink over to a booth in the far corner, beneath metal signs for Bacardi and Budweiser. She took her first sip, hoping it might settle the nausea which kept coming in waves.

I just spoke to Unity.

And?

Hope danced within her, buoyant and light.

Even if we wanted a removal, the earliest they can see us is in a month. They are completely booked up.

Fuck.

I know.

What if it's an emergency?

Is it?

I'm not happy having a faulty chip, Eli.

Okay, but we've made it this far with it. Other than the headaches and soreness, are there other problems? Have you had any hallucinations?

I wish I could see your face.

You too. Where are you? Your tracker has dipped out again. I thought you were going home?

Oh, I . . . I went for a walk. Needed the fresh air.

Anna sipped her drink, ice knocking against glass. She'd forgotten about the cameras outside her house, looking on to the street. How they didn't just capture the movements of visitors but of her too. How Elijah could always see her.

Anna liked it in the pub. There was something comforting about the dim lighting, the velvet stools by the bar, the cardboard coasters she kept turning over in her hands. The air smelt of hops and old port. It reminded her of her grandmother's living room. Where there were always toffees out in a bowl, a young Anna hopelessly drawn to their rainbow wrappers.

Within her bag her phone began to ring. Anna reached for it, gave a smile of relief.

'Mandie, hey.'

'How did it go?'

Anna wanted to speak but she felt a lump in her throat. 'B-badly, it went badly.'

'No! What happened?'

Anna sniffed, peered around, noticing that the bartender had drifted away, leaving her completely alone. 'My chip is fucking faulty.'

'Oh shit, hon. Could they at least give you the mute thing?' Mandie sounded out of breath, like she was running.

Please be running.

'No, they can't. At least not yet. I'm worried Eli can mute me, though.'

'Really?'

'Yeah, I asked about it at Unity.'

'And they said he can?'

Anna groaned awkwardly. 'More like, they didn't say anything one way or another.'

'Okay . . . well . . . maybe . . .' Mandie was panting as she spoke. 'Don't . . . you know . . . jump to conclusions. At least . . . not until . . . you know . . . more.'

'Pretty mature advice there, Mand.'

'I know . . . Next I'll be . . . getting a blue rinse.'

'Are you alone?' Anna wondered.

'Yeah, just out for a jog. I know, right, who am I? I'm up before noon and I'm in Lycra.'

'Maybe someone placed a faulty chip in you.'

'Maybe.' Mandie's tone was light. 'But what about yours? Can they fix it?'

'Yeah, in a month.'

'A month? Jeeze!'

'Elijah even called and told them we wanted a removal, but still no budging on the date.'

'Hon, I'm sorry. That sounds shit.'

'It is.' Anna sipped on her drink, the vodka managing to even out her headache. 'And . . .' She looked to the leaded window beside her, at the cars gliding by outside. She felt safe in the pub, secluded. 'That's not the only issue.'

'It isn't?'

'They said that sometimes, with chips embedded too deeply, you start to share your conscious and subconscious thoughts.'

'Meaning?'

'Access to memories,' Anna said thinly.

'Well, that is just fucked up.'

'Where are you running? Regent's Park?'

'You know it.'

'Do you,' Anna tapped her nails against her glass, 'do you fancy ruining your healthy start to the day by indulging in some day drinking?'

Mandie's reply was instant and bright. 'Always.'

'I'm at The Moon on the Water.'

A tight breath from Mandie. 'That place? Why? It's so . . . old.'

'I think that's why I like it.'

'You've always been strange. It's why we're friends.'

'Exactly.' Anna nervously drummed her fingers against the table. 'Do you think you could jog over here? Sit with me a bit.'

'Of course,' Mandie enthused. 'I'll head that way now. You'll just need to excuse the sweat.'

'I need to tell you something,' Anna realised decisively.

'Okay, hon, I'll be there soon.'

The call ended with a light beep. Anna stared at her phone, moved her hand to touch the chip behind her ear, skin hot. Tender.

Murray had been clear in his advice not to remove it. But

could it really be so dangerous? She opened up the internet on her phone and quickly typed in –

Self-removal of Unity chip

The Wi-Fi in the pub was slow, but eventually her screen was flooded with stories. All of them hailing doom.

Several medical journals cited how people should never, under any circumstances, remove their chips themselves. Lower down the page there was a news story of a woman who'd pulled hers out with pliers, only to then suffer brain damage that had left her in a vegetative state for the last two months. Anna used her fingers to enlarge the image of the woman. She appeared to be early thirties, blonde hair, a bright smile.

She could be anyone.

She and her wife had been married for six years before deciding to partake in Unity. They had twin sons.

What made her take it out?

Behind her ear, Anna's stitches began to pulse.

The article mentioned a mood shift in the woman prior to the accident. She complained of headaches. Loss of appetite.

Hallucinations.

Anna's head was pounding now.

Hallucinations.

Suddenly it was the only word on her phone that she could see.

'Dreams?' Anna shouted at the device, needing to release the thought rather than think it. 'Dreams and memories? Was she having those?'

A squeak of a floorboard as the bartender drifted back into view; he gave her a wary smile.

Embarrassed, Anna lowered her head, and her voice.

'Fuck.' She looked at her phone, drank the last of her vodka and tonic. 'I need this thing out.'

Pliers felt extreme.

Perhaps something less destructive, a simple knife or—

I know a month feels like a long time but it isn't. Just be calm. Why aren't you home yet?

I'm meeting Mandie for lunch.

Anna gave a quick glance around the pub, doubting they served food.

I don't need her filling your head with any more of her outlandish theories. Do you need me to come home early?

No, I'm okay.

I'll be back for six, then. Maybe half past if this meeting goes on.

Did Gavin turn up?

About twenty minutes ago, looking like butter wouldn't melt. He's actually managed to sweet talk the clients and save the day. Typical.

You said everyone likes him.

He definitely has his moments.

You love him really.

Doesn't everyone? Isn't that the problem?

The door to the pub creaked open, allowing the hum of car engines to briefly creep in.

'I'm a sweat . . . ridden . . . mess,' Mandie gasped as she joined Anna in her booth and collapsed against the red velvet upholstery. 'I literally *ran* here.'

'Thanks, I appreciate it.'

'They best serve decent wine.' Mandie was eyeing the bar. 'I'll at least make it a spritzer since it's early.' She clocked Anna's empty glass. 'Seems I've some catching-up to do.'

As Mandie went to the bar Anna tried to calm herself. She knew what she needed to say. How she needed to say it. She just couldn't risk her thoughts betraying her. Not now.

Peter, Peter, pumpkin eater,
Had a wife but couldn't keep her;
He put her in a pumpkin shell,
And there he kept her very well.

I really don't get the nursery rhyme thing.
It calms me.
It creeps me out. That one is about a guy who found out his wife was screwing around, so he killed her and baked her in a pumpkin pie.
How do you know so much about the origins of nursery rhymes?
I look them up when you sing them.
Of course you do.

'You're smiling,' Mandie noted as she brought their drinks over. 'That's good. You sounded proper tense on the phone.'

'It won't last,' Anna admitted as her face promptly fell, 'not when I tell you what I'm scared is going to happen.'

28

'Okay, well, spill.' Mandie was frowning as she watched Anna from the other side of the table. 'What's wrong?'

Anna had met Mandie almost nine years ago, back when Anna and Helen still had the energy to maintain the façade of friendship. Anna had been at Junction, a nightclub in the centre of town that, even at twenty-eight, she felt too old for. It felt like everyone there had their stomach out, or their arse cheeks, wearing outfits that looked incomplete. They gathered on a dark dance floor, undulating to songs Anna didn't even recognise. Her nights at the Student Union, getting drunk on cheap vodka, suddenly felt so horribly far away. Helen, whose birthday they were meant to be celebrating, dipped out a little after eleven. She failed to tell Anna, who spent an hour searching the club in vain. Finally, giving up, she went outside to smoke. And that was when she met Mandie.

'You got a light?' Mandie strutted over to her, glorious in a sequin jumpsuit. When she realised Anna was holding an e-cigarette she doubled over in laughter. 'Shit, I'm, like, so drunk right now.' Her energy, her jubilance, it was infectious. Anna started laughing too, forgetting about the stress of her fertility battle, of failing to find any buyers for her artwork.

Being around Mandie was like being around the sun; she warmed her.

'Seriously, you're freaking me out.' Mandie gave Anna a kick under the table. 'What is going on with you? Is it the chip?'

'Sort of.'

'*Sort of?*'

'At Unity they told me that sometimes, in some cases, the subconscious can be linked.'

'Like when you thought you saw Elijah's dream?'

'I think it was a memory.' Anna tightened her hand around her glass. 'And the . . . the guy at Unity admitted that sometimes when a chip is embedded too deeply, that can happen.'

'Okay.' Mandie eyed her warily.

'And when that does happen, people usually have a reaction on waking up. Like vomiting.'

Mandie's eyes widened fearfully. 'Shit. Oh, shit. Right . . . so you . . .' She tapped her fingers to her forehead. 'You really are seeing his memories?'

'I think so, and I think he might be lying to me.'

'Oh?' Mandie's mouth formed a circle of surprise. 'I mean, he already lied about there being a mute function.'

'He didn't lie, he just didn't tell me about it,' Anna countered, defensive of her husband, a reflex she couldn't shake even though she knew he was in the wrong.

'So it's a lie by omission, same thing.'

'It's beside the point.' Anna drummed her fingers against the table. 'The thing is something bad happened to our friend at uni. Years ago. And I know I'm seeing something about that in this . . . this dream.'

'Something bad happen to your friend?'

'Oscar died,' Anna admitted quietly, unable to meet Mandie's gaze.

'Shit. Okay. That *is* bad.'

'And it seems like . . . like Eli and Gav were *there* when he died. Even though they always told the rest of us that they weren't, that Oscar got pissed and wandered off alone that night.'

'I see . . .'

'So now I keep worrying about Elijah lying and . . .'

'And?'

'And if I can see his memories, he might be seeing mine,' Anna said gravely.

'Wow. Christ. Okay. I'm guessing that's also a bad thing?'

'A very bad thing.' Anna began to feel queasy again. She lifted her glass with a shaking hand and took a sip of her drink.

'Can they not fix it sooner? Like, before a month?'

'No.'

'Honey, what is the memory you're so worried about Eli seeing?'

Anna blinked quickly, vision blurring, unable to speak.

Lavender's blue, dilly dilly.

Lavender's green.

'And with the thing about Oscar — why not just ask Eli?' Mandie pressed.

'I can't.' Anna folded into herself. 'Because—' She exhaled uneasily. 'If he's been lying to me all this time, I just . . . I'm scared.'

When I am king, dilly dilly.

'Shh, okay. Just, just breathe. Be calm. I'm sure it isn't as bad as you think it is. Sometimes, we build things up in our heads. That's all. And Elijah might not even be seeing your memories like you are his. And you might be misinterpreting what you are seeing.'

You shall be queen.

Anna sniffed, wishing she could believe that.

Who told you so, dilly dilly?

'He's . . . I don't think he's seen anything.'

Who told you so?

'Well, there you go.'

'Twas my own heart, dilly dilly. That told me so.

'Yet,' Anna added darkly, 'I'm worried that a month . . . that it's so long he'll definitely, you know . . .' She couldn't finish her sentence.

Shit.

Does he know?

Has he seen something?

'Look,' Mandie began confidently, 'I'm sure whatever it is you *don't* want him to see, that it really isn't that bad. That man *adores* you, Anna. He'd do anything for you. Forgive anything.'

'No. Not this.'

'You don't know that.'

'I do.' Anna felt tears on her cheeks which she didn't bother to brush away. 'I fucked up.'

'Breathe. Let's talk it out, okay? It's why I'm here. You fucked up, sure. But it sounds like so did he.'

'Mandie, I don't know.'

'Sweetie, it's me. You can legit tell me anything.'

'I just don't want you to see me differently.'

'It'll be fine, I swear.'

'I don't . . .' Anna sucked in a breath, wishing it wasn't so hard.

'I'm here,' Mandie assured her, reaching for her hands and clutching them atop the table. 'Whatever it is, I'm here. Got it?'

Anna nodded. Mandie was so unlike Helen and her icy judgement whenever she fucked up. Mandie was open. Kind. Patient.

'Do you remember what I told you happened in university? With the,' she dropped her voice, finished in a pained whisper, 'abortion?'

'Yeah, I remember. It sounded horrific.'

'It was.'

Sometimes Anna swore she could still hear the scream that tore from Helen's mouth as she walked in. How her friend saw the pool of blood and wilted within the doorframe, one bony hand clamped over her mouth. Anna tried to remind herself that it had all looked worse than it was. Only that wasn't really true.

'I went and had it, had the reaction. Eli . . . he's always supported me through it. Understood the implications from it all. Accepted them. Unwaveringly.'

'Because he loves you.'

'But the thing is . . .' Anna had to release Mandie's hand to drink again from her glass. She'd needed a double vodka instead of a single. 'It was not his baby.'

Anna tore the truth from herself quickly, cleanly. Let it land between them on the table. The one thing she had never said aloud to anybody. Ever.

'Oh.' Mandie processed it, lips pursed. Then she gave a light shrug. 'Well, hon, that certainly doesn't make you a monster. And can you be, like, *sure* sure it wasn't his? I'm no stranger to enjoying myself, things can get complicated sometimes.'

'I'm *sure* sure.' Anna leaned in close, sweat gathering down her back. 'When we . . .' She winced at what she was about to impart, burning with betrayal. But it was Mandie, her best friend, and she needed to share the truth. All of it. 'When I met Elijah, he was a virgin.'

'Okay.'

'And during that first year, I think he felt, I don't know . . . Pressure. Anxiety. Either way, he could never get hard.'

'Never?'

'Well,' Anna backtracked, 'sometimes, a bit. At first. But it never lasted. His nerves got the better of him. He'd get frustrated, then he'd go out and get off his head, which also didn't help things down there. It became a vicious cycle.'

'How did you eventually break this cycle?'

'He went on beta blockers from the GP for a while, they helped with his nerves.'

'Okay.'

'But, for almost a year, we never actually properly had sex. Not, like . . .'

'He didn't finish in you,' Mandie stated factually.

Anna blushed. 'Yeah, exactly that.'

'But he *thinks* he did.' Mandie eyed her thoughtfully.

Anna squirmed within her chair. 'Yeah, most mornings after, when we hadn't, when he'd get frustrated and upset, I'd tell him we'd done it.'

'And he couldn't remember otherwise?'

'No.'

'So if Elijah wasn't the father,' Mandie whispered even though they were alone, 'who was?'

Anna began shaking her head, releasing fresh tears.

Call up your men, dilly dilly,
Set them to work.

'Take a breath, take a breath,' Mandie insisted.

Some to the plough, dilly dilly. Some to the fork.

'That's the worst part,' Anna panted, gripping the table for support. 'It was Gavin.'

Some to make hay, dilly dilly, some to reap corn.

'Oh, shit. *Shit.*' Mandie raised her glass and downed her entire spritzer, throat pulsating as she looked at the ceiling. 'Okay, well, that is—'

'I'm a terrible person. I'm a fucking terrible person.'
While you and I, dilly dilly.
Keep ourselves warm.

'One, you are not.' Mandie clicked her fingers at her. 'You are human. You were young. Horny. And then when you got pregnant, scared. I'm guessing he was with Helen at that point?'

'Yes.'

'And you didn't want to hurt your friend or your boyfriend, I get that.'

'Please don't think I'm that person.' Anna gave her a pleading look. 'I don't . . . I don't sleep with friends' boyfriends. I just don't. But with Gavin it was . . .'

'Two,' Mandie said softly, 'it was a long time ago.'

'Not long enough.' Anna sniffed. 'If it was anyone else, *anyone*, I'd have a shot at Elijah forgiving me. But not with Gavin. The two of them, they've had this rivalry since . . . since—'

'Uni,' Mandie finished flatly for her. 'It's all making a lot more sense now.'

'What is?' Anna rubbed her eyes, hands coming away wet.

'The way Gavin looks at you. How Elijah looks at Gavin. How Helen looks at you. The way you look at Gavin.'

'Fuck.'

'Is there really a chance that Elijah will see a memory involving Gavin?'

'Yes,' Anna admitted, hating herself.

'It happened more than once?'

A shameful nod.

'You don't think there's a chance he'd forgive you?'

Anna peered up woefully at Mandie. 'No,' she rasped. 'He won't forgive me because I lied. Because it was with Gavin. He . . . he thinks that the whole reason we can't have children is because of something we did together. A burden we share.'

'So he finds out, what then?'

'He'll kill me.' The words came so instantly, so unbidden, that Anna clamped a hand to her mouth in shock while Mandie stared at her, stunned.

'Come on, hon. He'll be pissed, sure. But kill you?'

'His . . . his thoughts at work. Sometimes . . . sometimes they are *so* dark. Like, scarily dark.'

Her neck. In a noose. Listening for the snap.

'Okay, well,' Mandie leaned back, studied her friend with a soft expression, 'we all have dark thoughts. Some of the stuff I think,' she pattered her long nails against her temple, 'especially about some of my exes. It's not pretty. But that doesn't make me a bad person. Or capable of doing something awful. We're not defined by our thoughts, hon. Just our actions.'

'Sure.'

'There's absolutely no way Elijah would hurt you. You're his entire world.'

'Yeah,' Anna agreed unsteadily, 'that's . . . that's crazy. Right?'

'Right.'

'Only . . . he hates Gavin so much. He's so jealous of him.' Screwing up her face, she grabbed fistfuls of her hair. 'It's such a fucking mess.'

'It is,' Mandie nodded, 'but all messes can be cleaned up. Even this one.'

Anna looked at her, unsure.

'You've got to last one more month, right? And then no chip?'

'One more month and then no chip.'

'Protect your thoughts.' Mandie pointed a stern finger at

her. 'Keep doing the nursery rhyme stuff. Don't falter. Whatever you do, don't go home and think about this conversation.'

Anna's shoulders sank low. 'I'm exhausted from trying to keep it together, from trying to hide all this. And I keep getting these . . . these headaches.'

Mandie clicked her fingers. 'Yes, good idea. Sleep. You said you can't access each other's thoughts when you're sleeping.'

'That's right.'

'I know a guy who can hook you up with these insane sleeping pills. They're basically tranquillisers. I use them whenever I get on a plane.'

'Okay . . .'

'Just don't drink on them. Another time I've got a story for you about me and an Amish guy on a transatlantic to New York. But not now.'

'I'm scared, Mandie. I'm scared he's going to find out and my whole world is just going to . . . to blow up.'

'Don't be scared, we can figure this out.'

'I should never have done it.' Anna scraped a hand down her face, eyes red. 'Any of it.'

'The stuff with Gavin,' Mandie asked delicately, 'why did it end?'

Anna gave a sad smile. 'Because I chose Eli. It all came to a head with us and Gavin made me choose.'

'And you're happy with that choice?'

Anna flinched.

'You can see why I'm asking,' Mandie explained, 'given what you've just told me.'

'Yeah, yes. I'm happy.'

'Then let's keep it that way.' Mandie reached again for Anna's hands, held them tight. 'Keep doing the rhymes. I'll get you the knock-out pills. Tell Elijah you're sick, blame your period, it'll stop him probing too much. It's one month. Four short weeks. I've got milk in my fridge older than that.'

'Thank you.' Anna felt the weight of fat tears gathering in her eyelashes, the onset of hiccups in her throat. 'Th-thank you for being a . . . a . . . friend.'

'Of course.' Mandie smiled warmly at her. 'I'm here for you and I'm not going anywhere.'

He'll kill me.

The thought chased Anna as she walked back towards her house, legs shaking.

Who will kill you?

My . . . my dad. I forgot Elaine's birthday.

Isn't that next month?

Shit, you're right. He won't kill me then. I'm just all over the place. The stuff at Unity, it's left me shaken.

Need me to come home? I can try and nip out early.

No, no it's fine. I'm actually planning on going back to bed for a bit.

Okay, sweetheart. Get some rest.

Anna had made it to their front door, she peered at the camera beside the bell, knowing that Elijah would be watching. Hoping that she didn't look as grim as she felt.

Turning, she noticed a woman walking down her street, pushing a pram, leaning down to coo adoringly at the child inside. As the wheels clicked by, the bright bell-like sound of young laughter peeled out. Catching Anna. Her gaze followed the woman, the pram, like a moth drawn to the flame. She pictured them going home to somewhere cosy with playmats and muslins strewn about, CBeebies still playing on the television as the mother had forgotten to turn it off before she headed out. She'd lift the baby from the pram and they'd beam at her, a gummy smile, filled with love. And she'd smile back.

Anna was still staring down the road, the woman long gone. With a jolt, she brought herself back into the moment.

Elijah?

She turned again to her front door, camera flashing green, access granted.

Sometimes walking through life felt so much like chasing ghosts, glimpses of what might have been.

Eli, are you still there?

Anna strained to find him within her thoughts. To focus. To tune in.

Elijah? Are you in a meeting?
Eli?

She found only silence.
Roses are red, dilly dilly,
Violets are blue,
Because you love me, dilly dilly,
I will love you,
Let the birds sing, dilly dilly,
And let the lambs play,
We shall be safe, dilly dilly.

He was gone. She was alone.
Out of harm's way.

29
THEN

'It's fine, it's fine,' Anna muttered soothingly as Elijah rolled off her, hair matted with sweat. 'Don't worry about it.'

For a moment he stared up at the ceiling of her uni room, at the pale blue lampshade, panting. 'I don't—'

He stank of lager. He was drunk. Too drunk. Anna had known that the second they left the Union. The way he snaked his arm around her waist and swayed to and fro as they walked back to halls. The way he kept telling her over and over how beautiful she was.

'Baby, I'm sorry,' he mumbled as he turned onto his side.

'Really, it's fine.' Anna dusted her hair out of her eyes, hugged her knees to her chest, naked and growing cold. 'Maybe . . .' She gently traced a circle with the tip of her finger against Elijah's back, between his spattering of moles, the white line of a small scar on his upper shoulder from when he'd fallen from a climbing frame. 'Maybe try drinking less tomorrow night. See if that helps.'

'But you know how Oscar and Gavin are. Always going hard,' he mumbled.

'I know, but maybe, try. For me.'

'He annoys me.'

'Gavin?'

'Oscar,' Elijah grumbled, voice low and raspy. 'Always trying to stir shit up. Get between me and Gav. I get that he's, you know, troubled, but it's too much. He parties way too hard.'

'Sure.' Anna pressed her full palm against Elijah's back. 'But maybe, you know, you could also try to drink less. Please.'

She heard his breathing deepen, knew he could no longer hear her. With a sigh she lowered her hand and climbed off the bed, pulling on Elijah's discarded T-shirt from the floor. A faded maroon, she wasn't sure if it was meant to look vintage or was just old. Already her room smelt musty. She considered cracking a window, letting the cool of the night creep in. But then so too would the sounds of passing cars and she'd struggle to drift off. So often she thought how she wasn't cut out for city life, that a home buried deep within open fields would best suit her. Away from everything, where she could just paint and create undisturbed. That was the dream.

Quietly creaking her door open she stepped into the hallway, padded along to the shared kitchen and leaned over the sink to fix herself a glass of water.

'Hey.'

She jumped as she span around, having not heard Gavin saunter in over the sound of the tap. His cheeks were flushed, hair tousled. He wore baggy jeans ripped at the knees, an emerald T-shirt of a band she'd never heard of.

'Sorry, didn't mean to startle you.'

'It's okay.' She gestured to the sink. 'Water?'

'Sure.'

When she turned her back to pour a second glass she felt the heat of his gaze upon her. It made her skin prickle.

'Here.'

He stepped closer. Like Elijah, he smelt of lager. Of cigarettes. But also cologne, a woody scent that still clung to him. Or was it freshly applied? Anna's nose crinkled, unsure.

'Thanks.' He took the glass from her, drinking it down quickly. When he'd finished he wiped his hand across his mouth, smirked at her as he placed the glass on the nearby table. 'We the only ones still up?'

'Yeah.' Anna sipped lightly from her glass. 'Elijah's already passed out.'

'Again, huh?' His gaze never left her face as they spoke.

'Again. He's been hitting it pretty hard lately.'

'I've noticed.'

'You and Oscar encourage him,' Anna noted, challenge flaring in her eyes. 'He only gets so drunk because he tries to keep up with you two.'

'Then he shouldn't try to keep up,' Gavin noted with a half-smile. 'I'm used to heavy nights. He's not.'

'Anyway, it doesn't matter. He's sleeping it off now.'

'Helen is also asleep.' He raised a hand to massage the back of his neck. 'She's got an early lecture tomorrow so she kicked me out so she could listen to that meditative crap she needs to help her drop off.'

'The rainforest sounds? Urgh those drive me crazy when I'm in her room. They make me need to piss.'

'Same.' Gavin laughed and his entire face lit up. There was something luminous about him. Anna figured it accounted for why he had so many friends. Already at uni he couldn't walk a corridor without fist-bumping or high-fiving someone.

'So why not just slink off to your own room?' Anna wondered. It was late. Or early. Depending how you looked at it.

'Maybe I'm thirsty.' Gavin stepped closer to her.

Anna nodded, sipped her drink.

'Or maybe I heard you come out of your room and figured you'd need some company.'

He stared at her, unblinking.

Anna felt her stomach flip.

'When I tell Helen I want to spend my life travelling, trying new things, she laughs. She tells me you get a gap year to live like that, at most. That after that, you need to buckle down, get a job. A career. A mortgage.' His face crinkled with disdain on the final word. 'Eli's the same.' He threw the comment over his shoulder, towards the bedrooms just metres away. 'But you and Oscar get it.' He took a step closer to Anna. She didn't move. 'You see the world like I do: rich in colour, full of possibilities.'

'Helen and Elijah, they're just pragmatic.' Anna placed her glass on the table, used the movement to back over towards the kitchen counter. Gavin mirrored her steps but still kept his distance.

'Pragmatic is just a polite way of calling someone boring.'

'If you're so bored, why are you in Helen's room every night?' Anna demanded boldly.

'You seem awfully concerned about who I share a bed with.' He moved closer to her, close enough that she could see the green flecks in his eyes.

'I'm not,' Anna whispered, heart beginning to race.

'You sure about that?' He frowned at her. 'Because I sure as hell care about who you're sleeping with.'

'Gavin—'

With one step he destroyed the space between them, his lips finding hers. Anna's hands lifted, wrapped around his neck, drew him to her as she kissed him back. Hard. His movements weren't sloppy from drink, or awkward. He kissed her in a way that made her entire body tingle. When he reached for the edge of the T-shirt she wore, Anna didn't resist. He moved to kiss her neck and she let out a groan.

'I want you,' he murmured into her ear. 'It's killing me how much I want you.'

When he entered her, Anna slipped over into bliss. Their bodies so seamlessly fit together. There was no awkward manoeuvring, no muttered apologies of putting something in the wrong place. Gavin was well versed in the way of women, acting like he'd pleasured her a thousand times before.

'Don't stop,' she heard herself pant as her bare arse bounced atop the kitchen counter, the curtain-less windows shining out into the darkened street, giving anyone passing by a show. Anna didn't care. She was in the moment. She was so deliciously, so wonderfully alive. Every part of her tingled.

Later, as she padded barefoot into her bedroom, the guilt met her like a tidal wave, trying to drown her. She gulped for breath as she joined a sleeping Elijah on her single bed, curling her body up around his spine, listening to him breathing.

She told herself it had been a one-time thing. A lapse in judgement. But then it happened again. And again. She felt them getting bolder, taking greater risks. He'd bend her over the kitchen table, she'd straddle him upon one of the stiff plastic dining chairs. 'I'm wrecking my back for you,' he said through a smile as he entered her.

And every night Elijah drank too much, passed out within her bed. Helen fell deep into her studies, stopped joining them at the Union on weeknights.

'I've just too much to do,' she'd insist before closing her door, disappearing behind it. Leaving Anna and Gavin alone. Unwatched.

*

'We need to tell them.'

Easter break was looming, supermarket shelves crammed full of chocolate eggs and bunnies.

Anna pulled her pants back up and studied Gavin's face to see if he was being serious. 'You know we can't do that.'

'Why not?'

'Because it will devastate them,' Anna stated tersely. The last few nights, as Elijah stumbled home, he'd progressed from saying how beautiful she was to declaring his undying love. 'Elijah, he's your best friend.'

'And Helen is yours.' Gavin met her gaze.

'Which is why we need to stop.'

'No,' he reached for her hand, grabbed it, 'we need to tell them. Because this is real, Anna. This, here,' he gestured to the space between them, 'you and I, we could be something wonderful.'

Anna thought of Elijah sleeping just metres away, blissfully unaware of what she'd been doing. How she'd betrayed him. 'I love Elijah.'

'No you don't,' Gavin declared forcefully. 'You're just saying that because you should love him. Because he's the easy option, the safe one.'

'Look, I just—'

'I get it. You don't want to hurt anyone. Yes, when we tell them shit is going to blow up. It's going to be bad.'

'I don't want stuff to be bad.' Anna felt her chin begin to tremble. 'I don't want to blow anything up, to see our world burn.'

'News flash,' Gavin growled at her, 'the world is burning, Anna. Whether you like it or not. But you and me, we can burn together.'

'Gavin—'

He cupped her chin in his hand; he was hot to the touch.

'I can't give you what he can, I know that. I don't come from money. I'll need to work for everything, work hard. But I *will* work, Anna.'

'You barely show up for lectures.' Anna tried to twist away from his gaze but he held her in place.

'I'd show up for you.'

'I don't want to hurt anyone.'

'It's you and me; it was always meant to be you and me.' He looked into her eyes, his gaze watery. 'That first night, at the SU, I came to dance with you. I saw *you*. But then Helen caught my hand, you went to sit with Eli and the world just . . . it shifted. You feel it between us too, I know you do.'

'Helen is my friend.' Anna felt a tear slide down her face, reach Gavin's hand upon her chin. This wasn't who she was. She didn't cheat. She didn't sleep with a friend's boyfriend. She closed her eyes, tried to rationalise it all away, that she was merely lashing out because of what had happened to her mum. Trying to self-destruct the second she had something good to destroy. She opened her eyes and felt her stomach flip, the way it did every time she looked at Gavin. It was a dizzying sensation. One she both loved and loathed. She pictured Elijah's face when she told him about her and Gavin. Helen's. The pain. Then the hatred. Anna took a long, steadying breath. This wasn't her. She didn't hurt people. Elijah. Helen. They didn't deserve to be hurt.

'I love Elijah,' she told him through her tears.

'You don't mean that.'

'I do.'

'If you mean it, if you truly mean it,' he dropped his hand, ran it through his sandy mass of hair, 'then this,' he looked at her, anguished, 'this stops. Right here, right now, it stops. I won't . . .' His eyes briefly closed over the effort of it all. 'I won't get in your way. I won't say anything. If you love him.

But,' he inched closer to her, hopeful, 'if you want this, me and you, I'll march over and wake Helen up this second, tell her I'm done. For you, I'd burn it all to the ground. I'm crazy about you.' He searched her face for answers.

Anna pictured it. All the hurt. The grief. The words shouted along a corridor, in her face. She couldn't meet Gavin's gaze as she spoke. 'I love Elijah.' She heard him storm from the room, slam the kitchen door behind him, leaving her alone where she crumpled to the floor and wept.

When she eventually made it back to her bed Elijah was sleeping, he didn't even move as she climbed in beside him. In the darkness she grazed a finger down the length of his bare back.

Loving Elijah. Stable, always waiting. He was someone she could form a future with, a future where she wouldn't need to worry about the ground shifting beneath her feet. About his mood changing with the tide. Gavin claimed to love her now, but how long could that last? Anna was curled on her side, staring at the wall, when she eventually joined Elijah in slumber.

The following morning, she and Gavin passed in the corridor like ghosts.

30
NOW

Sleep would not come. Anna willed it as hard as she could. She lay in the bed, curtains drawn. She sprawled across the sofa, draped in a blanket. She made herself a mug of warm milk, put on her softest flannel pyjamas. Still her mind whirred, her limbs jittery with energy.

'Just fucking sleep,' she commanded herself as she stood waiting for the bathtub to fill, another attempt to lull her body into a state of relaxation. She heard her phone buzz from the bedroom and paced over to check it. A new message from Mandie.

>Thinking of you xxx

Anna held back a sob. That was the entire problem, wasn't it? The thinking of it all.

Fuck.

Anna? You all right?

I'm just so tired. And feel like shit.

Try and get some rest.

'Rest, yeah,' Anna muttered to herself as she went back to the bathroom, the air sweet on account of the strawberry bubble bath she'd used. The water foamed deliciously as steam gathered against the window. 'I need to rest. To sleep. To stop fucking . . . thinking.' She angrily smacked her forehead, aware that from the outside she must surely look like she was losing her mind. And in some ways she was, wasn't she? Her mind was no longer her own. Shedding her pyjamas she climbed into the bath, let her body sink into the warm water. She had to keep her mind clear, couldn't risk replaying her conversation with Mandie.

Little Boy Blue, come blow your horn.
'I did the right thing telling her.'
The sheep's in the meadow, the cow's in the corn.
'She understands how serious it all is.'
Where is the boy who looks after the sheep?
'And she doesn't hate me.'
He's under the haystack, fast asleep.
'But Eli will. Eli will hate me.'

Anna lifted her toes, studied them, pink nail polish chipped and cracked. She used to be so on top of things like that; regularly dyeing her hair, getting her nails done at a little salon on the outskirts of the city. Waxing. So much waxing. Ripping her skin raw until there wasn't an errant hair left on her body.

'He said it's embedded too deep,' she explained to herself aloud. 'To remove it risks cerebral damage.'

The woman from the article. In a vegetative state.

Dipping her toes back beneath the bubbles, Anna's hand strayed to her left ear. To her chip.

'Shit,' she lamented, fingers pressing hard against the chip, ignoring how it smarted beneath her touch.

Why does it have to be broken?
I need quiet now, going into a big meeting.
I'm doing my best here, Eli. You try managing all this.

I guess my thoughts just don't run away from me like yours do.

What's that supposed to mean?

Anna swallowed, throat dry.

Nothing.

Christ, Elijah, why do you have to be such a dick sometimes?

I'm in a meeting now, Anna. Be. Quiet.

Anna screamed and kicked her legs out, feet smacking the porcelain of the bath, bubbles tumbling over the top towards the tiled floor. She screamed until her throat ached. Then she grabbed the sides of the bath and waited for the water to cease rolling, felt it growing cold around her. Climbing out, she dried herself and then put her flannel pyjamas back on and approached the mirror above the sink. How pale she looked. How tired. Her eyes pitted with shadows, skin waxy.

'I'm a fucking mess.' Anna pulled at her cheeks, the skin under her eyes. Then she noticed her manicure set on a nearby shelf. A birthday gift from Elijah: a pink, moulded leather case then opened to reveal a gold nail file, scissors and nail clippers. The scissors, she remembered, had seemed especially sharp. Anna reached for the set, unwound the zip. Carefully she picked up the scissors and then looked back at her reflection.

'There was the risk of cerebral damage,' she told the ghost looking back at her. 'No certainty in it.'

But *were* her thoughts running away from her? Betraying her?

What had she said?

What had Elijah heard?

One hand held the scissors while the other grazed the chip. She could feel it so certainly, hard and raised beneath her skin. Tilting her head she tried to glimpse it, but it was so well concealed behind her ear, it made it difficult to see.

'It's right . . . there.' She kept pressing atop it. 'How hard could it be to get it out? I could just . . .'

Pull.

Anna stared at her forlorn reflection. 'You fucking do this, or you let him stay inside your head. Either way, you're fucked,' she whispered, voice cracking.

She imagined the tear of flesh, a metallic prize within her grasp, and then blood. A river of it, running down her neck, her shoulders, darkening her pyjamas. But she'd be free.

'You can keep it in and live the next month in fear,' Anna told herself, 'or pull it out now and everything will be fine. Worst case you're in hospital. But Eli won't know. Make sure he never knows.' She stared at the dark centre of her own pupils. 'Make sure he never knows.'

Pulling back her ear she raised the scissors, brought them close to the chip. The sharpened point connected with her skin, just for a split second, causing Anna to inhale sharply.

'What do I need to do? Dig in around it? Pluck it straight out?' She kept tapping the chip with the scissors. 'I sound like a fucking weirdo. It needs to come out. Just . . . just do it. Take a deep breath. Then, on three, make a cut. There, just below it . . .' She positioned the scissors just beneath the ridge of the chip.

'One.'

Her hand wavered, unsteady.

'Two.'

Sweat beaded across her temple, down her neck.

'Three.'

Anna dug the scissors into her skin, screaming as she felt the warmth of her blood on her fingertips. She kept screaming, knowing she needed to increase the pressure, move towards the chip, wrestle it free.

But what if it all goes dark?

'Fuck!' with a cry of anguish Anna flung the scissors into the sink, their tip red and glossy. Then she pressed a hand to her neck, felt blood running between her fingers. She looked at herself, filled with disdain. 'Baby,' she seethed, 'you fucking baby.'

An hour later and she was on the sofa, a plaster placed beneath her chip, cushions held to her chest as she lay on her side and absently watched the television. She'd sent Mandie a message as soon as she'd cleaned herself up.

Any word on those tablets? Xx

And was now impatiently waiting on a reply. Anna needed darkness. An endless ocean of it to swim in. She couldn't survive an entire month this way, on the knife-edge of being discovered. Of everything being ruined.

Her phone beeped and she leapt up to grab it.

Working on it. Will be a few days, tops xxx

A few days.

Anna groaned. What was she supposed to do during that time, while her sanity slowly drained away? Her neck throbbed from the freshly inflicted wound. What was she going to tell Elijah when he came home and noticed the plaster?

The truth.

Not all of it, of course. But some. Although . . .

He won't understand. He won't.

Upon the sofa Anna twisted with indecision. If she told him too much, he might suspect she was keeping something from him. Better he thought she'd had an accident rather than something deliberate.

Everyone has accidents. They happen all the time.

Anna looked to the television, then she got to her feet and wandered to the kitchen, to the window which overlooked her studio. All her pictures of cats. She looked to the far fence, thinking of the large ginger tom who would strut along it.

'I could say I went to stroke him,' she conspired aloud, 'I could say he became agitated by a noise, I turned and he scratched me.' She studied the pale outline of her reflection in the glass. 'Behind the ear, though?' Anna frowned, trying to iron out the logistics. She needed the scratch to look authentic. If the ginger tom had caught her behind the ear, he'd have surely caught her face a bit too, the front of her ear. Anna closed her eyes, stomach dropping as she realised what needed to be done.

First, she took some paracetamol to stave off the worst of the sting. Then she returned to the upstairs bathroom and the mirror above the sink, for it offered the best lighting. This time, she didn't hold the scissors from her manicure set, she held a small kitchen knife, one she usually used for peeling apples.

'Do it quick,' she commanded herself, one hand tightly gripping the cold edge of the sink. 'Three, four slashes, nothing more.'

I could ask Mandie to do it.

Anna knew that there was little her friend wouldn't do in the name of protecting a loved one, but this might be straying too far from her limit. And was there even time? Anna had been so preoccupied with her plan that she'd failed to check the time on her phone.

How was your meeting?

She waited for several elongated beats of her heart, breathing hard. Nothing. He must still be in it. Good. That meant she had more time. Palm slick with sweat, she raised the knife to her face, practised the stroke she wanted against her cheek. Her ear.

'I can't do this.' Her entire body was prickled with sweat, breathing shallow. She swallowed, stared at herself. 'You can do this.' Then she lifted the knife to her cheek, pushed down hard, hard enough to break the skin, and drew it back in one quick, fluid motion, gasping and trembling as blood began to drip down her face.

Shit.

Be still.

There was no time to recover. Anna raised her hand, repeated the movement three more times, until she looked to have been repeatedly slashed.

Don't . . . move.

Tears smarting her eyes, she dropped the knife and pressed a towel to the side of her face as loud, heaving sobs began to escape from her.

Anna downed a glass of whiskey from the liquor cupboard before attempting to clean up, needing something to calm herself. She cleaned away the knife, the blood, applied fresh dressings. She looked out to the garden, satisfied her plan was almost complete, and then froze as fear stabbed through her.

A single camera, facing the far end of the garden. Her studio.

'Mother fucker,' Anna mumbled as she pulled on her coat, her sheepskin-lined boots, turned up the hood. 'Out we go,' she told herself. 'Studio, then head to the far corner of the garden, where the camera can't quite see.'

In the golden light of dusk she acted out her plan. She went into the studio, paced around, refused to let guilt creep in over her lack of progress on her painting that day.

Refusing to lock eyes with her overturned image of a beach. It was still turned to the wall, unmoved. That was good. That meant it had as yet gone unseen. At some point she really needed to remove it altogether. But then a part of her liked it, liked the sense of unease she'd captured even though it was just a landscape.

Dammit.

She was drifting from her plan. Anna inhaled, then she stepped outside, made her movements seem as though she'd been alerted by a sound. Over to the fence she went. And then –

A light scream.

Argh! Fucking cat! Shit!

Turning, clutching the already bandaged side of her head, concealed by her hood, she ran towards the house.

Argh, shit, this really hurts. He got me. The bugger. Urgh, it's bleeding. Where are the plasters?

She went to great lengths to grab the medical box, scatter some plasters on top of the island in the kitchen. Making everything look haphazard. Panicked.

Anna! What's happened?

I was in my studio and heard that ginger tom passing by so thought I'd go and give him a fuss. He must have heard something that scared him as he turned, hissed and scratched me.

Oh, shit. Are you all right?

Not really.

I'm just stuck in this sodding meeting, it overran.

I've managed to stop the bleeding and get some gauze and plasters on, it should be okay now.

We should take you to a doctor, get you checked over.

No, no, really I think it'll be fine.

Cat scratches can be toxic.

I've put some antiseptic cream on them.

You can't be too careful.

Honestly, it looks worse than it is. You can check it when you come home if you like?

Baby, I'm so sorry you're having such a hard time of it. First the stupid chip and now this.

Anna steadied herself against the island, crying.

He's usually so friendly; I didn't expect him to lash out.

I'll grab some takeaway on the way home. What are you in the mood for?

Pizza would be nice, she lied. Her stomach felt like it was filled with stones. And the cuts across her face stung.

It's just a scratch.

And her thoughts strayed to the hours she'd spent, happily, watching *Romeo and Juliet* for her English studies. Mercutio upon the beach: 'Ay, ay, a scratch, a scratch; marry, 'tis enough.' And then, moments later, 'Ask for me tomorrow and you shall find me a grave man.'

Really, just a scratch. Don't worry yourself.

31

It had been years since she'd waited at the window for Elijah to come home. As a newlywed she'd stalked through their big house, unsure of what she was actually supposed to do. This life as a wife felt strange to her. Anna had her paintings, her studio, and within those little wooden walls she felt safe. At ease. But in the three-storey terrace they called home, with the magnolia walls and white doors, she felt uncertain. In those first months as Mrs Weston she kept waiting for someone to come and pound their fists upon the front door, drag her out by her elbows, telling her that it was time to stop pretending. That this life wasn't for her.

Elijah had been born into it. He didn't baulk at the prices in their local supermarket, or scoff when he noticed all the various imported cheeses. This was his world. And now Anna was in it. When they dated she felt like she'd been dipping her toe into the pool of excess, but now marriage had cemented her position and she'd been thrown in and she felt like she was drowning.

Every evening in those first months Anna would wait at the living-room bay window, arms hugged to her chest, watching the street outside. It was only when the days darkened and she placed a fir tree strung with lights in the window that she ceased her vigil. Began to feel secure enough to stay in her studio all afternoon, to let Elijah come to her, to not feel the need to always have dinner ready the second he walked through the door.

Anna was at the window now, face throbbing.

She glanced back towards the fireplace, above which hung an ornate mirror – a previous anniversary gift from Elijah. She remembered ripping off the crisp wrapping paper, a bow falling to the floor.

'I thought this would be perfect for the lounge,' he told her proudly as she stared at her own reflection.

'The lounge?'

'Above the fireplace.'

'Oh?' She watched her smile fall. 'Only . . . didn't you say we could buy a piece from that American painter I like? The one who does landscapes?'

'Randall?' Elijah said the name with distaste. 'You mean the guy with the long dark hair who paints topless?'

'You said you liked his work, you said it was—'

'I like the mirror, Anna. It adds a fresh dimension to the room.'

'Right.' Anna looked into the smooth surface, pictured instead the dramatic rise of snow-capped mountains or rolling green prairie fields. 'Perhaps we could buy a Randall to put elsewhere?'

They could easily afford to have an original piece shipped over.

'You did say—'

'He's not the right fit for my house, Anna,' Elijah told her with a hard look.

My house.

Anna gave a tight nod, still clutching the mirror. She became all too aware of the fact that she was sitting within the lounge of a home for which she'd never contributed towards a single mortgage payment. It was all Elijah. Always.

'I think the mirror is great,' she told him with forced brightness. The hard angles of Elijah's face melted away as he smiled at her.

'I knew you'd like it.' He came over to kiss her, lips cold. 'I always know what you'd like, Anna.'

Anna shifted to look again out the window, to the street, unable to stand her forlorn expression in that gaudy mirror for a second longer.

That sodding cat.
Elijah, are you okay?
She looked out on the static cars lining the street.
Are you on your way home?
A minute passed. Then another.
Is everything okay?
Where was he? He knew she was hurt, why had he suddenly gone silent?
Elijah!
She heard herself shouting within her own mind, yelling into a vacuum.
You said you were on your way home. Where are you? What's going on?
Have you muted me?
She was hurt. He wouldn't ignore her when he knew that she was hurt. Would he?
Elijah, please.
Anna searched her thoughts, tried to find him, to tune in to what he was thinking. It felt like floating through an endless void.
Elijah?
Fuck my sodding shitty chip!
Elijah!

The living room was dark behind her. She tapped the screen of her phone, wishing she had the app that alerted her to movement at the doorbell. To her husband's location. 'Tonight,' she told herself, 'I'll get them all installed tonight.'

A click at the door. Key twisting within a lock. Elijah was home.

'Anna?'

Where are you, sweetheart?

Christ! Where have you been? I've been so bloody worried. I'm in the front room.

Elijah stepped in from the hallway, clicking on the lights, causing Anna to blanch beneath them. She felt jittery, unnerved.

'Oh my God, your face.' Still wearing his coat he strode over to her, gingerly touched her chin, raising her face to the light. 'Oh, sweetheart, he really got you.'

'Where were you?' she rasped, peering into his eyes.

'On the way home.'

'I . . . I kept speaking to you.'

'I didn't hear anything.' He twisted her face to assess the damage, the plasters barely concealing her handiwork. 'This looks bad.'

'I know.'

'He's made a right mess of your face.'

'It all happened so quickly, and it's so unlike him.'

'Hmm.' Elijah tilted her head to the left, then the right, studying her. 'I really would rather we go to the doctor's.'

'Why didn't you answer me? On the way home?'

'I told you, I didn't hear anything. Let me look at you.'

Anna flinched beneath his touch.

'I looked it up on the way home. If the cuts get swollen, or you start to feel unwell – like flu-type symptoms – we go straight to the doctor's. Got it?'

She gave a nod. 'Got it.'

Elijah dropped his hand and carefully kissed her lips. 'It must have really shaken you up.'

'It did.' She could still feel the cold tip of the scissors slicing through her skin.

'I picked up dinner on the way back.' Elijah nodded towards the hallway. 'Are you feeling up to eating something?'

'Yes, sure.' Her scratches stung as she forced a smile.

The cheese on the pizza felt like clay in her mouth. She chewed it over and over, struggling to swallow.

Elijah had a pepperoni pizza which he happily ate as they sat at the island, his tie loose, jacket gone. Anna kept picking at her margherita, feeling nauseous yet again.

'You're proper in the wars at the moment.' Elijah dabbed his mouth with a napkin and pointed to the assortment of plasters covering his wife. Her face. Her hand. She looked like she had fought with a bear and lost.

'I feel in the wars,' she admitted.

'I can't believe your chip is faulty.' He got up and walked over to the fridge, opening its smooth, silver doors and reaching inside for a bottle of beer. 'I mean, I paid for the *Executive* Package. It's not good enough.'

Executive Package but with no mute function.

'I know.' Gravel in his voice.

We've been over this.

He twisted the bottle cap and frowned. 'Want one?'

Anna shook her head.

You drinking tonight then?

She watched Elijah roll his eyes, a sneer on his lips.

Let's not. This evening has been stressful enough as it is.

'I called them again, this afternoon, to complain. Unity,' he told her.

See? I'm trying to fix this. For you. Going out of my way during my busy day to help.

'Oh?'

'They gave me some bullshit about the waiver, that it can be a known but rare issue. Assured me it would all be fine, and so on and so on.'

'I just . . .' Anna went to touch her chip and flinched, the skin surrounding it too sore. Too broken.

'I don't want you being upset,' Elijah continued, pausing only to sip from his beer, 'and I'm worried about the . . . the hallucinations they said you might have. Did you read about that woman, the one who tried to remove her chip herself?'

Anna froze, fighting to keep her face a mask of indifference. 'Oh?'

'Apparently she was getting driven crazy by, like, visions. So she pulled the chip out and it really fucked with her brain. She's on life support now, in a coma.'

A vegetable.

'Christ.'

'But, you know,' Elijah dragged a hand through his hair, displacing all the gel he'd so carefully applied that morning, 'you can see how it happens. I never thought we'd get a faulty chip. The tech . . . They assured me all the kinks had been worked out. And now you've got a dud and I'm sick to my stomach worrying about you.'

'It's a month.' Anna did her best to sound breezy. 'We can last a month, surely?'

'She used pliers,' Elijah was looking at her, at her scratches, 'just yanked it straight out.'

'Sounds brutal.'

'Perhaps she didn't know how dangerous it could be to mess with the chip.'

'Mmm.' Anna shoved a piece of pizza into her mouth just so she wouldn't have to talk. Slowly she chewed it, the tomato sauce, cheese and dough forming a claggy paste.

'It's so awful, the cat scratching you.' Elijah gave her a sad look.

'Mmm.' Anna gulped down her pizza, felt it moving against the sides of her throat, landing like an anchor in the pit of her stomach.

'You need to be more careful,' he told her, still looking at her. 'I'd hate for something to happen to you, Anna.'

'Actually,' she coughed and gestured to the fridge, 'I'll take a beer.'

Elijah was upstairs, shedding the trappings of his work life and slipping into joggers and a hoodie. Anna was in the garden, smoking.

Make sure you're keeping away from that cat.
I will.

She held her phone, its faint glow turning her face blue as she peered at it, navigating the screen with only her thumb while her other hand lifted her e-cigarette to and from her mouth. Elijah hated her smoking, but she needed it tonight. Needed something to calm her tempest of nerves.

She tapped out a message to Mandie.

Am feeling proper shit. Need those pills xxx

A reply pinged through in less than a minute.

> Patience, babe. Am working on it xxx

Pacing across the lawn, back to the house, Anna scrolled through her contacts, blowing blueberry smoke high into the air. Her thumb hovered over Gavin's name. She swiftly turned towards the house, all windows dark. The only light from her home came from the open back door, a golden rectangle beckoning her back inside.

The impulse to call him. She felt it within her gut.

'We need to talk,' she said aloud, pacing faster. 'I need to know about Kavos. About Oscar.' Her eyes flicked upwards, certain there had been movement at a window. Anna lowered her voice to a whisper. 'I need to know for sure if it's a memory or a dream. You were there, you should know.' Anna stalked over to her studio, leaned against it as she craned her neck to study each of the six windows of the house. All were still.

You okay?

Fine, just doing some last-minute emails. What shall we watch tonight?

I don't mind.

I wish you'd stop smoking.

I'm trying to.

She wasn't.

Can you come inside? I don't want you lingering in the garden in case the cat comes back.

Are you mocking me?

How could she tell? She could only hear Elijah, not see him. She was unable to read his expression.

Of course not. I'm worried about you. Come inside, please.

She took one last, longing look around the garden. The shadows that gathered within the flower beds. This was her safe place, her calm place. Elijah had little interest in the garden, every decision made outside had been hers, from which plants to grow to where to place the shed.

Anna blew one final plume of smoke up towards the pale curve of the moon.

Okay, I'm coming.

She found Elijah in the living room, sprawled across the sofa, a fresh bottle of beer in his hand.

'I've had a shit day,' he groaned as she walked in, clocking the judgemental look she gave him. 'I know you have too,' he added.

'Why was it so bad?' Anna curled up on her armchair, dragged a soft cream throw over her legs and looked up at the wall where the concealed television had glimmered into life.

'Gavin.' Elijah said the name with disdain.

'Oh?' Anna felt the pizza in her stomach shift.

'He's just being, you know, typical Gavin. But it's driving me up the wall.'

'I bet.'

'Sometimes I wonder why I'm even friends with him.' He gave a shake of his head, sipped his beer.

'You guys have been through a lot, there's history there,' she offered.

'Yeah,' Elijah took a longer sip, 'a whole lot of history. I couldn't get rid of him now even if I wanted to.' The way he said it. The tightness in his voice. Anna tried to see his expression, but she was looking at him in profile, his gaze tilted up towards the television. 'Should we watch that HBO show?' he said suddenly, brightly.

'Sure,' Anna agreed, scratches throbbing, 'whatever you like.'

*

In bed she waited for sleep to take Elijah. It didn't take long, thanks to the beers. As his breathing levelled out, Anna peered into the darkness, lifted a hand to touch at her plasters.

He knows.

She tried not to tip over into panic.

No, he doesn't. Breathe. Focus.

Her eyes were wide and unblinking.

He knows you tried to cut the chip out.

Anna kept fingering the dressings. Cautiously she turned to study her husband, rolled towards her, eyes closed. So peaceful. Reaching out, she tucked a stray chestnut curl behind his ear. She wondered if he was already dreaming. If he was on a sandy beach with Gavin by his side. Or was he somewhere else, within one of her memories? A tear slid down her cheek.

Just because it happened doesn't mean he'll dream about it.

She knew there was no certainty to any of it.

Just the threat.

Looming over her like a vast, black cloud. Anna shivered beneath the weight of it. She knew how often Gavin slipped into her thoughts, her dreams.

Too often.

Far too often.

And now did Elijah know that too?

One month. I need to last one month. Four weeks. Twenty-eight days. That's it. I can do it.

Her body ached while her mind whirred. The story about the cat, had it been convincing enough?

I could just ask Elijah about Kavos.

With a sniff she sucked back fresh tears.

But if I ask him he'll know about the memories. And what if . . . ?

Anna squeezed her eyes shut, unable to finish the thought.

If Elijah had seen her and Gavin together, she'd know, wouldn't she? There was no way he could be so composed, so normal. So caring. If he knew, he'd . . . he'd explode. She was sure of it. How could he not? His thoughts . . . he'd think about it. Reveal something.

One month.

Anna panted as she lay on her back. The tablets would come through from Mandie, they would help. And until then she just needed to keep a handle on her thoughts. Keep up with the nursery rhymes.

Elijah didn't know anything.

One month.

That's it.

I can do it.

Doubt spread through her like a cancer as she rolled on to her side, body turning cold, clutching the pillow tight to the side of her face that hadn't been maimed by her own hand.

I'm going to go mad, she decided with awful clarity.

Over the next four weeks I'm going to lose my fucking mind.

She pictured the woman who'd been driven to remove her chip with pliers, exhausted and pushed to the brink, blood seeping down her face, dripping from her chin as she smiled manically, finally free.

32

When sleep finally took her, she was back there. On the beach. In Elijah's mind . . . memory.

Only this time it all felt sharper. Focused. And no one was running.

'I'm sick of this.' Oscar was staring at her, red hair whipped by the wind, eyes screwed up in anger. 'I'm sick of you having a fucking drink and being unable to take a sodding joke.'

'Just leave it, Oscar.' Gavin's voice was behind them, tight with warning.

'I'm just trying to have a *laugh*.' Oscar kept looking at her, Elijah, a goading spark lighting his eyes. His white Lacoste polo shirt was splashed with lager, browning in the fading light. In one hand he held a bottle of Corona, the other gave Elijah's shoulder a shove. 'You need to lighten up; you're always bringing down the mood.' He glanced back towards where Gavin stood in the sand.

There was the distant pulse of music, twisting on the breeze, trying to lure them back to the clubs, to the neon lights. Instead they lingered on the cliff top, felt their skin cool as the wind lifted off the sea and came up to meet them.

'Can we just *go*?' Gavin pleaded.

'Only if we stop pretending we don't know why Elijah's so goddam uptight all the time,' Oscar sneered angrily. 'You need to chill out.' He tipped his bottle to his mouth, lips cracked from too much time in the sun, drained the last of the amber liquid in a smooth, single swallow. 'You need to fuck your girl.'

'What?' Elijah's voice was small yet steely.

'I said you need to fuck your girl, limp dick. No wonder Anna is making eyes at Gav all the time; we know his actually works, I hear him at it enough through our paper-thin walls and—'

Oscar didn't get to finish his sentence. Elijah's fist collided with his mouth, sending a spray of blood into the air. Stunned, Oscar dropped his bottle, which landed in the sand at his feet, whole. He looked to Elijah, colour rising in his cheeks, when he was shoved, quickly, firmly, a hand to each shoulder. Oscar faltered on his feet, his blue Converse upon the edge of the cliff. A second shove, this one to the centre of his chest, to his heart. And he was falling, limbs flailing, eyes wide with shock, with horror, dropping like a stone towards the water. The rocks. When he landed upon them, even over the rushing whisper of the waves, they heard the snap of something vital.

'Fuck!' Gavin's voice was suddenly loud and close. 'Fuck, Eli, what did you do? What did you *do*?' He dragged his hands through his sandy hair, pacing back and forth.

Elijah looked down at his hands as though he suddenly didn't recognise them. 'I . . .'

Gavin cautiously approached the edge and peered over. 'Aww, fuck man, I'm pretty sure he's . . . he's dead. I—' His voice was breaking.

'We have to get out of here.' Elijah reached for Gavin, grabbed his elbow in a pincer grip. 'If we get caught here, with him like this, we're as good as dead too.'

'Oscar . . . he . . .' Tears were upon Gavin's cheeks, beer on his breath. 'He . . .' He began to breathe heavily, erratically. He clasped a hand to his chest, doubled over.

'Keep it together. We need to get out of here.'

'What? N-no . . .' Gavin peered up at him, broken, face red and twisted.

'Get. Up.' Elijah hauled him up by his collar, hands trembling, though his voice remained firm. 'We need to *go*.'

'Wait, we—'

'You want a criminal record?' Elijah hissed at his friend. 'You want to kiss any decent future goodbye?'

'Wait.' Gavin shook his head, trying to focus. 'I . . . I didn't do anything.' He eased away from the cliff edge, placing space between him and Elijah, one hand reflexively touching his own chest. '*You* hit him. You—'

'And I say it was you. What then?' Elijah challenged.

'Look, I—'

'I'm drunk.' Elijah threw his hands up, making fists of frustration. 'I'm drunk and I'm . . . I'm . . . Shit. I need to call my parents—'

'Let's get out of here first.' Gavin was reaching for Elijah, tugging him away from the cliff, the sea. 'We need to get back to the hotel, okay?' There was a tremor in Gavin's voice, pure fear in his eyes. 'Let's just back to the hotel before we do anything rash.'

Elijah stared at him for a few seconds.

'Come on, man, we need to go.'

And then they were running.

33

Anna awoke with a start. Like she'd been falling, jolted back into consciousness. She looked up, breath caught in her throat, waiting for her heart to stop hammering so hard within her chest. She'd been back on the beach. Back with Gavin. Just seconds ago. And now she was in her marital bed, Elijah sound asleep beside her.

Shit.

Sitting up, she rested her head in her hands, scratches instantly screaming at being touched.

Shit, shit, shit.

In a haze she left the bed, put on her slippers, her silk dressing gown, and headed downstairs, phone slipped into her pocket. Once in the kitchen she took painkillers, washing them down with icy water. Was it normal for her scratches to sting so much? Was it because of the chip? Was it doing something?

Punishing me.

Anna drained the last of the water, admonishing her thoughts for feeling so foolish. She went to the window, pulled up the blind to peer out into the garden, soaking up the stillness of it all. Phone in hand, she called up Gavin's details.

What to say . . .

What *did* she need to say?

Kavos. She needed answers about that. About Oscar. But she didn't want to be so brazen as to put it down in a message, where it could be seen. Anna still wanted to labour beneath the belief that Elijah could only hear her thoughts. That he wasn't journeying into her memories each night. Her secrets.

We need to talk.

The message she settled upon was blunt. To the point. Anna checked the time on the screen. Four in the morning. She imagined Gavin spread-eagled across his bed, snoring loudly, with Helen curled serenely on the far side. Anna paced into the living room, turned on the television with no intention of really watching it. She just wanted the comfort of sound, of voices in the room with her.

Her phone pinging in her pocket startled her. A message from Gavin:

Okay.

That was it. One word. How was she supposed to deduce from that if he was happy? Pissed off? Anna figured that at least he was being compliant.

The Moon on the Water. 1pm. Can you make that?

She watched three dots bounce across her screen as Gavin typed his response, wondering if he'd accept the invitation.

What am I doing?

The thought made her scratches burn brighter.

Anna never saw Gavin alone. Or Helen, for that matter. It was only ever the four of them, like a band that couldn't possibly be split up. Gavin and Elijah saw one another for work stuff. But Helen . . .

Anna stopped looking at her phone and thought of all the unanswered messages, all the vague responses to suggestions to days out.

'Do you fancy going to that new spa over on Boldwood Bank?'

'Maybe, sometime.'

'There's that new film out this weekend that everyone keeps raving about, we should go.'

'I can't this weekend.'

Eventually, Anna gave up asking. And then there was Mandie. Forever excited to go out, to have fun. Anna was pretty sure she'd yet to be turned down by her friend. Her phone pinged.

I'll have to dip out of work but yeah, okay.

Three more dots began to dance.

Anna wondered what she was doing, meeting him in the same pub she'd just met Mandie.

She reasoned it was dark in there. Quiet. They wouldn't risk bumping into anyone. Elijah would never suspect where she was. Anna could just tell him she was heading out for a jog. Turn off the data on her phone, make sure he couldn't track her. She could leave in her running gear, he'd clock her on the camera and then an hour later clock her again. She needed to do all she could not to arouse suspicion. Because if he knew she was meeting Gavin he'd—

A fresh message pinged.

What's going on?

Anna's heart fluttered nervously as she tapped out her response.

I'll tell you later.

She wanted Gavin to stare at her in pained confusion when she mentioned Kavos, to tell her that he and Elijah had already told her everything they knew about what happened to Oscar. That he'd been drunk, had wandered away from them. Had perhaps walked too close to the cliff edge. Had fallen.

I just need to ask, that's all.

Because in the dream, the memory, it felt like she was *there*. Gavin spoke of a dead body. As though they knew, had seen it all happen. Then why had they lied? Both of them?

Above, a floorboard creaked. Anna reached for the television remote, muted the screen.

Shit.

Barely breathing, she listened overhead, the house now still around her.

Baby, are you up?

There were two hours until Elijah was due to wake up, step in the shower and come downstairs for his beloved morning smoothie. A creature of habit, he never woke before his alarm, never stalked the rooms of their house in the small hours. Not like Anna.

Where are you?

Upon the sofa she bristled.

In the front room. I was feeling unwell so had to get up.

The cuts? Are they hurting? Do they feel hot to the touch?

No, no.

Anna stood, returned her phone to her pocket and left the room, making for the hallway and the stairs. She went up each steep, wooden step, house cracking like old bones around her. At the top she took the sharp turn into her bedroom, found Elijah sitting up in bed, squinting at her.

'You okay?' His voice was rough with sleep.

'I took some paracetamol, which has helped.'

He reached for her, drew her to him and placed a hand upon her temple. 'You don't feel hot.'

'Really, it was just a headache. You should try to get back to sleep.'

'No, no,' the springs of the bed sighed as he stood up, 'I'm awake now. Might as well get up.' He went over to the bathroom and moments later the sound of rushing water filled the room. Anna heard the old pipes banging in the walls. Their home was such a strange collision of old and new. Modern technology crammed on to a Victorian canvas. In some ways Anna liked it, the juxtaposition of it all. Other times, when the staircase creaked or the pipes sang, she wondered just how much their old house could take. Her father had approved of it when they bought it, peering up from the steps at the full three storeys.

'Houses like this are made to last,' he told his daughter. 'It's a solid home, Anna.'

'Solid home for a solid marriage,' Elijah had declared, beaming. 'And to think, we were almost outbid by some rival buyers. Good job I made some calls, chased them off.'

Must be nice, Anna had mused, while looking at her husband, *to always get what you want.*

From the bed Anna stared at the closed bathroom door.

I'm sorry I woke you.

She pressed a hand against her phone in her pocket, needing not to think about the messages she'd been writing. The plans she'd been making.

It's fine. Probably do me good to get an early start on the day. Fire off some emails. Got a big meeting later.

Oh?

Corporate coming in for an update. All hands on deck kind of thing.

I see.

Anna closed her eyes, tried to slow her breathing.

This little piggy went to market.

The hissing from the bathroom grew louder.

This little piggy stayed at home.

Within her pocket, her phone pinged.

This little piggy had roast beef.

Anna refused to look at it, didn't dare think about what it might say.

This little piggy had none.

The bathroom suddenly plunged into silence, shower off.

And this little piggy cried wee wee wee all the way home.

Stop that.

Anna swallowed.

Stop what?

The sodding nursery rhymes. It's infuriating.

I'm just . . . I'm trying to keep myself calm.

'Maybe.' The bathroom door creaked open and light pooled out on to the floor. Elijah had a towel wrapped around his waist, body damp, hair flat against his head. 'Or maybe you're trying to conceal your thoughts from me.'

'What?' Anna's voice was high, alarmed. 'That's ridiculous.'

'I can't help but feel like you're doing it to keep yourself from thinking.'

'I told you, it's a calming thing,' Anna said contritely. 'In case you hadn't noticed, I've been pretty fucking stressed lately.'

'I've noticed.' Elijah raised the towel, dried his hair.

'We're supposed to be able to mute the fucking thing,' Anna continued icily, 'but we can't. Because we didn't get *that package*. So apologies if my neurosis is *annoying* you. It's not much fun for me either.' One hand protectively pressed against her dressing-gown pocket, the phone within.

'Okay, okay,' Elijah muttered as he rubbed his hair with the towel. 'Just . . . just stop it. All right? It's distracting.'

'Sure.' Anna eyed him darkly. 'I'll just stop thinking.'

'Don't be like that.'

'Like what?'

'Difficult.'

'Maybe I'll go and see if we have some pliers in your toolbox,' Anna threatened.

Elijah lowered the towel, stared at her. 'Or maybe see if that cat's about to finish the job.'

She flinched.

'Stop hiding things from me,' he told her as he went over to their walk-in wardrobe, disappearing inside. Anna heard the soft rattle of coat hangers sliding back and forth.

I'm not hiding anything from you.

Stop with the nursery rhymes.

I did this for you.

'For us,' Elijah loudly corrected her, stepping out in a shirt he was buttoning up. 'We did this for *us*, Anna. Don't lose sight of that.'

'I'm not.'

Once fully clothed, Elijah left the room. She listened to his footsteps on the stairs, the creak of her home.

Want anything?

She imagined him in the kitchen angrily preparing his morning smoothie. Anna cast a longing glance at the bed. At the silence that came with sleep.

I'm going to try and get some more rest.

Okay.

Anna lowered herself to the pillow, drew the duvet up to her chin.

Keep an eye on those scratches today.
I will.

She closed her eyes, sleep coming sooner than she'd anticipated. When she opened them again the room was filled with light. Sunlight poured in from the windows, making the white of the walls scold Anna as she sat up, wincing. Still in her dressing gown, she fumbled for her phone, saw the message from Gavin that had come through earlier:

See you soon

She checked the time: half nine. Late for her. Anna got out of bed, went downstairs. The only trace of Elijah was the freshly washed-up glass draining on the sideboard. A hand went to her lips.

You left without saying goodbye.

Cars were sliding by outside, sparkling in the sun.

You were asleep.

I know but . . . you always kiss me goodbye. Always.

I was in a rush.

The scratches on her head pounded.

A rush? You got up at four?

Whose fault was that?

Anna opened the fridge, dipped her head inside, needing to do something. She scanned the shelves for juice. Eggs. As she withdrew them she kicked the silver door closed.

'He knows.' She stood there, bathed in sunlight, sensing the darkness gathering around her house like vines. 'He knows, he fucking knows. Elijah *always* kisses me goodbye.'

As she placed an egg in a pan of water, she realised she was shaking.

I hope your meeting goes well.

'Just be calm,' Anna commanded herself as she touched a button to activate the gas, small blue flames licking the base of the pan. 'He's probably just pissed that you woke him up; Eli loves routine. That's all.'

Well, it won't.

Elijah's voice thundered in her head.

Gavin has now dipped out of it. Apparently got some family emergency he can't get out of. A load of bullshit if you ask me. His house could be on fire and he wouldn't sit out a corporate meeting. He's up to something.

Maybe there really is an emergency. Should I check on Helen?

Don't bother. I'm pretty sure he's bullshitting. Probably off for an interview somewhere else.

Well, that'd be good.

Unless he's on more money.

It doesn't always have to be a competition with you two, you know?

Her mind was silent. Elijah gone. Anna watched her egg bob and turn as the water boiled, cooking it from the inside out. She watched the shell crack, some of the white insides seep out and harden.

I love you.

Anna saw her pinched face reflected in the black splashguard above the hob. She stared at it as the minutes passed and her egg overcooked.

34

Gavin was already in the pub when she arrived, casually sitting in a booth, a glass of lager slick with condensation in front of him. Anna took a deep breath, walked over. She was in leggings and a zip-through top, hair loose about her shoulders. She'd attempted a ponytail but felt the pinch of her scratches so gave up.

I'm going out for a run.

All morning she'd talked at Elijah, receiving radio silence in response.

Eli, is everything all right? Work okay?

Both her head and the house felt worryingly quiet. It was good to get outside, to step into the spring sunshine.

'Well, this is all rather clandestine,' Gavin noted when he saw her. He was in a suit, tie loose, jacket tossed across the chair beside him. 'What's your poison?' He nodded towards the bar and Anna suddenly fretted that it would be the same bartender, that he'd remember her, comment on her being in there again.

Just stay calm.

She blinked furiously, needing to control her thoughts. 'Vodka tonic,' she said as she lowered herself into the chair opposite Gavin. 'Double.'

'Shit.' Gavin recoiled when he fully looked at her. 'What

the hell happened to you? Get into a fight with a racoon or something?'

'Cat,' Anna deadpanned. 'And I can get my drink, don't worry about it.'

'No, no.' Gavin stretched a hand towards her, motioning for her to remain sitting. 'I'm sure you've scared enough people on the walk over; let's try to minimise the damage, eh?'

'Hilarious.'

Minutes later he was back. 'Here.' He handed her a drink and had bought himself a fresh pint. Anna raised her eyebrows at it.

Gavin shrugged. 'In for a penny, in for a pound. I figured if we're day drinking, I might as well go all-in.'

'Sure.' She drank down the vodka tonic, cool and sharp against the back of her throat. 'Thanks for meeting me,' she said as she lowered her glass.

'No problem.'

'Hope you're not missing anything important at work.'

Gavin gave a dismissive shake of the head. 'Nah, nothing serious.'

She frowned.

'What?'

'That's not the impression I got from Elijah.'

'Well, he's got a rod up his arse so large about that place I'm surprised he can sit down,' Gavin remarked, sipping his lager. 'No offence,' he added with a smirk.

'None taken.'

'So.' He slapped a hand against the table, making the cardboard coasters jump. 'To what do I owe the pleasure of your unexpected company this afternoon?'

Anna drank more from her glass, nerves mounting.

'I have to say the choice of venue is . . . questionable. I

reckon it's been a solid ten years since I've been in a regular pub.'

'I thought it'd be quiet,' Anna admitted.

'You thought right.'

'I wanted to talk to you about . . .' She drew in a shaky breath. 'How to begin . . .' She mumbled to herself.

'Talking to yourself: first sign of madness,' Gavin teased. 'He mutes his all the time, you know. Says it helps him focus.'

'What?' Anna shook herself, distracted. 'He *mutes* his chip?'

'Yep.' Gavin nodded as he sipped from his glass. 'All the time.'

'But . . . but we can't. We didn't get that model.'

'Is that the royal we? I'm pretty sure he can mute his chip.'

'No, no. He . . . we don't have that.'

I don't have that.

She tasted bile in the back of her throat.

'He does have it, doesn't he?' She stared wildly at Gavin, her pulse thick beside her chip, behind her scratches, causing her to wince. 'The mute function. He uses it, doesn't he?'

'Ah.' Gavin awkwardly cracked his knuckles, looking to the table.

'Has he been lying to me?' Anna demanded of him. 'All this time, has he been muting me? Lying about it?'

Is he muting it all the time?

'He's lying to one of us,' Gavin reasoned with a tilt of his head. 'Given his track record, let's assume it's me.'

'What does that mean?'

'He wouldn't lie to you, Anna. Not knowingly. He's too high and mighty for that.'

'Perhaps a lie by omission.' She twisted her glass, watched as the ice knocked together, thinking of what Mandie had said.

'Can you get it too?'

She raised her gaze to him.

'The mute thing,' Gavin explained, 'you said you don't have it, why not just get it? Can United sort that?'

'Unity.'

'Whatever.'

'Yes,' Anna nodded, 'they . . . they need to sort my chip. I've got an appointment there. In a month.'

'Oh, right. What's the hold-up?'

'They're busy.'

Gavin gave a swift roll of his eyes. 'Course they are.'

'Anyway,' Anna tightened her posture, needing to focus, 'I asked you here because, well, yes my chip is malfunctioning. And it . . . sometimes . . .' She groaned, wishing she had the luxury of thinking through what she was going to say. 'What happened in Kavos?' she suddenly blurted.

'Kavos?' Gavin flinched. 'Why are you bringing that up?'

'I just . . .' Anna sighed, unsure how much she could risk saying. 'I need to know what happened there. What happened to . . .' She took an uneasy breath. 'To Oscar.'

Gavin paled. 'Why?'

'Because.'

'Kavos was a long time ago,' Gavin eyed her warily. 'Oscar . . .' He blinked, gaze watery. 'It was a fucking tragedy, but, you know . . .' Reaching for his glass, he drank from it deeply. 'Like I said, a long time ago.'

'You guys said you weren't with him when he fell.'

'Right,' Gavin confirmed stiffly.

'But is that really true?'

'What the fuck, Anna?'

'Please.' She held her hands tight around her glass, its coolness seeping into her palms. 'Just tell me what happened on the beach. The truth. I can take it.'

I need to know if what I saw was real.

Gavin's eyes went wide. 'What the hell, Anna? Why are you asking about all this?'

'Because . . .' She chewed her lip. Frustrated. 'Just tell me, *please*.'

'Anna, I'm really not—'

'You both always said that Oscar just disappeared after a heavy night.'

'And what? Is Elijah now trying to spin things? Say he's protecting me or some bullshit? How fucking typical.' Gavin laughed sharply.

'I've not talked to him about it; I've come straight to you,' Anna admitted, feeling a pinch in her chest over the reality of not approaching Elijah. Why *had* she done that? Was she afraid of what he might say? That he might lie?

'Tell me why you're asking.' Gavin stared at her, eyes burning with challenge. 'And don't bullshit me.'

'Okay.' Anna inhaled, then raised her glass to her lips, drinking down until only ice remained. 'So, basically, one of the, er, issues with the chip – with *my* chip – is that it got implanted too deep and now I can . . . I can sometimes see what I think are Elijah's memories. As dreams. As, like, my dreams.'

She watched an array of emotions ripple across Gavin's face. Surprise. Anger. Fear. 'Anna,' he lowered his voice, leaning towards her, eyes darting around the empty pub, 'are you serious right now?'

'Yes,' she confirmed nervously. 'I'm serious.'

'And you're asking me to confirm what happened on that beach in Kavos? What happened to Oscar?'

'Yes.'

'I guess I should have figured he'd never tell you.' Gavin leaned back and drained the last of his lager.

'Tell me what?'

'That he killed him, Anna. Oscar is dead because Elijah killed him. But you already knew that, right? It's why you're here talking to me about it and not him.'

Anna closed her eyes as the truth washed over her, Gavin giving her the confirmation she'd been seeking.

Elijah killed him.

The dream . . . the memory . . . it's all real.

How distant he had been at the start of second year. How haunted. Each time Anna went to hold him he'd withdraw from her. A part of her feared it was because he knew about her and Gavin. Or that he'd cheated while on the island. It could have happened so easily: too many shots, too many girls about. And guilt had left him a ghost to her. He flinched every time someone said Oscar's name. Eventually he opened up to her, drunk and distressed – 'It was so awful, Anna. So, so awful. I just keep thinking about how we should have stopped him, forced him to come back to the hotel with us.'

At the time, she assumed he was just a mess because of guilt. But now . . .

Anna had never seen a dead body. Her mother passed away in the hospital, away from her, to an orchestra of beeps and buzzes from the machines gathered around her. She imagined that seeing someone once the life had left them was truly distressing. That losing a friend was something you never got over. But was it different when you were the hand that pushed them? Had she mistaken fear for grief?

'I'm here,' she had told Elijah time and again that year as he shuffled between lectures and the Student Union. 'I'm here.'

Anna held the table, stared at Gavin.

'You're lying,' she rasped, even though she knew he wasn't.

The memory. Elijah's constant desire to banish Oscar to the archives of their life, to never speak of him.

'I wish I was,' he said drily. 'Look,' he stood abruptly, reaching into his pocket for his bank card, 'given the dark turn this meeting has taken, I think we're going to need more drinks. You sticking with a double?'

'Yes.'

In the dream – the memory – Gavin and Elijah were on the beach. Running away from something. Afraid.

'You helped him,' Anna recalled as Gavin placed down fresh drinks.

'Yes,' he said slowly, awkwardly. 'Everything happened pretty fast. I didn't really know what to do. And he . . . he was threatening to call his parents. You know what they're like. How that goes. He'd have pinned it all on me. I know he would, if I refused to help.'

'So what happened?'

Gavin ran a hand through his hair, pained. 'He . . .' he began and then trailed off.

'Tell me,' Anna urged.

'You're in his head now,' Gavin looked at her, tone cautious, 'you've surely had some insight into his . . . temper.'

'Sometimes,' she admitted. 'Some of what I've heard . . . it's been, ugly. Hateful.'

'Shocker,' Gavin deadpanned.

'What are you saying?'

'Elijah has a temper,' he told her, dragging the words out like she were a confused toddler. 'A bad one. A really fucking bad one. Before Kavos I'd seen him go off a few times on nights out. Throw the odd punch. But usually I could rein him in. He just struck me as someone who, you know, ran too cold during the day so sometimes at night they burned too hot.'

'And in Kavos?'

'In Kavos . . .' Gavin groaned, clasped a hand over his mouth. 'You know, I'm really not supposed to talk about it. His parents made me sign a waiver thing.'

'Diane and Henry did?'

'Yeah, they cleaned the whole mess up. We called them the night it happened and his dad sent some lawyer over. Made it so we were never on the beach that night. Framed it that Oscar was always a flight risk because of all the shit with his brother. That he was troubled, and so on. I was told to hold my tongue. Threatened with jail time. A record. We were friends, and I was in shock, afraid, so . . .'

'So you went along with it?'

'Don't judge me,' Gavin said icily, 'not when you weren't there. He was my friend, things got out of hand.'

'What happened with Oscar? He was your friend too.'

'They got into an argument on the beach. It was . . .' Gavin sighed, dragged a hand across his face. 'It happened so fast. One second Oscar was there, the next he was tumbling over the side, hitting the rocks.'

'And you knew he was dead?'

'We knew.' Gavin swallowed uneasily.

'In the dream,' Anna closed her eyes, 'you're on the beach. Both of you. Running away. Back to your hotel.'

'Yeah, it . . . There was a sandy path from the cliff to the main beach. We . . . we panicked. Both of us. We were in shock. At least, I was. Elijah kept telling me that if we got caught out there, with Oscar in the state he was in, both our lives would be over.'

'So why'd you do it?' Anna asked, eyes opening to look at Gavin, searching for remorse within his features. 'Why did you help him?'

'Because he was – is – my friend. Because I was fucking afraid, Anna.'

'Does Elijah ever . . . ever talk about it?'

'No,' Gavin said flatly. 'Clearly he dreams about it, though. Or at least, it's a core memory.'

'I don't . . .' Anna lowered her head, clasped her hands together. 'I just don't . . .'

'Didn't realise he had it in him, did you?' Gavin watched her over his glass as he drank his fresh pint. 'To lie like that?'

'You lied too,' Anna pointed out sharply. 'Why not just tell me, or Helen? We all knew Oscar, cared about him. And to think . . .' The burn of betrayal began to sting.

'Don't sit there and judge me,' Gavin said scornfully. 'I was eighteen and foolish. I made a lot of mistakes back then. Don't you think *I* miss Oscar? He was one of my best fucking friends!'

'Why keep being around Elijah? Why protect him?'

'Think about it.' Gavin eyed her icily. 'If I came out with the truth, what then? He counters it and says it was me who pushed our friend. That I'm the monster. Who would people believe? The clean-cut guy from money or the screw-up?'

'You think he could do it again?' Anna wondered fearfully. 'Hurt someone?'

Gavin gave a shrug. 'Maybe. Maybe not. I didn't think it'd happen the first time. But it did. Like I said, he's got a hair-trigger temper.'

'Do you think he's dangerous?'

Gavin sucked in his cheeks, frowning.

'Do you?' Anna pressed.

'Do *you*?' He turned the question on her. 'I'm guessing you must do, to be sitting here with me in some shitty old pub covered in plasters and scratches. Anna, has he threatened you?' His face flushed with concern. He reached out to stroke her cheek beside her largest scratch. 'Did he do this to you?'

She flinched, swatted him away. 'No . . . no this was all me.' She blinked back tears of shame. Fear.

'What has Eli said to you?' Gavin pressed, urgency creeping into his voice. 'What has he been *thinking*?'

Anna said nothing, cheeks burning. The beach. Oscar. She felt tainted by it all, as though she'd been part of it.

'You're suddenly asking about Kavos, worried about this dream. Memory. Whatever. Why?'

'Like I said, I'm . . . with the chip. I'm seeing Elijah's memories. And I'm afraid . . .'

Rub a dub dub.

'Afraid of what?'

Three men in a tub.

Anna remained silent.

'Don't fuck with me on this, Anna. What's going on in that head of yours?'

And who do you think they be?

The butcher. The baker.

The candlestick maker.

'I think,' her voice trembled as she spoke, 'that there's a chance that . . . that Eli can see my memories too.'

'Fuck,' Gavin roared, smacking the table. 'So you're saying he might know about us?'

All put out to sea.

Anna nodded, body growing cold. 'Yes. I think – I fear – maybe he already knows.'

35

'Why?' Gavin's features twisted with rage. 'Why would you ever agree to that sodding chip, Anna? Why put us at risk like this?'

'I didn't know this would happen,' she countered sharply. 'I thought we would share thoughts, that's it. My chip . . . it was imbedded too deep.'

'Fuck me.' Gavin shook his head, cracked his knuckles, full of nervous energy. 'What did you think it would be like? All sunshine and rainbows, like those ridiculous couples on the beach in the holograms?'

Anna clenched her jaw, met his stare.

'Those are adverts, Anna. *Adverts*. How could you have been so stupid? So reckless?'

'I was trying to keep my husband happy, to . . . to *fulfil* him in at least this one way.' She teetered on the edge of crying but managed to pull herself back. 'Don't . . . don't judge me on this.'

'Don't judge you?' Gavin asked, aghast. 'You did this, Anna. You decided to burn the roof over your head.'

'I'm not even totally sure he does know,' she explained angrily. 'I just . . . With the beach, Kavos, I was afraid he might.'

'And you should be afraid,' Gavin told her. 'As should

I. Because what do you think he's going to do to us when he realises we betrayed him all those years ago?'

Anna swallowed, throat tight.

'I've seen what he's capable of when he's in a rage. I'm not risking being collateral damage of his temper. I can't go back to the office.' He took his phone from his pocket.

'No, please.' Anna reached for his wrist to stop him. 'If you don't go back Elijah might suspect something is wrong. He already thinks you're at a job interview right now.'

'Better that than the truth,' Gavin said quickly.

'Please, just face him, be around him. Be normal,' Anna pleaded.

'No fucking way.' Gavin began typing on his phone. 'If he knows, I'm fucked. A click of his privileged fingers and my job, my life, all of it's in jeopardy. He *knows* people, Anna. Powerful people. I worked for what I have. He didn't. And what about you?' He looked across at her, expression stern.

Anna's chin trembled.

'Him, his family, people like them. They are cold, Anna. Ice fucking cold. Used to cleaning up messes and making sure they come away clean.'

Anna's hand lifted to her plasters, eyes smarting.

'Are you scared he's going to hurt you?' Gavin's voice became low, gaze soft.

Her voice was small. 'No.'

Yes.

'Then why are you here? Why have you never told him the truth about us? About what happened?'

'Because it was your baby,' Anna declared, a single tear upon her cheek. 'The baby I aborted.'

'The baby you . . .'

'Helen must have told you.' Anna sniffed. Gavin managed a single, slow nod.

'It was *yours*. That's why I can't have children now. And he's . . . he's going to find out.'

Gavin stared at her and his pale eyes grew misty. 'It was . . .' His voice was hoarse. 'It was *mine*?'

'Don't act surprised,' Anna sniffed and scolded him. 'You must have known.'

'How?' Gavin touched a hand to his chest. 'How could I have known? Anna, you were *with* Elijah. All the time that we were together.'

'No.' Anna shook her head, wishing it wasn't all so monstrous, so messy. 'Elijah and I . . . he struggled. For a long time. With his anxiety, the drinking.'

'You're telling me you two weren't fucking then?'

Anna stared at her hands. 'No. Not really.'

'Which is how you'd know it was my baby?' Gavin continued.

'Yes.'

'But he thinks you were fucking back then?'

Anna squirmed, bunched her hands together. 'He thinks . . . sometimes we did.'

'But your dreams, memories, whatever, they will relieve him of that notion?'

Slowly she raised her head to look at him, tasting salt on her lips. 'Yes.'

'Anna.' With a groan of despair Gavin dropped his head into his hands. 'Anna, Anna, Anna. What have you done?'

'Please, Gavin, I'm just trying to figure it all out and—'

'Back then, back at uni, I told you what I wanted. To tell Helen. Tell Elijah. Stop living a lie. But you stopped me. You picked Eli with his money, his connections, his fast track to an easy life and security. And *now* you want to raze it all to the ground. Now, when we have careers, mortgages, marriages to think about.'

'I didn't want any of this,' Anna declared desperately. 'I thought . . . I thought we'd share thoughts for a few weeks. That Elijah would get bored of it, move on to the next new thing, and the chips would be removed by Easter.'

'You thought wrong.'

'You think I don't know that?!' Anna was almost shouting. She gestured at her maimed face. 'I'm desperate, Gavin. Desperate and fucking . . .' She felt more tears run down her cheeks. 'Afraid. I'm afraid.'

'You should be.' Gavin's expression was dark. 'If Elijah does know, then we are both in trouble. This isn't just about us cheating together. This is bigger than that. This is about . . .' He leaned back, looked briefly at the ceiling. 'I mean, you're telling me that *I'm* part of the reason he can't have kids with you. That is seriously going to fuck him up, trust me. He struggled with all the fertility stuff – like, really struggled.'

'He did?'

'He's driven by success,' Gavin explained. 'He always has to be the smartest guy in the room, drive the flashiest car. He felt like a failure over it all.' Gavin lifted his glass, finished his lager. 'Only it was never his failure. His issue. It was mine.'

'Gavin—'

'You should have told me,' He gazed at her, pained.

Anna shrugged angrily. 'What good would that have done? It's not like you'd have told me to keep it.'

Gavin exhaled loudly. 'Well, I guess we'll never know. But it seems like you made your mind up about me years ago.' He stood, began pulling on his jacket. Anna hurried to follow him out of the pub, out on to the street.

'You never would have wanted it,' she explained.

'Is that what you think?' Gavin was walking briskly down the street, looking ahead, trying to get away from her.

'I did you a favour,' she blurted. This made him stop, turn to look at her. People trickled by them as they stood outside a bakery, the sun warm on their backs.

'For the record, I'd have told you to keep it.' Gavin didn't meet her gaze as he spoke. 'You know how I felt about you. I'd have changed my whole world for you, but you never let me.'

Anna stood motionless beside him, cowed into silence.

'Clearly, I still care about you,' he laughed at his own weakness, 'which is why I'm here right now. When I should be at fucking work. Telling you all the shit that went down in Kavos even though it could ruin me.' His tone suddenly grew serious as he reached for her shoulders. 'Believe me when I say that you're not safe around Elijah. He'll know. If not from your dreams then from our meeting today. Our thoughts always end up betraying us, Anna. Go home, pack a bag, go stay with your dad. Or Mandie. Just don't be home when he gets in from work.'

'I . . .'

'Do you think about me? About us?'

Anna's face burned.

'Because I still think about you. Our thoughts, they're not something we can contain. Lock away. Control. Anna . . .'

She couldn't stem the flow of tears. 'He's . . .' She could barely find her voice. 'Eli wouldn't hurt me.'

'I watched him shove our friend over a cliff and then use his status to coerce me into helping him cover it up. And that was just an argument over you *possibly* liking me. What you've done,' he inhaled sharply, 'what *we've* done is deceive him. In the worst possible way.'

'I never meant to hurt anyone,' Anna rasped.

'Yet here we are.' Gavin glanced along the length of the street. 'I am heading home and will be avoiding Elijah at all costs. I strongly suggest you do the same.' He went to move from her but hesitated, something holding him in place. 'Fuck it.' He grabbed her chin, kissed her lightly upon her lips, just the once, and then turned, taking long, deliberate strides away from her. Anna stood and watched him leave, until he was gone from view and she was surrounded only by strangers.

Anna's pace was sluggish as she walked home. She tried to focus only on what was around her, not the fallout from her drinks with Gavin. All that she had learned.

Daffodils looking pretty. Staying late this year.

I should really get some for a vase in the kitchen. Living room, too. They'd look so nice, really brighten the place up.

She rounded a corner, made it to her street.

Why is it always so busy even in the middle of the day? So many parked cars?

It was nonsense, thoughts like fluff, but she needed to keep herself occupied.

What shall I have for dinner? Maybe lasagne.

Where have you been?

Anna physically stopped when Elijah's voice entered her head, suddenly breathless.

Just . . . just out for a run. Like I told you.

It was a long run.

I had a lot of energy to burn. How's . . . how's work?

Shit. Gavin is completely MIA. I've tried calling him and he's ignoring my calls. So unlike him. He at least normally checks in, or answers to boast about how late he's going to be.

Didn't he say he had a family emergency?

I phoned Helen and she knew nothing about it.

Oh? You did?

Maybe I've dropped him in it doing that, but I needed to know. The meeting he missed, it was serious. And Helen had absolutely no idea where he might be. Said she'd call me as soon as he got home.

She did?

I feel bad for her. He's clearly messing around behind her back. I told you I think he's been seeing someone.

You don't know that.

I do. And now he's fucked me with all his philandering. I'm going to go bloody ape shit at him when I see him.

What time will you be back?

Where did you say you went for your run?

Just the park. When are you home?

She was on the doorstep now, body slick with sweat even though she'd only been walking, her fear beaded upon her skin for all to see. She pictured Elijah slipping his phone from his pocket to check the notification that alerted him to her arrival, studying her outfit, expression. Watching her.

Late. I need to cover for Gavin's mess.

That's a shame.

Go for something low effort for dinner. I'm not in the mood for a big meal.

Oh, okay, if you're sure?

I'm sure. How are your scratches?

Not too bad.

Beneath the plasters they burned, a reminder of her desperation.

Did you . . . ? Are you sure you can't mute me?

Not this again.

I just—

We remain connected, Anna. What you see, I see.

Anna felt bile creep up to her throat.

See?

Hear, I meant hear. It's already been a long day. Thanks to Gavin.

Sorry.

I'll talk to you later.

Okay. Bye. Love you.

The wind whispered past her ear but her mind was silent. There was birdsong, the sweet melody of spring, the grumble of a passing car. The camera beside her front door flashed green, permitting entry. She took a moment to steel herself before reaching for the handle, a long inhale. Then she stretched forward, opened the door and she was inside, everything looking as she'd left it.

Eli? You okay? She walked down the hallway, towards the kitchen, peering through each doorway as though she expected to be ambushed any second.

I said I love you.

Nothing. Just the pulse of her veins, the gathering of saliva in her mouth. Anna leaned against the island, folded her body over it and pressed her cheek to the cool marble, her warm breath fogging the surface.

'He knows,' she whispered, eyes wide.

Unity

Unity changed my life. For my husband and me, this kind of togetherness is invaluable. I know where he is at all times. And he I. Allowing him into my thoughts was the best thing I've ever done. And why not? He was already in my heart. Becoming OneMind was the next logical step. Try Unity today and discover a level of happiness I didn't even know existed.

M. Daniels, Unity User

36

A shrill beep. From the other side of the room. Anna straightened quickly, blood rushing from her head. She looked around and noticed the digital display for the inbuilt oven glowing blue.

'What the hell?' She walked towards it, examined the setting – a hundred and eighty degrees for two hours. Glancing over her shoulder, Anna tried to figure out what was happening.

Elijah? She felt her blood starting to run cold. *Sweetheart, did you just turn the oven on? Didn't you want something simple for dinner?* Quickly she pressed the power button, blue light dying, the oven ceasing to hum.

'Fuck's sake,' she said aloud. For a moment she studied the oven, puzzled, then she turned her back on it, heading for the hallway. She'd barely reached the doorway when there was a beep behind her. Followed by a gentle humming sound.

Elijah, what the hell? Is that you? Either this is you on that ridiculous app or the oven is malfunctioning.

Turning to the kitchen, Anna glowered at the oven, at its glowing instructions.

This isn't funny.

The oven continued to hum.

'Fine,' she threw up her hands, 'have the oven on. See if I care.'

As Anna walked through the hallway, she glanced up the stairs, then eyed the utility room that led to the back door. She was suddenly acutely aware of every little dot of light. Every slice of automation through her home. It was atop doorways, along windows. In high corners where security cameras peered out. Elijah could see – and control – *everything*. Checking her phone was in her pocket, Anna marched to the utility room, flung open the back door and strode out into the garden, making for her studio. It was the one place in her home absent of cameras. Or gadgets. Other than her ancient heater.

'We should really fit cameras and a locking device out there,' Elijah had suggested when he was kitting out the house. 'We need to protect your art.'

'No,' Anna had told him quickly. 'I need that space to be . . . simpler. It helps me focus.'

In truth, she was just sick of it all. The apps. The monitors. She didn't need to use her phone to turn on the oven, or lock a window. She was more than capable of doing those things herself.

'It's about ease,' Elijah kept reminding her.

'Well, it's easier for me if we don't have it all.'

The door to the studio slapped shut behind her. Anna breathed in the pine, the oils. With a shuddery breath she went to the small single window and peered up at her house.

'He's trying to scare me,' she concluded over the incident with the oven. And the worst part was it had worked. Taking out her phone, she opened up her contacts and pressed Mandie's name, foot tapping loudly against the floor as she waited on each drawn-out bleat of the ring tone.

Finally –

'Hey.' Mandie's voice, as bright and welcoming as the sun after a dark day.

'Oh, Mandie, thank God.' It was only as she spoke that Anna realised how knotted her chest felt, how laboured her breaths were.

'Everything all right?'

'No.' Anna pressed a hand to her forehead, twisted her back to the window. 'Can I . . . can I come and stay at yours for a bit?'

'My place? Yeah, hon, of course. What's wrong? What's happened?' There was a murmur of voices behind Mandie. 'Sorry,' she said loudly, 'I'm just at Westfield picking up some bits.'

'It's fine.'

'No, no, let me . . .' A muffled sound on the other end. 'Here, I've dipped into a quiet shop. Oh, Christ, scented candles. We both know I'll leave with three minimum. I'll grab you one too.'

'Thanks.' Although Elijah wouldn't allow Anna to burn scented candles within the house.

'Not only are they a fire hazard, Anna, some studies have shown that the smoke they create can be toxic,' he'd told her, face poker straight.

'They're just candles, Eli. To make the house smell like cotton or vanilla.'

'I won't have us inhaling the fumes.'

'Fine.' Anna had relented, the guilt she carried over her broken womb always weakening her resolve. Sometimes she felt that he knew that, exploited it.

'Babe, what's wrong?' Mandie asked, serious.

'I just need to not be here,' Anna explained, speaking quickly, nervously.

'Okay, well, come be at mine. You know you're always more than welcome. But . . . what's happened at home?'

'He knows.'

She heard the intake of breath from Mandie. 'He knows? Like, for real? Are you sure?'

'I'm sure.' Anna glanced over her shoulder at the window framing the structure of her house. How it loomed like a tower over her little slice of garden. Of freedom.

'What's he said?'

'He hasn't said anything yet. He's just acting strange.'

'And it's definitely that?'

'I think . . .' Anna closed her eyes.

No I love you.

The oven.

Oscar.

The silence.

Muting the chip. All the time.

Gavin.

Gavin.

He knows.

'It's definitely that.' It wasn't like Elijah to fuck with her. Toy with her like this.

'Okay, well then, yeah, come to mine. I'll head straight there now.'

'Great, thanks.'

'You don't think it's worth, maybe, talking to him about it all?'

'No.' The refusal came instantly.

'I'm only saying that, because, well, it's Elijah and, hon, he's your husband. I know the whole situation is a mess, but I'm sure you guys can work it out. If you want to.'

'No.' Anna was shaking her head back and forth. 'I can't . . . I can't talk to him.'

'Are you sure?'

'I think about him too much.'

'Elijah?'

Gavin.

'No,' Anna admitted so quietly she wondered if her friend had heard. 'My thoughts . . . I think they . . . I thought I was in control and . . .' She couldn't finish the sentence.

'Okay, deep breath, stay calm.'

'He'll . . .' She closed her eyes, held back tears. 'Mandie, I'm worried he'll hurt me.'

'Right, okay. Shit. Yeah. Get your arse over here right now then.'

'It's just . . .' Anna slumped against the wall of her studio. Her shed. 'Gavin told me something about him and now I'm . . . I'm scared.'

'What did Gavin say?' Mandie's voice was sharp in her ear. 'Wait, you saw Gavin today?'

'Mmm.'

'Why? You know what, doesn't matter. Where are you now?'

'My studio.'

'Right, I need you to march into the house, go to your bedroom, bundle up some shit and come straight to mine. Got it?'

Anna sniffed loudly.

'Don't bother with the tube; I'll set up a car to collect you, okay?'

'I've fucked up.' Anna felt her knees begin to tremble. 'The chip. Unity. I should never—'

'Sweetheart, have a pity party later. Okay? Right now, let's focus on getting you somewhere *safe*. Do you need me to come get you? Would that help?'

The first time she'd seen Mandie, in that sequin bodysuit, she glittered like a star. Anna couldn't help but be drawn to her as they laughed over her e-cigarette.

'Mandie Simone,' she'd said, elegantly extending a hand for Anna to shake, as though she were royalty. 'Like Nina,' she'd added with a cheeky smirk. 'One day I'm going to be headlining the Grammys, just you wait and see.'

Anna had laughed, admiring her confidence. 'Anna Weston,' she'd said as she shook Mandie's hand, 'one day I'm going to have my art hanging in the Tate.'

Mandie's eyes had shone approvingly. 'A fellow dreamer, I love it. Yes, girl. One day we are going to have it all.'

Only having it all looked like painting cat portraits that didn't sell in a shed. And living in a studio flat above a kebab shop and taking any paid gigs they could find. Sometimes Anna wondered how long you were able to keep chasing a dream. How long until you had to admit it had slipped from your grasp, or that you were never holding it at all.

'Anna? You still there?'

'Can you . . . ?' Anna was still looking up at her house, at the blank windows. 'Mandie, come get me.'

'On my way. Like, literally, I'm backing away from the candles and I'll order a car – it'll be faster than walking between tube stations. Do you need me to stay on the phone to you?'

'No, no, I need to pack.'

'Okay. Okay.' She could almost hear Mandie's mind racing, processing everything. 'So, I'll come get you, we go straight to mine?'

'Please.'

'Are you . . . are you all right?'

'No.' Anna swept a hand across her cheeks. 'But this is a mess of my own making. I can't . . .' She blew out an uneasy breath. 'I guess I always feared this was coming.'

'Everyone makes mistakes,' Mandie told her gently.

'I know. See you soon.' Anna hung up, turned to look at the half-complete landscape of a beach she'd previously turned towards the wall. Would she ever get the chance to finish it? If she fled now, what would become of her and Elijah?

If she stayed...

'He killed someone.' Anna whispered the truth aloud, needing to say it. To hear it. Elijah, her Elijah. Her husband. He was a killer. And it wasn't just someone. He'd killed their friend. Oscar. Someone they all cared about, someone they drank with, laughed with. One of their *best* friends. All over a suggestion of something existing between Anna and Gavin. What she had done to Elijah – what she had put him through – that was far, far worse.

Pushing open the shed door, Anna stepped into the garden, the air cooling. She looked down at her phone. It was almost three in the afternoon. That gave her enough time. Elijah was never home before five. And he'd even mentioned that work was extra busy. That he'd be late.

Because of Gavin.

Anna scrolled down her screen, found his name. She was tapping out a message to him before she had chance to think better of it.

I'm going to go and stay at Mandie's.

She was halfway across the lawn when her phone pinged with his reply.

I think that's for the best. He called Helen.

Anna hung her head guiltily, writing her response.

I know.

How had Helen reacted to Elijah's call? Did her cool composure crack, just for a second?

Was she worried?

'Stop fucking thinking,' Anna snapped aloud, knowing she needed to safeguard her mind now more than ever. She made it to the back door when her phone pinged within her hand.

She's majorly pissed. He crossed a line calling her, he'll know that. You need to get out of that house before he gets home.

Anna whimpered, fear tight in her chest. She opened the door, stepped inside, a chirp announcing a sensor had detected her movement. So often she ignored these small noises; now they were like gunshots. Flinching, she went through the utility room, towards the hallway. Pausing at the entrance to the kitchen she peered in to see the oven aglow.

Calm. She needed to be calm.

Babe, the oven is still on. Want me to put something in it?

'Don't let him know you're freaking out, that you're leaving,' Anna loudly told herself.

Did you fancy that frozen pizza we've got? Or there's that veggie casserole your mum made we still have in there.

The staircase wheezed as Anna powered up the wooden steps.

Little Bo Peep.

Has lost her sheep.

She was at the top of the stairs, making the sharp turn into their bedroom.

And doesn't know where to find them.

'Mandie is on her way,' she whispered to herself, needing to calm her nerves.

Leave them alone and they will come home.

'Just pack your shit up and get out of here. You need to be gone before he's back.'

Wagging their tails behind them.

37

It was a small, cream holdall with soft brown leather straps. The last time Anna had filled it, she'd been preparing to go on a weekend away with Elijah. To the cabin they were so fond of. Within the woodlands, among the trees.

'How is this happening?' she asked herself as she hastily opened drawers, grabbed at knickers, socks, a T-shirt, a jumper. Stuffing them all inside the bag without any consideration, any care. It just needed to be done.

Little Miss Muffet, sat on her tuffet, eating her curds and whey.

In went some pyjamas. Navy satin and lace. A pale pink zip-through hoodie. Then Anna was pacing towards the bathroom, grabbing her rose-gold electric toothbrush, the hard, glittery shell of her tangle teaser.

Along came a spider who sat down beside her.

Anna chucked everything from the bathroom in with her clothes.

And frightened Miss Muffet away.

With a loud rip the zip was closed. Anna was packed. For a moment she looked down at her bag, breathing hard.

Don't think.

Her phone buzzed from where she'd dropped it on the bed. Anna grabbed it, grateful for the distraction. It was a message from Mandie.

Babe, traffic is shocking but I'm on my way xx

Anna was about to phone her when a call came, phone vibrating in her hand, Helen's name flashing on the screen.

Shit.

Chewing on a thumbnail, Anna looked to the bed, then the window.

'Hello?' she answered tightly.

'Hey.' Helen's voice was clipped in her ear.

'Look,' Anna moved back to the window, hung behind the thick grey curtain as she studied the street, 'this isn't a good time.'

'I figured.'

'I'm just in the middle of—'

'I'll make this quick,' Helen declared sharply. 'I've always known, Anna. About you and Gavin.'

Anna felt dizzy. She doubled back to the bed, perched on the end of it, phone pressed tight to her ear.

'Honestly, you'd have to be blind not to see it,' she added bitterly. 'But, well, it seems Elijah didn't know. I suppose they say love makes us blind, which must account for it.'

Anna could feel the panicked rising and falling of her chest. 'He said he'd called you,' she managed to mutter.

'When Elijah phoned to ask after Gavin, where he was, he began asking about you. About what happened at uni. When I shared with him what I knew, he went very quiet, and I didn't like that.'

Anna pressed a hand to her chest, skin damp with sweat.

'I thought perhaps he was just, you know, processing it all. That he'd shout, scream, whatever, in private. But Gavin has just come home and disturbed me in my office, white as a sheet, and told me about Kavos. What happened there with Oscar.' Now Helen's voice was on the brink of breaking. 'I never,' she continued, almost breathless, 'I never knew they'd been there, Anna. That Elijah had—' Helen stopped speaking and Anna imagined her clamping a hand over her mouth to calm herself, to suppress her sorrow.

It felt like the world was spinning. Anna's head pounded. She clutched the phone, trying to remain upright. A tight cough on the other end of the line: Helen composing herself.

'I'm phoning because in spite of everything I care about you, Anna. Elijah knows about you and Gavin, and the implications of what you two did. Now I know what he could be capable of. I wouldn't be able to live with myself if I didn't call you now to warn you.'

Anna couldn't speak. Head bowed, her shoulders shook as she held in sobs.

'Gavin says you're heading to Mandie's. Good.' She drew in a feathery breath. 'Maybe text me when you get there, all right? Let me know you are safe.'

'I'm . . .' Anna was shaking, needing to find the words. 'Helen, I'm sorry.'

'I don't want your platitudes.'

'I never meant to—'

'I'm hanging up now. Text me when you're safe.'

The ensuing silence after the call was deafening.

When you're safe.

Anna looked around. Her bedroom, the bed she'd made that very morning, carefully pulling up the dove-grey duvet, peeling it back at the top. The mirrored surface of her vanity, a nightmare to clean, forever getting smeared, now casting back her shifted, anxious image.

I'm a mess.

Sweat gathered under her armpits, darkening the fabric of her T-shirt. Her cheeks were blotchy, the dressings bulky.

'Get out,' she whispered to herself. 'Get the fuck out of the house.'

She stood, grabbed the handles of her holdall, made for the door, when her phone buzzed against her palm: an incoming call from Mandie.

'I'm about to leave.'

'The traffic remains horrific,' her friend told her briskly. 'I've been stuck over by Dormer Street for the last ten minutes and I'm,' her voice began to rise, 'losing my shit. What are you doing? Where are you?'

'Packed.' Anna lifted the holdall even though Mandie couldn't see her.

'Okay, perfect. The satnav thing says I'll be at yours in twenty. Can you hang on that long?'

'Yeah, I should be fine.'

'Any sign of Elijah yet?'

'No. None.'

Elijah?

'Okay, good. We still have time. Are you happy to wait at home?'

Eli? Talk to me. Please.

'Anna?'

'Y-yeah. I can wait here. He's still at work.'

'Just hold tight. Okay?'

'Okay.'

'I love you.'

'Love you too.'

Anna pushed her phone into a pocket of her holdall. She was about to leave the bedroom when she spotted the picture on the wall. She and Elijah on their wedding day, the image in black and white, placed in a silver frame. They looked so happy. Anna, elegant in her gown, hair drawn back in a bun, tendrils falling into her face as she laughed so hard she was doubling over, her new husband swooping in to catch her, his own face cracking with laughter. He was so handsome in his suit. She could remember how he smelt, of limes and whiskey, as he kissed her that day. How he'd held her close and whispered in her ear, 'This is the start of forever.'

With a start Anna realised she was crying. Sniffing, she used her free hand to wipe at her eyes.

This is the start of forever.

She looked at the couple in the photograph. Caught in a moment of pure joy. Sand at their feet, the sun at their back.

Elijah?

Nothing.

Had he muted her?

Anna looked down to the grey carpet at her feet, remembering the sand from her dream. She detached from the past, hurried on to the landing, taking the sharp corner towards the staircase. The house was beeping and chirping as though it had come alive. Anna had no idea what Elijah was furiously turning on and off: the oven, the kettle. It didn't matter. She'd soon be outside. She could wait for Mandie on the street if she had to.

Less chance of a scene out there.

The thought of being beyond the house, around people, was suddenly extremely appealing. Anna moved faster down the stairs, the hallway in sight. Within her bag she felt the tremor of her phone buzzing. Pausing at the bottom step, Anna pulled her phone from the pocket, saw the message from Gavin on the screen –

> Sorry about Helen. I felt I had to tell her about Oscar. About the beach.

Transparency.
　Unity.

How had their marriage ultimately had that when hers had not? And more than that ... were they now working through it?

How long had Helen known about what happened in their shabby kitchen back at uni?

'She said she'd always known. Which means she forgave him all along,' Anna whispered aloud.

Hope fluttered in her chest.

'Elijah could forgive me.' She tried the notion on for size, placing it on her tongue and breathing life into it. 'We might be okay. This might be something we look back on and laugh about in twenty years.' But the words, as she said them, she didn't feel them. The question which Mandie had originally asked her came back to haunt her.

'What would he do if he found out?'

In her mind's eye she saw Oscar falling, fluttering through the air before breaking upon dark rocks, waves rising up to greet him.

Anna breathed out her answer as a figure appeared behind the glass of the front door. 'He'd kill me.'

She knew it was him. The height. The shape. She was both drawn to him and repelled. Anna went with the latter feeling, turning and sprinting back up the stairs, bag in hand. She disappeared into the bedroom just as the door clicked open.

The concept of Unity came from a simple one – my partner and I were on separate continents for work. Phone calls were becoming troublesome; we struggled to make the time difference work. She was in Africa, on location as a wildlife photographer. Her signal could be intermittent at best. More than anything, I wanted to be able to tell her that I loved her. Like I told her every night when we were together.

That simple desire for connection, that was the foundation for developing the microchip. Wanting to be able to tell somebody, anytime, anywhere, that you love them. We used state-of-the-art nano-technology, expanding on previous research into cerebral states and cognitive enhancements. It took ten years to progress from the prototype stage. Ten years of blood, sweat and a lot of tears. But myself and my team, we never gave up. Because we understood the importance of being able to connect. Of being able to share your love, your feelings, regardless of distance.

Now, when my partner goes away we are in constant contact. I no longer need to worry about where she is, if she's safe. And I tell you, that kind of peace of mind is invaluable. You truly cannot put a price on it. I worked to make my dream a reality not just for myself, but for everyone. I tell her every night that I love her. And hearing it straight back is the best feeling in the world.

> Unity is true connection. OneMind is true peace and I'm so blessed to be able to share this with the world.
>
> Emerald Reeve, Unity Co-founder

38

Anna stood motionless, straining to hear if her husband was coming up the stairs. Her holdall was tossed on the bed behind her.

A click.

From downstairs.

The front door closing. The twist of the lock.

Anna's breath felt unbearably loud as she edged towards the bedroom door, a floorboard creaking beneath her.

Shit.

Anna.

His voice in her head was suddenly dizzying, she staggered back from the door, stretching out a hand to the bed, which she sagged against as she crumpled to the ground.

Elijah? Are you okay?

She squeezed her eyes shut, panicking.

You've been so quiet today.

There were no sounds in the house below her. No footsteps pounding up the stairs. Had she been expecting fireworks? An eruption as soon as Elijah walked through the door?

Where was he?

Elijah, you're scaring me.

Did you enjoy your lunch with Gavin?

Her head pounded.

Let me . . . let me just explain.

He told me it was a family emergency. I suppose in a warped way it was. The two of you, always so close.

Eli—

To think I was actually worried about him when I called Helen. I should have done it years ago, shouldn't I? Called her. Voiced my worries. Maybe she'd have spoken up sooner and saved me all this mess. All these wasted years.

Anna slunk down from the window, pressing a hand to her chest.

Don't say that.

I loved you, Anna. Like truly. A sort of love I used to think didn't exist. I would have done anything for you. I gave you everything.

Elijah, I know, just let me—

All along you were harbouring this secret. This deception.

Eli—

How could you lie to me like that, Anna? Beyond the cheating. The lying. That's what burns the worst. And to think it was with him.

Look, there's no way—

Don't say it. Don't say there's no way of knowing whose baby it was. Don't shame yourself further, Anna. We both knew my struggles when we began dating. It took me a year to get my anxiety in check. There was no way that baby could have been mine. But you fooled me. Back when I was doe-eyed and in love, you told me it was mine. Let me console you as you wept after your

botched abortion. You did that. Do you have any idea how fucked up that is? How scheming?

Elijah, if you'd just calm down, we can talk about this.

Calm down? Where? Here? In our home? In the house I bought for us. The mortgage I pay. The world I gave to you. In exchange for what? A nest of lies?

I don't know what Helen told you but—

Never mind what Helen said; this is about you, Anna. How your thoughts have been betraying you since we got the Unity chips. Half the time I don't think you're even aware of what's going on in your own head. Do you dream of him often, Anna?

I had a dream about you. About a beach.

Back at the cabin, you thought of him. Of your little tryst in the kitchen. Of how good it all felt. It made me sick to my stomach.

Eli—

A part of me always knew – or at least, always feared it. When I heard about Unity I knew it was what I'd been looking for, a way to get definite answers from you. About Gav. Then with our anniversary looming, it all fell into place. A chance to finally know what secrets you were keeping from me, once and for all.

What about your secrets? What about all that you kept from me?

Anna found the fight within her, got to her feet, eyes burning a hole into the bedroom door she kept expecting her husband to walk through.

I had a dream of a beach in Kavos. Of a dead man. Of Oscar.

I see Gavin sang like a canary. How typical of him.

Elijah, I've seen it. What you did to Oscar.

And do you know what I've seen? A spoilt wife playing house in a home she doesn't deserve.

You're a murderer!

I see a woman on the edge. Driven to madness by her faulty Unity chip. You talk of dreams. Memories. Hallucinations. It's all on your file at Unity.

My chip is faulty! They . . . they checked it there for me. Told me it had been embedded too deep.

And you told me you couldn't wait a month for it to be removed. That you couldn't cope. You even tried to claw it out yourself. Using manicure scissors, of all things. And you failed at that. Like you fail at everything.

Anna made her hands into fists as she stood within the bedroom, straining to listen beyond the whirr of words in her head.

Have you had the mute function all along?

Of course I could always mute my chip, Anna. Do you really think I'd be so foolish as to get mine installed without it?

You lied to me!

And you to me. Only yours was much, much worse. Wasn't it?

Why didn't you tell me the truth about Oscar?

Whose truth? Gavin's? Did he tell you I pushed him? Is that what he said? And let me guess, you believed it, drank it all in like the idiot you are.

He told me what you did. How you convinced him to protect you.

Of course. Because he has no free will. And you never considered that he is just lying to you, and that what we told you about Oscar has always been the truth.

I've seen what you did.

In what? A dream? Well then, it must be fact.

She knew he was mocking her.

It's a memory, Eli. Your memory, of what you did.

How awful it must be for you to be on the edge like this. You could do anything in this vulnerable state of mind. Anything.

Her hands went instantly limp at her sides. There was no ambiguity over Elijah's words. His threat. Anna looked to her holdall, perched on the bed.

Mandie is on her way over.

So she gets to find you. Lucky her.

This isn't you, Elijah.

Anna was shaking.

You wouldn't hurt me. She bit down on her lip to stop herself from crying out, wishing she believed her own thoughts.

Tears silently dripped down her cheeks.

You didn't stop to ask for my version of events, just accepted his. Do you not think I'd be in jail if I'd killed someone?

Anna was staring at her holdall.

Come on, Mandie. Hurry up.

How could it be possible for Gavin to know about this supposed murder and no one else?

Your parents.

Anna swallowed, throat coarse.

They covered everything up. Had him sign an NDA.

Of course you think that. You never have liked them.

They've never liked me! They avoid coming over as much as they can.

Do you feel like they treat you as a second-rate wife, that they blame you for their lack of grandchildren?

Anna clenched her jaw, teeth grinding together.

You're being unfair.

I think that role belongs to you, Anna. You've been more than unfair to me. You've been cruel. Cold. I loved you; did that ever matter to you?

Of course it did.

She surveyed the room, the window, her only potential exit point.

It does. It does matter.

All these years you've let me resent Gavin. Bemoan him at every chance. And you knew. You always knew what had gone on between you. Were the two of you laughing behind my back?

No! Of course not! We never . . . we never—

And today. It was him you went running to.

Elijah, can we—

A click. Downstairs. Anna heard it distinctly.

I'm a good husband. I deserve better than what I got. I deserve more than your regret.

She looked again to her bag, grabbed its leather handle and bundled it into the walk-in wardrobe, following closely behind, carefully clicking the door closed behind her.

I want a family, Anna. There is no shame in that. None at all. I want a new start. A fresh start. With someone who hasn't fucked me over, repeatedly.

Anna pulled herself into a tight ball, resting her chin atop her knees.

I wanted forever with you, Anna. I'm sorry that wasn't good enough for you.

A chirp. Loud and close. The snap of locks twisting.

Anna whimpered. She recognised the sound. The locks on the doors, the windows. He'd activated them all, trapping her inside.

39

Anna didn't dare breathe. A tear sliced down her cheek.

Why bother hiding? I know you're here. I see everything. Remember?

Don't think.

Don't. Think.

It was dark within the walk-in wardrobe. The only movement the gentle rocking as Anna shifted back and forth, knees bunched up tight to her chest.

Don't think.

She wanted to listen out for a creak. The thud of a footstep. Anything. But each time she stilled her breath enough to focus, her thoughts began to betray her.

Jack and Jill.

Anna felt the heat of a tear streak down her cheek, tasted its salty death on her lips.

Went up the hill.

She just needed to wait. Wait and not think. She could do that, couldn't she? Her thoughts were hers alone to control. Only—

To fetch a pail of water.

There was movement just beyond the wardrobe. Was someone in the bedroom?

Jack fell down.

She rocked back and forth. Back and forth.

Rain whispered against the windows but Anna couldn't hear it, barely any sounds reached her within the wardrobe, her chosen prison. Pressed suits and elegant tea dresses hung just inches above her. Carrying the scent of him. Of her.

And broke his crown.

Perhaps it wasn't perfect, but she had to hide somewhere. Hide and gather her thoughts. Smother them.

Another noise. This one closer. Anna clenched the breath within her chest, refused to release it, ceased rocking.

And Jill came tumbling after.

Will you stop with the fucking nursery rhymes? They are driving me insane. Do you think I don't know what you're doing? Trying to stop me getting in your head.

She could smell the sweat that had gathered in her armpits. Saliva thick in her mouth, tasting sour.

Not in the shed, then. Sorry, studio. I built it, for you. To let you carry out your fantasy of being a painter. To keep you happy. Always doing everything for you. Everything. And for me . . . well. You fucked me, Anna. Truly.

Anna closed her eyes, pictured her little studio, Elijah storming in, thunderous with anger, toppling over the heater. Knocking down the easel and the unfinished picture upon it, her incomplete beach ending up on the floor, on its side. She looked to the closed door of the wardrobe.

Come on, Mandie.

I've locked the house, Anna. Through the app which you refused to even try to use. The doors and windows only open for me now. The house thinks it is on high alert. Mandie can knock on the front door all she wants, she won't get in.

She'll call the police.

Let her. And when they arrive I'll tell them how you've been driven mad by your faulty Unity chip. We might even make the news.

Mandie knows everything.

Great. Shall I call Gav, ask him to come round? Make this a full-blown party?

You're being insane.

Are you upstairs?

Anna was stone. Cold and unmoving. She didn't even blink.

Foolish place to hide, don't you think? Backing yourself into a corner.

Don't think.

Think as much as you want. I'll find you either way. There're only so many places you can hide in this house.

More chirps.

Anna's breath was shaky. She tried to decipher the sound, like something being scanned. Cameras?

You're sweeping the rooms.

Bingo.

Fuck.

Fuck indeed. If you'd only bothered to try the app you'd see that we have cameras placed on the landing, in the hallway, the kitchen, the lounge.

Anna quietly unfurled her body, crept close to the wardrobe door, and pressed her ear against it, listening.

Do you cum thinking about him? When it's me inside you, do you wish it was him?

Buzzing. Loud and close.

'Shit.' Anna scurried back to the holdall, pulling her phone free from the front pouch. A message from Mandie.

> Babe I've tried to call but your phone keeps going to voicemail.
> Are you okay? I'm about ten mins away xxx

Anna looked at the screen, noticing the icon in the top corner flickering.

You're blocking the phone signal.

Only yours. Another benefit of my app: I can control which devices can be active within the house. You seriously should have downloaded this for yourself. So practical. So useful.

Anna tossed her phone back into the bag, moved towards the wardrobe door, dared to crack it open a fraction, enough to allow her to peer out into her bedroom. The day had grown dark, rain peppering the window.

I wish there was a way to erase memories. I bet in ten years the tech will be there. Because I'd love to forget about you. And him. Together. I worry that whenever I close my eyes, or whenever I think of you, that's all I'll see.

Through the crack Anna studied the room, eyes wide.

A creak.

She knew that sound. It was from the staircase. Third step from the bottom. It cracked like an old man's back whenever she stepped on it. How she loathed that step when sleeplessness claimed her and she'd wander downstairs for a glass of water. Or when she'd return home late from a night out with Mandie, giggly and clumsy.

Anna didn't think. She just acted. She threw open the wardrobe door, sprang to her feet and bolted from the bedroom, straight onto the landing, to the top of the stairs.

Unity gave me what I needed. For years I feared what my husband was doing when he was out of the house, where he went. My paranoia threatened to destroy us. I'd try to go through his phone, his emails. I struggled to build trust. After we got the chips, everything changed. I realised I didn't need to worry, ever. That I was the only woman ever on his mind. Through Unity, we built the trust I'd always longed for. We became OneMind, just like we were already One Heart and One Soul.

I can't thank Unity enough for what they did for my marriage. How they saved me.

Connie S. Roberts, Unity User

40

Anna was on the small landing, rounding to the top of the stairs, heart like a jackhammer in her chest. Elijah was rising up to meet her, face distorted with anger, nostrils flared wide.

'Stay the fuck away from me!' she screamed as he reached the top step, thrusting her hands forward. They connected with his chest. He toppled backwards and stared at her, fear suddenly filling his eyes as he felt gravity's grasp against him.

The snap of bone hitting wood. Elijah fell on to his back and then tumbled awkwardly down into the hallway, his body spread across the three lower steps. Still and unmoving.

'Shit,' Anna squeaked from where she remained on the landing, hands still outstretched. 'Shit.' Shaking, she reached for the banister, gripped it tight.

'Elijah?' She whispered his name, watching his body for a twitch. Anything. 'Elijah?'

Her husband was like stone.

'Fuck.' She twisted back to the landing, grimacing.

Fuck, fuck, fuck. Elijah! Elijah, speak to me!

She needed a murmur, a groan. Something.

'Fuck,' Anna repeated as she forced her legs to stand and carefully plotted her way down the stairs. When she was just above Elijah's feet, where they were caught on the creaking third step, she froze. It made her think of the games she'd play as a child, where someone would pretend to be sleeping and then lash out when you crept too close. Was Elijah going to suddenly kick out at her? Was this all just an act?

Elijah, just tell me you're okay.

Hers was the only voice in her mind. The hallway filled with her harried breathing. 'Shit. Come on.' She made herself descend completely into the hallway, crouched beside her husband. Elijah's eyes were closed, bringing a peacefulness to him which was completely at odds with the man who'd been climbing the stairs to reach her. Tenderly, Anna reached out and stroked his hair. It felt like the monster had retreated and her husband had been returned to her.

Speak to me, please. Let me know you're all right.

Crouching beside him, Anna lifted his hand, warm within hers. Pressed her fingers to his wrist, felt the thin presence of a pulse. 'Okay, okay, good.' She dropped his hand to stroke his forehead. She was about to edge closer to his face when the sound of the doorbell split through the room.

'Fuck,' Anna gasped, falling away from Elijah. Turning she saw a figure at the door.

Mandie.

She scrambled to her feet, went to pull on the handle. Only –

It didn't budge. Above the door an alarm gave a single beep in warning.

The locks. The stupid, sodding locks.

Anna glanced back at Elijah. His phone. She needed his phone.

'Just wait there,' she shouted through the door.

'Is everything all right?' Mandie called back, pressing her face up against the glass, peering inside.

'One moment.'

Anna was again on her knees at Elijah's side, rooting in his pockets. She quickly found his phone, withdrawing it carefully, still expecting a hand to close, iron tight around her wrist, stopping her. But he remained still. When she leaned close to him she heard his shallow breaths.

'Right, okay . . .' She held his phone before her. 'Pin code. Shit.'

Elijah, I need you. I need to get you help. Please, please answer me. Pin code for your phone. What is it?

'Hon? Are you all right? Is he there?' Mandie shouted to her.

'One second!'

Anna studied the phone in her grasp. It was asking her for six digits.

'Come on, come on.' Her foot tapped anxiously against the wooden floor. She entered her wedding date. Declined.

'Okay, Anna, think. Think.'

This is Elijah. What six numbers would he have as his pin?

Her temple throbbed. Knowing her husband, it would be six random numbers, unconnected to anything, to make it harder to guess. He was the kind of person who had different passwords for everything. And miraculously remembered them all. Anna had used the same pin code for over ten years; it matched the pin number for her cards. And still there were times when she struggled to remember it.

A groan. Very slight. At her feet.

'Elijah?' Anna panicked, looked at him, eyes still closed. 'Your pin, I need your pin.'

If not their wedding day then—

My birthday. Like the alarm. Dammit, Eli.

She entered her date of birth, mouth dry. The phone unlocked with a bright chirp. The same code for the house alarm. It was always about her. Always.

'Find the app . . .' Anna scanned the numerous icons,

recognising the silhouette of a house with a green heart within it. The app Elijah had kept telling her to install. She clicked it, pressed the prompt saying that everything was fine. Around her the house beeped with relief, locks and bolts untwisting. With a gasp Anna reached for the front door, Mandie bursting in.

'Oh my God, are you all right? Thank God you're all right.' Mandie was looking at her, frantic. 'Jesus, your face. What happened to your face?' Then she turned and saw Elijah's figure at the foot at the stairs. Screamed. 'Fuck! Fuck, Anna, what's happened?'

'He . . . he . . .' Anna felt like she was being strangled by her own nerves. She drank in air, looked desperately at her husband. 'He fell. He was coming up to get me and he took the stairs too fast.'

'Oh my God.' Mandie was kneeling at his side, holding her hand before his mouth. 'He's still breathing.'

'He needs an ambulance.' Anna looked down at the phone, typed in three nines.

'Okay, okay. Just breathe, honey. Everything will be okay.'

Two rings.

'999, please state your emergency.'

'It's my husband . . .' Anna dragged a hand through her hair. 'He fell down the stairs and now he's . . . he's unconscious.'

'Sixty-two Lemmington Park, is this you?'

'Yes.'

'Is he breathing?'

'Yes.'

'Can you see any blood?'

Anna shook her head. 'N-no.'

'An ambulance is on the way. Do you need me to stay on the line with you?'

'My . . .' Anna felt dizzy.

This can't be happening.

'No, it's all right. My friend is here with me.'

'Okay, good. Try to stay calm. The ambulance is six minutes out.'

Anna hung up.

'He's got a pulse but it's weak.' Mandie got up, looked at Anna, face drained of colour.

'What do we do?'

'We wait.' Mandie gripped her friend's slim shoulders. 'The ambulance will soon be here; they'll help.'

'He was so angry with me.' Anna felt her face beginning to crumble. 'He was shouting and making threats.'

Mandie embraced her. 'Shh, honey. I know, I know. But it's over now, just breathe.'

'H-Helen called and—' She couldn't speak. The sobs came heavy and fast, choking her.

'It'll be okay, it'll be okay,' Mandie said over and over as she held her in the hallway. 'It was just a terrible accident. Breathe.'

And people have accidents all the time.

They heard the peel of sirens before they saw the ambulance. The pulse of blue lights blocked the road as paramedics ran in, firing questions at her.

'How long has he been like this?'

'Have you tried to move him?'

'Any underlying medical conditions?'

She answered as best she could. And then Elijah was being raised up onto a gurney, strapped into place, eyes still closed. Anna could only sputter and sob.

'Are you coming with him?' The shorter paramedic, a stocky brunette with an overly tight bun, was looking at her.

'I—' Anna turned to Mandie, feeling lost.

'She's going.' Mandie nudged her out of the front door. 'I'll get back in the taxi and be right behind you, okay?'

Anna stumbled out into the street, rain soaking into her clothes, mingling with the sweat they were already stained with. A crowd of onlookers had gathered outside her house, gawping and gossiping. Mandie's hands reached for hers, held them tight.

'Go to the hospital, be with Elijah, tell them what happened. Okay?'

Anna sniffed and nodded.

'You can do this.'

'I can't . . .' Anna's tears swirled with rain upon her cheeks. 'I can't hear him.'

'That doesn't mean anything.'

'Have I—'

Mandie drew her close, whispering directly into her ear, 'Go to the hospital, tell them how he fell. It's all going to be all right, got it?'

Anna gave a shaky nod and then climbed into the back of the ambulance. The metal doors slammed shut, sealing her in. She perched beside the gurney and Elijah's lifeless body.

Please, please just say something.

'So you're his wife?'

The brunette was in the back with her, fixing an oxygen mask over Elijah's face.

'Yes.' Anna jolted as the ambulance lurched forwards.

'You did the right thing calling as soon as you did.' Now the paramedic was leaning over Elijah, furiously tapping the back of his hand.

'Will he be all right?' Anna asked, watching as a cold

feeling of terror gathered in the pit of her stomach. The woman inserted a cannula into the back of Elijah's hand, then wound a clear tube from it, up towards a bag of fluid.

'Let's hope so,' the woman said briskly. 'He's breathing, has a slow but steady pulse. In cases like these, we worry about spinal and cerebral damage.'

Cerebral damage.

Anna swallowed as the ambulance took a corner, rocking her. Sirens wailing.

'But try to remain calm. We won't know anything until we're at the hospital and tests have been done.'

Anna clutched the edge of the metal seat she was perched on.

'These old houses are hazardous,' the woman continued, 'old, hard staircases. Treacherous. We've had many call-outs like these.'

'I kept telling him we needed to carpet them.'

'Definitely makes them safer,' the woman agreed. She then carefully picked her way to the front of the ambulance, to the open window where Anna could see the driver swerving through traffic. She said something to him. The ambulance went faster.

Are you there? Can you hear me?
Elijah, this wasn't supposed to happen.
I just wanted to stop you.
Do you understand?
Please . . . please don't ignore me.

The paramedic was back beside Elijah, checking his pulse for a second time, opening his eyelids and flashing a small torch against his pupils. With a frown she looked first to Anna and then back to Elijah, drawing his left ear forward.

'You got those chips?'

'Yes.' Anna blushed, wanting to confirm that they were

Unity, that they were great for togetherness. A knee-jerk reaction to needing to believe the lie. 'It's . . . er, relatively new for us and—'

'Anything?' The woman was staring at her, brown eyes bright.

'Sorry?'

'Anything?' She gestured between Elijah and Anna. 'Can you hear him at all?'

Anna's shoulders dropped. 'No.'

'Nothing?'

'No.'

'Okay, well let me know if that changes.' She continued with her checks.

Elijah, you're in an ambulance. This is real. This is happening.

'Did you see him fall?' the woman asked, pausing after reading the thermometer she'd placed in Elijah's ear.

'Y-yes.'

'Where were you?'

'The hallway,' Anna said shakily. 'He . . . I heard him tumbling and ran into there.'

'So he hit a lot of the stairs on the way down?'

'I . . . think so. Yes.'

The paramedic was again moving to the front of the cab. 'Call ahead and say we'll need an urgent CT,' she told her partner.

'I just . . .' Anna dropped her head into her hands and began to wail.

'There now,' the woman said soothingly, patting her back with a gloved hand. 'Please, try not to panic. I know you must be extremely distressed but you did the right thing. If your husband gets through this, it will be because of you, okay?'

If.

Because of you.

Anna fought the urge to vomit.

'He was lucky that you were home when it happened. Imagine if you'd not been there.'

Anna could only nod.

The ambulance bounced over a speed bump.

This wasn't my fault, Elijah. Any of it. I don't know if you can hear me, but if you can: know that this was an accident. It was all just a horrible, horrible accident. And I'm here. At your side. Where a good wife should be. Because despite what you think, Elijah, I am a good wife. A great one.

Here at Unity we promise a level of togetherness that has been previously unimaginable. To be within your partner's mind is so intimate, so bonding, that all our chips come with a ten-year guarantee. That's how satisfied we know you will be. All of our customers report on how their relationships have been vastly improved thanks to the Unity experience.

From the seamless implantation procedure to our state-of-the-art facilities in the heart of London, you'll be in the very best of hands. Why not come and visit us today for a free consultation? Or order one of our exclusive packages as a special anniversary gift to really show someone how much you love them?

OneMind.

One heart.

True Unity.

41

ONE MONTH LATER

Anna stood facing the car park, hands clasped around a plastic cup of tea which had long gone cold. Pale sunlight spread across a nearby patch of daisies whose tiny heads gently bobbed in the breeze.

Anna tried to focus on the movement of cars, the constant interchanging of vehicles between parking spaces, the gentle hum of their electric engines. One thing she had learned over the last four weeks was that the hospital was always busy. No matter what time she arrived, what time she left, there were always cars vying for spaces, people gathered on the bench beside the small stretch of lawn, the patch of daisies. Anna shivered just beyond the main entrance, loitering on the edge of the car park, cold in her jeans and T-shirt. But soon she would be warm. It was unbearably hot in the unit where they kept Elijah, the air so sticky it instantly caught in her throat when she walked in. Anna drank down her tea, then she turned and headed back through the glass-doored entrance, crushing the empty cup with one hand and tossing it into a bin.

Visiting hour didn't start for another five minutes but she

hadn't been quick enough. As she was rubbing antibacterial gel into her hands, feeling the unpleasant burn against a fresh cut she'd gained while preparing dinner the previous night, she spotted Helen and Gavin just ahead of her, turning a corner.

'Shit.'

Helen had briefly messaged the night before, saying they wanted to swing by ahead of their holiday. Anna had groaned the second she saw it, the last thing she needed was an audience.

Hurrying, she followed the all too familiar path down long corridors, past a sign for HDU, shoes squeaking against the floor. When she walked into Elijah's room they were already at his bedside. Gavin turned and offered a tight smile, while Helen, occupying the room's single plastic chair, stared primly at Elijah.

'Hey.' Anna lingered at the end of the bed, already too hot. She wished the nurses would consider opening the window behind the bed, even just a fraction, to allow some fresh air to circulate. But they insisted the threat of infection was too high. 'Th-thanks for coming.'

'Of course.' Gavin nodded, pushed his hands into his trouser pockets.

'You've come from work?' Anna noted his shirt, though there was no tie.

'Yeah, yeah, just came out during lunch. Wanted to see him before we went away. I wasn't expecting him to be so . . .' His voice trailed off as he assessed the array of machines surrounding the bed.

'What have the doctors said?' Helen asked, still looking at Elijah.

'You know,' Anna clasped her elbows in her hands, arms to her chest, 'that he's . . . stable. No changes. But then, no change can be good.'

Helen spoke again: 'Do they expect him to wake up soon?'

Anna chewed her lip. 'They're . . . they're not sure.'

A silence settled between them as this sank in.

'Are you . . . are you excited for your holiday?' Anna needed to shift the stifling weight of discomfort in the room.

'Yeah, though I'll feel better once I've clocked off.' Gavin glanced nervously at Helen, whose hands were clasped in her lap. 'We've never done Mexico before; it'll be a nice change for us.'

'Sure.' Anna felt like she'd become queen of the one-word answer over the last month. Struggling to rustle up any kind of embellishment.

'If you need anything,' Gavin peered at her from hooded eyes, 'anything at all. Or if anything, you know, changes. Just call. Okay?'

'Okay.'

'Do you come here every day?' The question came from Helen, though she failed to look up as she spoke.

'Yeah.' Anna sighed as she looked to her husband upon the hospital bed. Currently half man, half machine. His face was hidden behind a ventilator, which hissed loudly with every breath he was unable to take for himself. 'Every day.'

'I suppose it could happen at any moment, right?' Now Helen turned to look at her, blue eyes icy. 'Him waking up?'

'It could, yes.' Anna gave what she hoped was an enthusiastic smile. 'It seems with comas, there really is no exact answer or anything. You just have to keep hoping for the best.'

'Hmm.' Helen kept looking at her.

'It feels so strange to keep seeing him like this,' Anna added, growing nervous. Usually she was alone for her bedside vigil. At first, people had gathered eagerly. Elijah's parents, her father. But they all dropped off after the second week. And now Anna knew Helen and Gavin were only there through guilt. They were about to jet off on a three-week luxury holiday while she waited around to see if, or when, her husband might wake up. 'We washed his hair yesterday.' She turned towards the door, hoping a nurse might be coming in to empty Elijah's catheter or check his obs. Anything to stop her needing to fill the space. 'And I've been cutting his toenails. I'd try and shave him but,' she gestured to her own mouth, 'it's hard to get to.' Curled hairs had sprouted along Elijah's jawline like errant pubic hairs. Anna felt repulsed each time she discovered a new one, her husband slowly slipping from handsome to bedraggled.

'Still nothing on the . . .' Helen tapped behind her ear. 'The chip?'

'No, nothing.' Anna's fingers instinctively strayed towards her left ear, the fading ridges of the scratches that surrounded it.

'Isn't yours due to be taken out soon?' Gavin looked at her. 'Or fixed? Wasn't it faulty?'

'Actually, it was meant to be today,' Anna confirmed tightly, remembering the pained phone call she'd had with Murray from Unity.

'Well, you see, Mrs Weston, given the circumstances, with your husband being in a coma, it would be unsafe to do anything with your chip. There's a risk of causing a cerebral imbalance his end. Once his situation *changes*, we can look to either update or remove your chip.'

'So I'm stuck with my faulty chip,' she told them after relaying the update. 'It all feels pointless now, since it doesn't do anything.'

'But it might,' Helen's tone was insistent, 'if he does start having thoughts again, you may well be the first to know.'

'Exactly.' Anna was smiling so hard her face ached. 'So I definitely want to keep it in.'

'Well, I don't know how you're holding it all together.' Helen gave her a flat smile. 'You look simply exhausted, which isn't surprising.'

'Thanks.' Anna gave a nervous laugh. She knew Helen spoke the truth. Each morning when she went to wash her face she was met with a spectre in the mirror. Her skin ashen, stretched too tight over her bones. Dark circles beneath her eyes. Every time Anna pulled on a T-shirt, a pair of jeans, she felt the poke of her ribs, her pelvis, the strange airiness of items no longer fitting properly.

'Are you eating okay?' Gavin turned to her, concerned. He reached out and touched her elbow, then, face burning, promptly dropped his hand. 'Helen and I, we could bring over some takeaway or something.'

'You don't look like you're eating properly,' Helen stated. 'Or sleeping.'

'Well . . .' Anna wasn't sure how to respond. In truth, she wasn't doing either properly. Eating or sleeping. She was just . . . existing. Flitting between her home and the hospital. Slowly going mad.

'When I'm back, let me handle some shifts here,' Gavin offered. 'You don't need to be at his bedside all day every day.'

'But she's the concerned wife,' Helen stared at Anna, 'and she's playing the part so perfectly.'

Anna opened her mouth to object when the door behind her opened, a red-haired nurse with a thick neck walking in. 'How's our boy today then?' she asked with so much brightness Anna was nearly blinded.

'The same,' she muttered, dazed.

'We just keep praying he'll wake up soon,' Helen announced with a sharp glance at Anna.

'Don't we all?' The nurse nodded sympathetically. Numbers noted, she was drawing back to the end of the bed, activating the tablet attached to the frame. 'None more than this one.' She nodded towards Anna as she typed. 'Here every day she is. Such devotion. Such love. I've told my fella, if I end up in a coma, if he showed even half the commitment she has I'd be happy.'

'She's certainly . . . committed,' Helen agreed pointedly.

'We all are,' Gavin rushed in, 'we all care deeply about Elijah.'

'I keep telling her, he's doing *well*.' The nurse withdrew from the tablet and placed a hand on Anna's forearm. 'You don't need to worry so much, my dear. I know it's easier said than done. But trust me, he's showing great signs of sustaining his stats. Which is *good*. No drops is *good*. You need to go home, run yourself a hot bath and try to *relax*.'

'Oh, I just . . .' Anna blinked, forever feeling like she lingered on the edge of exhaustion. That she was one drop of her eyelids from just collapsing on the floor. 'It's just not the same, at home, without him.'

'Such love,' the nurse smiled warmly at her, 'and he knows. So many coma patients wake up and say they heard everything while we thought they were completely oblivious.'

The nurse gave a final smile and left the room.

'You really do need to rest,' Gavin confirmed.

'I know . . .' Anna sniffed.

'So awful, to just fall down the stairs like that.' Helen's eyebrow gave a slight twitch as she looked over at Anna.

'Yes,' Anna agreed, it was. Again she was having to fan herself with her hands. She feared she'd pass out from exhaustion or heat stroke in the room. 'I kept telling him to get them carpeted. But he wouldn't listen.'

'Helen, come on.' Gavin nodded at the door, cheeks ruddy.

'It's bloody baking in here; I'm sweating like a sinner in church. Let's go.'

Helen rose from her chair, poised and regal. She walked over to Gavin, patent nude heels clicking against the floor.

'Thank you for coming.' Anna smiled at them, as though they were leaving after a dinner date. 'I – we – appreciate it.'

'It's no problem.' Gavin's hand flexed towards her and then got pushed deep into his pocket. 'Really, we should have come sooner.'

'It's fine. Have a wonderful holiday,' Anna gushed with faux sincerity.

'We will,' Helen smoothly assured her as she glided towards the door. In the corridor she waited for Gavin, took his hand in hers.

'Remember, any changes, any at all, call,' Gavin urged, but he was already being led away, Helen at his side, directing him.

Anna collapsed into the freshly vacated chair at Elijah's bedside, cradled her head in her hands, chin pressed against her chest. She'd remain there until the light dimmed outside, until her legs went numb. Then, stiffly, she'd stand up, stretch. Make her way to the door, smile at any nurses she saw along the way. Go home, fail to sleep. Fail to eat. Only to wake up the next day and repeat the ritual anew. Trapped in a cage. A hot, horrible cage.

And every day the on-duty doctor would take her aside, tablet in hand, and ask after her Unity chip.

'Anything at all?'

And every day, Anna gave the same answer: 'No, nothing. Nothing at all.'

42

It had been six weeks since the accident. Helen and Gavin were sunning themselves on a beach; each night Anna's social media feed was flooded with images of them grinning, sun drenched, cocktails in hand.

She felt herself wasting away, like a corpse left to decompose. Anna was hungry, tired. Often that tipped over into ravenous, exhausted.

It was a morning that brought golden light, so Anna made the decision to not drive over to the hospital, to not sit for hours in God's waiting room, listening to the beeps and hisses which cut her to the bone. Instead, she would paint. Perhaps if she attempted to claw back this tiny part of herself, the rest would return in time. If she found her love of creating, she might then find her love of eating. Be able to sleep again. The image of the beach, she could return to it. There was something there, within it, she knew it.

Anna propped open the door to her studio with a brick and stepped inside. She expected to find everything toppled and destroyed. It was the first time she'd ventured inside it in over a month. But all was as she'd left it, waiting for her. Tentatively she turned the easel containing the vista of the beach around. How she'd missed painting. The smell of the oils. The whisper of brush on canvas. Quietly, she mixed a few shades in her palette, then she stood before the easel, took a steadying breath, extended her brush. If she could just add some definition to the sand, the cliff, then maybe this was a piece that could actually do something, sell, could actually—

Bitch! Where are you? Why aren't you here? I can hear the stomping of that heavy-footed nurse. She said you're not coming. Bitch!

With a whimper the brush left her hand, clattered to the floor.

Elijah, please—

Every day. I expect you to be here every day. Don't think you can hide from me, Anna. I want you here when I wake up, at my bedside. So I can tell everyone what you've done.

That's if you wake up.

I'll tell everyone how you lied. How you pushed me. How you continue to lie. You can hear me, Anna!

Maybe I should tell everyone how you killed Oscar! How you pushed him!

Imagine doing something awful and lying to protect yourself. You and I, we're not so different, Anna.

Shut up.

You understand now, don't you, the way things went down on that beach? That I'm no monster.

Shut up!

Or if I am a monster, so are you. You nearly killed me.

God, just shut up!

With a groan she crouched down, retrieved her brush. Elijah had begun talking in her mind on his second day in hospital. She had been at his bedside when a machine bleated sharply and then he was asking questions.

Where was he?

What was going on?

To everyone at the hospital Anna's distractedness just seemed like worry, concern. As the weeks dragged on and he continued to haunt her mind, she presented like a wife wracked with anxiety. Fearful for her husband. No one questioned her when she zoned out, when she failed to follow conversations. They just nodded sympathetically and told her it would be all right.

No one knew that her husband screamed at her throughout the day. Even the night. Managing to infect her dreams. It would seem that the chip didn't disconnect when one mind was forever active. Anna had tried to talk to Murray at Unity, tried to ask for a removal, but been told no. And if she pushed for one, if she mentioned anything about Elijah already being active in her thoughts, she risked arousing suspicion. She had to play the part of the concerned spouse. That meant keeping the chip. That meant being subjected to Elijah's every thought.

Just tell them, tell them the chip is connecting us.

No.

Anna clenched her jaw, tried again to paint.

Because I'm going to wake up, Anna. And then your life is over. Do you hear me? Over! I'm going to destroy you. I'll see you behind bars for what you've done to me. And I'll make sure to come and visit you and watch you while you rot.

I'm already behind bars.

Good, it's what you deserve! You vicious, self-serving bitch.

I'm going to tell them to turn off your life support.

You can't. I still have time. We both know that.

You might never wake up.
I might wake up tomorrow.
Just fuck off and die already.
Anna blew hot air through her nose, angry.
I'm trapped here in the darkness and I'm going to trap you too.

'Just fuck off!' Anna screamed aloud. Even to Mandie she had to keep putting on a façade, pretending everything was fine while her sanity slowly eroded. All night Elijah sang and screamed at her. Going through endless renditions of 'I'm Henry VIII, I Am'. Over and over. In his comatose abyss there was no dawn. No night. It was all just endless, his mind left to wander indefinitely.

Anna's left eye twitched. She was being driven to madness, she knew that. The only comfort came from the fact that it had to end. Elijah would either wake up or die.

And then it's your word against mine, she thought sourly. The home app on her phone, she'd finally got to grips with it. Deleting any incriminating footage of herself. Contacting the company to announce it was faulty; appliances turning on and off at will, rendering the whole thing unreliable.
I'll ruin you.
Anna reached her brush towards her picture, hand quivering.
You already have.
Good, you heartless, vile bitch! Gavin, too; I'll ruin you both.
They're having a wonderful time in Mexico.
Fuck them both.
How funny that they are out there, happy. And we are here, trapped.
That's because you're a lying cunt.
Or maybe it's because you placed me on a pedestal so high I was always fated to fall. Anna sighed and placed the paintbrush

down on the side, accepting she'd get no work done. Over and over she fought with Elijah, her mind a warzone.

I'm so fucking tired of this.

Head down, she trudged back to the house, hoping she could swallow down some tea and toast. Her stomach felt so hollow, but each time she went to fill it her nerves swelled up like a tempest.

Jail.

Disgrace.

Was this what awaited her once Elijah broke free from his coma?

She'd considered how she could end him in there. A bubble in an IV perhaps?

They'll see, Anna. They'll know. You think the place is run by fools? There are cameras. I'm monitored. If I die while you're in the room they'll know you have blood on your hands.

Everyone thinks you fell. I can be pretty convincing.

Try it, then. See how it feels to be convicted of not just manslaughter, but murder. Because that's what awaits you. Prison. A slow death. And that's what you deserve.

Anna flicked on the kettle, wilting against the kitchen counter. She should go and find her phone, tell Mandie she still needed those pills. Anna desperately needed the sweet silence of being knocked out.

It doesn't matter what you take. The moment you wake, I'll be there. Waiting. I'm always here, Anna. You saw to that.

Just leave me alone.

The kettle clicked off and Anna poured hot water over what she thought was a teabag. When she looked down she saw kernels of pepper floating. 'Fuck.'

Whatever you do, wherever you go, I'll be there.

Anna cradled her head in her hands. So very exhausted. So very weary.

Until death do us part, right, sweetheart?

She wished she was on a beach, sipping something sweet, dipping her toes into turquoise waters.

I'll be here in your mind, Anna. Always.

> Unity changed my life. It is that simple. I thought I knew what happiness was, then my husband and I got the chips implanted and just . . . wow. I feel so much closer to him, so much more connected. It really is true – complete connection does bring complete unity. I have never known peace like this. Every day we talk internally together, make plans, discuss the kids. The logistics of everything is so seamless, so natural. I wish everyone could get to experience this. There is no way I would go back. Not for a second. My husband is in my mind now and that's where I intend for him to stay.
>
> Hannah Edwards, Unity User

43

It was becoming increasingly hard to keep track of the days, they all melted into each other as the sun burned and the grass in the garden faded from a soft green to shrivelled brown. A heatwave. Social media was abuzz with it. Not that Anna cared. She moved through her days in a fog until she realised she could go no further. Which was why on a Tuesday afternoon she was entering the lobby of Unity, the sweat of the city damp against her skin.

'Do you have an appointment?' the prim blonde behind the desk enquired coolly.

'I'm here to see Murray,' Anna blurted, before adding, 'it's an emergency.' From anyone else, the statement might have been challenged. But Anna was vaguely aware of how she looked. The thick shadows beneath her eyes, her matted hair, the track marks of old scratches across her cheek. She saw the pinch of worry on the face of every nurse she passed when she dragged herself to visit Elijah. She saw it in the way Mandie puckered her lips and smoothed hair out of her eyes.

'Really, babe, we need to pull you out of this.'

At night, when Anna should have been sleeping, she stared into the darkness and considered how long the machines pumping around Elijah might keep him alive. Days. Weeks. Months.

Where are you?

Anna winced as her husband's voice echoed in her head. The sternness in the blonde at reception eased as she clicked a finger to her headset. 'I'll call and tell him to come right down.'

Anna had called. Emailed. Been told over and over that nothing could be done. That she was stuck with her faulty chip and comatose husband until something cracked and she feared it was going to be her. It was that fear which had led her to schedule a taxi into the city, to numbly enter it an hour earlier and watch her home slip from view in the rear-view mirror. And for moments, the journey had been peaceful. Quiet. But, as always, Elijah returned, never slipping far from her consciousness.

'Ah, Mrs Weston.' Murray greeted her with his usual smile as he exited a nearby lift and came over to her, though when he took in her appearance it promptly fell, along with his arms. 'My goodness. You look . . .'

'Please,' Anna looked him directly in the eye, 'I'm . . . I'm desperate.'

'Come, come.' He ushered her away from the lobby, towards the lift and up to the waiting area Anna remembered all too well. 'Please, sit,' he instructed, heading over to the coffee machine and making her a fresh drink and then carefully placing it on the table in front of her. 'Everyone at Unity is so, so worried about your husband. We are all praying for Mr Weston to have a swift recovery.'

'That's just it . . .' Anna blinked back tears. 'I'm so . . . so distressed. All the time. Worrying about things. Thinking the worst.' She reached for her drink with shaking hands, then thought better of it and clasped them within her lap. 'My fear is that . . .' She sniffed, drew her greasy hair behind her ear. 'I worry he can *hear* me. All the things I'm scared of, scared of for him. And I don't want that . . .' Here she wobbled, chin quivering. 'What if I'm making things worse,' she asked Murray in a panicked whisper, 'because he can hear how upset I am? I don't want—' Unable to go on, Anna buried her head in her hands and wept.

'There, there.' Murray nervously placed a hand upon her shoulder. 'I can't imagine how stressful this must all be for you.'

'If only . . . if only I could mute my chip. Give me . . .' Anna hiccuped over her words, 'give me some . . . some peace of mind. When I need it . . . most.'

'I understand.'

'Won't Unity help me?' She twisted her head to peer up at Murray, who was deep in thought.

'I . . .' He sighed, looked towards the windows and the distant city skyline. 'Goodness, as I've said before, unfortunately we can't perform any procedures on your chip while your husband isn't conscious.'

'I'm so . . . so terrified of my thoughts *hurting* him,' Anna whimpered. 'What if it's all he can hear?'

'I . . .' Murray traced his jawline with manicured nails and then shook his head. 'You know,' he suddenly strode away from her to retrieve a spare tablet from a nearby docking station, 'I can't bear to see you suffering like this, Mrs Weston. Truly, I can't. This isn't what Unity is about. While officially we cannot perform a procedure at this time,' a sparkle entered his eyes, 'we could do a routine diagnostic, given your . . . issues. And if during that someone *happened* to activate your mute function, might that help?'

Anna blinked in grateful surprise, managing to nod.

'Though of course, officially, you only ever came in for a diagnostic check. And normally, those must be scheduled, but this is an emergency.' His fingers moved quickly across the illuminated screen of the tablet. 'And luckily we have two surgeons working until ten tonight and one has a brief opening in half an hour.'

'I don't . . .' Anna could barely rasp out her words.

'I want to help.' Murray clasped her hands, his skin warm and golden. 'You've already been through so, so much. Let me do this.'

While Anna waited and a hazy sky lingered above the city she tried and failed to drink her coffee. It all still felt too good to be true and she remained braced for some fly to appear in the ointment of it all.

Where are you?

Why aren't you here?

Seriously, Anna. You should be here. I know you're not. All I can hear are those fucking nurses gossiping about some reality show. Anna!

She closed her eyes, took a deep breath.

Soon.

What?

I'll be there soon.

44

She woke groggy, the room cool and still around her. Anna inhaled, waiting for her vision to settle. With a turn of her head she could make out the rainforest imagery on one wall, hear the gentle rushing of rain.

'Everything went great.' A gentle hand upon her shoulder, a voice she didn't know. 'It was actually simple to align your chip to a more temperate level and enable the mute function. And because we were so swift, there should be no disruption to your connection with your husband.' A clinician slid into view, slim in pale blue scrubs. And then they were gone. Anna swung her legs over the side of the bed and stood up. There was no rising nausea, no dizziness. She felt tired, but okay. With a soft hiss, the door to her room opened and Murray came in, carrying a tablet.

'How are we feeling?'

'Good.' Anna nodded at him, already feeling brighter.

Where have you been?

Anna!

I've been calling for you! What the fuck!

'So, does it work now? The mute function?' Anna asked quickly.

'Let's give it a whirl.' Murray beamed at her. 'Press your

fingers to your chip, apply pressure and hold it there for ten seconds.'

Anna raised her hand, felt the ridges of old and new stitches, the pulse of aching skin. She pressed down.

Anna! Seriously! When I find out where you have gone I'll—

Silence.

Sweet, glorious silence.

'Of course, without your husband's thoughts it will be difficult to know for sure if it's working,' Murray was explaining to her as he scrolled across the tablet, 'but we ran a diagnostic check *as scheduled* and all looked well.'

'Great.' Anna felt both exhausted and exhilarated as her hand fell to her side. 'Thank you, it's . . . it's the peace of mind I needed.'

'And, that's not all.' Murray was sitting beside her on the edge of the bed, both of them facing the rainforest wall. 'As is standard procedure, we took a blood test ahead of the diagnostic check.'

Anna threw him a wary glance. 'Okay?'

'Mrs Weston, it would seem you are pregnant.'

'Pregnant?' She spat out the word in disbelief. 'What? Seriously? No. No. That can't be. I was told that the last time . . .'

Would be the last time.

Her head throbbed.

'I know you've been through a lot lately,' Murray commented kindly, 'but sometimes when God pisses on us he does send a rainbow.'

'I can't get pregnant,' Anna told him, heart rate beginning to climb. 'Not . . . not any more. I . . . the doctors told me there'd been . . . too much damage. Too much . . .' She swallowed against the lump forming in her throat. 'Too much loss.'

'Your bloodwork would suggest otherwise.' Murray smiled at her, even proffering the screen of the tablet so that she could see the results for herself.

'I don't . . .' It was there, beneath her name. In cold, clinical detail.

HcG – 140

'We always run thorough checks on bloodwork as part of our commitment to monitoring the well-being of our valued clients.'

'I'm not meant to be pregnant,' Anna told him, dazed by it all.

'Yet here we are. Life still has the capacity to surprise us.'

Anna blinked, in shock.

'Have you been more tired lately? Nauseous?' Murray enquired gently. Anna found herself nodding.

She was exhausted but Elijah kept tormenting her so she couldn't sleep.

And back when they'd gone to Nicco's, she had been so sick she assumed it was from drinking too much. Now she wasn't so sure.

Could it really be?

'Go home, absorb it all, get some over-the-counter tests,' Murray advised. 'And please rest, Mrs Weston. Your thoughts will no longer be troubling your husband. His mind can be silent now while he recovers.'

'Thank you.' Anna threw her arms around Murray, buried herself into him, forgetting that she hadn't showered in days, breathing in his light minty odour. 'Thank you,' she whispered again as the tears began to fall.

'Happy to help,' he told her earnestly as he hugged her back.

In the taxi on the way home Anna peered at her ghostly reflection in the window and the blurred city beyond.

When?

If she *was* pregnant, when had it even happened?

Her stomach churned as the memory of the cabin came to her. The hot tub. The bedroom. The island in the kitchen. Back when things had been normal with Elijah. Back when they had been happy. Then she'd dreamed of the beach and a shadow had settled over their world.

I'm pregnant with Elijah's baby.

Of course she was. The thing she'd wanted more than anything was happening now, when everything was a mess. When she was alone.

She touched her ear, skin tender and raw, but mute function very much working. Anna smiled as the taxi pulled out of the city, turning towards home.

45

The next seven days proved to be the strangest of weeks. There were pockets of silence deep enough for Anna to lose herself in. To entertain her own thoughts. It was both wonderful and terrifying.

After her procedure at Unity she slept deeply but awoke sweat clad and anxious.

Can it be true?

She instantly pressed her chip, something which was already becoming habit, and planned her day. First, she went to the nearest chemist and bought a dozen pregnancy tests. Then she spent a surreal morning, pissing on them in turn and staring in disbelief as a solid line appeared.

Anna kept repeating a pattern: seeing a positive result, assuming the test was faulty and necking down a glass of water to start again. It was only when she had twelve empty boxes crammed into her recycling bin that she began to think that perhaps it was actually true. But even then so many other intrusive thoughts prevented her from being happy.

It could be something else.
Hormone imbalance.
A tumour.
A phantom pregnancy.

By the end of the week she was in the plush office of a fertility specialist who was assessing her most recent blood-work. 'It would seem you are definitely pregnant,' she declared, kind brown eyes settling on Anna, who was positioned stiffly across the desk from her. 'But, to allay any fears your end, let's do a scan this afternoon.'

'A scan?' Anna felt dizzy.

'Just to check everything is in order, given your history.'

The jelly was cold against her stomach, the room dark. Just before the Doppler touched her skin, Anna raised a hand to her chip, pressed hard.

'There we are.' It didn't take long for a small, grainy curled figure to appear on the screen before Anna. 'You're carrying one embryo, and I'd estimate you're about ten weeks.'

Anna did the maths. It placed her at the cabin. She kept her gaze on the screen, unblinking. 'But I don't ... I was always told that with my scarring ...' She didn't even look at the consultant as she spoke, afraid that if she tore her eyes away from the screen for a second her baby would disappear.

'I can see some scarring,' the consultant nodded, tracing a finger along a curve upon the screen, 'and while substantial, it has clearly healed enough to permit a foetus to attach. But we will monitor you closely throughout your pregnancy to ensure you don't come into any difficulty.'

'Thank you,' Anna whispered breathily, feeling the heat of a tear upon her cheek. 'Thank you.'

She told Mandie. She cleared out the spare room. Anna did all she could to keep herself busy, knowing that eventually she'd need to go to the hospital. To tell her husband.

He might not even wake up.

The morning before she was due to visit him Anna found herself in her bedroom, rummaging underneath the bed for a certain box. It had once held a pair of Louboutin heels, now it was coated in a thin layer of dust and when Anna popped the lid she went back in time. All the photographs she had kept from her time at university were wedged inside. Her friends had mocked her for insisting on printing them all out, but she used to like to pin them to her walls, to surround herself with smiles and good times. Anna flicked through them; here was one of her and Helen, arms around each other's shoulders, laughing. Both so young. So beautiful. How had they not known back then all that they had? All that they were? Other pictures with Gavin, always red-eyed and a little drunk. Elijah, dark-haired and brooding. And Oscar. He flitted in and out of the group photos; even frozen within the images his energy radiated off him. Oscar who was always ordering shots, always shouting merrily for the DJ to turn a song up. Oscar who had been more alive than any of them.

And now he was gone.

Because of Elijah.

Anna kept shuffling through the photographs, looking upon ghosts of the past. She hated the lump of certainty that had settled in her stomach the moment Gavin told her. Elijah had always been a prudent pragmatist, thinking ahead, ensuring a strong future.

But surely it had been an accident?

Anna stared down at a picture of the three boys: Gavin, Oscar and Elijah.

They didn't tell anyone. Either of them.

She returned the picture to the box and firmly attached the lid. While Elijah was the one supposedly with blood on his hands, Gavin was far from innocent. She touched a hand protectively to her stomach.

'Things are going to be different,' she whispered to the life growing within her. 'We are going to do things right. You and me. I'm going to protect you.'

It had only been a few days since she'd last visited the hospital but Anna had forgotten how acrid the stench of the place could be – how ammonia crawled up her nostrils and burned her senses. In the corridor, she passed by one of her husband's nurses.

'I wish I could visit more,' she told her, face the perfect picture of regret, 'but I've found out I'm expecting and I'm really struggling with HG.'

'Oh my goodness, dear, that's wonderful news. But yes, if you're unwell, you must put yourself first. Don't worry about your husband; he's in good hands here and we'll update you of any changes,' the woman told her earnestly.

'I just wanted to come today, while I had the energy.'

'Of course, of course.'

When Anna entered Elijah's room, the hiss and wheeze of beeps greeting her, the nurse closed the door, giving them privacy.

Where have you been?
What is going on?
Anna? Anna! Why can't I hear you?

She took a long breath and looked at her husband upon the bed. So pale. So still. If it wasn't for the chip she'd doubt he was even there at all any more.

I installed the mute function.

Nothing. Just the pulse and throb of the machines that were breathing for Elijah. Keeping him alive.

Nothing to say on that? How nice it must have been for you to use yours as and when you wanted.

Anna . . . please, just let me—

This may well be my last visit. Things have changed for me. You see I'm . . . I'm pregnant. I'm sure you're as shocked as I am. And please don't ask anything distasteful like is it yours. I'm ten weeks. You knocked me up at the cabin.

Anna . . .

Even in his thoughts she could hear his voice breaking.

And it's not like it's some miracle; the consultant just said that my scar tissue had healed enough for a baby to attach. I might still have issues down the line. I'm scared. But I'm also elated. So . . . so fucking elated. And grateful. And happy. And I'm telling you because . . . because I felt like I should. I wanted you to know. Everything with us, it's a mess. I'm not really sure how we got here. But I wanted you to know. You're hopefully going to be a father.

Anna—

One day, if you wake up, we can talk more. About so many things. Including Oscar. I feel like I was only ever married to the idea of you. Not the real you.

Anna, I never—

I lied about something . . . something that I feared would ruin us. But it only ruined us because you let it. You could have just forgiven me, Eli. You could have understood that I was young and scared. Instead, you became a monster. And with Oscar . . . I don't know you. At all. And that scares me more than anything. But I'm ready to raise my baby alone. I don't need you any more.

Can you just—

Anna lifted her hand, pressed behind her ear and Elijah's thoughts abruptly ended. When she left the hospital she paused on the car park to breathe in the fresh air, feeling hopeful. Feeling determined.

> I'll always be forever grateful to Unity for what it gave me – a fresh start. A life I didn't dare believe I could have. Unity showed me who I really was, who my husband was. Unity set me free.
>
> Anna Weston, Unity User

Acknowledgements

I feel extremely fortunate to have worked with so many wonderful people on this book.

Firstly, huge thanks to my wonderful agent, Liza DeBlock. You were instantly enthusiastic about the book and I couldn't have asked for a better advocate on this journey. Thank you for saving the ending and for working so hard. You are truly a star.

I was also lucky to work with other members of the Mushens team throughout my submission process, notably Kiya Evans – you were wonderful when you stepped in during Liza's maternity leave. I loved working with you. Also, Rachel Neely, thank you for coming along on my first trip to the Penguin Random House offices. It was so nice to chat books (and eat biscuits).

The team at Harvill Secker have been incredible, right from our first exciting Zoom meeting. You all understood and connected with the book in the best possible way.

Katie Ellis-Brown – you have been an utter joy to work with. You make editing fun (which is no easy feat)! I'm excited for what the future holds for us!

Sania Riaz – thank you for being so passionate about the book, and for loving the characters as much as I do!

My copy-edit team: Alison Tulett and Graeme Hall, thank you for all your support. I'm sorry that at some points in the book I seemed to have literally made up words; thank you for going through it all with a fine-toothed comb and really helping it shine.

*

I'm beyond fortunate to have made some incredible writer friends over the past few years. This book wouldn't exist the way it does without them. Their guidance, support and kindness emboldened me to become the writer I wanted to be. Sandra, Amy, Tess, Jenny. You are all rockstars and push me to be better.

Finally, my family. The people who put up with me.

Mum and Dad, thank you for always giving me the space to be myself. I hope I make you guys proud. I'm certainly proud of both of you and feel lucky to be your daughter.

Sam, it would be unfair to say you inspired this book, because you're a bloody good husband, but you encouraged me to write something out of genre, and never doubted that I could do it. You always saw a studio, and for that I'm forever grateful.

Rose, it will be a good while until you can read my books but I hope that one day, when you do, you enjoy them. Every day you inspire me to be the best I can possibly be (though every day I fall short of that, but I'm always, always trying).

And Rollo. You have been my loyal writing companion for all of your almost twelve years. I love you, my big fluffy man. Thank you for being an incredible dog. I miss our walks but still love our cuddles.

Last, but by no means least, thank you dear reader. For picking up my book, for reading and hopefully enjoying it. I was a reader long before I became a writer and I think there's no greater feeling than losing yourself in a decent book. Thank you for spending your time with mine.

Credits

Vintage would like to thank everyone who worked on the publication of
ALWAYS ON MY MIND

Agent
Liza DeBlock

Editor
Katie Ellis-Brown

Editorial
Sania Riaz

Copy-editor
Alison Tulett

Proofreader
Jane Howard

Managing Editorial
Graeme Hall

Contracts
Emma D'Cruz
Gemma Avery
Ceri Cooper
Rebecca Smith
Anne Porter
Rita Omoro
Hayley Morgan

Design
Dan Mogford

Digital
Anna Baggaley
Claire Dolan
Brydie Scott
Charlotte Ridsdale
Zaheerah Khalik

Inventory
Nadine Hart

Publicity
Susie Merry
Amrit Bhullar

Finance
Ed Grande
Samuel Uwague

Marketing
Sophie Painter
Lucy Upton
Preetnoor Nagi

Production
Konrad Kirkham
Polly Dorner
Eoin Dunne

Sales
Nathaniel Breakwell
Nick Cordingly

Malissa Mistry
Elspeth Dougall
Caitlin Knight
Rohan Hope
Jade Perez
Erica Conway
Maiya Grant
Neil Green
Amanda Dean
Andy Taylor
David Atkinson
David Devaney
Helen Evans
Lewis Cain
Phoebe Edwards
Justin Ward-Turner
Charlotte Owens

Rights
Catherine Wood
Lucie Deacon
Lucy Beresford-Knox
Beth Wood
Maddie Stephenson
Agnes Watters
Sophie Brownlow
Amy Moss

Audio
Nile Faure-Bryan

About the Author

Carys Green is a thriller writer based in Shropshire, where she lives with her husband, daughter and dog. When she's not writing she can be found indulging her two greatest passions – either walking round the local woodland or catching up on all things Disney related.